The Gazette:
From Detroit to the Trenches

The Gazette:
From Detroit to the Trenches

Catherine Paonessa

While this book is based on actual family newspapers written between 1915 and 1918 by Robert Randolph Stevens, it is a work of fiction. The Stevens and Robinson families were real families. I have used the names and characteristics of the members of these families but the book does not necessarily reflect their everyday actions and feelings. The Stevens family did live in a house on Crane Avenue then moved to a house on Fisher Avenue in Detroit, Michigan. The places in Detroit are all real and many of the places mentioned still exist today.

Any other names, characters, businesses, places, events and incidents are either the products of my imagination or used in a fictitious manner. Any resemblance to actual persons, living or dead, or actual events is purely coincidental.

To view The Gazette newspapers online along with photographs of the Stevens and Robinson families go to:

www.catherinepaonessa.com

ISBN-13: 9780692894729 (Seavoy Press)
ISBN-10: 0692894721

Dedications

To my grandfather, Robert Randolph Stevens for writing his newspapers way back when.
To my mom, Sue Paonessa and grandmother, Margaret Stevens for keeping them safe.
To my dad, Joe Paonessa for teaching me the difference between there, they're and their.
To my dedicated first readers and lovely daughters, Erin & Megan
And to my husband Andy for believing in me, listening to my ideas as the story took shape, and reading and re-reading it part by part as it grew into this novel.

Darkness descended on no man's land. The chaos of battle was gone. It was quiet, dead quiet. The stars that had decorated the sky earlier were hidden behind thick clouds. Every now and then a warm breeze lifted a collar here or a lock of hair there. Bodies, the result of the surprise attack, littered the eerie landscape. And two men moved slowly over the hideous terrain. Once fresh, young soldiers, now deserters, part of the living dead that haunted the void between the opposing armies. They moved silently from body to body, looking for provisions and perhaps, a lucky soul that might have survived the attack.

"This chap has fine boots," one of the men whispered, "must have just come over." He sat down and measured his own worn boot against the corpse's new one. "Too small," he mumbled with regret.

They continued scavenging, taking only what had been issued by the army; boots, canteens and food, then they moved on, leaving their dead countrymen alone with their personal treasures, their photographs, letters, sometimes a pocket edition of a favorite book or a Bible.

One of the men picked up a canteen and examined it in the darkness. He shook it. It was empty, but maybe still useful. He inspected it with his fingers and discovered a large hole. As he dropped the worthless canteen next its unfortunate owner, he heard a low, hoarse moan.

"Oi, this chap is still alive," the man said in a gruff voice.

CHAPTER 1

New to Detroit
~ Bob Stevens

Bob put down his pencil, took off his round wire glasses and rubbed his eyes. He looked out the window. He could make out the gray sky and patches of white, icy snow, but not much else. *Dumb eyes, stupid glasses,* he thought. He ran his fingers through his mop of curly, red hair and wondered if he could avoid getting a haircut before starting at his new school. Mother was already nagging him about it. He wiped his glasses on his shirtsleeve and put them on again. Now he could see the small city yard clearly. Two big trees, a place for Mother's garden and an alley running along the back. Bob shrugged, it wasn't as nice as the yard in Beaver Dam, but it would do. He looked back at the newspaper he was writing, the CRANE AVE GAZETTE. He liked it. With the black and red ink and the date stamp, **DEC 15 1915**, it looked very professional. He flipped it over, making sure he had included everything. The advertisement for the Detroit Delivery service and information about the Detroit Savings Bank.

Newspaper clippings were pinned to the wall and stacked in piles on his shelf. There were articles about cops and robbers, crooked politicians, disasters, but mostly articles about the war. Bob was going to be a war correspondent after high school.

His stomach rumbled. Dad had a rule about no "eating between meals", but if he looked pitiful, Mother would give him a snack, a big slice of bread with honey or jam. Dad was at work anyway. He headed downstairs to deliver his first edition. Mother was in the kitchen, her hands busy peeling potatoes.

"Do you want the first issue of the CRANE AVE GAZETTE?" Bob asked, holding the newspaper out to Mother. She smiled and dried her hands before taking the newspaper.

"Oh, my, isn't this nice." Mother said as she read the headline. Bob knew she'd like the newspaper, but he didn't tell her he was practicing to be a war correspondent. She hoped President Wilson would keep the U.S. out of war. Bob hoped it would last long enough for him to write about it.

"I was kind of thinking about a snack," Bob said, sheepishly. His empty stomach rumbled loudly, as if on cue.

Mother frowned at him, but she spread a thick piece of bread with jam, handed it over and said, "Don't tell your father." Bob grinned, and stuffed a big bite in his mouth.

Mother scolded, "Please dear, don't inhale your food like that." She handed him a small pail full of potato peels and other kitchen scraps, "Run this out to the alley for me."

"Sure," Bob said between chews and headed toward the back door.

Mother called after him, "Robin, put your coat on, it's cold out."

Mother always called him Robin, like he was still a baby. His full name was Robert Randolph Stevens. He planned on using Bob at his new school. Dad sometimes called him Bob. Robin was a fine name for a kid, but Bob was better now.

Mother was right. It was cold and damp. He licked his sticky fingers and buttoned his coat up under his chin. After dumping the scraps in the scrap pile, he sat down on the back step. He liked this house. Maybe they would stay here. Dad was a machinist, and he thought Bob should be a machinist after high school. They moved to where new industries were popping up. Detroit seemed like a good place for a machinist. Dad got a job at Burroughs Adding Machine Company. It was the biggest adding machine company in America, and Dad was a second shift lead machinist. Bob hated the idea of being a machinist. He was going to be a reporter.

As he sat on the step, Bob thought about the other places he'd lived, at least the ones he remembered. There was the house in Ilion, New York. Ilion was cold and snowy, but he didn't remember much else. There was a big tree in the yard with a great swing. As his thoughts wandered back to Ilion, he absentmindedly picked up some stones lying at his feet. He tried to throw them through a knothole in the next-door neighbor's fence. His aim wasn't very good.

When he was in first grade, they packed up and moved away from Ilion. Thinking of the move made him mad. Why did they move so much? He threw more stones, each one a little harder than the last. They hit the damp wooden fence with a dull thud. He was running out of stones, when, finally one sailed through the knothole. *Oh, wow, I made it*, Bob thought, surprised. He was searching the ground for another stone when the one he had just thrown fell at the toe of his boot. Someone had thrown it back. "Hey! Sorry!" he shouted, but no one answered. It was a six-foot fence, he couldn't see over it, so he got up, and peered through the knothole. He caught a glimpse of the back door closing. Sleeping by the door was a huge German shepherd. The dog lifted her head and looked right at him, then, unconcerned, returned to her nap. Bob went back to his seat on the step and his memories.

After Ilion, came their adventure in the Wild West, as Mother called it. They took the train to Sandon, British Columbia; Dad thought he'd try his hand working for a mining company. He hated it, and Mother didn't like the mountains. They made her feel small, she complained, and the town was uncivilized, but Bob had though it was grand. Even school was exciting. There were boys there from the all over the world, and they all had a story to tell. Come to think of it, those stories may not have been completely true. Sam's granddad probably didn't beat Big Joe

Mufferaw in a log-splitting contest and Jack's dad probably wasn't the greatest hero of the North-West Rebellion. It was a wild place, too wild for his little family. They only stayed there two years.

They moved from Sandon to Beaver Dam, Wisconsin when Bob was nine. In Beaver Dam there was a gang of boys that played ball together after school. He wasn't very good at it, he was small for his age and not very coordinated. But, the fellas didn't care as long as they had enough boys to cover all the bases.

Bob threw a bigger stone, this time at the oak in the middle of the yard. He missed.

While they were living in Beaver Dam, he and his pal Tommy Masters had started a delivery service. At first, they picked up the groceries for their mothers from Mr. Scott's dry goods store, but they had big plans. Their mothers had paid them a penny each. They'd scoured junkyards and alleys for pieces of this and that and were able to make a great cart. Bob thought about the day they'd painted the cart. Tommy had scratched the name on the side and said aloud, "Masters and Stevens Delivery Service".

Bob had been mad. "Wait a minute," he'd said, "I thought it was "Stevens and Masters".

"Well, M comes before S," Tommy had replied.

They'd stared at each other for a few seconds, fists clenched. It wouldn't have been the first time they'd fought.

"I'm older by two weeks, so I'm the senior partner," Bob had claimed. But then he'd had an idea. He smiled, and picked up a sharp rock and scratched a beaver, big teeth and all, on the side of the cart and wrote, BEAVER DAM DELIVERY SERVICE in big letters. They agreed, and had great fun enhancing the beaver, adding a hat, a really big tail and goofy eyes. Dad had donated some old paint. They may have gotten more paint on themselves than on the cart, but when they finished, the cart looked great. They added more customers in the couple of years that followed, and were making pretty good money.

Bob left the cart with Tommy when he moved, but had saved enough to buy a used cart here in Detroit. He knew it wouldn't be the same, but at least he could start again by picking up Mother's groceries.

"Robin?" Mother said as she appeared around the corner of the house. "Oh, here you are." She sat down on the step next to him. "This is rather a cold perch," she smiled.

"I know, I was just thinking about Tommy and wondering how the delivery service was going."

"Well, I'll have a big list for you tomorrow. And I was thinking, Christmas is only ten days away. Come in for dinner, and we'll start making plans for our first Detroit Christmas. Oh, and your dad and I have decided that you're probably right, starting school now, right before the holiday break, would be silly. You can start fresh, first thing in January," she smiled and patted him on the knee, "Brrrr, let's go in."

He followed her inside thinking: *Reprieve. No new school for two whole weeks.*

EXTRA   DEC 15 1915

The Crane Ave. Gazette
PRINTED BY THE DETROIT DELIVERY DPT.
PRICE 2 CENTS
NO 1   VOL 1

NOTICE —   SEE LAST PAGE

The name and form
of the g.o. has been
changed as you
know. This paper
will be published
regular every
Saturday.
          EDITOR

NEW YEARS NUMBER

The Crane Ave. Gazette
Published every
Sat. Price 2 cents
a copy

Do you read the
g.o. sign
changed every Sat.

THE DETROIT
DELIVERY
DPT
PROMPT SERVICE —

December 15, 1915
www.catherinepaonessa.com/thegazette

New Neighbors
~ Aunty McLeod

Aunty McLeod put down her pencil and sighed; usually she enjoyed writing to her grandson. When she and her husband, Alan, moved to Detroit almost twenty years ago, they left behind their grown son Andrew, his wife, and, their only grandchild, Davy. Davy was just a wee bairn at the time; he was a young man now.

Her husband had worked with Ransom Olds at Detroit's first automobile plant on East Jefferson near Belle Isle. He passed away last year. She thought about leaving Detroit, but where would she go? Back to Scotland? Maybe. She had considered it, but her son had died in a mining accident eight years ago and his wife had since remarried. Scotland wasn't her home anymore, Detroit was her home now.

She picked her pencil up again. She had been writing to Davy since he was quite young. She wanted him to know his Nana in America. She wrote every Saturday afternoon. Letters about life in the growing city of Detroit. And Davy wrote delightful letters back. First, childish little "I love you Nana" notes, then as he grew, letters filled with the tales of boyish life. After his father died, Davy wrote about him. He would ask her questions about when Andrew was a little boy. In a way, the loss brought them closer together. They shared their grief across a vast ocean.

This letter was especially hard to write because Davy was no longer at his home in Bothwell, Scotland, but in an English army training camp. He would be going to France to fight. She was shocked, saddened, and worried by his last letter. It was filled with dreams of war; travel, courage, heroism. In a way, she didn't blame him; he had started working in the coalmines a year ago, when he turned eighteen. He hated it. Hidden between the lines of his letters, she could feel the sadness he felt spending his days in the dark and breathless hole. The dark hole that had taken his father from him far too early.

She smoothed the blank paper with her gnarled hands and wrote,

Dear Davy,

I want to ask you why, but I think I understand. Your Grandfather hated mining, and left everything, friends, family, country and you to escape from it. Your father, may he rest in peace, never seemed to mind the confinement of the mine and even enjoyed the camaraderie with his boyhood friends who shared the mine with him. The world is changing, and I understand that you want to be part of it. I hope the army is feeding you and preparing you for what is to come. Please try to write. I will write, as always, every week. I will try to include the usual comings and goings of your old Nana's quiet life, and hope my letters give you some comfort while you face the trials of war.

As Always, Your Loving Nana

She sat for a moment, seeing in her mind's eye Davy, dressed as a soldier, prepared for war, and she signed. She looked out the window into the backyard. A movement caught her eye. It was a boy. He was in the yard just north of hers beyond the ally. He was sitting on the back step of his house. He looked rather like her Davy. She could see red curls sticking out from under his cap, Davy's hair was wavy too, but dark brown. This boy was younger than Davy, but only by a couple of years. She watched him for a bit. He was picking up stones and tossing them toward a nearby fence.

Christmas in Detroit
~ Bob Stevens

Bob and his parents had a quiet first Christmas in Detroit. Dad worked a regular half-day shift on Christmas Eve and arrived home at noon. After a quick lunch, he and Bob were off to buy a tree. Mother stayed home to find the decorations among the pile of boxes in the basement.

"I saw a pretty good tree lot a few blocks away; at E. Jefferson and Hibbard. We should be able to carry the tree home from there," Dad said.

"That sounds good. Do you want to take my cart?" asked Bob.

"Good idea," Dad said looking up at the gray sky. He continued, "The fellas at work were talking about a Christmas Eve snowstorm, but I'm sure we'll be home before it hits."

They went to the little shed in the yard and retrieved the cart. Bob bought it used within a week of arriving in Detroit. They walked down Crane Avenue toward Jefferson. The air was crisp and delicate flurries danced about. The tree lot was busy. People were browsing, each looking for their perfect Christmas tree. The trees were a mix of bushy white pine, picky blue spruce and soft Douglas-fir. The strong, crisp smell of fresh cut fir trees filled the air. People chatted as they moved from tree to tree.

"What about this one?" one mother said.

"It's too small" her children shouted in unison.

Bob eavesdropped on a young couple.

"We want a big tree, right?" the man asked his young wife.

"But not too big, the living room is so small, and we don't have many decorations."

Maybe it's their first Christmas in Detroit too, Bob thought.

He and Dad wandered around. A Salvation Army band was playing Christmas music on the corner, adding to the jolly spirit of the lot. Dad whistled along, and dropped a few coins in the kettle as they passed. They found their perfect tree: a tall, and not too fat, Douglas-fir. Dad examined the trunk to ensure that it was straight. They discussed whether Mother would approve and after agreeing that she would, they made their decision. Each tree had a small tag with the price, so there was no need to barter with the salesman. Dad looked relieved, he never liked arguing about the price of something and believed it was the duty of the seller to pick a price. They loaded the tree in the cart and headed home, whistling Christmas music together. The flurries had turned into a steady snowfall that was quickly covering them and the tree.

Mother was watching for them from the front bay window. She waved and smiled when she saw them coming.

"Mother looks happy, she must like the tree," Dad said. "We must look like a scene from a Christmas snow globe that has just been given a quick shake."

On Christmas Day they went to church services at Fort Street Presbyterian Church. They opened presents after church. A couple of weeks ago Bob had distributed the savings from the Detroit Weekly Savings Bank.

Mother had the idea of starting a family bank last summer while they were still in Beaver Dam. She said it would be fun. Bob thought she was worried they wouldn't be able to put aside any extra savings with the expense of moving and setting up house in Detroit. He was beginning to see that while Dad was the head of the household, Mother was much more than the "sweet dear" Dad called her. She provided a ledger and put Bob in charge of managing the bank. He collected money from his parents each week and logged it in the "Detroit Weekly Savings Bank" ledger. He also added some savings from his delivery money. They each had their own accounts. He kept the money in a strong box hidden behind some shoes and stuff in his closet. By December, they each had a bit of savings to spend on Christmas presents for each other. He gave Mother a new pair of gloves. They were soft and a warm taupe color.

She opened her present and was so surprised. "Robin, dear, they're perfect. How did you know what size to get?

Oh, and just feel how soft." She loved them, and kept them on as she watched Bob and Dad open their presents.

Dad opened the warm wool scarf and socks Mother made for him. "These are great," he said as he wrapped the scarf around this neck. He continued, "These Detroit winters seem colder, damper, than even the winters in Beaver Dam. These will keep me nice and warm, thank you dear."

Bob handed Dad his gift with a sly smile. He thought back to the day he got it. It had been a cold day at the end of November. They had just arrived in Detroit. It had been Dad's first day at Burroughs. Bob was helping his mom unpack the kitchen boxes, but he was anxious to go out and explore the city. He started stacking plates on a convenient shelf in the closest cupboard and, cups on the shelf above. *This wouldn't take long at all,* he was thinking.

"Oh, no, Bob, the plates can't go there." Mother said.

His mom's voice startled him. He bashed the cup he was stacking against the edge of the shelf, a small chip appeared. "Oops, sorry." Bob mumbled.

Mother frowned, took the cup from him and said, "How about you go out for a bit, and let me decide where everything will go. A kitchen requires a certain organization." He was more than happy to escape the cramped kitchen, even if it meant braving the cold November day.

Out on the street, he headed toward Jefferson Avenue. He and Dad had talked about going to see the Tigers play at Navin Field in the spring. He decided to check out the ball park and see how long it took to get there. Bob had already studied the streetcar map. He hurried to a nearby stop and took the westbound Jefferson car to Fort Street.

From there he walked up Trumbull to Navin Field at the corner of Michigan and Trumbull. The ball park was huge, much bigger than he had imagined. *It must hold thousands of people*, he thought. A cold wind tugged at the collar of his coat, reminding him that spring, and baseball, were a long way off. As he was standing there, a door at the base of the concrete structure opened and a man came out. Bob knew instantly who it was, he had seen his picture in the paper hundreds of times. It was Ty Cobb, "The Georgia Peach". Bob stared, frozen in place. The papers said Mr. Cobb killed a man, they said he was a dirty player, but they loved him in Detroit.

Mr. Cobb was walking straight toward him, and then the famous ball player said, "Hey, kid, I hope you haven't been messing with that car."

Bob looked over his shoulder and realized he was standing between Mr. Cobb and his car.

"Oh, no sir, I was, ah just, looking at the ball park." Bob stammered.

"Last season was exciting. We'll get those Red Sox next year," Mr. Cobb said.

"Yes, sir, I'm sure you will sir." Bob couldn't believe he was talking baseball with Ty Cobb. Mr. Cobb reached into his car and grabbed a baseball card and a pen. He signed the card and handed it to Bob.

"Here, now scram," Mr. Cobb said, then he got into his car and sped away.

Bob couldn't believe it. A Ty Cobb autographed baseball card. He watched the car until it turned a corner, then he headed for home. He put the card in his overcoat pocket, afraid the wind would steal it from him. All the way home, he kept patting the pocket, making sure the card was safe. Bob framed the card between two pieces of glass neatly held together with some straps of leather.

It was that baseball card, wrapped in Christmas paper that Bob now handed to Dad. It was the perfect gift. He could give it to Dad, and still see it whenever he wanted. Dad put the glass frame in a plate spot in the corner cabinet, displacing one of Mother's china plates, but she didn't seem to mind. It stayed there for many years, and was a favorite family story – the day Bob met Ty Cobb.

From his parents Bob got a new, much needed, gray felt wool overcoat. Mother said he was growing like a weed. He also got some colored pencils. "For your newspaper project," Dad said. Next he opened three packs of baseball cards. They laughed at the coincidence. Although there were some good players, there was no Ty Cobb card. He also got the popular card game Pit.

"Unfortunately, we'll have to wait until tomorrow to play, remember, no cards on Christmas Day," Dad said.

"But this isn't really a card game, it's ah, well, a table game," Bob argued. "They're not regular cards at all," Bob showed Dad the cards, "see, wheat, barley, and corn." Bob tried to convince his dad that playing Pit on Christmas would not break the No Cards on Sunday Rule. Bob never understood this hard and fast family rule. They weren't particularly religious, but dad had strict "Sunday" rules; including, no card playing, no marbles, no fun. It was a day for quiet reflection and reading.

"We'll see," Dad said. "Maybe after supper."

But, instead of playing cards after supper, they had an unexpected visitor. A Mrs. Mary McLeod came tapping on their door.

"Happy Christmas to you all," Mrs. McLeod said with a smile, "I'm Mary McLeod, and I live behind you, one house to the south. I have to confess, I watched you move in a couple of weeks ago and feel awful that I haven't been to welcome you until now. I hope I'm not disturbing your Christmas evening?"

"Not at all," Mother said. "I'm Susie Stevens, this is my husband Robert and our son Robin." Dad and Bob rose. "This is Mrs. McLeod our new neighbor," Mother continued. Bob was just about to ask Mrs. McLeod to call him Bob, but, she was already making her own introduction.

"Please, call me Aunty McLeod, all the neighbors do. I've lived in Detroit for almost twenty years. I've watched the streets get longer and longer as the city has grown bigger and bigger with each passing year. It will be an important city one day," Aunty McLeod said. She handed Mother a tin and added, "Scottish shortbread, it's my specialty."

Shortbread, Bob thought, *too bad it's such a small tin.*

"How thoughtful, we were just about to have a nice cup of Christmas eggnog. Would you like to join us? Shortbread is Robin's," Mother paused and looked at Bob, "Bob's favorite."

As much as Bob had begged her to stop, Mother couldn't get out of the habit of calling him, Robin.

Aunty McLeod joined them for eggnog and she filled them in on the neighborhood. Who had a new baby, whose dog was not well mannered, and whose husband went to the pub too often. Bob sighed. Everyone in the neighborhood would be calling him Robin before he even got a chance to meet them.

"We haven't met our right-side neighbors yet, do you know them?" Dad asked.

"Oh, yes, that would be Professor Ackermann. Now there's a sad story. He teaches English literature and German language courses at the new college. He came here from Germany with his wife and daughter about ten years ago. He lost them both. Poor dears, his wife to influenza three years ago, and his daughter to polio a year later. He's been a recluse ever since, he's still grieving. Women, they need each other to grieve, they talk and talk until they've talked it out. Men, some of them anyway, just want to be left alone."

The conversation moved on to Detroit and how it was growing. Bob was disappointed. He was hoping a boy like Tommy might live next-door. Professor Ackermann, Bob realized, must have been the one who threw the stone back over the fence.

As Aunty McLeod was leaving she asked Bob, "I notice you pick up your mother's groceries. Could you do the same for me? I'll pay you of course."

Bob couldn't believe his luck, his first real customer. "Sure."

"Wonderful, stop by tomorrow and we'll work out the details." And with that, Aunty McLeod disappeared out the door, through the snowy yard and into the alley.

Professor Ackermann
~ Bob Stevens

Bob was busy the last couple of days of the Christmas holiday. He visited Aunty McLeod and made arrangements to deliver her groceries once a week. He also sold her a copy of his newspaper. He thought she might be a good source of information for his columns. As he was walking home through the alley and yard, he could hear someone chopping wood on the other side of the fence. *It must be Professor Ackermann*, he thought. Bob remembered Aunty McLeod saying that he taught classes at the new junior college. Maybe he could read The Gazette and tell Bob if it was any good. Bob rushed to his room and carefully wrote out another copy of the second issue. But when Bob went back out to the yard, the chopping had stopped. So, he went back to his room and wrote a note:

Dear Professor Ackermann,

Let me introduce myself. My name is Robert Stevens and I live next-door. I would like to start by apologizing for throwing rocks at your fence, I won't do it again. I have a favor to ask. I would like to be a journalist or war correspondent someday. For practice I'm working on a newspaper, The Crane Ave Gazette. Because you're a professor, I was wondering if you could read it and let me know if it's any good.

Sincerely,
Robert Randolph Stevens

p.s. Please call me Bob.

He thought about going to the side door, but remembered what Aunty McLeod said about Professor Ackermann being a recluse. And there was the big dog to think about. Instead, he rolled up the paper and note and put it in the knothole. He hurried back into the house. It was cold and a heavy snow was beginning to fall. A blizzard was on the way. Bob checked the knothole later that afternoon, the newspaper and note were gone.

It snowed through the night and Bob spent the next morning digging out. Every now and then he checked the knothole, but it remained empty. Bob spent the cold afternoon in his room working on the next issue of The Gazette. He discovered he could see the knothole in the fence from his window. Actually, he could see most of Professor Ackermann's yard. It was bigger than their yard. The shrubs were big, overgrown and loaded down with snow. At the far end of the yard was a small building, Bob thought, *ah, what are those things called, a kind of garden room with a roof, but no walls. They always seemed kind of worthless. Why didn't they have walls anyway? Whatever it's called, it needs a fresh coat of paint.* He went back to work on his paper, but kept looking at the knothole hoping to see Professor Ackermann. After a while, he became engrossed in his paper, adding stamps, drawing pictures and writing a poem. The New Year's issue would be the best yet. The next time he looked at the fence, he was surprised and excited to see a rolled piece of paper in the knothole. He rushed down the stairs and out the kitchen door. When his stocking feet hit the slush at the bottom of the steps, he regretted not stopping to pull on his boots. *Too late now*, he thought and continued into the foot deep snow to the fence. He pulled out the note and unrolled it:

Look Down

At his feet, a package stuck out of the snow. It was wrapped in waxed cotton and tied with a piece of twine. He picked it up, and started to untie the twine, then decided to wait until he was back inside. His feet were cold. The snow pulled at his wet socks with each step back to the house. When he reached the steps, his socks were heavy with snow and ice and hanging off his feet.

Bob left his soaked socks by the kitchen door and headed back to his room where he laid the package on the desk and untied the twine. Inside was a typed note, a copy of the *"Electric Railway Service"* magazine and a list of words. The note said:

```
Dear Bob,
     Thank you for not throwing more rocks at the
fence, the noise was quite distracting. I am will-
ing to edit your newspaper under the following
conditions:
     1.  Your spelling is appalling.  Please use a
         dictionary. I'll return a list of misspelled
         words - learn them.
     2.  You need more content for the paper to be
         interesting.  Enclosed is last week's copy
         of the "Electric Railway Service" magazine.
         You might be able to find some interesting
         information in it.  You can borrow my copy
         each week as long as you return it in good
         condition.
```

> 3. In return, you can shovel my walk each morn-
>   ing as needed and, in the summer, cut the
>   lawn and trim the shrubs in the yard.
>
> If you agree to these conditions, put each issue
> and the ERS magazine in the milk box by the kitchen
> door. I'll put the corrected issue and a newer ERS
> magazine in the box within two days. Don't worry
> about Nietzsche (Neat-cha), she's big, but she'll get
> used to you.
>
> > Sincerely,
> > Professor Ackermann

Bob read the note over twice. He was surprised and a little worried. Professor Ackermann seemed very serious and stricter than his teachers back in Beaver Dam. He hoped the teachers at Eastern High weren't this tough. And shoveling the snow, cutting the grass, wow, Professor Ackermann was asking a lot. And Nietzsche must be the giant German Shepard. *Great, how would she get used to me,* Bob thought, *one bite at a time?*

Bob picked up the *"Electric Railway Service"* magazine and thumbed through the pages. Professor Ackermann was right, the ERS contained lots of good information. *Shoveling the snow and the cutting the grass will be a lot of work, but it will be worth it for Professor Ackermann's corrections and getting to use the ERS,* Bob thought.

Bob started to work on The Gazette again, but remembered what Professor Ackermann's note said about spelling errors. D*rat,* Bob thought. *Where is my dictionary? Blast, it's probably in the basement in one of the unpacked boxes.* Bob stood from his desk and stomped off to find the old dictionary.

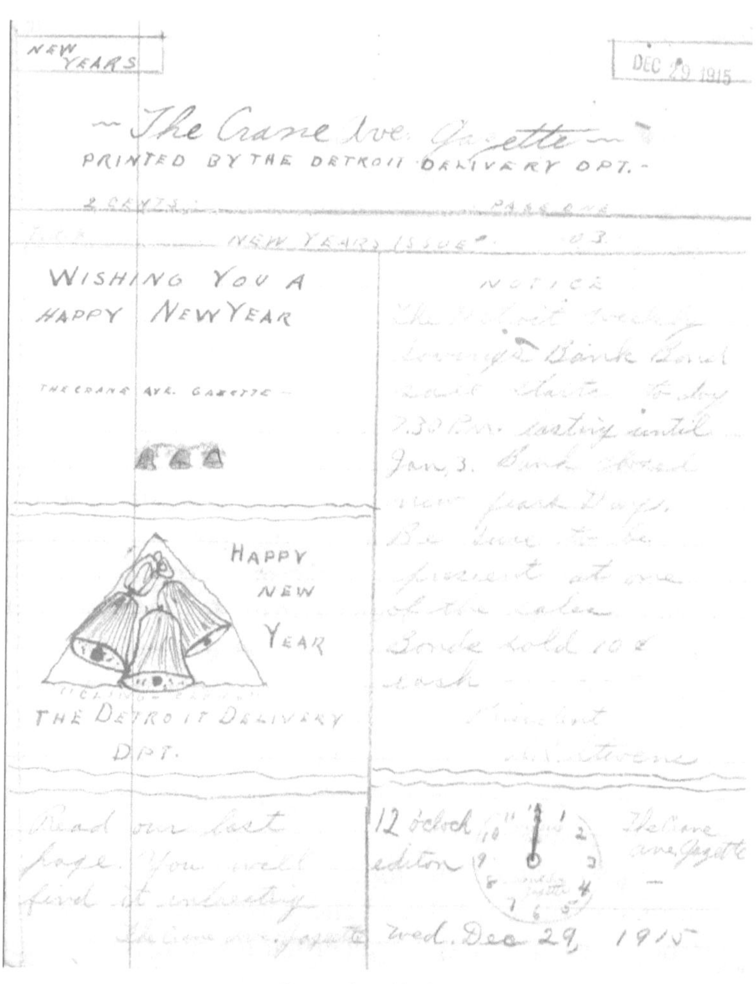

December 29, 1915
www.catherinepaonessa.com/thegazette

Eastern High School
~ Bob Stevens

After much nagging and negotiating, Bob reached a haircut compromise with Mother. She accepted that he was too old for her to be cutting his hair, and he agreed to get it trimmed at regular barber shop.

On the first day of school after Christmas break Bob reported to the Eastern High School office. *This school is huge,* he thought. He had registered for classes before the break and was told to stop by the office to pick up his schedule. He was a freshman. The office was busy. Teachers were talking, a group of students were changing the display on a large bulletin board, and the receptionist, Mrs. Truesdale, was on the phone. Bob waited, trying to look inconspicuous. He took off his glasses, wiped them on his shirtsleeve and put them on again. He opened a notebook he was carrying and pretended to study the forms he was supposed to turn in.

"Can I help you?" Mrs. Truesdale asked. "Excuse me, young man."

It was a minute before Bob realized she was talking to him. "Oh, yeah," Bob stammered, "This is my first day." He handed the paperwork to Mrs. Truesdale. "I was told to drop this off and pick up my schedule."

"Name?" Mrs. Truesdale asked.

"Robert Stevens," Bob answered.

"Let's see," Mrs. Truesdale rifled through some stacks of papers on her desk. "Oh yes, here you are," she said. "Robert Randolph Stevens?"

"Yes, ma'am."

"Welcome to Eastern High School," Mrs. Truesdale said with a smile. "Here is your schedule, a map of the school, and give this note to your first hour teacher." Her phone rang and as she answered crisply, "Eastern High School, how may I help you?" she dismissed him with a quick wave of her hand.

Bob stepped into the crowded hall. He pressed up against the wall and looked at his schedule, first hour was in room 204. He located 204 on the map. The stairs were at the end of the hall. He stepped into the flow of students and was propelled toward the stairway.

As Bob reached the top of the stairs, the bell rang and the halls quickly emptied. It was eerily quiet. *Crap,* he thought, *late for my first class.* He needed room 204. He passed 211, 210, and 209. There, 204. His heart was pounding and the note for the teacher was getting moist in his sweaty hand. He took a deep breath, and opened the door. All heads turned and stared. He could feel his face turning as red as his curly hair, and his glasses slipping down his nose. He handed the note to the pretty, fair-haired teacher.

"Hello there," she said as she looked at the note. She looked back at Bob and smiled, "Welcome to English Composition. Class, please welcome Robert Stevens."

"Ah, Bob, please," he corrected. There was a chorus of Hi's and Hello's.

"Oh, yes fine, Bob Stevens," Miss Stewart replied. She continued, "I'm Miss Stewart. Let's see, I guess you'll have to take that desk at the back, near the window. We've been discussing post-graduation careers."

Bob nodded, worked his way to the appointed desk, and sat down. *At least I got a good seat,* he thought. Miss Stewart continued talking. Bob's heart was slowing down; he was glad that was over with. He took a deep breath, and looked out the window. He could see the tall buildings of downtown Detroit in the distance. His mind wandered back to Beaver Dam. *What were the fellas doing after school today? Skating, ice fishing on the lake or sledding down by the waterworks. There was always something fun to do.*

"Mr. Stevens, have you considered what you would like to do after you graduate from high school?" Miss Stewart was saying. "Mr. Stevens?"

Bob's thoughts were yanked back to the classroom by a low murmur from his classmates. He realized the question was for him. Everyone was looking at him, expectantly.

"Ah, a war correspondent," he blurted out. But, before the word correspondent had left his lips, he was interrupted.

"War, that's all you boys think about!" a girl on the other side of the room burst out, "I'll have to be a nurse, or even a doctor just to take care of you when you come home without arms and legs."

"That will be enough Miss Robinson, and what have I told you about wearing a cap to class?" Miss Stewart said.

The girl sat down mumbling something about how the rule against hats doesn't apply to girls, but she took off the cap, set it on her desk, set her jaw stubbornly and stared at the green chalkboard.

Bob wondered why this strange, cap-wearing girl yelled at him. He didn't know that while his mind had been back in Beaver Dam, five or six of the other chaps had also mentioned the war in their post-graduation responses. He looked again at the outspoken girl. She was staring at the chalkboard, wisps of brown wavy hair had escaped her thick braid. Light brown freckles were sprinkled over her nose. Not too many, but just enough. Bob realized he was staring and looked again out the window at the Detroit skyline.

The day wore on. Bob entered each class as the new kid, and couldn't wait for it to end. The second day would be better, maybe he could disappear in this crowd of kids. As he left his last class and headed for the huge wooden front doors of the high school, someone behind him yelled, "Hey, wait, new kid." Bob considered running for the exit, but instead, clenched his fists as he turned around, not sure what to expect. Before him stood a tall upper-classman with dark hair and beady eyes. He extended his hand for Bob to shake.

"Miss Stewart said you might be interested in the school newspaper class. I'm John Edwards, the editor. You can't take it until junior year, but don't forget to put it on your schedule. Here's a copy of the latest edition."

Bob took the paper and said, "Great. Thanks, I. . ." but John Edwards had already turned and was walking away. Bob sighed and thought *Mr. Edwards must be a senior with no time for a crummy freshman.* Bob headed toward the exit and escaped through the doors and into the fresh, cold air of a Detroit winter.

The Snowball
~ Maggie Robinson

A couple of days later Maggie Robinson was shoveling snow from the front walk. With Sam and Bill gone, keeping the walk clear was her job. She pushed the shovel into the heavy snow and threw it into the rising snow bank next to the walk. Her family had moved from Toronto to Detroit last summer. Her father was a mason, and with Detroit growing so fast, there was plenty of work. She was used to snow, and usually liked to help Sam and Bill shovel, but shoveling alone was, well lonely. She tossed another shovel full of snow into the air, but a cold wind blew it back into her face. She grimaced. Maggie was fifteen, third oldest after the boys, so she got stuck with the shoveling. Jeannie was ten and old enough to help, but she coughed and whined about the cold and Mum let her stay in the nice warm kitchen. *Faker,* Maggie thought. She threw another shovel full of snow, to the other side of the walk this time, with the wind. She should have talked Sara into helping, she was only six so she wasn't much help, but at least she was company.

Bill and Sam had joined the Canadian Army in the fall. They'd been gone for four months. Maggie's mind traveled back to the day they left. She had been in the backyard, picking up soft apples from the ground and throwing them, hard, at the trunk of the old oak. But she kept missing. That had been her and Sam's game. Sam had been teaching her how not to "throw like a girl."

She had bent down to pick up another apple, when from behind her Sam had said, "You still throw like a girl." She hadn't answered; she threw another apple, but missed, again. Sam continued, "Aren't you going to come and say a proper goodbye? Everyone will be disappointed if you don't see us off."

She remembered looking at him. He looked so grown-up in his new khaki uniform.

"I don't want you to go. It's not even our fight. That's what all the newspapers say," she said.

"But it is Great Britain's fight, which makes it Canada's fight, and my fight. All the boys from the old neighbor-hood are signing up." Sam had his cap in his hand, it was his favorite cap, he plopped it on her head, gave it a jaunty tilt, and placed a piece of brown hair that had escaped her pony tail behind her ear. "You take good care of my cap, okay, I'm going to want it back when I get home. Now come on, it's time for us to leave." And he had walked away.

A strange squeaking sound brought her back to the January day and the icy walkway. She looked across the street. It was the new boy, the war correspondent boy, pull-ing a squeaky cart. Why was he staring at her? Before she could stop herself, she bent over, made a snowball and threw it at him. The snowball sailed straight and true, over the street and, to her surprise and horror, hit him right in the face. She was shocked. She never hit anything she was actually aiming at. Bother, she thought, he was walking faster now, almost running, wiping the snow and ice from his face.

"Hey, wait, wait, I'm sorry," she yelled after him. But he didn't look back. He turned the corner and disappeared down the street. "Well, if you're going to be like that, fine!" she shouted after him. "It's not polite to stare anyway, and why don't you oil those squeaky wheels." She felt bad, but he was staring and well, Sam would be really proud of that throw. Sam's cap had fallen into the snow. She picked it up, brushed it off, and plopped it back on her brown curls.

Snowballed
~ Bob Stevens

Bob couldn't believe it. Why would she throw a snowball at him? She didn't even know him. He wiped the snow and ice from his face and glasses. He could still hear her yelling something about staring and the squeaky cart wheels. *I'll show her what for,* he thought. He was steaming mad. He stopped around the corner and made a couple hard snowballs. He even included a few small rocks for good measure. He and Tommy had had their fair share of snowball fights. But he couldn't throw a snowball at a girl. Drat. He threw the snowballs at a nearby tree. They exploded hard against the trunk, surprising even himself. *No,* he thought, *he couldn't hit a girl with a snowball. She would probably cry and tell everyone at school how mean he was, even though she started it. He could probably even get arrested for it.* For a moment, he imagined the police coming and taking him away in handcuffs. Mother would cry, and Dad would plead with the officer to let him go. It would be the beginning of his life as a criminal.

He was heading home after making a grocery delivery to Aunty McLeod. It felt great to have the delivery service up and running again, then that crazy girl hit him with a snowball. *Ugh, snowballed by a girl,* he thought. O*kay,* he admitted to himself, *I was staring.* He recognized her from school. She was the one who yelled at him about the war. She was kind of pretty, even with the boy's cap on. He was staring and thinking about how her brown curls glistened in the late afternoon sun. And how her cheeks were pink from the cold. No, it just wouldn't do to hit her with a snowball. How stupid. He didn't even see her making the snowball, didn't even try to duck. Gosh, he felt like such a dingbat.

Maggie Tries to Make Amends
~ Maggie Robinson

Maggie watched the boy disappear around the corner. She thought about chasing after him, but couldn't seem to get her feet to obey. She was so embarrassed. What must he think of her? Throwing snowballs? So un-lady like, as Mum was always telling her. As the evening wore on, she felt even worse. What an awful thing to do, she was too ashamed to tell anyone. Oh, why had Sam taught her to throw so well? She resolved to apologize first thing in the morning. The boy was in her first hour English Composition class. She would do it then.

And she tried. For the next few days she tried to catch him on the way out of class, but he always seemed to disappear in the crowded hallway. She got to class early, but he arrived right as class started. Then she was stuck home sick with a cold for three days. She needed another plan, but first, she needed to know more about the war correspondent boy. She would visit Aunty McLeod. Aunty McLeod knew everything about everyone in the neighborhood, and always welcomed a visitor, especially if the visitor brought a treat. Mum still had homemade jelly from last summer in the pantry. Maggie suggested that it would be neighborly to deliver a jar to Aunty McLeod. Mum agreed and Maggie was off. It was cold and a light snow was falling. She hurried around the block and tapped on Aunty McLeod's kitchen door.

Aunty McLeod answered with a big smile. "Well, what a nice surprise, come in, come in."

"My mum sent me over with some jelly. She thought you might like it." Maggie offered the bright, little jar of strawberry jelly.

"Why how thoughtful. It's like a bit of summer in a jar." The kettle was whistling on the stove. "And look, you're just in time for tea. You must stay." Aunty McLeod said.

Maggie unwrapped from her layers of coat, scarf, mittens and Sam's hat. Aunty McLeod took her things and set them aside. She directed Maggie to a chair at the kitchen table and, after gently brushing the snow from it, she hung Sam's hat on the back of the chair.

"Tea would be wonderful," Maggie said, hoping Aunty McLeod would put out some shortbread. They sat down in the cozy kitchen to "enjoy a visit" as Mum would say. To Maggie's surprise, she didn't even have to ask the question she came to ask.

Aunty McLeod said, "Have you meet any of the Stevens family yet? Robin, the boy, should be in the same class as you at school. Oh, but his mother told me he goes by Bob at school."

Maggie decided she would stick to Bob, as he was already mad at her.

Aunty McLeod went on. "They live on Crane Avenue, one house north of mine. Such a nice little family, Mrs. Stevens has stopped by for tea a couple of times. Her husband works at Burroughs, up at the corner of Burroughs and Amsterdam. They make adding machines. Do you know anything about adding machines?" Maggie nodded, and was about to answer, but Aunty McLeod went on, "Someday you'll have to explain them to me. Bob is their only child."

Maggie felt even guiltier about the snowball. She always thought being an only child would be the saddest thing ever.

Aunty McLeod was still talking, "He's started a delivery service, and he has been delivering my groceries." She moved a plate of shortbread cookies closer to Maggie with a smile. "He's a nice young man and very reliable. You should get to know him; he might be welcome company with your brothers gone." Aunty McLeod caught Maggie's eye, and Maggie saw understanding in her face. Aunty

McLeod continued, "It's hard for you and your family. Me too, your brothers and my Davy are fighting over there, but America is trying to stay neutral. They don't understand, not yet. You can't blame them really. It's hard to think of our young men, any of them, British, Canadian, or American in harm's way." Aunty McLeod's voice trailed away as she spoke of the young soldiers.

"I didn't know you had family fighting. Who's Davy?" Maggie asked.

"Oh, he's my grandson. He lives in Scotland, and joined up with the Highland Light Infantry. I've been writing to him since he was a boy. So, you see, we have to help each other through these trying times." She patted Maggie's hand. "If you start missing them, you just pop over and see me, maybe Davy will run into your brothers, wouldn't that be something? I'll tell him to look out for them in my next letter. Oh, now, look at the time, your mum will be looking for you."

Maggie thanked Aunty McLeod for the tea and shortbread, and promised to visit again. As she walked home she thought about her plan to apologize to Bob.

The next day, she returned home from school as quickly as possible and asked her Mum if she could borrow the little oilcan Da kept in the shed. A friend wanted to use it. With the can in hand, she headed over to the Stevens house. She debated front door, or side door. She decided on the side door. Front doors were for important company, not neighborhood visits.

She tapped at the kitchen door window and Mrs. Stevens answered.

"Why hello there?"

"Hello, I'm Maggie Robinson, I'm ah, a friend of Bob's" Maggie stammered.

"Oh, I'm sorry dear, Bob's not home from school yet. He's been getting home later and later these last couple of weeks."

Maggie hadn't planned on him not being home, "Ah, can you give him this, ah oilcan, ah for his cart and tell him to drop it by my house when he's done with it." With that, she turned and briskly walked away. *Bother*, she thought, *that didn't go as planned. Oh, that will make things even worse. He'll think I'm teasing him about the squeaky wheels. Oh, this is horrible.*

A Proper Introduction
~ Bob Stevens

Bob had been busy learning his way around school, working on his newspaper and avoiding the girl with the cap. Plus, it seemed like it had snowed every day since he'd agreed to shovel Professor Ackermann's walk.

He started taking the long way home, avoiding the path he thought she would take. In English Composition, he sat on the other side of the room, and when class ended, he was able to escape and disappear in the crowded hall. All the same, he couldn't help glancing over at her. She caught him a few times, and sort of smiled back, but maybe, he thought, she was just laughing to herself about how she nailed him with that snowball.

Bob got home later than usual one afternoon. He went into the kitchen to say hello to Mother and see what was for dinner, thinking a snack would be great. An oilcan was sitting in the middle of the kitchen table.

"Hello, Robin, you're late today," she said.

"Oh, sorry, do you need something oiled?"

"Oh, no, not me. A girl, um, Maggie Robinson was her name, stopped by and dropped that oilcan off for you. We have an oilcan. You didn't need to borrow one, but she's a pretty little thing, so, I guess I understand."

"But I didn't…" Bob started to protest, but stopped. If he told her why the girl dropped off the oilcan, he would have to tell her about the snowball, and he was too embarrassed to tell his mother he got hit in the face with a snowball by a girl. Plus, for some reason, he didn't want his mother to think Maggie Robinson was the kind of girl that went around hitting people with snowballs. He continued, "Oh, yeah, I, ah, couldn't find ours. I thought it got lost in the move or something."

"Oh, I see," Mother said with a smile. "Well, don't forget to return that one." She nodded toward the oilcan on the table. "I don't want the neighbors to think we're the type of people who borrow things without returning them."

"I'll return it after school tomorrow. I have lots of homework to do tonight, and I want to work on my newspaper." He took the oilcan and headed up to his room.

He set it on his shelf and tried to concentrate on his geometry homework, but he kept looking over at the oilcan. He would have to meet her face to face. Why did she have to bring over that stupid oilcan? Did she think they didn't have one? Everyone has an oilcan. There was no avoiding her now. He looked back at the geometry problem. God, he hated geometry.

After finally finishing his homework, he worked on The Gazette. He wanted to try a new method of transferring pictures from the real newspaper to his newspaper. Professor Ackermann wrote him a note explaining just how to do it. First, you soften up a bit of wax with the heat from your hands. Then, spread it on the picture you want to copy. Next, you peel it off and press it on a fresh sheet of paper. He tried it with a picture in the *Detroit News*. It worked great. Professor Ackermann was really helpful, but super critical. Bob figured he would have to get used to that if he was going to be in the newspaper business. It was strange though, he still hadn't met Professor Ackermann in person. As directed, Bob put the latest edition of The Gazette in the milk box, which was tricky for the first couple of weeks because of Nietzsche.

The first time he tried, Nietzsche had growled and barked when he attempted to open the gate. Bob had gone back to his room in disgust and waited until Nietzsche was in the house for the night. *This wouldn't do* he thought, he couldn't be sneaking around the neighbors at night, but he had an idea. The next time he was at the grocery store, he used some of his delivery earnings to buy a bag of dog biscuits. Then, when he went to drop off his newspaper, he threw a biscuit to the back of the yard and when Nietzsche ran after it, he quickly went in and made the drop-off. But, Bob was beginning to think Nietzsche's bark was worse than her bite. The silly dog watched him through the fence as he shoveled the snow, and yesterday, when he went to pick up Professor Ackermann's corrections, Nietzsche got the biscuit, but instead of eating it at the back of the yard, she ran back and dropped it a few feet away from where Bob was standing. Bob picked it up and threw it, and again Nietzsche brought it back. They played fetch until Bob's hands were freezing, the biscuit was soggy and he had to go in for dinner. As he walked home, Bob realized he'd just made his first real friend in Detroit. *Okay, it was a dog*, he thought, *but it's a start.*

After dinner, Bob looked through the *Detroit News* and found some car pictures from the auto show. He'd been to the show with his dad, so he used the new wax method to copy some car pictures to the latest edition of the gazette. It looked great.

The next day, Bob covered the tip of the oilcan with a bit of wax and carefully positioned it in his book bag so it wouldn't spill. He planned on leaving it at the Robinson's back door after school.

Bob took the long way home, delaying the moment he might have to face Snowball Girl. On Mack Avenue, he noticed a team of horses with a buggy speeding down the street toward him. They were moving much too fast and heading straight for the congested intersections at E. Grand Boulevard and a block later, at Mt. Elliott Street. Bob watched the horses careen through the first intersection. Cars honked and swerved out of the way. One stopped so fast, that the car behind it slammed into its rear end. The commotion and noise of honking horns, screaming people and their own hooves on the cobblestone made the horses frantic. Bob watched in amazement as a policeman, who was standing at the corner of E. Grand Boulevard and Mack, took surprisingly quick action. The officer jumped on the running board of a car that was following the team. He indicated to the driver to speed up next to the horses. When he was abreast of the horses, he grasped the bit of one and brought the team to a stop before they reached the busy traffic at Mt. Elliott Street.

Bob continued to watch, amazed, as people gathered around. They shook the officer's hand and patted him on the back. *Wow*, Bob thought, *someone could have been killed had he not stopped the team.* The officer was a hero. Bob realized he had just witnessed a real news event. This would be great for his newspaper. He sat down on a bench at a nearby bus stop, pulled a notebook and pencil from his book bag and started to write. He made notes about the speed of the horses and the excitement of the crowd. Bob was so engrossed in his writing, that he didn't see her until she stuck her mitten covered hand in front of his face.

"Hello," she said, "let me introduce myself. I'm Maggie Roberson, and I'm really sorry I hit you with that snowball."

Her abrupt appearance made him jump. He dropped his pencil, and they both watched as it rolled off the curb and into a puddle of slush.

"Oh, bother!" Maggie said as she rushed to retrieve the pencil. She wiped it off with her mitten and handed it back to him with an uneasy smile. "What are doing?" she asked as she sat down next to him on the bench.

Bob couldn't believe it. It was her. Snowball Girl. He started to explain, hoping for an escape, "I'm, ah, writing about the runaway horses, I. . ."

"Oh wasn't that amazing!" she interrupted. "I saw the whole thing. I was standing right over there." She pointed down the street. "Were you standing here? I didn't even see you. I suppose you're writing it for practice, like a war correspondent. Very interesting, but I don't believe in this terrible war. It's enormously wrong. And such a waste. It's an awful way to settle anything. Why can't sensible people just talk out their differences? President Wilson's right in keeping out of it."

She could talk anyone out of anything, Bob thought.

With barely a breath, she continued, "My brothers are there, for Canada." She paused, adjusted her cap and started up again. "Do you know Mrs. McLeod, um, Aunty McLeod we call her? Her grandson is in France fighting for Britain. We commiserate about the war, but Americans don't understand, not yet. That's what Aunty McLeod says."

"But, I–" Bob tried to get a word in, but Maggie continued.

"Are you done with your story? It's getting cold. Do you want to walk home with me? We're going the same direction anyway and it would be silly for you to walk a few feet behind me. And you can't still be mad about the snowball because I didn't really mean to hit you. I usually miss everything I aim at. And you were staring. Actually, it's really Sam's fault, because he's the one who taught me to throw anyway. He's my brother. I felt so bad. I hardly slept that night and then I found out you're an only child, and that made me feel even worse because I can't imagine being an only child. So you see, you can't stay mad because I really am sorry and now Sam and Bill are fighting in France and you can't be mad at someone whose brothers are away fighting in a war, can you?"

With that she stopped talking. Bob thought she only stopped to breathe, but when she didn't start up again, he said, "I guess you're right, seeing as we're going the same way and I was staring." That didn't seem to make much sense to him, but she seemed satisfied.

"So, now we can be friends," she said.

"Oh, I have your oilcan," Bob replied, thinking that was a kind of stupid thing to say.

Maggie smiled. They headed down Mack Avenue chatting about the runaway horses. Actually, Maggie chatted, Bob listened and thought she was really easy to talk too.

JAN 22 1916

JAN 22 1916

The Crane Ave. Gazette

A DETROIT WEEKLY —

JANUARY 22, 1916, SAT. 2¢ A COPY —

SEE PAGE 3 — JAN 22 1916 DETROIT AUTO SHOW —

New Sign Board
for Crane Ave.

A wonderful new electric lighted sign board proposed by the Crane Ave. Advertising Co. It will be placed above the door of the Bank. It is hoped it will be installed before next Saturday. Watch the sign board.

Manager
C. R. Stevens

CURRENT
HAPPENINGS

OVERTAKES RUNAWAY
TEAM —

Leaping from the running board of an automobile Tue. afternoon Jan. 11 Patrolman Emil Hoff stopped a team of Horses which was dashing madly on Mack Ave., into the congested traffic at the intersection of Mt. Elliot Ave.

See Notice on page Four —

January 22, 1916
www.catherinepaonessa.com/thegazette

CHAPTER 2

Scotland
~ Davy McLeod

Davy McLeod was awake. Gavin Campbell was on the floor next to him snoring loudly. Earlier, Gavin had discovered he couldn't fit all 6 foot 4 inches and 230 pounds of himself in the small army cot. Disgusted, he had thrown the thin mattress on the floor, thrown himself down on top of it and promptly fallen sound asleep. Mac Sutherland was sleeping in the cot next to Davy. Mac wasn't really snoring, but every now and then he sputtered, or puffed. In the bunk above Davy a chap named Jamie Patterson was quiet.

Davy rolled over, pressed one ear to the mattress, covered the other with his pillow, and wondered how he could have known Gavin for so long without knowing that he snored like a pride of lions. God, he had known Gavin and Mac for as long as he could remember. The three of them had been inseparable as boys. Gavin was the brawn of the trio, Mac the joker, and Davy was the brains. They had explored the countryside around the small mining town of Bothwell together, poached pheasants and rabbits off the Earl of Homme's estate, and played hours and hours of football on the pitch by the train station.

When they all turned 18, they started in the mine together. Davy hated mining. He hated the long hours and the heavy work, but most of all, he hated the mine itself. Davy shivered in the dark, thinking about the deep, cold, damp abyss that was the mine. For most of the year, he went down into the abyss before the sun came up, and didn't emerge until it had set.

In early December 1915, after Gavin, the youngest, turned 19, they enlisted together. They had worried that the war would be over before they could join, but despite all the early predictions that it would end before Christmas, it was still raging and the armies of Europe were digging in. Once they passed their physicals and signed the paperwork, things had moved quickly. This morning they said goodbye to family and friends, boarded the train in Bothwell, and now, they were sleeping in a barrack, or some of them were sleeping, ready to start training tomorrow.

When Davy was a boy, the ladies of the village cooed over his cute dimples and wavy brown hair. As he grew, the chiseled features of some unknown roman ancestor appeared. His eyes were a steel, sometimes cold blue gray, but by nature, he wasn't cold. He was good looking. He had always been good looking, and he knew he was good looking, not in a conceded sort of way, but in the same way Gavin knew he was strong, and Mac knew he was funny.

It was too hard to breath with the pillow over his head and Gavin's snores penetrated the cheap pillow anyway, Davy rolled onto his back, put his hands under his head and stared up at the lump that was the chap sleeping in the bunk above him. His thoughts kept going back to the events of the last 24 hours. His last night at home.

He, Mac and Gavin had been deciding how to spend their last evening of freedom.

"We could get drunk," Mac had suggested. "Billy didn't have to pay for a single drink on his last night in town."

"That would be an excellent start," Gavin had agreed, "but, then maybe we can find some pretty girls to keep us company."

"And what pretty girls do you have in mind, and which girl's father and brothers are you willing to deal with?" Mac asked.

"I didn't mean one of them girls, I mean, well, I have money," Gavin said, somewhat sheepishly.

"You mean pay for it?" Davy asked. The thought was both intriguing and revolting.

"Well, you might be able to get any girl in town, but some of us aren't so blessed," Mac said as he wiggled his oversized ears, a trick he'd been doing since he was eight years old. He flashed a broad grin and chuckled.

Gavin guffawed and said, "Let's start at the pub."

Once there, they discovered that Mac was right, everyone was willing to buy them a drink, so they drank. And after a few, maybe more than a few, and a jolly farewell from the pub regulars, the boys stumbled out in hopes of finding, as Gavin said, some pretty girls to keep them company. Thinking about it now, in the cold, dark barracks, Davy decided this was where he had made his first mistake. He should have stayed with Mac and Gavin, but he knew the prettiest girl in town was Alice. He'd been walking out with Alice for the last few months. He had even promised to stop by and say goodbye to her, so he had wished Mac and Gavin good luck, and they parted company. Davy got to Alice's house to find her waiting on the porch.

"I didn't think you were coming," Alice scolded.

"I'm here now," Davy said. Alice smiled, took his hand and led him into the sitting room. The house was quiet.

"Where is everyone?" Davy asked, Alice lived with her parents and three sisters.

"Oh, they've all gone to a social at church. I told them I had a headache," Alice said with a sly smile. She sat down on the sofa and indicated for Davy to sit next to her. That he figured was his second mistake.

"Um, you're sure it's okay," Davy said. "What time will they be back?"

"Why, not for a while," Alice said, sliding closer to him. "Isn't this a lovely going away present? A little time alone together."

Davy could smell her. She was fresh, and clean and flowery. He kissed her, and she kissed him back eagerly. And one thing led to another and, Davy couldn't remember exactly how it happened, maybe it was the drinks, maybe it was the way she smelled, but before he left Alice's house that night, they had made love right there on the sofa while Alice's parents were away at the church social, and they were engaged to be married.

The thrill of it lasted until this morning at the train station, then realization and regret set in. Alice, her parents and sisters had all come to congratulate them and wish him good luck. His mother had cried because he was going to war and because he was engaged to marry Alice, the prettiest girl in town. And as he stood there on the platform, he realized that he had enlisted in the army to escape both the town and the mine, but with a few drinks, a smile, a sofa and a church social, he had condemned his future to the very place he wanted so much to escape. He was trapped.

Gavin gave a mighty snore, Mac puffed, and Davy sighed.

"Are you awake?" came a voice from the bunk above him. It was the chap from the train, Jamie Patterson. Jamie was tall and skinny. He had black hair and a pale, friendly face. He had helped Davy and his mates find the right connection in Hamilton. On the train they learned that Jamie was a few years older than them. Before enlisting he worked as a bank clerk. He was recently married and proudly showed them a picture of his new wife Nora. He fit in easily with the lads from Bothwell, although, Davy thought it was a little strange that he had the train schedule memorized.

"Yeah, I don't know how anyone can sleep through this racket," Davy said, gruffly. He continued, "Do all bank clerks travel a lot?"

"Um, no, why?" Jamie said, confused.

"Well at the train station, you had the schedule memorized," Davy said.

"Oh, I just remember things," Jamie said.

"Everyone remembers things, but not the bloody train schedule," Davy said.

"No, I mean I really remember things, like pages of books and maps and train schedules. If I look at them once, I remember them," Jamie explained.

"No, like you remember every page of a book?" Davy said, skeptical.

"Well, not every page, but pretty close, it's kind of weird. Most people don't believe me and ask me to re-member something from some primer we all used in first grade," Jamie said.

Davy smiled and changed his next question, "Can you conjure up the pages of a book you read a while ago and read them, say out loud?"

"Kind of, it's not as much like reading as it is telling, but it depends on the book, if it was boring, I probably forgot it," Jamie said. He continued, "What book did you have in mind?"

"Did you read *The Adventures of Sherlock Holmes?*" Davy asked.

"Yeah, twice," Jamie said. "It's one of my favorite books."

"Mine too," Davy said. "Could you read some now?"

Jamie was quiet for a minute, then he began, "To Sherlock Holmes she is always the woman. I have seldom heard him mention her under any other name. In his eyes she eclipses and predominates the whole of her sex. It was not that he felt any emotion akin to love for Irene Adler. . ."

Davy fell sound asleep.

Sergeant Angus Macgregor
~ Davy McLeod

"AAAttennnntionnnn," someone was yelling. Davy woke with a start. He jumped up, hit his head on the upper bunk, and bumped into Gavin. Gavin in turn tripped on his mattress and stumbled into the open area at the end of the bed. Mac was still sound asleep. Jamie had jumped down from the end of the upper bunk and was standing at attention.

The sergeant went over to Mac, kicked the leg of the bed and yelled, "Attention!"

Mac rolled over, and said, "Bloody hell, stop it, let a bloke get a bit of bloody sleep." He rolled over again and opened his eyes. The sergeant's angry red face was an inch from his own, "Bloody hell," Mac said again, then added, "Sir," as he jumped off the bed. There were fifty men in the long narrow barrack ranging in age from nineteen to thirty, a few even older. They had all lined up at the end of their beds and were standing at attention, well as best they could in their bare feet, boxer shorts and t-shirts.

"I'm Sergeant Macgregor," the sergeant said. "Welcome to the army. It is my job to turn you from whatever it was you lousy lot were as civilians, into soldiers." He eyed Davy, Mac and Gavin. Davy had the feeling that he had met the Sergeant before, but he couldn't place him. Sergeant Macgregor continued, "We will start with conditioning, because conditioning will win this war. If you're strong, and I know you all think you're strong," he looked at Gavin, "but I mean really strong, you might just survive." The Sergeant walked briskly up and down the line of new recruits, he stopped occasionally to reprimand someone for not standing up straight.

Davy looked at the men around him. They would be the men of his platoon. Some of them looked familiar. Davy and his mates had enlisted with the Highland Light Infantry, Hamilton Pals Battalion. Pals Battalions were made up of men from the same local area. Most had arrived yesterday to report for duty. Each was issued a kit. The kit consisted of a woolen tunic, shirt and trousers all dyed khaki, long puttees, which Davy soon learned were wound from the ankle to the knee, a battle helmet and liner. Most soldiers called the helmet a battle bowler, because it was shaped like a bowler hat. They were also given a broad waist belt that held a canteen, an entrenching tool, bayonet scabbard, ammunition and first aid pouches, a meatcan, or mess kit, with knife, fork and spoon, and a haversack, or webbing and black shoes. They were told that gas masks and firearms would be issued later. Gavin had taken an especially long time getting outfitted, everything was too short.

Sergeant Macgregor stopped in front of Davy and stared at him, considering, then he said, "I remember you, you're Davy McLeod." At that moment Davy realized where he'd seen Sergeant Macgregor before. He was Angus Macgregor. The Angus Macgregor who was the agent on the Earl of Homme's estate. *Bloody hell,* Davy thought. Davy's expression revealed his recognition of the agent, Sergeant Macgregor said, "So, you remember me too. Good, and after the next three months, you'll never forget me. You'll take the memory of me with you to the grave."

Sergeant Macgregor stepped back from Davy and said to the men watching, "We'll start today with a little trench digging practice. The trench size is marked with stakes outside," the Sergeant stopped, sized up Gavin and asked, "What's your name Private?"

"Gavin Campbell, sir," Gavin answered.

"You must be about six feet two inches?" Sergeant Macgregor asked.

"Six four, sir" Gavin corrected.

"Ah, six four, well we don't want Private Campbell to get his head blown off, so your trench should be six feet four inches deep. You should have been issued an entrenching tool and there are shovels outside, get dressed, and report outside in five minutes. Breakfast will be served when the trench is completed." Sergeant Angus Macgregor turned on his heels and left the barrack.

Mac looked at Gavin and mocked, "Six four great, you couldn't just let him think you was six two, could you? Why do you think he was asking? Did you think he was going to offer you a bigger bed?"

Gavin shrugged, pulled on his trousers, which were at least three inches too short, grabbed his entrenching tool, and headed out the door. In the field in front of the barrack, a long rectangle was laid out with stakes. A pile of shovels lay at one end of the trench site. As the men dug, a cloud of dirt, flying elbows and shiny shovel blades danced over the sinking trench. Jamie and Davy were digging next to each other. Jamie asked Davy, "So, what does the sergeant have against you?"

Trench Digging 101
~ Davy McLeod

As the trench began to take shape, Davy told Jamie about his past with Sergeant Macgregor.

"Mr. Angus Macgregor was the agent on the estate by Bothwell, the Earl of Homme's estate," Davy began with a snort as he heaved a large shovelful of dirt from the hole. He continued, "After my da died, my mam and I had things a little rough. I was thirteen and it seemed like I was always hungry. Mam took in washing, but it was never quite enough. So…"

"Enough talking and more digging," Sergeant Macgregor said from behind them. Davy shrugged and put his back into the task at hand. A year in the pit had made him strong. He knew how to work, especially with a shovel. As he dug, his mind wandered back to his last encounter with Angus Macgregor.

Davy had been hunting the dells, highlands and woodlands that surrounded Bothwell Castle on the Earls estate for over a year. At first, he hadn't been very lucky. He didn't have a gun, just a slingshot he'd made from an oak branch and a bit of rubber from an old bicycle tire he'd found in the dump. But with practice, he'd discovered he was a pretty good shot. He had modified the slingshot, adjusting the length of the rubber, adding a pocket and experimented with different size branches and stones.

Davy remembered his first kill. He'd been shooting at rabbits for a couple of weeks, but either he'd missed all together, or he'd hit them in the rump and they'd scurried away. On the afternoon of his first kill, he found what looked like a small animal trail. The trail went right through a patch of fresh clover. Davy thought, *if I was a rabbit, this is where I'd be. Munching on that clover.* He stood very still, the breeze ruffling his hair. He could smell the clover. Before long, a small brown rabbit came hopping along the trail, tasting the clover as it went. Davy pulled back his slingshot, let out his breath, slowly, quietly, and released. The small, hard stone flew fast and straight. It hit the rabbit square in the side of the head. The rabbit rolled to its side from the force of the stone, its legs gave a few quick jerks, and then it went limp on the trail. Davy couldn't believe it.

Quickly, he looked around, taking game, even small rabbits, from the Earl's property was poaching. It was against the law. He picked up the rabbit. It was soft and warm. Hiding it inside his coat, he hurried home. His mam didn't ask where he got it, but Davy could hear her humming softly to herself as she cooked it into a wonderful rabbit stew.

Davy's success with his slingshot improved. Sometimes Mac and Gavin joined him, but usually, he hunted alone. He brought home rabbit, squirrel and best of all, but hardest to hit, pheasant. He figured that it was taking the pheasant that alerted Angus MacGregor. As time went on, he began to suspect he wasn't always alone in the woods. Then one afternoon, after having just killed a pheasant, Davy heard a gruff voice yell, "Hey, you there? What are you doing?"

Davy didn't wait to discover who was yelling at him. He grabbed the plump bird and took off. The voice gave chase, but Davy was faster.

Davy stayed off the estate for a week and lived in fear that 'the voice' would show up at his door and carry him off to prison. He told Mac and Gavin about 'the voice' while they were kicking a football around the pitch, and Gavin said, "I bet it was that Angus Macgregor. He's the Earl's agent. I hear he's a mean bugger."

"Do you think you'll stop hunting?" Mac asked, thinking about his own stomach. Davy had been so successful killing rabbits and squirrels, he'd even shared a few with Mac and Gavin's families. They appreciated the extra meat, so no one asked where the game came from.

"Um, no probably not. I'll just be more careful," Davy said as he bounced the ball off his knee toward Gavin.

Davy and Angus Macgregor entered into a game of cat and mouse that lasted almost a year. Davy knew the agent needed to catch him red handed to prove he was poaching, so he was careful. He'd grown quite tall and skinny, so he took one of his father's old coats and sewed two big pockets into the lining, big enough to hold a rabbit, or a pheasant. And because the coat was wide for him, no one would ever know he was walking around with dinner in his pockets. He always tucked his slingshot into the waist of his trousers, under his untucked shirt.

On a couple of occasions, Mr. Macgregor stopped him, eyed him suspiciously, and asked where he was going. Davy said he was headed home, or just walking, and as he wasn't carrying a shotgun, Mr. Macgregor couldn't detain him. Then, one particularly beautiful afternoon, the mouse was playing, and the cat pounced.

Davy was happy. He'd taken a pheasant and a rabbit and they were tucked safely in his pockets. He was whistling gaily to himself as he walked toward home. Instead of taking the trail through the woods, he was on the lane. The sun was shining, and it was quite warm. Too warm for a coat.

Mr. Macgregor stepped from the woods into the lane, and stood, blocking Davy's way. "Now I've caught you," he growled at Davy.

Davy held up his empty hands and said, innocently, "I don't know what you mean, Sir."

"Not this time boy. I've been watching you," Mr. Macgregor said. He reached out and picked up a stick from the side of the lane, pointed it at Davy, and continued, "It's kind of warm for an overcoat."

Davy realized he was in trouble, he gave Mr. Macgregor a cold, defiant stare and said, "A fella can wear a coat if he wants too."

"Not if it has one of the Earl's pheasants stuffed in the pocket," Mr. Macgregor said. "Now, are you going to hand over that coat, or am I going to take it off you?" Mr. Macgregor raised the stick and took a threatening step toward Davy.

Davy started to slip his arms out of the overcoat, he was going to take off running as soon as it hit the ground. He figured he could out run Angus Macgregor, he'd done it before. But, he hated to leave his father's coat, or the beautiful pheasant. His mind flashed to an image of the cooked pheasant, golden brown and sizzling on a platter. *Damn you Angus Macgregor*, Davy thought. But, before the coat fell from his shoulders, Davy heard a commotion behind him. He turned to see two large horses charging toward them.

Davy and Mr. Macgregor moved quickly to the side of the lane to make way for the horses, but instead of passing by, the riders reared their horses to a stop directly in front of Mr. Macgregor.

They were beautiful horses. One, a chestnut brown with a black mane and tail, was being ridden by a tall, distinguished looking gentleman. The other horse was a small dapple gray ridden by a very pretty lady. A small round hat was sitting as precariously on her head, as she was sitting side saddle on the horse. Davy liked the way she looked, tall and straight. Both the lady and gentleman had been laughing.

"You only won because that monster of a horse is so much bigger than Charcoal," the lady said as she stroked the smooth, gray neck of her horse, but the gentleman was looking at Mr. Macgregor, the stick in Mr. Macgregor's hand, and Davy.

"What is this business about Angus?" he asked.

"Ah, good news, Sir, I've caught the poacher that's been decimating your flock of pheasants," Mr. Macgregor said, pleased. Davy realized he was looking at the Earl and Lady of Bothwell Castle.

"This boy?" the Earl asked, surprised.

"Yes, I believe so," Mr. Macgregor replied. He gave Davy a threatening look.

"This boy, but you said you thought it was a band of poachers?" the Earl asked. His horse was prancing around impatient to be running again. He continued, "And where is his gun? And has he taken any of my pheasants today?"

"I've caught him red handed. The bird is in his coat, and he must have hidden his gun somewhere in the woods," Mr. Macgregor replied, triumphantly.

The Earl turned to Davy and asked, "What is your name, lad?"

"Davy McLeod, Sir," Davy said, his gray eyes steady and unafraid.

"And do you have one of my pheasants in that over-sized coat of yours," the Earl asked.

At this point, Davy decided honesty was the best policy. "Yes Sir, I do, Sir, but I didn't shoot it with a gun." Davy took off his coat, reached into the large interior pocket and pulled out the pheasant.

"Did you trap it?" the Earl inquired, harshly; setting traps on the Earl's land was even worse than hunting.

"No, Sir, I used a slingshot," Davy said. He took his slingshot out of the waist of his trousers.

The Earl stared at Davy, then at Angus Macgregor, then back at Davy, then, to Davy's surprise, the Earl laughed and said, "So you're telling me that the gang of poachers that has been evading you for almost a year is really just this boy with a slingshot."

"No, I don't believe it, he must be using a shotgun, he's been taking a lot of game," Mr. MacGregor said.

"All with my slingshot, just check 'em for shot," Davy said, and he pulled the rabbit out of the other pocket. The Earl chuckled, but Davy realized he'd made a horrible mistake. He'd just admitted to regularly stealing game from the Earl's estate. He looked now from Mr. Macgregor, to the Earl, to the pretty lady. Davy had noticed her staring at him. He decided she may be his only hope of escaping a beating or worse, he softened his stormy gray eyes and gave her a sad, pitiful look.

Mr. Macgregor examined the bird and rabbit and said, "I can't believe it. Not a bit of shot in them," he eyed Davy angrily, "You must be very good with that slingshot."

"I am," Davy said, honestly.

"Well, there you have it, he's confessed," Mr. Macgregor said. "I'll take him over to the sheriff immediately and see that he gets the punishment. . ."

The Earl held up his hand, stopping Mr. Macgregor mid-sentence. "Not so fast, maybe he's not working alone after all," the Earl said. He looked down at Davy and said, "Does your father know you've been stealing game from this estate?"

"He's dead, sir. Died in the shaft accident." Davy said, simply.

"Oh, the poor lad," the Lady sighed softly. The Earl's expression softened. The shaft accident had been horrific. Eight men were killed when the shaft cable broke. The box carrying the miners plummeted to the bottom of the pit. The men were crushed to death.

"Tell me Davy McLeod, what do you do with all this game? Sell it?" the Earl asked.

"Why eat it, sir," Davy said, he continued, "Sometimes, if I'm especially lucky, I give some to my mates and they eat it."

"Honestly, sir, we should notify the sheriff, if he's not punished, every lad in the village will be up here, stealing from you," Mr. Macgregor said. The Lady leaned toward the Earl and whispered something. Davy heard the words, "fatherless", "sad", and "thin". He hated being pitied, but if it meant freedom, he would milk it. He lowered his head and slumped his shoulders. He would have conjured up a tear and let it run down his cheek and into the dirt lane, but he'd be damned before he'd cry in front of the likes of Angus Macgregor.

"Well, I don't think we have to go that far," the Earl said. He looked sternly at Davy and said, "Will you promise not to do any more hunting on my estate?"

"Yes, sir, I promise," Davy said honestly.

"If Mr. Macgregor catches you again, you will be severely punished. Do you understand?"

"Yes, sir," Davy said.

"Then, off with you," the Earl said.

Davy looked at the pheasant and rabbit at this feet, contemplated taking one or the other, but the Earl said, "No, you'll have to leave those."

Davy took one last, sad look at the Lady, but she had lost interest in the whole affair and was trying to adjust her hat while her horse pranced about. Davy picked up his coat and started down the lane with a shuffle. He could feel the eyes of the Earl and Mr. Macgregor on his back as he walked away, he let his head hang and his shoulders slump, but there was a relieved smile on his handsome face.

Davy had been shoveling steadily while his mind was in the past. Now, he looked around and found that the trench was taking shape. Jamie had stopped and was looking at the palms of his hands. Large ugly blisters were forming on his fingers. *I guess being a miner had some advantages,* Davy thought. His hands were used to the shovel.

At mail call that evening Davy received a letter from his grandmother in Detroit, Michigan, USA. He had hoped to save his army pay and maybe, after the war, immigrate to Detroit. It had been a dream of his since he was a boy. Only now, he would need enough money for himself and Alice. *But would Alice leave Scotland, leave her home and family and move to Detroit with him?* Davy wondered, *no she wouldn't.* He was trapped.

CHAPTER 3

Sisters and Suffragists
~ *Bob Stevens*

Bob and Maggie sat on Maggie's front steps talking. It was a cold, sunny day in early February. They had been walking home from school together since the day of the runaway buggy.

"You actually have a Victrola?" Maggie said, "You're so lucky. We've been so bored in the evenings without the boys." Bob watched as Maggie took Sam's hat from her brown curls, brushed off dust that wasn't really there, and put it on again. She continued, "Hey, we could have a musical. We could invite our parents, and Aunty McLeod. What records do you have?"

"Oh, we have some Caruso, John McCormak, Irving Berlin, but my favorite is the Sousa Band." Bob had mentioned the Victrola hoping to get up the nerve to ask

Maggie over to listen to records, he hadn't planned on inviting the entire neighborhood. *Drat*, he thought.

Maggie considered the selection. "Maybe we could charge admission, and use the money to buy more records for the next musical?"

"I don't know, do you think your parents and Aunty McLeod would come if we charged?" Bob said, thinking, *more records would be great, maybe a musical wasn't such a bad idea.*

"Sure, if it's not too much, and if the girls get in free. How about 10 cents?"

"What's 10 cents?" They hadn't heard little Sara come up behind them. She sat down between them on the step, put her mitten covered hand on Bob's knee, looked up at him and stuck out her tongue. He laughed and stuck his tongue out at her in return. Last weekend Bob had helped Maggie and her little sisters make a giant snowman.

"We're planning an evening musical program. Bob has a Victrola." Maggie explained.

"What's a Vic-tro-la?" Sara asked, eyes wide as she repeated the fancy word.

"Why, it's a machine that you crank and it plays music that's been etched onto a disk." Bob explained.

Sara looked skeptical. "Can I dance to the music?"

"Well, of course, silly." Maggie said.

"Then I'll dance at the musical. Are mummy and da coming? They have to come to see me dance." Sara wiggled with excitement. Maggie rolled her eyes at Bob over Sara's head.

"What musical?" Jeannie had joined them on the porch. She was shyer than her sisters with black hair, dark eyes, and fair skin. She sat down next to Maggie and stole a look at Bob. "Can I help?"

"Well, if it's okay with Bob, we can make it a joint family project." Maggie said. Bob looked from Maggie to Jeannie and Sara, their bright eyes stared at him expectantly.

He smiled and said, "Sure, it will be the best musical ever. Sara, you can dance, Jeannie, can you help with the decorations? I'll put an ad in The Gazette and Maggie; you can sell tickets and manage the refreshments. Maybe Aunty McLeod can bring some shortbread." The musical was shaping up to be quite different than the quiet evenings Bob's small family usually spent together. He hoped his parents wouldn't mind the house being overrun by little girls.

The front door opened behind them and they turned to see Mrs. Stevens emerge from the house. "Well, what a pleasant surprise, but aren't you cold?" Mrs. Stevens asked.

"I didn't know you were here." Bob said, surprised to see his mother.

"I was having a lovely visit with Mrs. Robinson, but it's about time we headed home for our supper." Bob got up and took his mother's arm to escort her home. He waved goodbye to Maggie and his little friends.

Bob told his mother about musical program as they walked down the street.

"I'm so glad you've made friends with the Robinson girls. They miss their brothers. It must be awful for Mrs. Robinson, having her boys so far away and in such danger.

I can't even imagine." A little sigh escaped from her throat, but she smiled. "A musical, that's a wonderful idea. Let me know if I can help with anything."

"I think I'll have plenty of helpers with the Robinson girls." Bob said.

They walked on in silence for a bit. The sun was low in the sky and the bitter cold made the snow crunch under their feet.

"I hope you don't mind if I'm not home for supper tomorrow evening. I'm going to a suffrage meeting with Mrs. Robinson." Mother said, she continued, almost to herself, "We'll have to take the street car." And to Robin, "Don't mention *that* to your father."

Bob couldn't believe it. His soft spoken, beautiful mother was joining the suffragettes. They protested at the White House. They were arrested and hauled off to jail. It was in the newspaper, pictures of them shouting and struggling with the police. And she wasn't going to tell dad. Bob's thoughts were racing, *they're rough women, trouble makers, aren't they? She's not like that, is she?*

His mother interrupted his thoughts, "Oh, don't look like that. I'll make you a nice stew and leave it on the stove. I'm sure you can manage eating one dinner without me, and I won't be late."

"Oh, yeah, I can manage," Bob said. But he thought, *it's not my stomach I was worried about, at least not this time.*

The next evening Bob ate his stew alone and waited for his mother. She arrived home safe and sound. He could tell she had enjoyed the meeting. She was excited as she told him about the speakers and the movement and how important it was for women to have the vote, especially with the possibility of war. "I have to look into becoming a citizen, I want to be ready when we get the vote. You know, if women have the vote, maybe we can keep the United States out of the war in Europe." He listened, and discovered that he agreed. *Why shouldn't women vote? Maggie was certainly smart enough to vote. She was smarter than most of the boys in his classes.* His mother continued, "Mr. Robinson escorted us, so we don't have to mention the streetcar to your father." *But, what would his dad think?* Bob wondered. *Would he agree with the suffrage movement, or would he be angry with mother for going to the meetings?*

A DETROIT WEEKLY
A SUNDAY EDITION
— ALSO —

C.AC.
PRESS
Nº 3

FEB 5 - 1916

The Crane Ave Gazette —

FRIDAY 4
PAGE ONE
EXTRA
FEB 4 - 1916

Nº SATURDAY FEBRUARY 5TH 1916 2ND PAGE

NOTICE

The Crane Ave. Gazette
has filmed a Sunday
Edition twice a month
instead of once a
month. The mid
month edition will
be 3¢ a copy probly
there will be no
story in this
issue but it
will have 6 pages.
The end of the
month Edition
will have 10 pages
a Story of corse
it will cost
6¢ a Copy.
Editor and Gen. Manager
A.R. Stevens

NOTICE

A surprise for you
it will be in
this space next
Saturday Edition
editor

The Story in the
end of month Sunday
edition is A Hot
Argument
by Robert L Stevens
watch for the
Sunday Gazette
program
editor

THATS GOOD YOU
have SUBSCRIBED
TO THE Gazette
20¢ a month Sunday
Editions (included)

February 5, 1916
www.catherinepaonessa.com/thegazette

Bob didn't have much time in the next couple of days to worry about his mother and the suffrage meetings. He was busy with the Gazette and preparations for the musical. He and Maggie figured out the program, and Jeannie copied it over eight times. After some debate, they decided they had to invite Professor Ackermann. He would see the announcement in the Gazette anyway. As it turned out, he was busy that evening. Bob thought it was strange. He still hadn't met Professor Ackermann in person. Bob kept up his end of the bargain and shoveled Professor Ackermann's snow. In return, Professor Ackermann left the ERS magazine and corrected newspapers in the box as promised. Still, it was a strange arrangement, getting advice and doing chores for someone he'd never met.

The afternoon of the performance, they all helped Jeannie hang decorations in the Stevens' parlor. She had made two long paper chains that they hung from corner to corner of the room. Paper stars decorated the walls. They arranged the dining room chairs, concert style. The stage was set. Bob was the master of ceremony.

"Ladies and gentleman, welcome to the Stevens' Musical program." The girls all groaned and Bob smiled sheepishly, corrected himself, and said, "I mean, the Crane Avenue Musical Extravaganza." Everyone applauded. "For our first selection, we will be listening to Irving Berlin's "Alexander's Ragtime Band." He gently placed the needle of the Victrola on the record and started turning the crank. The sounds of the Alexander's Ragtime Band filled the room. Soon, everyone was tapping their feet to the lively music. They played several popular pieces. He and Maggie took turns winding the Victrola. "Now we have a real treat." Bob announced as Maggie switched the records on the Victrola. "For our next two selections, the world famous dancer, Miss Sara Robinson will entertain us." Sara, dressed in her Sunday finest, and wearing a tiara Jeannie made of wire and ribbon, got up and bowed to the expectant audience. Maggie started cranking the Victrola and the sweet voice of Alma Gluck singing "Carry Me Back To Old Virginny" filled the room. Sara danced a slow and elaborate "ballet", swaying and spinning to the music. Sara ended her dance with a low, slow bow. Everyone clapped enthusiastically.

"Now, to liven things up a bit, we will hear the John Philip Sousa Band playing "The Fairest of the Fair". Sara picked up two wooden sticks. Each stick had an assortment of colored ribbons attached to the end with a tack. When she was ready, she nodded to Bob who started the Victrola. Sara danced a lively dance to the upbeat march. She swung the ribbons wildly and at one point almost fell into the lap of Mr. Stevens, who, to everyone's surprise joined her in the dance. To end the evening, they moved the chairs and played a couple waltzes so everyone could dance. They took turns winding the Victrola, Bob danced first with his mother and then with Aunty McLeod. As the third piece started, Aunty McLeod cunningly directed him into the arms of Maggie. Bob looked into Maggie's smiling face and, for the first time that evening, realized she wasn't wearing Sam's hat and she looked different, older. She caught his stare, crossed her eyes, and stuck out her tongue. He laughed, and they waltzed around the small, crowded room bumping into Sara dancing with her father and then into Bob's parents. When the music stopped, Mrs. Stevens announced that it was time for refreshments.

They were all happy for the punch and sweets provided by the mothers and Aunty McLeod. Bob listened as Mr. Robinson and Dad talked quietly together. They mentioned the fighting in West Africa and President Wilson's efforts to organize a peace conference. Then Mr. Robinson asked Dad about women's suffrage. *Would his dad be surprised or even angry? Had his mother told him about the meetings?* But the conversion was cut short, little Sara tugged at Dad's sleeve, and proudly showed him her tiara. Bob watched this simple exchange, his dad patting the little girl on the cheek and smiling, Bob forgot about the suffrage meetings and thought, *why am I an only child? Do Mother and Dad ever wish they had a daughter?*

"Bob," Maggie interrupted his thoughts. "Do you want us to help take down the decorations and put the chairs back?'

"Oh, no, I can do it, but thanks," Bob answered. Aunty McLeod approached with her coat, and Bob held it as she put it on.

"Well, children, thank you so much for the beautiful evening. Now I have something exciting to write to Davy. I'll tell him about the music and the dancing. He'll think us Americans are a jolly lot."

Mrs. Robinson smiled and signed, "Oh, if they would only end this terrible war, we could all be together."

They all said their goodbyes and headed out into the cold evening. After putting the front room back in order with his parents Bob went to his room, he could see the light in Aunty McLeod's window across the alley. *She must be writing to Davy*, he thought. *What must Davy think of American's, playing music, dancing, while he's fighting a war?* But Bob couldn't think any more, his head hurt.

❖ ❖ ❖

War Time Letters
~ Aunty McLeod

Aunty McLeod was indeed at her desk with, as she called it, a wee cup of tea in her hand. She continued to write Davy every week. Now she included Bob's newspaper in her letters. Davy was still at the training camp in England, Aunty McLeod was glad, at least he was being properly trained. She opened his last letter and re-read it.

Dear Nana,

Thank you for the letters and newspapers. I'm sorry I don't write as often as I should, and don't think for a minute that I don't appreciate getting your letters. We've been very busy getting ready to go over to France. And please try not to worry, the training has been very thorough. I hope you can keep sending the newspapers, I've been sharing them with my mates in my platoon. They give us something to talk about besides the war. We will be shipping over to France within a fortnight, and I've heard getting newspapers on the front is sometimes hard. I have to go now, take care, don't worry.

Davy

Aunty McLeod folded the letter, put it back in its envelope, opened the desk drawer and added it to a stack of letters, all in the same neat, bold hand. She thought about what Davy said about getting newspapers, she'd read that the British army didn't want the infantry to know the true details of how the war was going, so they controlled what newspapers were distributed to the men at the front. She was glad Davy was enjoying Bob's newspaper.

My Dearest Davy,   February 6, 1916

As always, I hope this letter finds you safe and warm. I have been busy with the usual things, church, ladies auxiliary, and baking, but the winter seems to be dragging on and I am anxious to get out to my garden.

Tonight I attended a musical at a neighbor's home. I want to tell you about it, but I realized that I have not properly introduced you to my new neighbors.

First, there is the Robinson family. They moved to Detroit from Canada over a year ago. Mr. McCoy Robinson is a mason. He is busy building this growing city. Margaret, his wife is an intelligent, caring mother. She's also an active member of the suffrage movement here in Detroit. They have five children. Bill and Sam are the oldest. They joined the Canadian forces and are over fighting with you. Maggie is next, she is in high school. Like her mother, she's a clever, spirited young lady. Jeannie and Sara are the two little girls. They are lively, adventuresome children and I enjoy their company. They make me feel young. I have been baking extra batches of shortbread cookies just so I have an excuse to invite them over.

The Stevens family is the other addition to our lively community. They live behind me across the alley. Mr. Stevens is a machinist at Burroughs Adding Machine Company. He reminds me of your grandfather, reserved, kind and proper. Mrs. Susie Stevens is his lovely wife and we enjoy tea together on many afternoons. Bob is their only child. You may feel you already know him. He is the author of the newspapers I've been sending. He has a small delivery service and delivers my groceries each week. It's a big help, especially in this cold winter weather. The Robinson girls have rather adopted Bob as a substitute big bother as their own brothers are so far away. It is amusing to watch Bob, who is so used to being the only child, surrounded by these new "little sisters".

Tonight, we all enjoyed music at the Stevens' on their Victrola. Little Sara danced and leapt about the room until we all felt compelled to join her. It was lovely to spend this cold winter evening in the company of warm friends, and I do hope this letter finds you warm and in the company of friends.

I hope you are doing well. Maybe after this terrible war is over you can come and visit me and meet all my nice neighbors. I've included the latest edition of the Gazette.

As Always, Your loving Nana

Aunty McLeod folded the letter and placed it in an envelope with the newspaper, ready for tomorrow's mail.

❖ ❖ ❖

Run Around
~ Bob Stevens

Bob woke up in the morning with a scratchy sore throat, but decided not to mention it to Mother. *She'll fuss,* Bob thought, *and it's just sore from all the talking last night.* Bob had not slept well, though. The image of Dad dancing with Sara kept floating through his head, and what Mother said about him being a big brother to the Robinson girls, played over and over in his ears. He tossed and turned. He couldn't stop wondering about being an only child. Before daybreak, he decided to ask his mother why he didn't have any brothers or sisters. When it was finely time to get up, he dressed and went down for breakfast, wondering how he would broach the subject.

Mother was in the kitchen. His breakfast was on the table ready for him. He thought, *it's kind of nice being an only child.*

"Good Morning." Mother said brightly, but her expression changed when she looked at his pale face. "Robin, I mean Bob, you look tired."

She reached up to put her hand on his forehead, but he pulled away saying. "I'm fine." Then, feeling bad, he said, "Did you enjoy the musical?"

"Oh yes. It was lovely. We have such nice neighbors."

"And all those little girls weren't too much trouble?" Bob asked.

"Why no, they're darlings. Little Sara simply won your father's heart." Noticing Bob's puzzled expression, she continued, "Don't you enjoy their company? I thought you did. And they look up to you. It's nice of you to fill in for their brothers."

"I was, well, just wondering," he paused, concerned, *would the question somehow hurt his mother*, then he blurted out, "why don't I have brothers or sisters?"

Bob watched the color drain from Mother's face. He instantly regretted the question. Mother sat down at the white kitchen table and motioned for him to do the same. She was studying the dish towel she was holding, picking at a loose thread. *She looks older*, Bob thought. *Did she have those lines around her eyes yesterday?*

She looked up, reached over, touched Bob's hand and said, "Oh Robin, I thought you knew, remembered, but how could you, you were only three, and I guess we just never talk about her." She paused, choosing her next words carefully. "You did have a sister, but she only lived a few days. I had a hard time with her. The doctor said I shouldn't have any more children. I'm sorry, I should have told you. It was a sad time for us, it was easier not to talk about it."

"Oh," was all Bob could think of to say.

She continued. "I will always miss the little girl we lost, but I enjoy our little family. I wouldn't change it for the world."

"I'm sorry, I shouldn't have mentioned it," Bob said.

He watched as his mother brushed a single tear from her check. She said, "We're fine, just us three. Right?" She looked at Bob, waiting now for a reply.

"Why yes, of course. I like our little family too." He smiled at this mother. He told himself he liked being an only child. He wouldn't like a little sister, always tagging along, always in the way.

Mother changed the subject, "I'm going to another meeting with Mrs. Robinson tonight, and of course, your father will be at work, so you'll be on your own for supper. I'll leave a pot of soup on the stove, and there will be fresh bread."

"Oh, I have track today. I'll be home late anyway."

"Then that works out fine. Now, off with you, Maggie will be waiting."

Bob grabbed his school pack and his gear for track and headed out the door. It was cold. He thought it was a little early in the season to start track practice, but Eastern had a pretty good team and they started conditioning in the gymnasium before running outside.

Maggie was waiting at the corner. She smiled as he approached and started chatting about the musical. Bob was thinking about what his mother had told him, and about eating dinner alone because of the suffrage meeting, and not really listening to Maggie. They walked about a block before Maggie noticed that Bob was quieter than usual. "Didn't you like the musical?" she asked, and this time she waited for an answer.

"Well, yeah, it was fine."

"Well, okay. Fine is okay, I guess."

They walked in silence for a few minutes. Bob wasn't used to this quiet Maggie so he said, "I can't walk home today. I have track practice."

"Track practice?" Maggie said rolling her eyes. "That's silly. It's too cold for track." But Bob heard "Track practice!" and thought Maggie was questioning his decision to be on the track team.

He exploded, "Well, a fella has a right to run track if he wants. He can't sit around having musicals all the time." They stopped walking and faced each other. Bob continued, "And while we're talking about people doing things they should or shouldn't do, why does your mother have to go dragging my mother to the stupid suffrage meetings? She should stay home and take care of you girls." Bob looked at Maggie. She was staring at him. Her mouth was open as if she was going to say something, but couldn't. Bob saw Sam's hat on Maggie's head. He thought about how she looked without it. His own head was pounding. And before he could stop himself, he said, "And why do you wear that hat all the time?"

It was too much. Maggie turned and walked away, but before she did, Bob saw tears forming in her eyes. He wanted to call after her. Explain that he didn't mean it. That he understood about the hat, about Sam. But he couldn't form the words. His head hurt. His throat hurt. He continued his walk to school, alone.

He made it through each long hour. He tried to talk to Maggie, but she was avoiding him. He decided he had to fix it somehow, but he couldn't think how.

He met up with Henry Harding in the gymnasium before track practice. Henry moved to Detroit in January, and as the new kids, they became chums. Henry was tall, blond and good looking. At a smaller school, he would have become popular the minute he walked in the door. But at a big school like Eastern, there were lots of tall, good looking lads.

As Bob walked up, Henry said, "Gosh, you look terrible."

"Don't worry. I'm sure I feel worse than I look," Bob said with a weary smile.

"Maybe it was something you ate. You'll feel better once you get moving." Henry said.

"Yeah, maybe, at least I hope so." Bob said.

Coach Jones was in the gymnasium waiting for the boys to arrive. They started with a warm up, and stretching. And Bob thought, *Okay, this is okay, I can do this.* Then they moved to sit-ups, push-ups and jumping jacks. And Bob thought, *Oh no, this is not good.* His head started to swim. He felt like he was underwater and he couldn't seem to breathe right, and *why were his arms so heavy?* He stopped.

Coach Jones yelled, "Stevens, don't stop, we just started; keep moving." One look at Bob's pale face and slouched shoulders told Coach Jones that he wasn't just worn out, he was sick. "Stevens, go home. Come back when you feel better."

Bob left the gymnasium. Normally, he would have been embarrassed to be singled out by a coach or teacher, but today, he didn't care. He got dressed, packed up his stuff, and headed home. The sun was low in the sky. Bob pulled up his collar against the cold, damp air. A stiff wind blew into his face. He figured he was about as miserable as a fella could be. He thought about Maggie and missed her chatter as he walked home alone. The house was dark, he didn't remember that Mother was at a suffrage meeting until he entered the back door and realized that the house was empty. *Okay, a fella could be even more miserable,* he thought. As promised, the soup was on the stove. He felt the side of the pot, it was still hot, but he didn't really feel like eating. He decided to lay down for a bit. Maybe his headache would go away. He would eat in a bit; after a little nap. He climbed the stairs to his room, kicked off his shoes, and climbed into bed, clothes and all. He was cold, and then hot. Bob fell into a fitful sleep.

Sam's Hat
~ Maggie Robinson

Maggie walked home alone. Bob was at track practice, and she didn't want to see him anyway. She was able to avoid him all day. *How could he be so mean?* When she got home she remembered that Mum was at a suffrage meeting with Mrs. Stevens. Jeannie and Sara were at Aunty McLeod's. She went upstairs. The door to the boy's room was slightly open. Mum must have been in there during the day. They didn't keep the room like a shrine or anything, but Mum kept it dusted and aired so it would be ready for them when they came home.

Maggie went into the room. She looked at the smooth beds. The quilts looked fresh and bright. The sun was low in the sky. A square of warm sunlight lay across Sam's bed. Maggie was holding Sam's hat in her hands. She set it down on the bed and laid down next to it. She had made it through the day without crying. She would never cry at school. But, she started crying softly now, her tears soaked into the quilt. *Where were they now? Were they okay? What if. . .* but she wouldn't think that. She cried herself to sleep.

Voices woke Maggie up. "Maggie, are you home?" It was Mum, and the girls.

Maggie shivered. The sun had set and the warm sunlight she fell asleep in was gone. She got up. Sam's hat had fallen to the floor. She picked it up and set it on the bed, thinking, *maybe. . .*, then she picked it up again and plopped it stubbornly on her head. She wouldn't stop wearing it, at least, not completely.

"I'll be down in a minute." She called. She checked her face in the hall mirror, wiped away any evidence of her tears and joined her family in the kitchen.

❖ ❖ ❖

Influenza
~ Bob Stevens

Voices interrupted his sleep. *Was he dreaming?*
"The speaker was very interesting?"
"Absolutely, and I agree. But I can't agree with some of their methods."
"Well, if women just ask politely, it will never happen."

Bob woke up, and was confused, where was he? His mouth was dry, and his head still hurt. *Who is that talking, are they arguing?*

"Bob, are you home? You didn't eat your dinner." He heard Mother's voice coming up the stairs. She opened the door to his bedroom. Bob tried to sit up and moaned.

"Robin, dear." Her cool hand was on his forehead. "You're burning up." Dad had followed her into his room. Bob was confused. *Why wasn't Dad at work? Did he sleep all night?*

"Dad, what are you doing home? Is it morning? Are you mad at Mother?" Bob asked.

"Shh" Mother said.

"Power outage at the plant" Dad explained.

Bob laid back on the pillow. Mother took charge and sent Dad for the doctor. Bob felt like a little boy again. Mother gave him some cool water to drink and placed a cool cloth on his forehead. He dozed while Mother waited for the doctor.

Bob had the influenza. It was not a bad case, but he was sick with a high fever for four days. During those fever-ish days, he dreamt about Mother being arrested as a suffragette, and about Maggie and Sam's hat. The hat grew bigger and bigger until Maggie disappeared beneath it. In another dream, he was running on the school track, and Maggie, Jeannie and Sara were chasing him.

Mother sat with him on the morning after his fever broke. "You're looking better." She felt his forehead. "I think that fever is gone for good. You'll feel much better in a few days." She smiled. It was Friday, Bob got sick on Monday.

"Will I be able to go to school next week?" Bob asked.

"Well, I don't know about that. I think it would be best if you stay home and regain your strength. Maggie and the girls stopped by every day after school to see how you were. Maggie said she would collect your classwork for you."

"Oh, she did?" Bob thought about his argument with Maggie. *Was she still mad?*

"The doctor's going to stop by this afternoon to check on you. If he says you're not contagious, Maggie can come and visit. You did lots of mumbling in your sleep the last couple of days. Have you been worried about me being a suffragette?"

"Um, well, yeah, I guess, what does Dad think? Is he mad?" Bob stammered. *What else did I say in my sleep*, he wondered.

"Why of course not, he thinks women should have the vote. He actually went to the meeting with Mrs. Robinson and me on Monday. The night you got sick. I'm sorry, I guess you haven't had much time to talk with your dad since he's been working second shift."

Bob was still weak on Saturday, and stayed in bed, but on Sunday he was able to get up and sit in the front room. Mother wouldn't let him work on any classwork or on his newspaper. She didn't want him to overdo. But, that was okay. Dad read the newspaper, and they discussed the up-coming baseball season and whether the Tigers would have another good year. They talked about plans for the yard, where they should put the garden and how big it should be. They also talked about the war in Europe. Aunty McLeod stopped by with shortbread, and Bob discovered that he was getting his appetite back. His mother joined them and they talked about the suffrage movement and how important it was for women to have the vote. Bob went to bed that evening feeling much better.

On Monday, Bob started on the pile of school work Maggie had been dropping off. He was able to get through the composition assignments. The reading was easy. So was the geography. He enjoyed those subjects. But the geometry was terrible. Gosh, he hated geometry.

Maggie stopped by with another list of assignments. Bob's mother said they could use the dining room table to review the classwork.

"You look better. How do you feel?" Maggie asked as sat down at the table.

Bob didn't know what to say. He kept thinking about their fight. He felt so bad. *How could he have been so mean to her?* He said, "Oh, I'm better, but, well, I. . . um the day I got sick, I said um. . ."

"It's okay," Maggie said. "You were sick. And, well, I know, I look silly, wearing Sam's hat around. I've been thinking, maybe I shouldn't wear it to school anymore. People don't understand. Maybe if America was in the war, but, maybe I'll just wear it at home and, well, at friends." She looked over at the hat sitting on the table next to the pile of books.

"Well, you should be able to wear it to school if you want. And if any of the fella's give you a hard time, well, you just send them to me. I'll tell them what's what," Bob said. And then he added, "And you don't look silly at all."

Maggie smiled at his gallantry, and said, "Why, thank you." She picked up Sam's hat and put it on Bob's head. "Now, what about this geometry. I'm a wizard at geometry."

CHAPTER 4

Ready for War
~ Davy McLeod

During the winter and early spring of 1916 and under the harsh training of Sergeant Macgregor, the men of Davy's platoon were transformed from civilians into soldiers. They grew strong digging trenches, and then filling them in again. Blisters that erupted, burning and bloody, developed into tough calluses. They gained endurance on long runs in cold winter sleet and drenching spring rains. They learned discipline during marching drills, and field craft at evening lectures. There were first aid demonstrations and map reading courses. And through it all, they hated Sergeant Macgregor. He pushed them hard, harder than any of the other sergeants, at least that's what they thought.

During the evenings, if they didn't have a lecture, they had free time to play cards, write letters, read or rest. Davy,

Mac, Gavin and Jamie were sitting at a table in the barrack. They had just finished playing pontoon, or blackjack as some of the chaps called it, Jamie won, he always won, and Davy was beginning to think he had some sort of advantage because of his memory. It didn't really matter, they played for cigarettes and Jamie didn't smoke so he always gave them back, but it was frustrating all the same.

"You win again," Davy said to Jamie. "How is it you always win?"

Jamie shrugged and said, "Don't know, I guess I'm lucky."

Gavin threw his cards into the center of the table and said, accusingly, "Lucky, ah, or maybe he's cheating?"

"No way," Jamie replied angrily, pushing his chair back from the table, clinching his fists, ready to defend his honor. "Take that back, or I'll…"

"Now, Gavin, didn't mean cheating, exactly," Mac interrupted, trying to calm Jamie down. "He was just wondering how you do it, how you seem to know where all the cards are?"

"Well, I guess, I pay attention to what's been played, you know, what cards are used and what ones are still in the deck, doesn't everyone do that?" Jamie asked.

"Bloody hell, you're counting cards and don't even realize you're doing it," Davy said.

"But I'm not cheating," Jamie said defiantly.

"You know, this might come in handy, you know, when we get over. If we worked together, worked out a little card scam, we would never need to buy cigarettes," Mac said with a smile. He reached over, took one of Jamie's cigarettes, put it in his mouth, lit it and took a long drag. He blew out a blue cloud of satisfied smoke.

"That's true, but Jamie doesn't smoke at all, and Davy and I only smoke occasionally," Gavin said. "But you'd be all set."

Mac chuckled and said, "True, but maybe we could trade cigarettes for other things."

Their plans for being a group of card sharks were interrupted by the sound of loud voices outside. Jamie got up and looked out the window. He held his hand up for the others to be quiet. "It's Sergeant Macgregor and that supply officer, I can't remember his name," Jamie whispered, which Davy thought was funny from the guy who remembers everything. Jamie motioned for them to join him by the windows. "They're really having it out," he added.

"These boys need rifles to train with," Sergeant Macgregor barked. "Their scheduled to go over in three weeks, and more than half of them have never fired a weapon, bloody hell, never even held one."

"Supplies are short. Especially firearms, the army is sending most of the new rifles over to the front," the supply officer said. "I put in the requisition, they will be here next week. And we would appreciate it if you didn't mention the supply shortage to the men, you now, keeping up moral and all that." With that the supply officer turned and walked bristly away.

Sergeant Macgregor yelled after him, "Well, what are we going to do until then, give them slingshots?"

"Bloody hell," Gavin groaned.

"They're going to send us to war without teaching us to shoot," Davy said.

"Well, at least we know how to use a bayonet," Mac said. They'd learned how to plunge the bayonet deep into the enemy's chest or throat and how to turn it as you pulled it out. But they practiced with bayonets mounted on wooden, fake guns. He continued sarcastically, "To bad we won't have guns to mount the bayonets to, maybe we can take the fake ones."

The next morning was clear and cool. The feeling of spring was in the air. The platoon lined up as usual waiting for the day's training schedule. Sergeant Macgregor arrived carrying a large box which he dropped at his feet.

"Attention," he shouted. The men stood to attention. "Before we begin firearm training, we're going to learn how to aim and shoot accurately using slingshots," Davy exchanged a quick look with Mac. They were both surprised. Sergeant Macgregor continued, "The principle is the same, a good eye, calm, steady breathing and practice. Don't you agree Private McLeod?"

Davy contemplated, and said, "I suppose so Sir, but I never fired a rifle."

"But you have lots of practice with a slingshot, isn't that right private?"

"Yes Sir," Davy answered cautiously, he didn't know what Sergeant Macgregor was up too. Was he going to finally get back at him for escaping punishment so many years ago?

"Private McLeod is an expert with a slingshot, and he has volunteered to help each of you make a slingshot and shoot it accurately. There's saws and everything else you'll need in here," he kicked the box with the toe of his boot, "take branches from the trees over there," he pointed to a stand of oak trees on the other side of the parade grounds, "and I'll be back at 1500 hours to see how it's going. Dismissed," to Davy he said, "Private McLeod, a word.

The men retrieved the box and started walking toward the oak trees.

"Yes Sir," Davy said as he joined Sergeant Macgregor.

The sergeant eyed Davy warily, "Can you do this?"

"Yes Sir, but it's been a long time since I hunted with a slingshot." Davy said honestly. Davy's mother had remarried around the same time he had promised the Earl he wouldn't hunt on the estate anymore. His mother's new husband was a widower with three small girls. A miner. They weren't rich, far from it, but they had food. Davy was able to keep his promise.

"You must have a good eye and a steady hand," Sergeant Macgregor said. A yell from the grove of trees caught their attention. Mac had climbed high into one of the trees, he was cutting off branches and dropping them to the ground. Sergeant MacGregor rolled his eyes, then looked seriously at Davy and said, "Show them how to aim steady and shoot without jerking the release. That will be enough for the time being, dismissed."

Davy hiked over to the trees and started examining the sticks, picking good ones and tossing aside ones that wouldn't work. He cut a couple of sticks to the right size for slingshots, and the men did the same. Some of them pealed the bark from the handle with their pocket knives. They used the rubber strips in the box for the bands and pieces of leather for the pockets. Soon everyone had a slingshot.

"Alright," Davy said. "I suppose most of you know how to shoot a slingshot, so if you have any questions, just let me know, otherwise, I guess you can just practice."

"Give us a demonstrations lad," one of the older men chuckled. "Serg says you're such a great shot, give us a show."

Davy sighed, and said, "It's been a while, um," he stretched the bands on his slingshot, getting the feel for the tightness. Next, he searched the ground by his feet for a good stone, found one, tossed it up and down and said, "Hmmm, this will do." He loaded the stone into the pocket of the sling-shot, then looked for something to hit. He spotted a wood-pecker hole on a dead tree about 20 yards away. He turned sideways to the tree, feet about shoulder length apart, hold-ing the slingshot in his left hand, arm extended and elbow locked. Davy pulled back on the bands. He could feel the stone through the rough leather of the pocket gripped tight-ly between his thumb and index finger. He eyed the hole, the men around disappeared from his sight and mind, he ex-haled slowly and steadily, relaxed and released the stone. It flew straight and hard, missing the hole by an inch, it became embedded in the soft wood of the rotten tree.

"Crack shot," Mac yelled excitedly. "You still got it mate."

"But I missed," Davy said.

"You hit the bloody tree lad," the man that asked for the demonstration said, "that's good enough for me, now, show me how the hell you did it."

Davy spent the morning and part of the afternoon showing the men how to shoot their slingshots. He told them about relaxing and breathing. Some were quite good shots, others, well maybe they just needed more practice. He, Mac, Gavin and Jamie knew why they were spending the day playing with slingshots, the army didn't have rifles for them to train with, but Davy wondered, *will this really help, aiming and shooting a rifle must be different.*

Mail Call
~ Davy McLeod

A few days later, the men of the platoon had gathered inside the mess hall. They had completed their evening lectures, so they had time to play cards, read or just relax. Some of the men were reading letters and opening packages. Outside a cold, heavy rain was falling. Davy often received mail. Alice had written daily in the first weeks after their engagement, then a couple of times a week, now it was barely once a week, but he didn't mind. Her letters were mostly about herself, her new dress, her new hair style, he didn't find them particularly interesting.

Tonight, Davy was reading a letter from his grandmother. She wrote weekly, and he enjoyed her letters. She had been writing him ever since he could remember, and even though he was only a baby when she left Scotland, he felt he knew her. After the sudden, tragic death of his father, her letters and those from his grandfather meant a lot to Davy.

His father had gone into the mine one morning and never came out. He and seven of his mates had loaded into the lift box as they did every morning, but then the unthinkable happened, the cable on the lift snapped. The lift box plummeting to the bottom of the shaft far below. The miner's bodies had been so smashed, so damaged, that the families weren't allowed to see them. All eight caskets were closed. Maybe if Davy had been able to see his father's body, say goodbye, it would have been easier. As Davy grieved for his father, his connection with his father's parents, his Detroit grandparents, became very important him.

Now again, it was his grandmother that came to his aid. Her cheery letters about Detroit and her neighbors, and the family newspapers she included helped relieve the boredom of camp. Today's letter was all about some new neighbors, the Stevens and the Robinsons, and how the Robinson girls had adopted Bob, the chap who wrote the newspaper, because their own big brothers had enlisted.

The rain drummed on the window as Davy skimmed through the letter a second time. He thought about his step sisters while he read about Maggie, Jeannie, Sara and Bob. His mam remarried about a year and a half after his father died. But Davy hadn't been ready to play big brother to three little girls. Or, maybe he hadn't been ready to share his mam. So, he had kept his distance. He was busy anyway. He spent his time kicking the football around with Mac and Gavin, doing homework and reading. He used to take a book to the attic and read for hours with the noise of giggling girls in the kitchen below. Davy signed, *maybe I should have tried harder to be part of the family*, he thought, *for mam, for myself.* He looked out the window and watched as fat rain drops splattered against the glass, then he shook off the feelings of regret, they wouldn't do any good now.

Davy's Nana had included the latest issue of Bob's newspaper with her letter. Davy opened it and read the announcements, then looked through the Around the World section for something worth sharing with his mates. Mac, Gavin and Jamie had read their mail and eaten all the cookies Gavin had received in a package from his mam, and now they were busy playing cards. Davy cleared his throat and said, "Did you know, baboons possess a remarkable instinct for finding water and are used for that purpose in South Africa?"

Mac looked at Davy and said, "Huh?" Surprised at the strange comment, "Oh, hey, did you get another newspaper from Detroit? Can I read it next?"

Davy laughed and said, "Sure." He handed Mac the newspaper. They spent the rest of the evening playing cards and talking about Detroit and America.

A week later the platoon was issued rifles. They learned how to handle, load, shoot and clean them. Davy was surprised to discover that aiming a rifle was similar to aiming a slingshot, and that he was an even better shot with the rifle. Most of the chaps in the platoon admitted that learning with the slingshots had helped them when they switched to rifles.

On the last evening at the training camp there was a celebration in the mess hall. There was plenty of food and beer provided by the local businesses, and the men talked boldly about how they were ready to take on the Hun. Sergeant Macgregor pulled Davy aside and said, "I want to thank you for helping out with the slingshots, you may not realize it, but you are a remarkable shot."

"Thank you sir," Davy said.

Sergeant Macgregor continued, "I've recommended you for a sniper training school in France. The Germans have excellent snipers and they're giving our boys hell in the trenches. Your commanding officer may send you to the school once you get over there." Sergeant Macgregor shook Davy's hand, and said, "Good luck to you Private McLeod," and left.

The platoon had a week's leave before going over to France. Davy, Mac and Gavin went back to Bothwell. Davy spent time with Alice, but they were never alone. At home, he slept, a lot, and ate a lot. And made a special effort to visit with his mother and stepsisters.

CHAPTER 5

The Detroit Electric

~ *Bob Stevens*

Bob and Maggie were friends again. It surprised Bob how easy it was to be friends with Maggie. He never had a girl for a friend before. And, he learned one thing about being friends with a girl, *whatever you do, never, ever, make them cry, because if you do, you feel just terrible.*

"Are you staying late for track today? It's so cold?" Maggie asked Bob as she pulled her coat tight against the cold morning breeze. As was typical for Detroit, winter was making a slow transition to spring. One day would be mild, and Bob would think that spring had finally arrived, only to be greeted the next morning by a cold wind.

"Coach Jones won't give us a day off just because it's cold. Our first meet is next week and we're not ready." Bob had recovered from his bout with influenza and was again busy with track practice. He wasn't the fastest boy on the track, so he was surprised when he made the team and was assigned to the 4 × 100-meter relay. "We have to work on passing the baton. We'll be disqualified if. . . " But he couldn't finish because Maggie was waving goodbye and hurrying off to meet her friend Edith.

After track practice Bob and Henry walked to Henry's father's tailor shop. The cold morning turned into a mild afternoon. They carried their coats over their shoulders and talked about cars, the Tigers, hiking trips they should plan and track practice.

"Gosh, Coach Jones is tough, I didn't think practice would ever end," Henry said.

Henry was tall, skinny and faster than Bob. He usually worked at the shop after school. His father lost a leg in a factory accident a couple of years ago. He used to make leather covers for seats on carriages, then automobiles. He joked that being a tailor was a good job for a man with one leg, that way, he could make his pants just the right length. Bob met him a couple of weeks ago, when he'd gone to Henry's house to study.

The little bell over the door made a soft tingling noise as the boys entered the tailor shop.

"Hi boy's, how was practice?" Mr. Harding asked from behind the counter.

"Long," the boys moaned in unison. The shop was small, but did very good business. The walls where lined with shelves that went from floor to ceiling. Each shelf was loaded with hundreds of different bolts of fabric, mostly for men's clothes. There were two large, glass topped counters with notions of all sorts, buttons, clasps, socks, ties. EVERYTHING FOR THE WELL DRESSED MAN as the sign painted on the window said.

"Well, lucky for you, the order of cloth I was expecting didn't arrive, so there's no inventory to log and shelve. Of course, it means you'll have extra work tomorrow. I do have a couple of deliveries for you to make," Mr. Harding said, pointing at the parcels on the counter.

Henry groaned, and said, "Oh, Pop, my legs are shot."

Mr. Harding chuckled, winked at his son, and said, "Mine too." Still chuckling he continued, "Well, I suppose you can take the car. Make the deliveries and drop Bob off at home. I'm sure his legs are shot too. But don't forget to come back and pick me up."

"Gee, Pop, thanks!" Henry grinned. He's father had invested in a Detroit Electric Car after the accident with his leg. It compensated for the loss of mobility and, in a way restored his independence.

"Ah thanks, Mr. Harding," Bob added. He couldn't believe his luck. He'd never ridden in a car.

"Let's go," Henry said, heading for the back door. His father cleared his throat loudly, and pointed at the parcels.

"The addresses are on the slips, and you *will* remember to come back and get me? Hmm?

"Sure thing, Pop." Henry and Bob gathered up the parcels and headed out the door, disturbing the bells with rather impatient jingling.

The shiny, black car was parked in the alley behind the shop. An electrical cord stretched from it to a plug just inside the back door. Bob watched, surprised, as Henry unplugged the car, coiled the cord, and placed it in the small trunk.

"Wow, a Detroit Electric," Bob said as he followed Henry into the car. "You don't even have to crank the starter?"

"No, that's why Pop got the electric. Managing a crank with his leg would be kind of hard. It's a Model 36 Brougham. He didn't spend the extra on the Edison battery, figured that he didn't really need it, most of our driving is around town."

Bob looked at the interior of the car. There was room for four people comfortably. The two leather seats at the back faced forward. The driver sat in one of these. Two more leather seats faced the driver. The passengers who sat in these would ride backward. Large pieces of glass enclosed the cab. The boys piled the packages on the back seat. Henry sat next to them facing the front window with the controls at his left hand. Bob sat in the passenger seat opposite Henry and to the right. Henry inserted a key, gave it a turn, and the car started with a shudder.

"Is it started?" Bob asked, "It's quieter than most cars."

"Yeah, the electric is nice that way," Henry said.

"I like the big windows. I bet it's nice in the rain; passing folks in open cars, watching them get drenched." Bob laughed.

"It's really nice on cold winter mornings. They should put a heater in. We keep some blankets in it, so it's warm enough." While he was talking, Henry maneuvered some levers, and the car started forward with a little jerk. "Hey, check the addresses on those packages. We should plan out the best route. Don't want to use too much battery."

Bob leaned over and, looking at the addresses, said, "Hmmm, I think," he shuffled the packages, putting them in the best order, "yeah, this should be good." He read Henry the first address and they were off.

The car picked up speed as Henry directed it out onto E. Grand Blvd. Bob watched Henry pull and turn the levers to control the car. The first stop was just a few blocks away. Once they arrived, Henry turned off the car and jumped out with the first parcel. As they rode to the second stop, Bob told Henry about his plans to become a war correspondent, and about his newspaper project.

"Wow, a war correspondent. I've read about how the British are trying to limit what gets reported in the British papers about the war. Some correspondents have even been arrested. Sure you want to do that?" Henry asked.

"I figure it's important for people to know what's going on over there. Do you think Wilson will be able to keep us out of it?"

Henry pulled the car over at the next stop and jumped out. He left the parcel with a maid who answered the door, hurried down the walk, and hopped back into the driver's seat. He continued talking as if they hadn't been interrupted by his delivery, "I don't know, I don't see how it's our fight anyway, at least that's what Pop says. There's a lot of ocean between us and that war – that's if Germany can keep its hands off our ships. It would be an adventure if we have to go over there."

"Hmm, hey, do you want to help me with the newspaper?" Bob asked.

Henry thought for a moment, "Gee, it might be fun, but with track, school work and working at the shop, I don't think I'll have much time. Writing isn't really my thing anyway. Pop's teaching me to run the shop. I don't really want to be a tailor, but I think I'd like to run a business someday."

They talked about school and complained about track practice as they continued to the last stop and then to Bob's house. Bob was surprised to see Mother and a tall gentleman standing on the porch as he and Henry drove up to the house. Mother was just as surprised when Bob jumped out of the car and it drove off.

"Well, here you are! Who was that?" Mother asked.

"Umm, that's Henry Harding," Bob mumbled, staring at the tall gentleman.

"Oh, I forgot, you haven't met Professor Ackermann yet." Bob's mother said. Bob shook hands with Professor Ackermann. He didn't look like the bearded, old man Bob had seen over the fence. He was younger than Bob thought, his beard was neatly trimmed, and he was dressed in a business suit.

"Nice to finally meet you Bob. You've done a great job shoveling for me this past winter." Professor Ackermann checked his pocket watch as he talked. "I hope my corrections on your newspaper haven't been too harsh, and that the *Electric Railway Service* magazine has been helpful." Bob began to answer, but Professor Ackermann kept talking, more quickly. "I've been called out of town, and will be gone for most of the summer. I can't take Nietzsche with me, so I'd like to hire you to take care of her. Oh, and the yard too." He checked his watch again. "I have a train to catch. I've left written instructions with your mother, and talked this plan over with your father this morning." Professor Ackermann started down the porch steps. "Goodbye, Mrs. Stevens, Bob, and thank you very much for your help in this." He walked across his front yard and retrieved a suitcase from his porch. Turning back, he said, "If you have any questions about the yard, what to plant, what to pull out, you know, ask Aunty McLeod, she's been at me to get it cleaned up for over a year now." With that he hurried down the street toward Mack Avenue.

Bob stood there for a moment, utterly surprised.

His mother turned to go inside. "Well, hasn't this been an exciting afternoon. Now, who was that in the car?" she said, smiling over her shoulder.

Bob followed her into the house, not quite sure what to think. His excitement over the car had faded. He started thinking about all the work he'd just been signed up for.

"Henry Harding." He replied absently. He thought, *they could have asked me before they filled my summer with yard work and dog sitting.* "I don't know how I'll have time for all this extra work. You could have asked me," he mumbled.

"Oh, there wasn't time." She frowned when she saw his sour expression. "I can't imagine what would call a man away from his home in such a hurry. He didn't even mention where he was going. But school and track will be over in a couple of weeks, and I'll help with the yard. It will be fun." Mother smiled.

Great, a summer of gardening with my mother, he thought sarcastically.

Seeing he wasn't convinced, she added, "I thought you liked that big dog."

"Yeah." He smiled a little. "I guess taking care of Nietzsche will be okay." He thought about sleeping with that big dog at the foot of his bed.

As if reading his mind, Mother said, "Professor Ackermann has assured me that the dog will be at his house, so don't get any ideas about bringing her in here." She handed Bob an envelope. "Here are the instructions Professor Ackermann mentioned, and some money. You won't complain about a little extra money in your pocket, will you? Now, I assume you have some homework? I have to make our supper. And then I want to hear all about your car ride."

Bob took the envelope from Mother, picked up his book bag and headed to his room. He opened the envelope; a letter, a ten-dollar bill, and a house key were inside. The letter began:

```
Nietzsche


1.  Food and Water - Please put two scoops of dry dog
    food in Nietzsche's bowl twice a day, once in the
    morning and again in the late afternoon. Fill her
    water bowl at the same time. The food is in a bar-
    rel in the shed. The scoop is on a hook over the
    barrel. While processed dog food is convenient,
    Nietzsche appreciates a little something from the
    butcher a couple of times a week. Mr. Carp, at the
    corner of Fischer and St. Paul (Aunty McLeod uses
    this butcher) knows what Nietzsche likes and will
```

> charge everything to my account. I also left in-
> structions with Mr. Jones, the grocer at the corner
> of Kercheval and East Grand Blvd, to sell you more
> dry food as needed. He too will charge my account.

Bob looked out the window at Nietzsche in the yard next store. *Lucky dog has better credit than most Detroiters.* He shook his head, now, along with picking up his Mothers and Aunty McLeod's groceries, he would be shopping for a dog. He looked at the ten-dollar bill, with all Nietzsche's expenses paid, maybe, just maybe the ten-dollars was his pay. He continued reading:

> 2. General Needs – Nietzsche sleeps in the house.
>   Please put her inside in the evening, around
>   dusk. She will serve as a guard dog in my absence
>   and will surely alert the neighborhood if any-
>   one but myself enters the house. That alert may
>   come after she deals with the intruder.

Well, I guess I'll stay out of the house. Bob thought.

> 3. Exercise – Nietzsche is quite happy in the yard
>   during the day, but she would be even happier if
>   you take her for a walk each afternoon. She enjoys
>   running in the open fields on Belle Isle. She will
>   come when called, and this outing usually cuts
>   down on the cleanup needed in the yard. She walks
>   well on a leash and should be leashed around
>   strangers. She is usually harmless, but because
>   of her size, can scare some people. She will gladly
>   join you when you pick up and deliver groceries,

I find it is fine to leave her on the sidewalk outside the stores. People rarely bother her.

*No kidding, people don't bother her, actually, having Nietzsche for
company will be kind of fun,* Bob thought.

Nietzsche is very important to me. If I could take
her with me, I would. Thank you for taking care of
her. I've watched you playing with her these last
couple of months, and can tell she likes you.

The Yard

1. Keep the grass trimmed, cut back some of the jun-
    gle in the back yard. Ask Mrs. McLeod for advice
    if needed. I assume you know what a yard should
    be like. Clippers, rakes, shovel, and the like
    are in the shed.
        The $10 is your pay. I will give you an addi-
    tional $10 when I return sometime in late August,
    and thanks again.

p.s. Sorry I will not be able to review your newspaper while I am away. Keep working on your spelling.
The post is redirecting my mail, but I notified the
Electric Railway Service. The magazine will be delivered directly to you.

Yours truly,
Professor Ackermann

Bob read through the letter again. The yard work would
be hard, but he was doing some of that anyway, for the
use of the *Electric Railway Service* magazine. Taking care of
Nietzsche would be fun. And twenty dollars, gosh, that's
more than worth it. Bob decided that Professor Ackermann

was odd. He hardly leaves his house all winter, then gets called away in big a hurry. What kind of Professor is he anyway? *Odd, very odd.* He pinned the letter on his wall, put the ten dollars in the money tin he kept hidden under his bed and headed out to feed and play with Nietzsche before supper. Homework could wait. Wasn't his job more important? He smiled to himself.

❖ ❖ ❖

About Little Girls and Big Dogs
~ Bob Stevens

Since the musical, little Sara had been meeting Bob when he was on his way home from delivering Aunty McLeod's groceries. Each Saturday and Wednesday, she waited on her porch, watching for him. When he turned the corner onto her street, she would run to meet him. She was a miniature version of her big sister. She had a round little face that was quick to smile, and just as quick to pout. The first time she had met Bob, she didn't say much, just took his hand, and walked along with him. Bob had been surprised and a little uncomfortable; he was still unsure whether he wanted to play the role of big brother. Nevertheless, Sara's happy chatter and unconditional friendship had won him over. Sometimes, Sara rode in the cart, sometimes she walked beside him holding his hand, and sometimes she pulled the cart for him. As the week's progressed, she started asking him questions about the war.

"Is the war going to be over soon, do you think?"

"What do the soldiers get to eat? Do you think they get chocolate cake? That's Bill's favorite."

"Sam said he would bring me a present? Do you think he really can? What do you think it will be?"

"They've been gone so long, and mum says I'm growing like a weed, do you think Sam and Bill will recognize me?

"Sam was teaching me to play checkers, do know how to play checkers? Maybe I could finish learning before he gets home. To surprise him."

"You'll like Sam and Bill."

Bob realized why she met him, she wanted, needed to talk about her big brothers. She talked about them to remember them. Maybe she couldn't talk about Bill and Sam at home. Maybe, even at her age, she sensed the worry her family felt. Maggie never said much about them. He assumed it was too painful. She was too worried. Unlike Sara, Maggie knew, understood, the real danger Sam and Bill were in. After each question, Bob tried to answer as honestly and carefully as possible. And he made a mental note to find his checkers.

The first time he took Nietzsche to the dry goods store and the butcher, he was surprised to discover that Nietzsche had quite a lot of friends. Mr. Carp came out of his butcher shop, patted Nietzsche, sized her up and decided she needed a little extra to eat. Maybe he was just taking advantage of Professor Ackermann's absence and looking for an excuse to charge him more, but Bob figured that was Professor Ackermann's problem, and anyway,

Nietzsche would be happy. Mr. Jones called his whole family out from the back of the grocery store to come and say hi to Nietzsche. His children jumped on her, rubbed her belly and scratched behind her ears. His wife gave her a large hand full of dog food. Nietzsche was a happy dog.

On his way home from Aunty McLeod's, Bob was excited to introduce Nietzsche to his little friend Sara. He turned the corner, and saw Sara heading down her front steps, but she looked at him, looked at Nietzsche, and turned on her heels and ran into the house. Bob thought, maybe her mother called her. But when it happened two days in a row, he thought he knew what the problem was. The next delivery day, he didn't bring Nietzsche with him.

When he turned onto Sara's street, he could see her waiting for him on the porch. She took a tentative step off the porch, watching. Then she came running to meet him.

"Why, hello Sara. I had almost given up on you. Where have you been these last few days?" Bob asked.

"I, well, I've had a cold." She coughed.

"Oh, I see. Maggie didn't mention that you were sick."

"Well, Maggie doesn't know everything," Sara said with a pout.

"Will you be walking, or riding today, milady?" Bob asked.

"Walking," Sara said and took his hand. They walked along quietly for a few minutes. She seemed to be considering something. Then she said, "You don't have to bring that big dog with you anymore, do you?"

"Why? Don't you like dogs?"

"I like dogs just fine," She said, defiantly.

"So, you can still walk with me if Nietzsche comes?"

"Well, I like small dogs."

"Oh, I see. I know she's kind of scary, but, she's as, , ,"

"I'm not scared of that old dog."

"I have to bring her with me, it's my job. And if you meet her, I'm sure you'd like her. She's as nice as can be."

"I'm sure she is, I just think she's too big, but I'm not scared, really. I'm not."

"I see, then, you wouldn't mind if we stopped by to check on her? I need to make sure she has enough water in her dish." Bob felt Sara's little hand stiffen in his.

"Um, I, ah may hear my Mum calling."

"Oh, come on, just take a look at her. You don't have to go into the yard. Just look through the fence."

"I guess I could do that. I don't have to get too close, seeing as she's so big, and I don't really favor big dogs."

They walked on in silence. When they reached Professor Ackermann's house Sara waited in the front yard, by the cart, while Bob went into the backyard. He shut the gate behind him and waved Sara over to the fence. Nietzsche ran up from the back of the yard and greeted them with a friendly bark. Sara gave a little start. The big dog nuzzled Bob's hand and sat down at his feet. Nietzsche and Bob watched and waited as Sara approached, ever so slowly.

"See how nice she is? Look, she's smiling at you." Bob grinned. And Nietzsche seemed to be grinning too. Sara slowly put her finger on the edge of one of the fence rails. Nietzsche took a step toward her. Sara pulled her hand away.

"Don't be afraid, she's nice, I promise." Bob encouraged.

"I'm not afraid," Sara protested. She set her jaw, stuck her hand through the fence and closed her eyes ready to sacrifice her hand to prove her bravery. Nietzsche stepped up and placed her cold, wet nose in Sara's outstretched palm. Surprised, Sara opened her eyes and giggled.

"It's cold," Sara said.

Nietzsche gave her a tiny lick.

"It tickles." Sara laughed.

And, this was the start of a true friendship.

Grey Marrow
~ Bob Stevens

March gave way to April, and winter gave way, completely, but not without a good dose of dampness, to spring. Bob was busy with schoolwork, track, deliveries, and taking care of Nietzsche. He was grateful that the snow had finally stopped, and because the grass hadn't started to grow, he had a break from yard work.

He also produced weekly issues of his newspaper. Aunty McLeod seemed especially happy to receive them, so in an effort to further please her, he recruited Jeannie to write a Women's page. He had asked Maggie to write the pages, but she was too busy with school. And, as she was perfectly happy to wear a boy's hat around, he figured that fashion news might not be her specialty. Jeannie was quieter than either Maggie or Sara, and she was truly excited to help. Bob gave her some supplies and taught her the trick of using wax to transfer pictures from the real newspaper. Soon, his newspaper had a very nice Women's page.

One afternoon in late April he was on his way home from delivering Aunty McLeod's groceries. He spotted Sara on her porch, and watched as she walked down the street to join him. She looked a little tired, Bob thought. Usually she'd run to give Nietzsche a hug.

"Riding, or walking today, milady?"

"Oh, I think I'll ride." She patted Nietzsche on the head and climbed into the cart. "I'm kind of tired."

Poor little thing, she's tuckered out, Bob thought as he began pulling the cart. He turned the corner, and headed toward Professor Ackermann's house. Sara enjoyed helping him feed Nietzsche and playing with her. Bob looked over his shoulder at Sara.

"Are you okay? You're rather quiet today?" he said.

"Well," Sara sighed, "This cart is just too bouncy today. It hurts my head. I think I'll walk."

"Sure." Bob stopped and Sara climbed out. She took Nietzsche's leash in one hand, and Bob's hand in the other. Bob was surprised. Her usually chilly little fingers were burning up. They walked a few steps.

"I think I want to go home …" but she didn't finish. As Bob watched, her eyes fluttered, then closed, and she began to fall. Bob reached out and caught her before she hit the ground. He lifted her up, surprised at how light she was.

"Sara, Sara!" He tried to wake her. She moaned softly. Bob left the cart and trying not to shake her, ran toward her house, Nietzsche close at his heels, barked loudly.

Mrs. Robinson was at the front window watering the old Christmas cactus. She had carefully moved it from Toronto and was pleasantly surprised at how much it had grown since coming to Detroit.   It had bloomed beautifully last Christmas. The barking caught her attention and she looked out the window and down the street. When she saw Bob, Sara draped in his arms, she dropped the watering can and ran to meet them.

"What's happened? Sara?" She took Sara from Bob. Calling to her, "Sara, Sara? Oh my, she's burning up."

Sara moaned, opened her eyes for a minute, and said, "Mummy, I don't feel so good."

"Bob, run, get Dr. Miller. You know Dr. Miller?"

"Yes Ma'am." Bob started out the door.

"Tell him to come right away. Then run and get my husband.   He's at the Leland school site on Antietam Avenue. Hurry." She turned, almost tripping on Nietzsche who was circling at her feet. "Oh, and take this blasted dog with you."

Bob grabbed Nietzsche's leash, he had to yank hard to get her to follow, to leave Sara. Together they headed out the door. They ran hard to Dr. Miller's office. Fortunately, it was only a few blocks away, and Dr. Miller was there. The doctor left for the Robinson's house right away.

From the doctor's office, Bob and Nietzsche headed down Lafayette toward the Leland school construction site. The street was crowded with people leaving work for home, anxious to enjoy the beautiful late afternoon weather. Nietzsche bowled over a businessman; the poor fella's hat went flying and he shook his fist at Bob from where he landed on the cobblestone. Bob shouted a "Sorry" over his shoulder. Children and old people scurried out of the way when they saw Nietzsche barreling down the sidewalk. At one corner, Bob caught his toe on a raised paving stone and fell hard, scrapping his knee and hands.

"Goddammit!" Bob swore. Nietzsche stopped and watched as Bob picked himself up. "What?" Bob said to her as he grabbed her leash and they continued. Finally, he could see the skeleton of the new Leland school at the end of the street. The site was big and confusing. Bob asked three different workers before being directed to the location where Mr. Robinson was working. The big Irishman was on a scaffolding laying bricks around what would be a second story window. Bob explained why he was needed at home, and Mr. Robinson was off.

Bob was breathing heavily and Nietzsche was panting just as hard. They sat down at a nearby bench to catch their breath. Bob looked at his scraped hands and knee. A spot of blood had soaked through his torn pants. He thought about finding a drinking fountain to clean the cuts, but instead, he picked out some of the dirt, spit on his hanky and wiped them as best he could. He figured that would do. After a short rest, they headed back to the Robinson's.

As he turned the corner to their street, he could see Dr. Miller posting a sign on the Robinson's porch. It read:

QUARANTINE AREA
KEEP OUT
POLIO

Dr. Miller turned and saw Bob approaching. "You can't go in there."

"How's Sara?" Bob asked. Bob let go of Nietzsche's leash as he spoke to Dr. Miller. The big dog scurried up the steps and sat down by the front door.

"She's a very sick little girl. Fortunately, her fever is coming down," Dr. Miller said. He continued, "What did you do to yourself young man. Is that blood?"

"Oh, I fell." Bob had completely forgotten about his hands and knee when he saw the quarantine sign. "They're fine. I cleaned them up a bit."

The doctor picked up Bob's hands, looked them over and said with a half-smile, "Oh, I can see that. Make sure you wash these good when you get home and you might want to keep them covered. I'm sure your mother will know what is needed."

Maggie and Jeanie where on the porch. Jeannie had been crying. Bob felt miserable as he remembered Sara's warm little hand and her sad expression as she passed out. Then he thought, *Maggie could get polio too. We all could.*

Girls in the House
~ Aunty McLeod

Maggie and Jeanie stayed with Aunty McLeod during the quarantine. She was more than happy to help.

"I hope you'll be comfortable girls," Aunty McLeod said as she and the girls prepared the guest bedroom. "My husband and I raised our only son in Scotland. This house has never had children staying in it. I have always hoped that my grandson Davy would make the crossing."

"Oh, I'm sure it will be just fine," Maggie said. She nudged Jeannie who, nodded and managed a weak smile.

"We'll have a nice little supper, and maybe enjoy sitting in the yard this evening," Aunty McLeod suggested. "I've ordered my seeds for the garden, but haven't decided how I'll be laying them out. Jeannie, maybe you can help with that while you're here." Mrs. Robinson had mentioned that Jeannie enjoyed working in the yard and Aunty McLeod hoped the idea would cheer her.

"Maggie, I thought you might like to use the desk in the room upstairs for your studies. It's quiet up there, and the view is nice."

"Oh, that will be perfect," Maggie said.

They had their supper and while Maggie settled in to study, Aunty McLeod showed Jeannie the garden. They examined the seed catalog and talked about which plants should be planted were.

Jeannie seemed to be taking an interest. "Mum likes to plant lots of tomatoes," she said as she flipped the pages of the catalog and looked at the garden.

"Oh, so do I, they can up so well," Aunty McLeod agreed. She continued, "And the zucchini does well here in this sunny spot. I have a wonderful recipe for zucchini bread that Mrs. Rossi gave me."

"Did someone say zucchini bread? I can't wait." Came a voice from the gate. Jeannie turned to see her father enter the yard.

"Oh, Da, how is Sara?" Jeannie ran to meet him.

"Well, her fever has dropped a bit."

Jeanie frowned. "She'll get better? She'll be her old self again in no time, right?" Before Mr. Robinson could answer, Maggie joined them in the yard.

"How is Sara?" Maggie repeated Jeannie's question.

"I'm afraid she's a very sick little girl, but," making his voice sound upbeat and reassuring, "Dr. Miller has assured us that children Sara's age usually recover from polio quite quickly." He looked over their heads towards Aunty McLeod, trying to conceal his real concern from the girls. "Are you girls all settled in then?" To Aunty McLeod, he said, "We really appreciate you taking the girls like this. I can't thank you enough."

"Oh, it is no trouble at all. I'm glad to help out any way I can. I just wish I could do more to help your wife with little Sara too."

"Mrs. Stevens is over there now helping Margaret get Sara comfortable in the guest room. That way, Margaret won't have to be running up and down the stairs to care for her." Jeannie's eyes were wide at this revelation, so Mr. Robinson changed the subject.

"And you girls won't believe who has moved in with us," he said.

"Who?" they asked in unison.

"Nietzsche! That bighearted dog. She sat on the porch just whining and waiting. Bob tried to get her to go home with him, but she wouldn't budge. Eventually,

Bob went home for his supper, promising to return and fetch Nietzsche this evening. We figured she'd be ready to go home when she got hungry. But when Mrs. Stevens arrived, Nietzsche just followed her into the house. She went straight down the hall and into the guest room. She put her big paws up on the bed and had a good look at Sara. Then she put her cold nose in Sara's hand and gave it a little lick. When I left Nietzsche was napping on the floor next to the bed like she owned the place."

"Oh, dear. What did Mum say?" Maggie asked.

"Well, you can imagine, she was not pleased to have "that animal", as she calls her, in the house. You know how she is with dogs. But, Sara actually attempted a smile when Nietzsche licked her and promised to drink some broth if we let Nietzsche stay. Honestly, I don't think any of us wanted to try to make the big dog leave. Between you and me, I think your Mum rather likes Nietzsche. I bet she's home giving "that animal" a meaty bone for supper."

"Gosh, replaced by a dog." Maggie frowned, and Mr. Robinson chuckled.

Later that evening, after Mr. Robinson said his good nights, and the girls were snug in bed in the guest room, Aunty McLeod sat down to write to Davy.

My Dearest Davy,   *April 30, 1916*

    As always, I hope this letter finds you safe and well. We have been getting news about the conditions in the trenches, and I dearly hope they are exaggerated. Do keep your feet dry, I've enclosed some nice socks that might be helpful.

It is finally spring here in Detroit and I am getting ready to put in my garden. I have a little helper this year, in fact, as of this afternoon, I have two young people staying with me. Let me explain. My good neighbors, the Robinson's, I think I've mentioned them in earlier letters, have 5 children. The two grown boys have joined the Canadian forces, and are fighting over in France with you. The three girls, Maggie, Jeannie and Sara are here with their Mum and Dad in Detroit. Well, this afternoon poor little Sara, just 6 years old, became quite sick. The doctor was called and, sadly, she has polio. The house has been quarantined, so Maggie and Jeannie have come to stay with me. I must confess that I rather enjoy the idea of having their company, which makes me feel a little guilty because of the circumstance that brings them here.

Having young people in the house makes me miss you, and hope that one day you will immigrate to Detroit. And now, I can offer to help make that happen. Last week I visited my banker. I carried with me a stack of stock certificates your grandfather left in a box in the bedroom closet. I have everything I need, and I am quite comfortable, so I haven't thought of cashing them in, but I thought it was time I discovered what they were worth. It seems your grandfather had an eye for a good investment. The money from the stocks would be more than enough to pay for you and Alice's crossing, once you're married of course. And once you're here, there would be enough to get you settled. Maybe you would like to go to college? Is there *anything particular you'd be interested in studying? I would be proud if you would let your grandfather help you chase a dream after this terrible war is over. I know your own mam would miss you, but she has her second husband and more children to keep her company. I believe she would support you if you chose to come. Please think about it.*

I will close now. I want to check on Maggie and especially Jeannie, I think she's a wee bit homesick. Take care; be safe.

As always, Your loving Nana

Aunty McLeod wrapped the letter, the latest editions of Bob's newspaper, and the socks in thick brown paper and prepared it for tomorrow's mail pickup.

❖ ❖ ❖

Fred Norman of Forestville
~ Bob Stevens

Bob, Maggie, and Jeannie sat in the shade outside Sara's open window. The sun was shining, and a beautifully warm breeze blew in from the west. The back of the yard was so bright with the yellow blooms of the forsythia that it almost hurt their eyes. A fat robin hopped around in search of nesting material. When she found a piece of dry straw, bit of string or scrap of bark, she flew with it to the large oak tree in the center of the yard.

Sara's had been seriously ill for a week, but yesterday, her fever broke. It left her worn out and frail, and worst of all, she had no feeling in her legs. The doctor was encouraging, saying that in most cases, the paralysis was only temporary, but everyone was concerned. He said she needed to rest.

Bob, Maggie, and Jeannie were still not allowed inside the house, so they had gathered outside Sara's window. Aunty McLeod had baked a batch of shortbread for Sara, hoping it would bring back her appetite. Bob, Maggie and Jeannie discovered that their appetites were just fine as they enjoyed their share of the buttery cookies. The doctor had also recommended that Sara be distracted from thinking about her legs, that if she fretted and worried, it could lengthen her recovery. Therefore, while Sara lay in her bed, Nietzsche at her feet, and the warm breeze blowing through the open window, Bob read her a serial story he had written for his newspaper.

"This is from the April 1st (www.catherinepaonessa. com/thegazette) issue of my paper. It's called Fred Norman of Forestville." Bob began:

"Extra, extra, read all about the big accident. Three cars run off the elevated!" A boy of about fifteen years was calling out on the busy corner of a large city. "Extra!"

"Was anyone killed?" Jeannie asked, concerned.

"Well, I don't know." Bob answered.

"How can you not know if anyone was killed? It's your story." Jeannie complained.

"Well, the story's not about the accident, that's just the start." Bob said, defensively.

"Hush now Jeannie, just let Bob tell the story." Maggie interceded. Bob continued.

"Fred, for this was the boy's name, Fred Norman, in full, perhaps, for he did not know whether it was Fred, Joe, or Bill. . ."

"He didn't know his own name?" Jeannie interrupted again.

"Well, um, no, but that will make sense when we get to the end." Bob answered, somewhat embarrassed.

"Jeannie, stop interrupting. I think it's a fine story." Sara's weak voice floated from the window.

Bob began to wish he hadn't offered to share a story he'd written, but he read on until Mrs. Robinson interrupted, "Sara, I think it's time you close your eyes and rest now."

"I've been closing my eyes while I listen, I want to know more about Fred!" Sara pleaded.

Her mother smiled, happy to see Sara taking an interest in something. "Very well, a little longer." She leaned toward the window and said, "Ten more minutes Maggie, and then I'm sure you children have homework to do."

Maggie sighed, rolled her eyes at being called a child, and said, "Yes, Mum."

Bob continued with the second installment, of the story from the April 8th (www.catherinepaonessa.com/thegazette) newspaper. It chronicled the adventures of Fred Norman and his friend, James Holms.

"Wait, who's James Holms again, the Grandfather?" Jeannie interrupted.

"No, the grandfather is dead. James is Fred's new friend."

"Oh, I see."

Bob continued, "Um, let's see, where was I?"

"At the station," whispered a little voice from the window. Bob and Maggie grinned at each other. Sara was on the mend.

"Oh, yeah. Thank you, Sara." Bob read on.

Mrs. Robinson face appeared at the window a few minutes later. "I'm sorry to interrupt, but it is really time for Sara to rest."

"Can you come back tomorrow?" they heard Sara say with a yawn.

"Sure," Bob said, "it's a serial, so it's better in installments."

"We'll walk Bob home," Maggie said. "Then head over to Aunty McLeod's."

"Oh, do we have to stay at Aunty McLeod's again tonight?" Jeannie asked, a quiver of homesickness in her voice.

Mrs. Robinson said, "I tell you what, I'll check with the doctor. He's coming to check on Sara it a bit. In the meantime, maybe you can keep me company in the garden while Sara naps."

"Okay," Jeannie said with a smile.

Bob and Maggie walked slowly to Bob's house. It was too beautiful to be inside studying.

The sun was warm and they could hear the buzz of the first bees of the season. The crocuses were in full bloom.

"Thank you for coming and telling Sara a story. I think it was just the thing," Maggie said. "Bill used to read to Sara," she added, almost in a whisper. They walked quietly, side by side. Maggie sniffed, Bob stole a sideways glance in her direction, afraid of the tears he might find there.

"Oh, what if Sara can't walk again. What will we do? Mum and Da are worried sick, but they try not to show it. It's just too much, first Sam and Bill go off to the stupid war, now Sara might be, be well, you know," Maggie blurted out.

Bob tried to think of something comforting to say, something that would help. He opened his mouth, closed it again, and in the end, draped his arm over Maggie's shoulders. Like he and his buddies sometimes did after a loss, or a win, on the track. He was taller than her by about six inches, his arm felt right there, but definitely different than with his buddies.

Bob and Maggie walked on in silence. The sun was getting lower in the sky. Bob felt Maggie's shoulders give a shutter under his arm. She took a deep breath, and wiped her eyes with her sleeve. When they got to Bob's house, Maggie ducked out from under his arm, looked up at him with a weak smile and said, "Thanks for understanding. See you tomorrow." And she headed off toward Aunty McLeod's house. Then, she turned, waved, smiled and shouted, "Study hard for geometry." Bob waved and thought, *Understanding, wow, I'm understanding, and I didn't even have to open my mouth. Girls were even more confusing than geometry.*

Bob was busy with exams and track, so it was a few days before they gathered again outside Sara's window. The doctor had given Maggie and Jeannie the all clear to return home, but it was another beautiful day, so again they gathered outside Sara's window. Sara had regained some feeling in her legs, but was still unable to walk.

Bob continued with the third installment of the Fred Norman story from the April 15th (www.catherinepaonessa.com/thegazette) issue of his newspaper. He read, "Seating themselves on one of the benches they began to talk to each other."

"Wait, I forget. Who sat down?" Jeanie asked.

"Fred and his new friend James." Bob explained, he read for a while, then took a break and drank some lemonade.

"Do you want me to read some?" Maggie asked.

"Sure," Bob said and handed over the newspaper. "But my spelling is really bad."

Maggie continued, until she finished the third installment.

"Oh, please read the next installment," Sara said through the open window.

"Sure," Bob said, "I'd rather sit here, in the sun and read to you, than study geometry.

"But only if you do your exercises while we listen," Maggie said, and she headed inside. Dr. Miller had recommended exercises to keep Sara's leg muscles strong while she recovered. He taught Maggie how to move Sara's legs, starting at the feet, and working each joint. He also showed her how to massage Sara's legs to help the circulation.

"Oh, I hate those horrible exercises," Sara whined. "My legs just need a little more rest, that's all. They'll start working again when there not so tired."

"No exercises, no story," Maggie said as she entered Sara's room. Bob and Jeannie watched through the window as Maggie started moving Sara's right foot gently back and forth.

"Be a good sport Sara and don't make me go home to my geometry," Bob added.

"Okay, but the massage tickles," Sara said.

Maggie smiled at Bob through the window, tickling meant feeling. Maybe Sara would be walking again soon. "Ready when you are, narrator," Maggie said out the window.

"Fred Norman of Forestville, Fourth Installment, from the April 22nd (www.catherinepaonessa.com/thegazette) issue." Bob continued. Reading his story out loud was embarrassing. He thought it was okay when he wrote it, but now he wished he'd suggested something else, but Sara seemed to be enjoying it, so he had to finish.

Bob read the fourth installment and concluded with, "Continued next week. And, I shouldn't put off my geometry any longer."

"That was the best part yet," Sara said.

"And we're all done with the horrible exercises," Maggie said.

Bob looked in the window. He noticed Nietzsche and thought, *that dog's getting fat and spoiled.* To the girls he said, "I think Nietzsche needs a little exercise too. I better take her for a walk before I hit the books. Come on Nietzsche". The big dog perked up at the prospect of a walk, but she looked at Sara as if for permission.

"Well, I had to do my exercise, you better go do yours," Sara said.

Bob headed to the front of the house wondering what Professor Ackermann will think when he discovers that Nietzsche has a new master.

Bob took Nietzsche to run in the open fields between Jefferson Avenue and the river. It felt good to be out and moving. They'd both been sitting too long. Bob found a good stick, not too heavy or long, but just right for a game of fetch. He threw it for Nietzsche to retrieve. She ran after it, but when she brought it back, she didn't drop it at Bob's feet. She dropped it 3 feet away. Bob had noticed this before. Sometimes to the right, and sometimes to the left or directly in front of him. But, she never brought it right to him. She stood by the stick and nudged it with her nose. She looked at Bob and gave a little yelp, as if to say, "here it is, you made me get it from way over there; you can meet me here."

"You silly dog," Bob said as he stepped over and picked up the stick. "What are you trying to prove anyway? That you can make me fetch too." Bob smiled at the big dog. He patted her head and scratched behind her ears. They played fetch for a while longer, each doing their share of the fetching. As the sun sank low on the horizon, the sky turned from pale blue to pink and then purple, and Bob realized it was getting late. He couldn't put off his geometry any longer.

Fetch

~ Bob Stevens

Bob and Henry were in the gazebo in Professor Ackermann's backyard. It was a good place to study. There was a picnic table, lots of shade, and no parents around to notice when they played a game of inside baseball instead of studying. A few weeks earlier, they had cleaned up the little gazebo, by sweeping out the dead leaves and cleaning up the cobwebs. Bob wondered why Professor Ackermann let it get so run down.

The boys were both struggling in geometry, Bob more so than Henry, and finals were only a week away.

"So, if this angle is 45 degrees, this one has to be 45 degrees too." Henry explained. Bob took off his glasses, wiped them on his sleeve, rubbed his eyes, and put his glasses back on.

"I guess," Bob agreed. "Gosh, I hope I can at least pass. My dad will have my head if I flunk geometry. He wants me to be a machinist."

"I thought you were going to be a war correspondent?"

"Well, my dad doesn't actually know that yet. He'll be disappointed, and my mom will be devastated if I go to Europe as a correspondent. One thing's for sure, I won't be anything that requires knowledge of geometry," Bob said, looking at the messy paper in front of him.

"Hey, why don't you get your sweetheart, what's her name, Maggie Robinson, to help you?" Henry asked with a smirk. "I hear she's a wizard at geometry. Kind of strange for a pretty girl. Usually it's the plain ones that are good at mathematics."

"Maggie's not my sweetheart, she's just a friend," Bob said.

"But you'd like her to be your sweetheart, huh? She's pretty, except for the silly cap she wears all the time. Why's she wear that cap around anyway?" Henry asked.

"It's her brother's cap. She has two brothers who enlisted for Canada. They're both over in France."

"Oh, gosh, what'd they go and do that for?"

"I guess King and country and all that," Bob said.

Henry said, "There's a rumor going around school that you two spend a lot of time together." He chuckled.

Bob was surprised; he'd never been part of the "rumor" crowd. "Oh, the Robinsons are just some kids that live in the neighborhood. The youngest has polio, so I've been reading to her, you know, to be neighborly."

"Hello? Bob, are you in there?" Mrs. Stevens called from the yard. She appeared from between the overgrown shrubs. "Oh, here you are? Hello Henry." She had met Henry a couple of weeks ago when he and Bob started studying together. To Bob she said, "Once school is out, you'll have to get to work trimming these shrubs. It's time for dinner. And didn't you promise to go over and read to Sara tonight?

"Gosh," Henry said, thinking about the time. "I have to head out too. Pop will be looking for me." He quickly gathered up his books and papers. "Nice seeing you again Mrs. Stevens. Have a nice evening, Bob." With a wink and a chuckle, he left.

"I have to get back and mind the stove, don't dally out here. Dinner will be on the table in five minutes."

As Bob gathered up his books, papers and the inside baseball game, he thought about Maggie. When they first met, he thought that maybe someday, he would court her. But somehow, in the last couple of months, she'd become a friend—actually, his best friend. He didn't want to ruin that. If they were courting, he'd have to act differently. Sit on the front porch or worse, in the front room, with her Mum in the kitchen, listening, making sure they behaved properly for a young couple that was courting. *That would ruin everything.* Bob decided. *And what does Maggie think? Would she want me for a beau?*

Bob and his mother shared a quiet dinner together. His dad was at work.

"I was thinking, when schools out we should eat dinner in the afternoon, before your father leaves for work. Then you and I could have a light lunch in the evening." Mother said as they sat down to dinner.

"That would be great. It will be strange having Dad home during the day."

"Just remember, he sleeps late so he can stay up at night. You'll have to be quiet."

"Oh, that's okay. I'm perfectly willing to sleep late too," Bob offered with a smile.

Mother frowned. "You know how your father feels about sleeping late. It's taken him months to get used to it, but it's not safe for him to go to the plant tired."

"I'll probably be in Professor Ackermann's yard all summer. It's like a jungle. And that gazebo is in really bad shape. I don't think it will make it through another winter if it doesn't get a coat of paint. Professor Ackermann didn't say anything about painting." Bob liked the idea of painting the gazebo. At least he liked it better than weeding and trimming. Henry even said he'd help. "Do you think Professor Ackermann would reimburse me if I bought some paint?"

"I don't know, you could ask Aunty McLeod. She knows the Professor better than we do." Bob's mother watched as he soaked the last bit of gravy off his plate with a piece of bread. "Robin, did you even chew any of that food?" she asked.

"Oh, sorry, I have to get over to the Robinsons'," Bob said as he buttered another piece of bread and started to stuff it into his mouth. His mother frowned; he slowed down, took a small bite, and ate it slowly.

"And you don't mind reading to Sara, and letting Jeannie help with the newspaper? I hope you understand what it means to them?" she asked.

Bob realized she had overheard him talking to Henry in the gazebo. "No, no it's fine. I don't mind, I, well, I just don't want the fella's to know I spend so much time with a group of little girls."

"Just so you know that they look up to you. They've rather adopted you as a big brother. Even Maggie. They miss their own brothers. It's been a month since they've had any news." Bob thought, *Maggie doesn't want a beau, she wants a brother.*

"I know, I guess I've rather adopted them too," Bob said. The image of Sara's eyes fluttering and her starting to fall came back to him. He missed her on his delivery days. *But, could he be just a brother to Maggie?* He wondered. "I understand Mom, really I do. But, may I please be excused? I have to go; they're expecting me." He got up, gave Mother a quick peck on the cheek, and headed out.

It was a beautiful evening. Sara still wasn't walking, she insisted that her legs were just tired and needed to rest. Dr. Miller was encouraged though. Her reflexes were improving, and she moved her legs while she slept. He said she just needed confidence to walk again. Mr. Robinson moved a chair out to the back yard for her and rigged a little canopy over it. During the last week or so, Sara spent more and more time outside. She and Nietzsche enjoyed being out of the confines of the house. When Bob arrived the family was in the yard finishing dinner – picnic style.

"Hello," Bob said as he walked into the yard. The Robinson family greeted him with a chorus of "Hi's" and "Hellos". Nietzsche greeted him with a yelp and a lick on the hand. Mrs. Robinson and the girls began clearing away the dishes.

"Did you remember the next installment of the story?" Sara asked.

"I did. It's from the April 26th (www.catherinepaonessa. com/thegazette) issue of the newspaper," Bob answered.

"Sara has been enjoying your story," Mr. Robinson said to Bob. "We really appreciate you taking the time to read to her. In fact, she's been retelling me the story. We're both anxious to know what happens to Fred." He turned to Sara and said, "Enjoy the next installment, pay close attention, I want to know all the details."

"Oh Da, you could stay and listen." Sara pleaded.

"But, if I did that, I would miss having you tell me the story tonight before you go to sleep." He stroked Sara's check and gave Bob a hearty pat on the back before gathering up the remaining dishes and heading inside. Maggie and Jeannie returned quickly from helping with the dishes. Jeannie sat down on the picnic table with Bob, but Maggie picked up a stick, threw it toward the back of the yard and watched Nietzsche run after it.

"Is it okay if we play fetch while you read?" Maggie asked Bob.

"Sure, but she has a different idea of how to play, you might get some exercise too," Bob said, then he began, "Fred Norman of Forestville, Fifth Installment."

When he got to a part about Fred and a boot black, Sara asked, "What's a boot black?"

"It's the same thing as a shoe shine boy. You know, we see them on the corner downtown sometimes," Maggie said. "And you're right about this silly dog, she never brings the stick back. Can't you train her to put it down at your feet?"

"But were all the shoes black? Didn't they have brown shoes?" Sara persisted.

"Sara, it doesn't matter what color the shoes are," Jeannie answered. To Maggie she said, "And Nietzsche knows that you want her to put the stick at your feet. She likes making you move for it. Now who's silly? To Bob, Jeannie added, "But, keep reading. I still have homework to finish."

Bob smiled as Sara stuck her tongue out at Jeannie. He continued to the end of the installment, and said, "To be continued."

"Oh, can't you keep going?" Sara asked.

"No, I have to go do my homework, and I don't want to miss any," Jeannie said as she got up and headed toward the kitchen door.

"I have a composition to finish. Did you finish yours?" Maggie asked Bob.

"All done." Bob said with a satisfied grin. "But," he continued, his smile fading, "I have reading to do for history." He looked at Sara; she looked so forlorn. Everyone was abandoning her. He added, "I could read out here, I could even read the history out loud to you Sara. Maybe that would help me remember it."

"I could help you study?" Sara asked, brightening.

"Exactly," Bob said. "I'll run home and get my history book." And he was off.

Maggie handed Sara the fetch stick and asked, "Will you and Nietzsche be okay until Bob gets back?"

"Sure," Sara said, and Maggie headed inside.

Sara looked at the now soggy stick. The bark was coming off and it had Nietzsche's teeth marks on it. It smelled like dog breath. Sara crinkled her nose, and threw it. It didn't go very far, but Nietzsche bounded after it. Sara smiled. Nietzsche retrieved the stick and ran back. But, as usual, she put the stick down five feet in front of Sara, and a little to the right. Bob was coming around the corner of the house, but stopped when he heard Sara say, "Oh Nietzsche, come on girl. Be good and bring me the stick." Bob waited. He wanted to see if Sara could get Nietzsche to fetch properly. He was sure Nietzsche would do anything for Sara. He watched quietly. "Bring it here girl." Sara pleaded. Nietzsche circled the stick. "I'll throw it again if you just bring it here." Nietzsche nudged the stick with her nose. She looked at Sara, sat down behind the stick and gave a little yelp. "I don't know if I can girl." Sara said, she was close to tears, but she placed her feet squarely on the ground and pushed herself up from the chair. Bob held his breath, frozen. Sara took a tentative step toward the stick. She held on to the picnic table for support and took another step. Nietzsche took a few steps toward Sara then backed away. Sara followed. Nietzsche barked and sat down next to the stick.

"Sara, you're walking." Maggie called from an upstairs window. Bob moved toward Sara, ready to take her arm if she needed help, but she waved him away. She took four more steps, until she was standing over the stick. She took hold of Nietzsche's head, bent down, picked up the stick, and tossed it into the yard.

"Go get it girl. Go on." Nietzsche barked and bounded after the stick. Sara reached out and took Bob's outstretched hand. "I think I should sit down now," she said.

By this time everyone else was in the yard. Mr. Robinson helped Sara back to the chair. Mrs. Robinson was crying. Nietzsche returned with the stick, dropped it five feet to the left of Sara's chair and yelped. Everyone looked at the silly dog and laughed.

"This calls for a celebration." Mr. Robinson laughed. Bob went home to get Mother, and Maggie invited Aunty McLeod. They filled the ice cream churn with cream, sugar and packed it with ice. The happy group stayed in the yard most of the evening, polio, homework and the war forgotten, at least for a time. They each took a turn cranking the ice cream churn, and soon they were enjoying the cold, creamy, treat.

Summer Time
~ Bob Stevens

Sara continued to improve. She still tired quickly and dragged her left foot slightly, but Dr. Miller said the fatigue and limp would both be gone before school started in the fall. Bob, Maggie and Jeannie finished the school year. Both Bob and Henry passed geometry, maybe not with flying colors, but they passed. On the first official day of summer, they gathered in Professor Ackermann's gazebo to finish reading the Fred Norman story. Bob, Maggie and Henry were playing inside baseball while they waited for Sara and Jeannie.

"You got an A in geometry?" Henry asked Maggie.

"Well, yes, why, what did you get?" Maggie answered, a little defensive. She had discovered that boys didn't like girls that were good at math.

"Not an A, that's for sure, I was just happy to pass. How about you Bob, was your Pop mad when he saw your C- in geometry?" Henry asked

"He wasn't jumping for joy. But I think he's accepted that I'm not going to be a machinist. It helped that my other grades were pretty good," Bob said. "But, come on, let's not talk about school. Whose turn is it?"

"Oh, mine." Henry said. "Let's see, I rolled an out my last two turns, so odds are I'll get on base this time."

Maggie gave him a disgusted look.

"What?" Henry asked.

"What you rolled last time doesn't change the odds of what you'll roll this time. You're still rolling the same number of dice, the odds don't change," Maggie explained.

"But, if I. . ." Henry started to say, but Bob interrupted.

"Just roll, we'll never finish if you guys keep at it." Henry rolled the dice.

"656, see," he said to Maggie.

"But that doesn't have anything. . ." Maggie was interrupted by the arrival of Sara and Jeannie. "Oh, never mind, let's finish the Fred Norman story."

"Sorry Henry, you missed the first five installments," Bob explained to Henry as he reached for the papers.

"Oh, that's okay, I'll just follow along best I can," Henry said. Henry met the Robinson girls a couple of days ago while he and Bob were studying in the gazebo.

Bob began, "Fred Norman of Forestville, Sixth Installment from the April 30th (www.catherinepaonessa. com/thegazette) issue. One day Fred saw Dick picking on a small boy." To Henry, Bob said, "Oh, Fred's the main character and Dick is a bully." Bob continued reading, "Fred stepped up to Dick and told him to give back the boys toy. Dick laughed and said he couldn't make him. Before he knew what was happening, Dick found himself on his back with a good strong boy holding him down."

"What strong boy?" Sara asked.

"Fred, you silly," said Jeannie.

"Oh, I see," said Sara. Bob stared at them. "Sorry, go on," they said together.

Bob finished the sixth installment and said, "That's the end of this installment. Do you want to continue? It's the last installment?"

"Oh, yes," Sara and Jeannie said.

Bob continued, "Fred Norman of Forestville, final installment from the May 3rd (www.catherinepaonessa.com/ thegazette) issue." The story continued to follow the adventures of Fred as he discovered he had been kidnapped as a child, and that he was really the only son of rich parents. Bob concluded, "Fred decided to become a lawyer. It looks as if he will be a very promising young man. The End."

"Oh, good, a happy ending. I do like happy endings," Sara said. Everyone laughed and clapped.

Bob was a little embarrassed. He never meant for the story to be read out loud, especially to a group of friends. He was glad that was over. "Hey, are we going to finish this game of baseball?" Bob asked.

"Oh, that game is no fun," Jeannie said. "And it takes so long. Do you have Pit? That's a fun game."

"Yeah, I'll go get it," Bob said, he gathered up his newspapers and the inside baseball game and headed toward his house. "I'll be right back."

Soon, a chorus of "Wheat" "Oats" "Oats" Barley" "Wheat" and loud laughter could be heard coming from the over grown gazebo. Summer had officially started.

CHAPTER 6

George's Bug Show
~ Dave McLeod

The air was damp and rancid. A soft pool of light fell through the door of the dugout onto eight large, dirty feet. A small tommy's cooker was burning. It providing a little heat to the otherwise chilly, damp room. The dugout was small, barely large enough for the four mates. On either side, a plank had been fitted into the earthen wall creating a bench. Davy and Mac sat on one side, Jamie and Gavin sat facing them. They were trying to get their feet dry after their work detail in the sap tunnel. They had their tunics on their laps, and they were chatting, or searching the seams of their clothing for lice and squishing the small, hard bugs between their thumbs and nails. The platoon had arrived in France in late March 1916, and after four weeks in the reserve trenches, they were sent up to the front to dig saps, underground tunnels that reached out under no man's land toward the enemy. Rumors of a pending German attach were rampant. After a week at the front, they were drained, dirty and discouraged.

"Bloody hell," Mac mumbled with each annoying bug he caught. While Davy hated the darkness of mining, Mac hated the dirt. They were dejected when their platoon was attached to a sapping group. They had joined the army to escape the mines, only to be stuck mining in a war zone. But, as Jamie explained, from the army's point of view, it made perfect sense, they came from mining communities; they knew how to dig.

Mac squished another bug, flicked it toward the tommy cooker and looked at his dirty hands, disgusted. Back in Bothwell, Mac had been the dandy of the group. He said that, because he hadn't been blessed with natural good looks, he had to make up for it with style.

"Bloody hell," said Mac as he scratched his head, picked off a louse, squished it and flicked it.

"Hey, I just remembered," Davy said. He stopped searching for lice and started searching the many pockets of his overcoat. "I got a package yesterday, I didn't have a chance to open it before our work detail, so I stuffed it in my pocket."

"Bloody hell, if it's shortbread, it will be ruined," Mac said.

"It wasn't heavy enough to be shortbread, it's from Detroit, so maybe there's a newspaper," Davy replied. He found the package and opened it. A letter, newspaper and pair of soft, clean socks fell onto his lap. Mac snatched the newspaper, opened it and started thumbing through the pages, but Davy didn't care because he had clean socks. He picked them up. Felt the soft yarn and held them up to check the size. Then he smelled them, and he thought he could smell his grandma, or what he imaged a grandma would smell like. He considered wrapping them back up, saving them until he could wash his feet before wearing them, but decided against it. He slid them over his smelly, dirty feet, wiggled his toes and smiled. His feet felt wonderful.

A snort from Mac disturbed Davy's foot bliss. Then Mac actually giggled, which was strange, he wasn't the giggling type. Then he laughed hard and loud and choked out, "Bloody hell." Mac stomped his feet, slapped his knee and almost upset the tommy cooker.

"What the hell?" Gavin said. Mac held the newspaper out to him, taping on an article. Gavin read the heading, "Georges Bug Show". He read the first couple of lines and looked at Mac confused, then chuckled at Mac's hysterical reaction and said, "It's not really funny."

April 9, 1916
www.catherinepaonessa.com/thegazette

"No?" Mac croaked. A couple large globules of spit few out of his mouth and sizzled as they hit the tommy cooker. Davy and Jamie exploded in laughter. "But it is funny!" Mac struggled through gasps to explain. "Don't you see, it's us, we're the bugs and King George has snatched us up and put us in his bug show," but by now, Gavin, Davy and Jamie were laughing too hard to care.

A loud explosion interrupted their laughter. The German attack had started.

❖ ❖ ❖

Battle at Vimy Ridge
~ Davy McLeod

The sound was louder than anything Davy had ever experienced. They quickly stuffed their dirty feet into their still wet boots. Once outside, they grabbed their gear. As they were strapping on their webbings and fixing their bayonets, Davy shouted, "Meet here after."

"What?" Jamie shouted back.

Davy pointed to the opening of the dugout and shouted again, "Here? After?"

Gavin, Mac and Jamie shook their heads in agreement. Mac and Jamie had been trained as gunners. They moved away quickly to their assigned position at a Lewis machine gun. Davy, because of his exceptional skill with a rifle, and Gavin, because of his sheer size and strength were assigned to positions on the fire step. *Bloody hell,* Davy thought nervously as he checked that his rifle was cocked and ready.

After the platoon had formed up, the commanding officers moved along the trenches ordering half the men to stand down. The guard would switch every hour for as long as the German artillery barrage lasted. The men not on guard, were told to rest, which was ridiculous, considering the noise. *Bloody hell,* Davy thought, *rest, with the world exploding around you, not bloody likely.* He took the first guard duty and Gavin sat against the parados, pulled his coat up under his beard, and closed his eyes. *He can't really plan on sleeping,* Davy thought impressed by Gavin's calm doggedness.

Using a periscope, Davy looked out over no man's land. Incoming artillery was exploding around him. Each hit caused a mountain of dirt to erupt into the air. The dirt showered down on him. Smoke encircled him. He felt down for his gas mask, it was there, in its pouch, hanging at his side. Davy looked again through the periscope, the landscape in front of him changed. Craters appeared, lines of barbed wire vanished. Some of the shells exploded behind the trenches, some directly into the trenches.

Davy watched in horror as a shell exploded in the trench 40 yards to his right. He heard the whistle, the explosion, then a high-pitched ringing. Dirt, wood, sandbags and men were flung into the air as if they were snatched up with a shovel and tossed aside. When the dirt settled, a single soldier remained, Davy thought he looked okay, but then he noticed, his arms, both arms, were missing. Just gone. Davy looked around, expecting to see the lost arms laying in the dirt, but they had disappeared. Time slowed down, and Davy could hear nothing but the steady high-pitched ringing. He watched as the armless man's knees buckled, then he fell, face first, into the dirt. *Why did it take so long for him to fall?* Davy thought. Other men filled the gap in the trench. Medics moved up and lifted the man onto a stretcher and carried him away. An explosion directly in front of him filled Davy's ears, he tore his gaze away from the carnage, and looked back into the periscope at the changing landscape of no man's land.

When the officers signaled, Davy and Gavin switched places. The barrage lasted 5 hours, and then the advance came. All men were ordered to the ready. Davy looked over the parapet. He maneuvered a sandbag to support his rifle. Gavin did the same. And they waited. And watched. Soon, they could make out figures advancing. Small at first, growing. Davy could hear the rattle of the machine guns. Numbers of the advancing Germans began to fall, but they kept coming, closer, and closer. Gavin prepared to shoot, but they were still too far. Davy reached out tapped his arm and signed for him to wait. They waited, and watched as the line of men advanced. When they were 120 yards away Davy shouted, "NOW!" He picked a figure, aimed and fired. The figure fell into the mud. His heart was racing, his breathing fast, his mind rushing, *a man, son, father, brother, mate, I've killed him,* he thought, but he buried the thought as soon as it formed. Davy slowed his breathing, calmed his racing heart and numbed his mind. He worked methodically, picking figures, aiming, firing and watching them fall.

Davy never new how long they stood there firing, or how many figures fell, but eventually the line stopped coming and Davy watched as they started to turn and retreat.

The Viking
~ Davy McLeod

A horn blew and the order to advance was given. Davy, Gavin and the other men of their platoon climbed over the top and into no man's land. Advancing on the retreating Germans. But the Germans were firing as they moved away. Now Davy was a figure in an advancing line. They moved forward, taking cover in the shell holes left by the artillery fire, aiming and shooting. The platoon had thinned and spread out. Gavin was now 15 feet to Davy's left. As they moved over a ridge, a single German soldier appeared. He was close, maybe he had tripped, or maybe he hadn't heard the order to retreat, but there he was, standing not 20 feet in front of Gavin. *Why, he's young, just a lad,* Davy thought. Gavin stood there. He was huge. Dirt covered his face, his thick blond hair was blowing in the wind. He looked every bit like his Viking ancestors. Davy took aim at the German, but as his finger was about to squeeze the trigger, Gavin gave a load roar, and the German dropped his rifle, turned and ran. A moment later, a shell exploded where the German had been standing. When the dirt and smoke cleared the German was gone, and so was Gavin. Davy continued the advance, but the retreating Germans were gone. He thought he heard someone yell stand down. He flattened himself out in a shell hole and listened. Stand down. There it was again. He moved slowly backward in the direction he'd come, over the parapet and into the relative safety of the trench. The artillery had moved further down the sector and this area was quiet. For Davy, the battle was over. He thought they had driven back

the German advance. He would learn later that British losses of both men and territory had been great.

❖ ❖ ❖

After the Fight
~ Davy McLeod

Davy made his way back to the dugout. The trenches
were lined with men, many wounded, all exhausted.
He hoped to find Mac, Gavin and Jamie already at the
dugout, but it was empty. Davy looked around, thinking maybe he was confused, maybe this was the wrong dugout. *But,
no, this is it, this is where we we're supposed to meet.* Davy thought.
Dammit, where are they? And for a moment, an awful realization hit him, *they could all be dead.* He might be the only one
left, alone in this living hell on earth. He was shaking. He
struggled to get his cigarette case from his haversack, open
it and remove a cigarette. *Dammit,* he thought, as he tried to
steady his hand to light the cigarette. He took a long drag,
and slowly blew the smoke into the heavy air. He stood there,
unable to move, unable to think, or decide what to do next.

"Bloody, hell," Mac shouted as he came up from behind Davy and thumped him on the back. Davy jumped,
and turned to find Mac and Jamie. They were covered with
mud, faces black, but he had never been so glad to see anyone in all his life. Mac continued, "That was a bloody awful
business. Where's Gavin?"

Davy shrugged, it took him a moment to recover his
voice, "The last time I saw him was out there," he said,
pointing to no man's land.

Mac squinted out over no man's land and mumbled, "Bloody hell."

The bond between the three friends was strong. They were more like bothers than mates. It had been Davy and Mac who took turns hiding Gavin when his father drank too much, at least until Gavin had grown big enough that his father left him alone. When Mac had fallen out of a tree and broken his leg, Gavin carried him home, and Davy ran for the doctor. And Mac and Gavin had been there for Davy when his father died.

"He probably just forgot where we're supposed to meet," Davy said, "You know Gavin, he's probably sleeping in some other dugout, not a care in the world, snoring to beat the band."

"Exactly what I was thinking," Mac agreed. But their eyes met, and they saw the thing that they feared, but were unable to speak.

"Let's ask around, someone's bound to have seen him?" Jamie suggested.

"He is hard to miss," Mac agreed. They moved up and down the trench, asking the men of their platoon if they had seen Gavin. And it seemed everyone had.

A bloke named Brice said, "Yeah, I saw him, the crazy fool, saw him go back over the top, again and again to carry out the wounded. And, mind you, this was before the battle had settled down, before the medics were willing to go up and over. He came back once with a chap over each shoulder."

"Do you know where he is now?" Davy asked.

"Nope," Brice said with a shrug.

Davy, Mac and Jamie wandered back to the dugout, hoping Gavin had shown up. As they approached, they heard a load, familiar noise. They looked inside. Gavin was spread out on the floor of the dugout, flat on his back, blood and dirt covered his tunic, but he seemed unhurt. He was snoring loudly.

Their commanding officer was moving up and down the trench with a rum ration, so they woke Gavin, retrieved their tin cups from their kits, and lined up for their share. They needed it. When the officer got to Gavin, he poured him an extra-large portion, seems Gavin's heroics hadn't gone unnoticed. The mates raised their cups.

"To Gavin" Davy said.

"To all of us" replied Gavin.

Mac added, "To knowing how to bloody shoot straight."

And Jamie said, "To Sergeant Angus Macgregor. The bastard. Without him I don't think we would have survived."

"To Sergeant Angus Macgregor," they said in unison, and they downed the rum.

An Invitation from Detroit
~ Davy McLeod

They settled back into the dugout, lit the tommy cooker, took off their boots and resumed picking lice out of their clothing. They had heard that the platoon would be going back to the reserve trench for some R&R. They were ready.

"I heard we get a bath, and they send our clothes out to get de-loused." Mac said.

Jamie rubbed the matted stubble on his chin and said, "I sure would like a shave."

Gavin stroked his thick, dirty beard and said, "I think I'll keep my beard. How do I look?" He grinned broadly.

"Like a bloody Viking," Mac said.

"Good, I'll keep it." Gavin declared.

Davy said, "I want to get some paper, I need to write a letter thanking Nana for the socks." He looked at the now mud-covered socks, wiggled his toes and sighed. "Hey, that reminds me, I never read her letter," he started searching his pockets for the letter, found it and began reading it, silently. Mac found the newspaper in his pocket, and read about the bug show again, but it wasn't so funny anymore. He yawned, put the newspaper between his head and the dirt wall and closed his eyes.

Davy read his letter. He was sad to discover that Nana's neighbor had polio. He continued reading and was astonished when he got to the end of the letter. *Can it be real? She's offering to pay for my passage to Detroit? Help me get started in a new life?* Then Davy remembered Alice, and his heart sank. Alice would never leave Bothwell. Her family was there, and friends and she was the prettiest girl in town. She liked being the prettiest girl in town, she wouldn't want to be just another girl, in a big American city. No, his life was in Scotland now, forever. Davy folded the letter, Mac, Jamie and Gavin were all sleeping. He pulled his coat around him, put his head back and tried to join them.

The platoon was issued R&R the next day. Back in the reserve trenches, Davy received a stack of mail that had been delayed. They spent two weeks washing, resting and reading the adventures of Fred Norman in Bob's newspapers.

CHAPTER 7

A Rude Awakening
~ Bob Stevens

Bob collected the Free Press from the front porch, retrieved the delivery cart from the shed, and headed next-door. He opened the gate and pulled the cart into Professor Ackermann's yard. The storms from the night before had blown over, and an early morning fog blanketed the city. The shrubs and flowers hung low with the weight of the rain. Delicate droplets illuminated the spider webs. It would be another hot and humid August day. Bob unlocked the door and opened it for Nietzsche. Usually, the big dog bounded through the door as soon as Bob opened it, but today, she sat, looked at Bob, looked up the steps leading to the kitchen, and looked at Bob again. She gave a soft whine.

"What's a matter girl?" Bob said. "Come on, we're going on a picnic." Bob opened the door wider. "It's just a little fog you silly dog. Nothing to be afraid of." Nietzsche stepped into the yard and Bob re-locked the door. Together, they walked to the gazebo. It had become a meeting place for Bob, the Robinson girls and Henry. Bob and Henry spent a few days in mid-June trimming back the overgrown shrubs and giving it a fresh coat of white paint. From the gazebo, they had planned a trip to Navin Field for a Tiger baseball game, an outing to the Boblo Island Amusement Park, numerous picnics on Belle Isle, and kite flying in Ascension Park. While for Sara and Jeannie, the summer seemed to last forever, for Bob, Maggie and Henry, it was over all too fast. They seemed to sense that the world was changing around them, that this might be their last real summer vacation. They each wondered, would the country be fighting in the war next summer? Would everything be different? Would they be different? The only other shadow in the summer sunshine was the fact that letters from Bill and Sam had stopped suddenly in late June. No telegrams came, no bad news, just, no letters either. Bob hoped that keeping his adopted sisters busy would help to lessen the worry they felt.

Today they were taking the river steamer Ossifrage up the Detroit River, into Lake St. Clair and across to Chatham, Ontario for the last picnic of the summer. School started next week. Bob sat down on the step of the gazebo to wait for the others. He opened the Detroit Free Press. Nietzsche nuzzled his hand. Bob rubbed Nietzsche's ears, poor girl seemed out of sorts. He skimmed the pages of the paper, he was looking for the latest news on the Black Tom Island explosion, and the Burroughs auto bandits.

The explosion on Black Tom Island had dominated the news since July 30th. Black Tom was a munitions depot on an island in New York Harbor, and on July 30 it exploded with the force of an earthquake. They say they felt it in Philadelphia. Windows were broken 25 miles away. It even damaged the Statue of Liberty. Seven people were killed and hundreds were injured. Bob was intrigued, maybe it was morbid, but he read every article about it. At first they thought it was caused by the night watchmen who lit smudge pots to keep away mosquitoes, but then investigators determined that the pots had not caused the blasts, and that it had not been an accident. Current reports said that sabotage was suspected, and that Germany was behind it.

Two weeks after the explosion, on August 14th, there was a robbery at Burroughs Adding Machine Company. Unlike the Black Tom Island explosion, this hit closer to home. Burroughs is where Father works. Three robbers held up the paymaster and armed guards and made away with over $33,000. They shot and injured one of the guards. Bob's father was on his way to work at the time, and even saw the robbers drive away. He told Bob all about it the next day, "When I got off the bus I saw their car speeding away. There was a commotion and one of the guards was lying on the sidewalk, bleeding. As the crowd gathered, I could hear the alarms of the police getting louder. I went into work, but to be honest, we didn't get much work done. We were too busy speculating as to whether the police would catch up with them, and wondering what the robbers would do with all that money." He had paused, shook his head and added, "I'm glad I didn't get there any earlier, I would have walked right into the thick of it. Don't tell your mother all this, it will only worry her." It had been two weeks since the robbery, and the police still hadn't made an arrest. Bob figured they were long gone.

THE Detroit Gazette

Base Ball Reports 4 pages	1st August Extra NIGHT — — EXTRA Aug 4th 1916	Final Extra page one

FIVE AUTO BANDITS LOOT-BURROUGHS-CAR OF $37,000; GET AWAY

Burroughs Scene of Sensational Robbery;
Robber and Clerk Wounded
— In Street Duel —
— FIRST Reports —

Three men drove up to the store
of the Burroughs Adding Machine Co.
this afternoon and held up clerks
and tore bags away from them
then escaped down Second Ave.
The police were given the alarm
at March in similar way —

August 4, 1916
www.catherinepaonessa.com/thegazette

Before he found any news about either investigation, he heard stomping feet and laughter. Maggie was the first to appear. She came running around the corner of the tall fence, her hair flying, one hand on her head holding Sam's hat in place. Next came Sara, then Jeannie, her hands on her hips looking indignant.

"I won," Maggie boasted.

"Well, it's not fair, I still have polio in my foot," Sara said frowning. She did still have a slight limp that was slightly worse when she thought about it. "Plus, your legs are longer."

"You're too old to be running around like a wild Indian," Jeannie said to Maggie with a stomp of her foot, "Mother said so. It's not lady like."

"Well, she doesn't have to know now, does she?" Maggie replied.

"Hi, everyone," Bob chuckled as he folded the newspaper and tossed it into the cart to read later.

"Gosh, I could hear you from a block away," Henry said as he entered the yard. "You're going to wake…" But before he could finish, the door to the house flew open.

"WHAT ARE YOU YOUNG RASCALS DOING IN HERE? GET OUT OF MY YARD! OUT! NOW!"

It was Professor Ackerman. He was wearing a gray night shirt. His graying hair floated over his head and unshaven face. He seemed to melt into the fog, but his eyes were blazing with anger, surprise and something else, grief? Sara hid behind Bob, taking his hand in her small one.

"We're sorry…" Bob started to explain. But Professor Ackermann had turned and was headed toward the house. "OUT!" He shouted over his shoulder. To Nietzsche he said,

"Nietzsche, inside, NOW." Professor Ackermann opened the door and the poor dog obeyed meekly, her tail limp and her head low. To the children, Professor Ackermann whispered, "Please leave." He followed Nietzsche into the house, locking the door behind him.

They stood there gaping. Sara was crying softly.

"Poor Nietzsche," she said. "She has to stay with that old meanie. She'll miss the picnic."

"Let's get out of here," Henry said. Bob got the cart and they headed, dejected, toward the Robinson's house.

"Well, come on. We can still have a fun picnic," Henry said, although his voice wasn't convincing.

"Sure," Jeannie said, "and mum has prepared a wonderful lunch for us. There's even a jar of lemonade."

"And we have the taffy we saved from Boblo," Maggie added. Joining in the effort to cheer everyone up.

"It just won't be the same without Nietzsche," Sara sniffed. "What if I never see her again? What will I do?"

"I'm sure Professor Ackermann didn't mean to be so, so well, mean," Bob said. "We just surprised him. He must have gotten home really late. We'll go see him later. You'll see. It will be fine."

They explained what had happened to Mrs. Robinson, who promised to talk it over with Aunty McLeod. Professor Ackermann will have to listen to Aunty McLeod; everyone listens to Aunty McLeod. Felling a little better, they loaded their picnic supplies in the cart and headed toward Randolph St. to board the steamer. Before they reached the end of the street, they heard loud barking.

Sara saw her as she rounded the corner off Crane onto Jefferson, "Nietzsche!" she shouted. "You've escaped, oh, what a good girl. Did you bite that old grump?" Nietzsche had bounded into Sara's outstretched arms, almost knocking her to the ground. They all gathered around, petting Nietzsche and talking at once. The picnic would be a success after all.

A Busy Man
~ Aunty McLeod

Aunty McLeod had heard the commotion beyond the ally and recognized the children's voices. After finishing her morning tea and tiding up the house she headed over to the Robinson's on a fact-finding mission. She discovered Mrs. Robinson and Mrs. Stevens deep in conversation.

"The children were quite upset, especially Sara," Mrs. Robinson concluded as she retold the tail to Aunty McLeod. "She's become quite attached to that dog. I suppose I should have seen this coming. Nietzsche doesn't belong to us. I should have discouraged the attachment. But Sara was so sick, and Nietzsche seemed to help." She shook her head, frowning.

"Well, if you ask me, Nietzsche needed Sara as much as Sara needed her. Poor dog." Aunty McLeod said. They were sitting on the Robinson's shady front porch enjoying a cool glass of lemonade. The bees buzzed in the black-eyed susans. "Let me explain," Aunty McLeod said. She paused, deciding where to begin, then continued, "When the Ackermanns moved here they were a beautiful little family, Karl, that's Professor Ackermann's name you know, his wife Hanne, and their daughter Gabriele. Gabriele was just a baby at the time. Karl was devoted to them. I think he was a bit older than his wife. Hanne was a beautiful woman, tall, thin and graceful, but delicate, too delicate if you ask me. I don't know if she ever really felt at home here. She missed Germany." Aunty McLeod sighed. She took a sip of lemonade.

"It's hard to move to a new country," Mrs. Robinson said, "I still miss Canada, and it's just across the river."

"Uprooting your family and trying to make a home in a different place as always hard." Mrs. Stevens added.

They each nodded in agreement, Aunty McLeod continued, "Gabriele was a sweet baby." She looked like a small version of her mother, but with her father's friendly, laughing eyes. They got Nietzsche, oh, five years ago, I guess, when Gabriele was about Sara's age. That dog is a little girl's dog. She and Gabriele were always together. I was never a dog person myself, they always rather scared me, but Nietzsche's special, very special."

"Remember, I didn't want to let her in the house when Sara got sick, but well, I didn't really have a choice. Nietzsche knew Sara needed her." Mrs. Robinson paused. "Imagine, I called that sweet dog a beast."

Aunty McLeod continued, "Hanne got influenza three years ago. It was a bad case, and, well, she just didn't make it, may she rest in peace." Aunty McLeod paused, looked down the sunny street toward the Ackermann's house and continued, "It was so sad. Karl and Gabriele were devastated, but they had each other, and Nietzsche. Then, two years ago, in the spring, like Sara, Gabriele got polio. But, she was much worse than Sara. Her fever went quite high, then broke. We thought she was out of the woods, but then the fever came back. It went like that for over a month, a high fever on and off. She lingered, growing weaker and weaker, then she just slipped away. Karl and Nietzsche were by her side when she passed." The women were quiet for a few minutes. Mrs. Robinson wiped away a silent tear. They sipped their lemonade, listened to the hum of the bugs and the hush of the hot summer day. Each was thinking about Professor Ackermann's loss, and their own losses and near losses.

Mrs. Robinson interrupted the silence, "No wonder Professor Ackermann keeps to himself. The grief must be, well, I can't even imagine."

"He mentioned his family to Robert, they've met for coffee several times," Mrs. Stevens said.

"That's good," Aunty McLeod said, "He was in a bad way after he lost Gabriele, very bad, to the point of not wanting to live himself. He seemed to be getting better, beginning to live again, then he left town so suddenly, now, well, I don't know what to think. I'll pop by to see him this afternoon. I'll take some cookies," Aunty McLeod concluded.

The conversation moved on to other things, the ladies discussed their gardens, the upcoming canning season, and the suffrage movement.

As promised, Aunty McLeod paid Professor Ackermann a visit later that day. She tapped on the side door, expecting to hear a welcoming bark from Nietzsche. Instead she heard some bumping and shuffling. She tapped again, and the door swung open.

"Ah, Mary," Professor Ackermann said with a weary smile. "I had a feeling you might stop by. Come in, come in." He held the door open for her. She went up the three narrow steps that led to the kitchen.

"Hello Karl. Welcome home," Aunty McLeod said. She looked around the room, her eyes adjusting to the darkness after the bright afternoon sunshine. The house had a stuffy, closed up smell. Professor Ackermann no longer looked like the haunted ghost the children had seen earlier. He was clean-shaven and dressed in a neat, white dress shirt.

"I'm sure you've heard about the surprise appearance of the crazy professor," Professor Ackermann said with a chuckle. "Oh," he said spotting the plate of cookies neatly covered with a cheese cloth in Aunty McLeod hand, "Those wouldn't be cookies, would they? I was just feeling rather sorry for myself, as I have nothing tasty to go with my afternoon tea. You will stay to tea?" Professor Ackermann asked.

"Why, that would be lovely," Aunty McLeod said, as Professor Ackermann led her through the dining room and into the parlor. He offered her a seat on the large, stuffed couch. She continued, "I really came to ..." but before she could finish, Professor Ackermann took the plate of cookies from her and disappeared into the kitchen. He knew Aunty McLeod well enough to know that once she started talking, she would be hard to stop. He wanted—actually needed—a cup of tea, and especially a cookie, before she began.

Aunty McLeod looked around the quiet room. It was cool, the shades drawn to keep out the afternoon heat. The dining room table was covered with books, papers and a typewriter. The morning issue of the Detroit Free Press was laid out covering much of the table, hiding many of the books and papers. One paper had escaped the table and was lying on the floor. Aunt McLeod picked it up. To her surprise, she couldn't read it; it wasn't English. And didn't appear to be French either, *German of course*, she thought. She set the paper down on the table and returned to the sofa. Dust floated and sparkled in the one shaft of light that shone through the only open window.

Professor Ackermann returned carrying a tray with two cups of tea and the plate of cookies. "Well now, how have you been Mary?" He asked.

"Oh, I've been fine, but I was rather wondering about you? You gave the neighborhood children quite a start this morning."

"Ah, that. Well, I can explain," Professor Ackermann said. Aunty McLeod sipped her tea. She was surprised to find Professor Ackermann in such good spirits. She had expected much worse. He looked well too. He was a handsome man, his hair graying only slightly at the temples, he had kind, intelligent eyes. *He could find a new wife, he could be happy again.* Aunty McLeod thought.

Professor Ackermann continued, "I arrived home quite late last night. It had been a long, exhausting day of travelling. I was sound asleep, dreaming about Gabriele, and I heard laughing and chatter of little girls in the yard." He paused, half smiling at the memory of the dream, "And Nietzsche barking. The sounds invaded my dream, but they were so real, and I think I was still half asleep when I jumped from my bed and ran out to the yard. I wanted to catch Gabriele there and see her well again. I even called out to her, but by the time my bare feet hit the hard gravel of the path, I was awake and the children were staring at me. And Nietzsche," Professor Ackermann chuckled sadly, "my dog, looked at me like I was the intruder." He paused, shook his head, and looked into Mary's understanding eyes, "I imagine you've heard the rest, I behaved rather badly." He paused again, ran his fingers through is hair, looked away. "I was astonished to discover how much it still hurts. To be honest, I thought I was getting better, moving on." He whispered.

Aunty McLeod patted his knee. "Oh, my dear, dear man. I'm so sorry," was all that she could say in reply.

They sat in silence for a long moment, then Professor Ackermann said, "Truly, I am getting better, I am trying to rejoin the world of the living." Brightening he said, "I'm working on a book, a history of European and US relations during the Second Industrial Revolution. Of course, the war is rather changing that history. That's what took me away this summer, research and meetings with publishers."

"Well, that explains the pile on the table. And you'll be going back to the classroom soon?" Aunty McLeod asked.

"Actually, no. I won't be returning to teaching," Professor Ackermann said sadly.

"Not teaching, but why?"

"Well, learning German has become rather unpopular at the moment, and German Professors of literature, even more so. Enrollment in my classes has been dwindling since the start of the war. It was only a matter of time before the college would have to let me go, I saved them the trouble and quit last spring," Professor Ackermann explained.

"Oh, but, that's a shame," Aunty McLeod said.

"I'm far too busy with my research, so it's probably for the best," Professor Ackermann said, and then added, "What I don't understand is how Nietzsche has turned against me too? She's as German as I am."

"Why, where is Nietzsche anyway?" Aunty McLeod asked, realizing Nietzsche wasn't there. "The children were so disappointed when she couldn't join them on the picnic."

"Well, so was Nietzsche. She whined and cried; I couldn't bear it. I finally sent her out to join the children," Professor Ackermann said with a frown. "Who has bewitched my dog?"

"Well, now, there's a story to tell," Aunty McLeod said. Professor Ackermann reached for another cookie, paused, took two, and sat back in his chair. Stories were Aunty McLeod's specialty, right behind baking shortbread cookies. Aunty McLeod filled Professor Ackermann in on Sara's illness and Nietzsche's part in making her well again. She also explained how the children had fixed up the gazebo and had been using it as a meeting place.

"I do hope you don't mind. If you do, well I'm at fault, I encouraged them to enjoy the gazebo. It may be their last summer as, well, children. I think this country will be joining the war before too long; God help us. And those children will be the ones to pay for it," Aunty McLeod finished with a sad sigh.

Professor Ackermann considered, then said, "I didn't get a good look at the backyard, but Nietzsche seems healthy and happy and the front of the house looks better than it has in years. Bob Stevens has done a great job. In fact, I was going to ask him to continue taking care of the outside for me. I just don't have the time, and I will be traveling quite a bit in the coming months," he paused, reading Aunty McLeod's steady gaze and continued, "And I suppose the children can continue to use the gazebo. But I would appreciate if they stayed away from the house, the noise of children playing would be a quite distracting."

Aunty McLeod smiled, "And what about Nietzsche?" she asked.

"Well, Nietzsche has made that clear. They can play with Nietzsche all they want, but I like to have her in the house at night, especially when I travel. She's a good guard dog. I'll settle things with Bob this evening."

Aunty McLeod rose to leave saying, "And you will take care of yourself? And you must come over for supper soon," she looked him over from head to toe and continued, "I don't think you're eating enough, and I would like the company."

"Of course, of course," Professor Ackermann chuckled, "and now, I'll see you home. We can go through the alley, I'd like to see the yard and gazebo."

Summers End
~ Bob Stevens

Bob and his friends were tired and hot as they headed home after the picnic. The cart's wheels squeaked on the hot pavement.

"I can't pull you anymore, it's too hot," Bob complained.

"Well, if Jeannie got out, it wouldn't be so heavy," Sara whined. "I hardly weigh anything at all."

"You've been riding the whole way! It's my turn!" Jeannie snapped.

"Ugh! Out! Both of you," Maggie ordered. The girls sheepishly obeyed and the group continued up the hot city sidewalk.

"I liked the boat the best," Jeannie said, "and the taffy."

"Me too," Sara said softly with a sigh. They walked on quietly. As they headed up Fischer Avenue, toward the Robinson's house, they noticed a man on the porch. They could tell it wasn't Mr. Robinson, this man was smaller, and, as they got closer, they could tell he was dressed in a suit.

Maggie squinted in the bright sunshine, "Who's that? The man in the suit?" she asked.

"Why, that's the crazy man from this morning," Henry said.

Sara took Nietzsche's collar, patted the big dogs head and said, "That's okay girl. He won't hurt you," It was hard to tell if she was talking to the dog, or herself. But Nietzsche recognized Professor Ackermann, escaped from Sara's grasp and ran to greet her owner. For a moment, the children thought she was going to attack. But, Nietzsche ran up to Professor Ackermann, barked a happy hello and nuzzled his hand. Then, she ran back to Sara, then back to Professor Ackermann, and again. Barking with each trip up the sidewalk. Silly dog, it was as if she wanted her two friends to meet.

"Why hello," Professor Ackermann called as the children arrived in the yard, "I've been waiting for you. I think Nietzsche is trying to introduce us."

As Bob was the only one to have actually met Professor Ackermann before, he shook the professor's outstretched hand and finished the introductions.

"How was the picnic?" Professor Ackermann asked.

"Great, Fine, Fun," the children answered in unison.

"Well, good, good. I wanted to stop by and apologize for my rude greeting this morning. You see, I was sound asleep when I heard you're voices in the yard. Truly, I didn't mean to scare you," Professor Ackermann said smiling at Sara, "and I wanted to thank all of you for taking such good care of Nietzsche. I hadn't realized how lonely she was with just old me to amuse her."

"She's the best dog in the whole world," Sara said earnestly.

"Well, any friend of Nietzsche's is a friend of mine," Professor Ackermann said. "I hope you will continue to come and play with her, and take her for walks." Sara beamed; she wouldn't lose Nietzsche after all. Professor Ackermann continued, "And Bob, I also wanted to thank you for doing such a terrific job on the yard. The gazebo looks very nice, so nice, that I want you children to feel free to use it as much as you like. All I ask," and Professor Ackermann became very serious, almost strict, "is that you stay away from the house. I'm very busy with my work, and I cannot be disturbed." They all nodded. "I will also be traveling again in the coming months, and Bob, I'd like you to continue to take care of the yard, rake the leaves this fall, and shovel the snow next winter, and take care of Nietzsche of course."

"Um, yeah, sure, that will be fine," Bob said.

"Wonderful, that's all settled then," Professor Ackermann said. He reached into the inner pocket of his suitcoat and pulled out a small pile of envelopes. He handed them to Bob, saying, "Here's your pay for this summer, and I think enough to cover you until the end of the year. There's also a little something for the rest of you, for helping Bob out.

Now, I really must be going, and remember, just please, stay away from the house, I have much work to do." With that, he escaped up the street. "Nietzsche," he called over his shoulder, "time to come home." The big dog obeyed silently.

Bob looked at the pile of envelopes in his hand. The top one was for him, he moved it to the bottom and handed out the rest of them. There was one for each of them, their names printed neatly on the front. They opened them and discovered that Professor Ackermann had paid them each two dollars. Bob's envelope held two ten dollar bills. They couldn't believe it. Sara and Jeannie ran in to show their mother. Maggie, Henry and Bob looked at each other surprised.

"Wow, that's a lot of money to be handing around," Henry said.

"Twenty Eight dollars in all," Maggie said.

"That's a lot of money to pay a bunch of kids just for watching his dog?" Henry said.

"Hey, I do a lot more than watch Nietzsche," Bob said defensively.

"We know," Maggie said, "but he didn't have to pay the rest of us."

"Well, I'm not going to complain, I'm going to think of something good to buy with my money," Bob said smiling.

4th
extra   The Detroit Gazette   Fri Aug 18

Anniversary Extravaganza

Detroit Wins All of Three
Games   Standing 8 - 5

To-days
3 games
Fri. Aug 18, 1916.

The first game
was a 2 to 0 game.
The Innings were
Det. —   1 2 3 4 5 6 7 8 9
              0 0 1 0 0 0 0 0 1 - 2
Kansas City 0 0 0 0 0 0 0 0 - 0

The Second game
another victory
with a score of
2 - 9
Indinplis 0 0 1 0 0 1 0 0 0 - 2
Detroit   0 0 0 0 0 3 6 0 0 - 9

The third game
the longest game
we played this
season, the score
being 5 - 7 and
14 innings

ST. P. 1 2 3 4 5 6 7 8 9 10 11 12 13 14
        0 1 0 0 0 3 2 1 0 0 0 0 0 0
Det   3 0 0 1 0 1 0 2 0 0 0 0 0 1

Total
Detroit 8
St Paul 7

(Game Monday)

August 18, 1916
www.catherinepaonessa.com/thegazette

But, Bob did think about the money. He thought about it that evening while he searched the Free Press for more information about the spy's who caused the explosion in New York. He thought about it while he wrote an article about the picnic for his newspaper. And, he thought about it some more while he shoved coal into the coal bin the next morning. *It was a lot of money.* He couldn't shake the idea that there was something strange about Professor Ackermann giving them so much money.

That afternoon while he was cutting the front grass a truck drove up and stopped at Professor Ackermann's house. The black truck had a gold emblem of a bell on it. MICHIGAN STATE TELEPHONE COMPANY was printed in bold letters around the bell. *Wow,* Bob thought, *a telephone, I bet he's the first in the neighborhood to get a telephone.* Two workmen got out and made several trips to and from the house carrying wire and equipment. They ran wire from the corner of the house to a pole in the alley. Bob hadn't noticed the pole before; they must have put it up when he wasn't home.

Bob had only used a telephone once, last June, at Mr. Jones' grocery store. He and his father and mother, dressed in their Sunday best, had walked down to the store and called his grandfather on his 77th birthday. The store clerk made the connections to the Barrington Passage General Story, where his grandparents were waiting for the call.

"Hello, Dad," Dad yelled in to the wall mounted phone. "Yes! Yes! This is amazing. Oh yes, I can hear you fine. Happy Birthday. I'll put Susie on the line." Mother had to tip toe to talk into the mouthpiece.

"Hello, Dad?" She said tentatively. "Oh, Hello. Oh, this is wonderful. Happy Birthday Dad! How are you? Hello Mother. Yes, yes we're all fine here. Oh yes, Detroit is a big city, but we have lovely neighbors. Say hello to Robin," Mother handed Bob the phone, tears were glistening on her cheeks.

"Hello, Granddad," Bob yelled into the phone. "Oh, it's fine. I'll be a sophomore in the fall. Oh, Happy Birthday," Dad motioned for the phone. "Here's dad again. Bye."

Dad said, "Have a nice Birthday Dad, yes, yes, we'll all write soon. Bye." And that was it. Mother was crying, people in the store were staring and Bob decided it had all been rather embarrassing.

Now, as he stared at the workmen running the wire to Professor Ackermann's house he thought, *having a phone in your own house would be grand.*

Later that day, while he was playing inside baseball in the gazebo with Maggie, Henry, Jeannie and Sara, he told them about Professor Ackerman's telephone.

"See that wire, going from the house to the pole in the alley," Bob explained, "That's for the telephone."

"And your voice gets squished up and travels through the wire," Jeannie said.

"If we had a telephone in our house, I'd call Bill and Sam every night. Then we wouldn't have to watch for the postman, and be sad every day when he doesn't bring any letters. It's mean of Bill and Sam not to write us, but Mum says that they are very busy fighting the mean Germans," Sara said.

"My pop's been thinking about getting a phone for the new shop," Henry said.

"If we all had phones, we could just sit around and talk to each other. We wouldn't even have to leave our houses," Bob added.

"Well, I don't think that would be much fun," Maggie said. "Whose turn is it anyway?"

❖ ❖ ❖

Sophomores
~ Maggie Robinson

On the Thursday before school started, Maggie, Bob and Henry walked over to Eastern High School to sign up for classes.

"Are either of you taking Solid Geometry?" Maggie asked.

"Uh, no," Bob said.

"Me either, I almost flunked Plain Geometry," Henry said, "Anyway, I'm taking bookkeeping. My dad wants me to learn how to keep the accounts so I can help with the business. He's expanding, maybe soldier uniforms, nap sacks, that kind of stuff. There's a big demand for stuff made out of canvas."

"Hey, I'm taking bookkeeping, let's get in the same class." Bob said to Henry, then he asked Maggie, "What else are you taking?"

"Oh, let's see," she pulled a neat list out of her book bag. She noticed Bob and Henry looking at her dumbfounded. "What, you can't just show up and take any old classes," she said defensively, realizing that's exactly what they planned on doing. She continued, stubbornly, "I'm taking Solid Geometry, English, Chemistry, Civics, I think we all have to take that, Biology and Latin. I couldn't take Ancient History," she said, disappointed, "It wouldn't fit."

"Wow, we won't ever see you, you'll be too busy," Bob said. Maggie couldn't tell if he was just stating a fact, teasing, or actually disappointed.

"I'm going to try and get English first hour, with Mr. Taylor. I here he's a good teacher. You boys should take it with me." Maggie said, excited, she continued, "Oh, and if we take Civics fourth hour, we can have two classes together."

They turned the corner and could see Eastern High School at the end of the block. Maggie smiled, *summer is great, but I'm ready for school to start,* she thought to herself, but would never confess it to Bob and Henry.

"I was going to take Latin, too," Bob said. Maggie checked her list.

"I'm going to try and get Latin sixth hour," she told Bob.

"Wait, what, your taking Chemistry, Biology and Solid Geometry all in the same year? And Latin?" Henry asked, "But, your head will explode." Maggie rolled her eyes and didn't reply. Henry continued, "Do you know if Mr. Taylor is hard or easy?"

"Oh, easy, English is my worse subject," Maggie said.

"But you got an A in English last year," Bob reminded her.

"Still, it's hard for me, I read so slowly. I'd much rather do math or science," Maggie explained. They entered the busy school and headed to the gymnasium. Students sat visiting in groups on the bleachers that lined two walls. Warm sunshine streamed in from high red and blue windows giving the room a festive look. The wooden floor glistened with a thick coat of new polish. Tables were set up around the large room. Each table had a department sign, English, Science, and so on. The science table had a large group of mostly boys in front of it. Maggie spotted Edith among the boys, "Gosh," she said to Bob and Henry, "look at this crowd. I hope I can get the all the classes I want.   Remember, English first hour, Civics forth hour" and" to Bob, "Latin sixth hour." Edith was waving her over. "Bye," Maggie said over her shoulder as she hurried to join her friend.

Maggie was happy. She knew Bob and Henry thought she was daffy, but she liked school. She liked the regular schedule. She liked getting the syllabus for each class mapping out the semester, what would be covered, what was expected and when things were due.

She and Edith waited by the Science table chatting excitedly. Finally it was Maggie's turn. She handed her schedule form to the teacher. "Chemistry and Biology please," she said, smiling.

"Hmmmm," the teacher said concerned, "I think you're mistaken," he said finding her name on the form, "Miss Robinson. You want to take both Chemistry and Biology in the same year? You realize that both are very difficult?"

"Yes sir, I realize that," Maggie said, "but, I want to fit in two years of physics."

"Young ladies don't usually take such a rigorous schedule," the teacher explained. Maggie could feel her face getting red. The others around the table were starting to stare.

"I'd like Chemistry and Biology also," Edith said quietly from behind Maggie.

"There's no rule against it, is there?" Maggie asked firmly, emboldened by Edith's timid voice. She'd heard many of the boys ask for the same classes, it was the only way a student could get all the science classes in before graduation.

"Why, no, we let the boy's do it if they are planning on attending college. Do you plan on attending college Miss Robinson?" the teacher asked.

Maggie was dumbfound, "I, um," she stammered. She dreamed of going to college, but she had never spoken that dream out loud. Not to anyone. *We can't afford college,* she thought. And, now, this teacher was asking her, in front of everyone, *what should I say?* But, she didn't have to say anything. She hadn't seen Bob get in line a few boys behind her, so she was surprised when he pushed in between them and spoke to her.

"Hello, Maggie, Edith," he said nodding to each in turn.

"I suppose you're signing up for the college prep courses, smart girls like you. With your fathers' always talking about you going off to college and all. Oh, I'm sorry," he said to the teacher, "am I interrupting?"

"Yes, young man, you are," the teacher said frowning. "Get back to your place in line."

"Sure thing. Bye ladies," Bob said, nodding and smiling.

"Now, let's see, you ladies want Chemistry and Biology? It's very uncommon, hmmm. It will be quite difficult.

Hmmm. And Miss Robinson, I see you don't have Home Economics on your schedule. We'll have to speak to each of your fathers before we can let you proceed with this plan," the teacher insisted.

"But, the boys can sign up for ..." Maggie began.

The teacher didn't let her finish, "Now, you've taken enough time. I'll pencil it in, but..." He took Maggie's and Edith's schedules and wrote, very faintly, Chemistry and Biology. "Your fathers will have to stop by the office and approve these schedules, otherwise, you'll have to select something more appropriate." With that he handed them their schedules and waved them away.

More appropriate! Maggie thought fuming. She was so mad. Tears were welling up in her eyes. *Oh, why do I cry when I get mad! I never used to cry.* Maggie thought exasperated. She headed straight to the ladies room in the hall. Edith followed.

"Oh, what am I going to do?" she asked Edith. "I'm not sure what my father will say. And oh, he won't be happy about having to stop by here on his way to work. Oh, what was Bob thinking?" She moaned.

"I think it was rather gallant of Bob to try to help," Edith said.

"But, my father never talks about me going to college," Maggie said. "He doesn't even know I've thought about it. What about your dad?"

"Well, um, my father expects me to go to college, so Bob was half right," Edith said sheepishly.

"Oh," Maggie said.

"Come on, we better go schedule for the rest of our classes, or we'll both be stuck in Penmanship," Edith said.

"At least Penmanship would be more appropriate for young ladies like us," Maggie smirked. She splashed a little cool water on her face and they were ready to go. Maggie was able to get her other classes as planned. She spotted Bob and Henry in line for their Bookkeeping class and joined them to see if they'd be ready to walk home soon.

"Did you get your science classes?" Bob asked.

"Well, kind of, thanks for trying to help. My da has to come to the office and tell them he approves of my schedule, if not, I can take something more appropriate," Maggie said, imitating the teachers nasally voice on the word appropriate.

"Oh, gosh, he actually said that, I'm sorry, did I make things worse? I didn't mean to," Bob said.

"I guess he might have said no if you hadn't come up talking about my da and college and all, but, now I have to convince my da," Maggie sighed.

"Oh, he'll agree. He's proud of you being so smart," Bob said.

"Thanks," Maggie said, she looked down at her schedule sheet, *bother, am I blushing? First crying, now blushing!* She thought, angry at herself. "Are you ready to go?" she asked.

"I have to head into the locker room, football practice starts tomorrow, and I need to talk to the coach," Henry said. Maggie stole a look at Henry, and thought, *wow, a football player.*

"And I'm going over to the Eastern office to see about a position on the school magazine," Bob added. Maggie looked up at Bob, and realized how much taller he was than herself. *Gosh, they're both rather dashing,* she thought, and wondered if anyone else noticed her talking to them. She felt herself starting to blush again. She said, "Did either of you get English first hour?"

"Yup, both of us," Henry said, "and I got in the fourth hour Civics course. But Bob didn't, it conflicted with Chemistry." Maggie noticed Henry's slight smile.

"Oh, I didn't know you were taking Chemistry," Maggie said to Bob. "But you have it forth hour?"

"No, fifth," Bob said. "And Latin sixth, he added, "Advertising conflicted with Civics."

"Oh, so we have Chemistry and Latin together," Maggie exclaimed.

"Yeah and English first hour," Bob said, now it was Bob's turn to smile, "and I hope I can count on you for lots of help."

"Sure, oh, this will be a fun year," Maggie said. Bob and Henry rolled their eyes and groaned. The three friends left the gymnasium in different directions. Maggie was glad Bob and Henry were busy; she needed to think about how she was going to ask Da about college.

When she got home, Maggie poured her soul out to Mum as they sat on the porch. She told her about the scheduling problem, and about her dream of going to college.

"Well, I don't see why you shouldn't dream of going to college. You're a very smart young lady. Maybe, if more women went to college, men would see that we can do more than cook and clean for them." Mum said exasperated. "Honestly, maybe I should go down to that school myself," Maggie had expected this, but she didn't think it was such a good idea.

"He specifically said, my father," Maggie said.

"Well, that just shows you, doesn't it?" Mum said angrily.

"But, we can't really afford college, can we?" Maggie asked, hopefully.

"Well, not exactly, but there may be a way." Mum said, considering, "Just last week I overheard some of the women at a Lady's Auxiliary meeting talking about scholarships for promising young women. So, it's not impossible." Maggie couldn't believe it. She never thought she might really be able to go to college. Mum continued, "I'll talk to Da about the schedule, I'm sure he won't mind stopping by the school to give his approval." Mum smiled, and said, "In the meantime, there's ironing that needs done, and dinner won't cook itself."

"Yes, Mum," Maggie said. Maggie didn't mind ironing. Actually, she liked it. She liked the smell of the clothes fresh off the clothes line. She liked the precision needed to heat the iron on the stove to just the right temperature, and she liked seeing the crisp clothes when she was done.

Although mum said not to worry, she was anxious for da to get home. When he did, she minded the stew that was simmering on the stove and kept Sara busy setting the table, so Mum could talk to Da in peace. She was finishing the last of the ironing when he came into the kitchen.

"Well, young lady, your mum tells me I have to go down to the school tomorrow," Da said. His voice was stern, but the twinkle in his eyes gave him away.

"Oh, I'm sorry, but I ..." Maggie began.

Da interrupted with a loud chuckle, "Now, now, let me finish, I think you taking college prep classes is a fine idea. As far as college goes, well, that would be a fine thing, a fine thing indeed. I'm not sure how we'll manage it, but we'll cross that bridge when we come to it."

"Really?" Maggie replied, stunned.

"I guess, we'll have to see," Da said, "In the meantime, mind that ironing, I think you've burned a hole clean through my hankie."

Maggie jerked up the iron she'd forgotten she was holding, and examined the scorched hankie, "Oops, sorry," she said sheepishly, secretly happy it was one of Da's hankies, and not one of her dresses.

An hour later the Robinson's sat down at the large dining room table for dinner. When Sam and Bill first went overseas, the family had continued sitting in their original spots, leaving empty chairs where the boys used to sit. But the lonely chairs made Sara sad, to the point of tears. Mum moved the chairs up against the dining room wall, ready for when they were needed, and the five remaining chairs were placed around the table. Da at the head, as always, Mum opposite him at the other end. Maggie on mum's left, closest to the kitchen so she could help Mum serve and Sara and Jeannie across from her. After Da said the blessing, Maggie told everyone how Bob had saved the day by interrupting the teacher.

"I like knowing you have someone looking out for you over at that school," Mum said. "The Stevens are such a nice family, we're lucky to have them in the neighborhood."

"Hmmm," Da said, to his wife, he continued, "I don't know Margaret, she spends a lot of time with that Bob and his friend, what's his name, Henry. And I know Bob was a great friend to Sara when she was sick, but have you seen either of them lately? They're not boys anymore; they're growing up. But, I'll leave such matters, courting and chaperoning, to you my dear." To Maggie he said, "Mind your mother, she knows what's proper regarding these things." Jeannie giggled. Maggie gave her a quick kick under the table.

"Yes, Da," Maggie said, blushing. *Dang-it, blushing again,* she thought. She decided she wouldn't mention the classes she, Bob, and Henry had together.

The Spy Next-door
~ Bob Stevens

Bob was tired as he walked to meet Maggie. It was the first day of school, Tuesday, September 5, 1916. Maggie was waiting when Bob turned the corner. She smiled and waved as he walked toward her.

"Hurry up," Maggie called out to him.

"Gosh, how can you be so excited this early in the morning, and on the first day of school?"

"We got letters, a whole stack of letters, from the boys. They're okay!" Maggie burst out. "They're just fine. I'm so happy." Bob could tell, her whole face was smiling, and her eyes were sparkling. Bob smiled back.

"Wow," he said, "that's great. Just great." Bob took Maggie's book bag and slung it over his shoulder on top of his own. He was surprised at how heavy it was, considering it was the first day of school.

"Oh, sorry," Maggie said sheepishly, "I know it's heavy, but I wasn't sure what I'd need. I brought extra notepads and a couple of books from last year." Bob rolled his eyes. He had started carrying Maggie's book bag when they started walking together last year.

"That's okay, I only have a notepad and a pencil, so my bag is light," Bob teased. "So, Sam and Bill are okay?"

"Yep, the letters must have been held up somewhere. We got four from Bill and two from Sam. Sam never was one for writing. And you'll never guess what?" Maggie asked.

"What? Are they coming home?" Bob asked, surprised.

"Well, no, not that good," Maggie said a little disappointed, then brightening again, "but Sam got a promotion. Well, they both got promoted last spring, from private to corporal, but Bill said that was just for staying alive, but now Sam is a sergeant."

"Sergeant? Really, that's great," Bob said.

"I figure that he'll be safer as a sergeant, I mean, the privates are in the most danger. Isn't that right?" Maggie asked.

Bob thought for a moment, "I suppose so," he said. He didn't mention that he'd read how the allies were having problems with Germen snipers shooting officers.

"Well of course, that's exactly what I thought," Maggie said, she added, "Hurry up, we don't want to be late on the first day."

"Ah, no," Bob grumbled and yawned, "But, I'm so tired, I hope I can stay awake."

"Well, you should go to bed earlier," Maggie told him.

"I went to bed plenty early, but it was so strange. On Saturday night, I dreamt I heard voices, German voices," Bob said, "I figured it was from the war news I read in the paper that morning, but then I had the same dream Sunday night. German voices, and I couldn't understand what they were saying, and in my dream, I was so frustrated because I felt like I was supposed to understand. I was supposed to know the answer to what they were asking."

"Oh, that's horrible," Maggie said, wide eyed, "I'd be afraid to sleep ever again."

Bob continued, "Then, last night, it all made sense. I woke up right in the middle of the dream and realized that the German voice wasn't in my dream at all, it was coming through the window, from Professor Ackermann's house."

"Gosh, that's strange, are you sure you weren't still dreaming?" Maggie asked.

"Yeah, I got up and went down and opened the living room window, I could hear him even better down there," Bob explained, yawning again.

"Well, I guess he was working," Maggie said with a shrug, "at least the mystery of your strange dream is solved. Anyway, I didn't get to tell you what else Bill said in his letters. He wrote about the food. They call the meat bully beef. It's actually canned corn beef. Bill said it wasn't that bad and that they have it with canned pork and beans and hard biscuits. But the worst stuff is called Maconochies Irish Stew. It's supposed to be, well, like stew. Bill said it was pretty terrible, and he wouldn't feed it to a dog if he was back home. He said some of the fellas don't mind it and even eat it cold, but he figures that's because their mum's weren't very good cooks. That part made Mum cry. Oh, I just wish they could come home. Bill said that Sam is rather good at being a soldier. That the other chaps look up to him as a leader. Maybe that's why he got a promotion."

Bob yawned again, but persisted, "But don't you think it's strange for Professor Ackermann to be talking German, at night, in his house, alone."

"Maybe he was on the telephone, you said he got one, right. Maybe he called some German friends," Maggie said, exasperated.

"Hmmm, I guess that makes sense," Bob said. *Why was Maggie always so logical?* He thought. They got to school and found their first classroom.

After school Bob and Henry went to see the building Henry's father was renting. He was opening a small canvas production shop. It was a brick building on Atwater Street. It had three stories and very high ceilings. An office was located at the back of the first floor. At the moment, the building was empty.

"Pop got a contract from Ford and one from GMC to produce canvas covers for trucks being sent over to Europe. The Allies use them for ambulances and transporting troops. They use canvas over the back-cargo area because it's lighter than wood, but still keeps the soldiers and injured out of the weather," Henry said. He pointed to the far corner of the large dusty first floor. "The sewing machines will be placed in rows here, and here. The cutting room will be upstairs. He'll be hiring about fifteen people. If you want a job for after school, I'm sure Pop would hire you. Especially since I'll be at football practice and all," Henry smiled, he was happy to have made the football team.

"I'll be pretty busy too, I'm going to be as an assistant editor for *The Eastern* but maybe a job would be good. I'll think about it," Bob said.

Mr. Harding came out of the office and joined the boys in the middle of the large room. "Hello boys, well isn't this exciting; we're on our way. The work-tables will be delivered and bolted in tomorrow, on this floor and upstairs. The sewing machines are coming Friday. Seven industrial machines! They should have no trouble sewing through the canvas. We'll do the cutting upstairs and the sewing, folding, and packing down here. How much homework do you have my boy?" He asked as he thumped Henry on the back. "We have to measure out the placement for the tables."

"None today Pop," Henry said, as he dropped his book bag on a nearby crate.

"I'll help," Bob said. *This was exciting, a brand-new business,* he thought.

"Great," Mr. Harding said. He explained where the tables would be placed and the boy's set to work measuring everything out and marking the corners of each table with chalk. They took a break on the stairs when they were done with the first floor. Bob told Henry about his strange dreams and Professor Ackermann's nighttime German conversions

"Wow, that's really strange," Henry agreed.

"That's what I thought," Bob said. *At least Henry agrees with me,* he thought remembering Maggie's logical explanation. "Do you think he could be, well, a spy or something?" Bob continued softly. "I've been reading about the explosion on Black Tom Island. They say it was sabotage. They're trying to track down the Germans that did it."

"Yeah, it's been in all the papers. You don't suppose he's mixed up with that? Henry asked.

"I don't know, but well, maybe, all that stuff about us staying away from his house, and he gave us all money," Bob said.

"I thought that was strange, but now, now it makes sense," Henry said, excited. "He was paying for silence—in advance!"

"Exactly!" Bob said, "But, what should we do?"

"I don't suppose we could go to the police," Henry said. "We don't have any real proof. Talking German on the telephone isn't exactly against the law."

"No, at least not yet," Bob said discouraged.

"But, you could listen, maybe you could pick out some words," Henry suggested.

"Unfortunately, sauerkraut and strudel are the only German words I know," Bob chuckled.

"What's that?" Henry asked.

"Some type of food," Bob explained. "We had a German neighbor in Beaver Dam. Strudel is pretty good."

"Well, write down some of the words and we can look them up at the library," Henry said.

"Oh, good idea," Bob agreed. "You know, he teaches over at the Detroit Junior College. We could go investigate, maybe something will turn up."

"Boys, how's the measuring going?" Mr. Harding's voice came from the office. The boys jumped up and went back to work. They agreed to go over to the college the next day to see what they could discover. That night Bob put paper and pencil next to his bed ready to take notes, but he soon fell sound asleep. He woke up in the morning, freezing. The weather had turned fall like overnight and Professor Ackermann had closed his windows.

As planned, Bob and Henry went over to Detroit Junior College the next afternoon. They decided they would go into the main office and ask for Professor Ackermann's room.

"What will we do if we actually run into Professor Ackermann?" Henry asked, concerned.

"Um, we'll just say we're thinking of enrolling here in a couple of years," Bob said.

"Oh, right, that'll work," Henry agreed. He was toying nervously with the strap of his book bag. "This place looks like a castle," Henry continued, looking at the large square tower and pointed chimneys of the main building. As they climbed the steps he said, "You ask, okay, I don't think I'm cut out for this investigation stuff, my heart's bounding."

"Relax, it's not like we're doing anything wrong," Bob said looking around, "this is kind of nice. Maybe I'll actually come here, in a couple of years." They entered the clean, efficient looking office. A young, pretty blond secretary sat at a desk near the door. Her nameplate said, Miss Jones. Bob smiled at her.

"Good afternoon boys, may I help you?" Miss Jones asked.

"Um, well, yes. We were wondering, um, where Professor Ackermann, I mean what room Professor Ackermann is in?" Bob stammered.

"Classes are done for today, I'm afraid you missed it," Miss Jones said, frowning.

"Um, well, we don't want to miss it tomorrow" Henry said quickly.

"I would guess not," Miss Jones replied, still frowning. "Let's see, Professor Ackermann you said? Hmmm, wait, Professor Ackermann, why there must be a mistake with your schedules. May I see them? Professor Ackermann no longer teaches here," she said, puzzled.

Bob and Henry looked at each other surprised. Miss Jones was looking at them, her hand extended, waiting for their schedules.

"Oh, right, we forgot," Henry blurted, and they backed quickly toward the door.

Bob grinned and said, "Sorry to have bothered you." They hurried out the door and down the steps before talking. "He doesn't even work there anymore?" Bob said, "I knew there was something strange going on."

"Yeah, maybe they suspected something. Maybe they fired him because he's German," Henry said, shaking his head. They continued walking as they talked.

"Well, you can't just fire someone for being German," Bob said, "Can you?"

"What do you think he's doing, for work, I mean?" Henry asked.

"That's the big question," Bob said. "A man can't have a house and get a phone and do all that travelling if he doesn't have a job. And he seems to have lots of money."

"But not having a job doesn't *prove* he's a spy. Now what do we do?" Henry asked. They stopped at the corner where they would have to head in different directions. "Do you want to come down to the shop and see the new machines?" He asked.

"No, I can't. I have to cut Professor Ackermann's grass, and I have a ton of chemistry homework," Bob sighed.

"I told you, you where nuts for taking chemistry," Henry said, adding, "But then, you could go do your homework with Maggie. Which is why you took it in the first place, right?"

"Well, maybe," Bob said, smiling sheepishly. "But, seriously, what should we do next, about Professor Ackermann, I mean."

"I guess we have to wait and watch. See if you can get anything from his phone calls," Henry suggested.

"Yeah, I guess, but it's getting kind of cold to sleep with the window open," Bob said. "I better get going. See you tomorrow."

"Good luck with that chemistry," Henry chucked, "Say hi to Maggie for me."

CHAPTER 8

The French Garden
~ Davy McLeod

Davy's platoon was rotated to the front-line trenches twice since the spring. Each tension filled day was the same as the next, and began the hour before dawn with 'stand-to'. During 'stand-to' the men were ordered to man their positions on the fire step to guard against a morning raid from the enemy. When the threat of attack was deemed unlikely, they had breakfast. Then, a few daily chores were assigned, things like filling sandbags, checking supplies and digging latrines. All daytime tasks must be down below the trench line out of view of the deadly German snipers. With these light chores completed, the soldiers were off duty and most of them found a dugout to crawl into and sleep. Men also used this time to clean their rifles and check their equipment. Nightfall meant a return to strenuous activity. Under the cover of darkness the trenches were maintained, repaired, drained, resupplied, troops were moved, raiding parties were sent out, and communication wiring and equipment was repaired. At dawn, the troops would stand-to once more and the whole process was repeated, until the soldiers' days and nights became a jumbled haze that was cleared only by the realization that a sniper's bullet, a stray shell or an all-out attack could make the day their last.

After their second rotation to the trenches, Davy's platoon was moved to the rear for R&R. It was late in the afternoon, and Davy, Mac, Gavin and Jamie sat in a small French garden opening their mail. Before the war, it was a pretty little garden in a pretty little village with flowers and a bubbling fountain. A statue of two fat children decorated the top of the fountain. One child held a pitcher that poured water into a large seashell held by the other child. But, the people who had tended this garden, left during the initial German invasion of 1914.

Now, in the summer of 1916, the flower beds are over gown with weeds, and the fountain no longer works. The pool around the fountain holds a puddle of rainwater. Mac flicked his cigarette butt into the puddle where it went out with a sad sizzle. Gavin gave Mac a disapproving look, but Mac just shrugged. He dug into his pocket for another cigarette, of which he had a good supply thanks to Jamie's card playing skills.

"What'd ya suppose happened to the people who own this garden?" Gavin wondered aloud. His mother had the prettiest garden in Bothwell.

"Some of the villagers came home after the German's were pushed back, and the trenches were dug." Jamie said, "I guess these folks didn't make it back."

Davy and his mates had been in the village for two days now. They had bathed and di-loused. Their uniforms had been cleaned or, if too damaged, replaced. Mac sighed, rubbed his clean-shaven chin and said, "Damn, I won't lie, it feels grand to be clean. I know it won't last, but all the same, I feel great."

Gavin scratched his thick red beard, grinned and said, "Bloody hell, you boys look like wee bairn with your clean-shaven faces. Honestly, now that I remember what ya looked like, the beards and dirt were an improvement." He laughed at his own joke then sighed.

Sleeping and eating was easier away from the trenches. There was still work to do, training to attend and orders to be followed, but the men were allowed to sleep through the night, given free time to read and write letters, play cards and, Davy's favorite pastime, play a game of football.

"When we're done reading this mail, let's head over to the pitch and see if anyone wants to get up a game?" Davy suggested.

"It's to bloody hot, don't you think?" Mac said.

"Worried you'll get sweaty?" Gavin mocked.

"Not at all," Mac replied defensively, "I'll play if every-one else wants to."

"I'm in," Jamie said.

"Me too," said Gavin, "Maybe the boys from the 83rd will be ready for a rematch. We slaughtered them last time."

"Great, let's read our mail first though, and maybe it'll cool off a bit," Davy suggested, smirking at Mac. They fell quiet as they opened their mail.

Gavin had a package. He gave it a shake and could tell it was biscuits from home. Mac was eyeing him expectantly. They usually shared whatever treats they received from home. Gavin smiled, and slowly, very slowly untied the string on the box. Mac smacked his lips. Gavin carefully unwrapped the brown paper covering the box and slowly lifted the cover. Mac's stomach gave a load rumble. Davy laughed.

"Ahh, ginger! My favorite," Gavin exclaimed. Many of the cookies were broken, and they were a little stale, but the lads didn't care. Gavin took what amounted to three biscuits and passed the box to Mac.

Mac grinned at Gavin, but took only a small piece, and passed the box to Davy. Davy shook his head and thought, *Mac may smoke like a fiend, and be crude and sometimes even rude, but no one will ever say he's stingy.* Davy took a couple pieces and passed the box to Jaime who did the same. Gavin put the box in the shell on the fountain, the fat child holding the shell seemed to look at the biscuits with longing and regret. The four friends help themselves as they read their mail.

Gavin opened the letter that came with the biscuits. It was from his mother.

My Dear Son,

I hope these biscuits get to you before they spoil. I know that they are your favorite. Share them with Mac and

Davy if you like. I hope you are all doing well, or as well as can be expected, considering. The war has everyone here very busy. The mine is running overtime. Did I mention in my last letter that I changed the whole garden over to vegetables this year? They haven't started rationing, but it's good to be prepared. You should see the tomatoes! They're as big as your fist, and I truly mean _your_ fist. I miss my flowers, but I will be glad to have a cellar full of canned vegetables this fall.

Your brothers and sisters are doing well and keeping busy. Bruce sprained his ankle playing football yesterday, so I didn't let him play today. He's sulking. He's a tough little lad, just like you, but don't tell him I said so.

Before I close, there is something I want to tell you. Everything with da has been fine. Actually, better than fine. I know you were worried that he would return to his rough ways, and that you wouldn't be here to watch out for us. But, your da is not a bad man, and he's only rough when he's had too much at the pub. Well, with the overtime, and so many of his mates over there, he doesn't go to the pub much. And if he does, he comes home and sleeps in the shed like he's done since that one awful night between the two of you. You must know that he's very proud of you, and he loves you. So, don't worry about us a bit.

I'll say goodbye for now, I want to get these biscuits in the mail, and I have a Ladies Auxiliary meeting. Please keep safe. We miss and love you, Mum

Mac opened an envelope from his family. It contained a page from each of his three siblings. The first page contained a hand drawn picture of a little girl with blond hair, dots for freckles and a big smile. A black block was drawn to show how her front teeth were missing. Written across the bottom of the picture, in his mother's hand, it said, "I lost both my front teeth since you went to war." Under this, in purple crayon, it was signed, Katy.

Mac laughed at the picture and passed it around.

"Your sister?" Jamie asked when the picture came to him. "How old is she?"

"She's five," Mac said, he took the picture back, looked at it again with a sign, "Gosh, she's getting big."

Mac's next letter was from his nine year old sister, Brenda.

Hello Mac,

I hope you are still okay. School is hard and I miss having you here to help me with my arithmetic. Robbie isn't as good a helper as you and he gets mad at me when I don't understand. Mum is teaching me to knit socks so I can send some to you, but it might be a little while before you get them. The heel is the hardest part and I had to rip the first one out three times before I got it right. I decided to wait until I finished the second sock and send them both at the same time. One sock would be silly. I'm off to meet the girls. We're going to go to the pitch and see who's playing today. Be careful and don't get hurt. I can't wait until you come home. Yours Respectfully,
Brenda

Mac chuckled at the formal closing. The last page was from his 17-year-old brother Robbie. He unfolded it and read,

Hey Mac,

I got your letter. And, well I guess you're right about my not asking Mum and Da to let me enlist early. Not that I'm a coward or anything. And I think I would be a great soldier. But, well, it sounds like all the stuff in the papers about being heroes and fighting for the King is malarkey. Actually, it sounds pretty awful. Good thing you don't put a lot of details in the letters to Mum, I don't blame you, she's worried enough. I didn't show her your last letter, but thanks for filling me in. Got to go, the fella's are waiting for me. Take care of yourself, and say hi to Davy and Gavin. We all miss you guys. -Robbie

"Robbie got my last letter, you know, I showed it to you, the one where I told him straight up how bad it is here. He's not going to try and join up early," Mac said, satisfied.

"That's good, he needed to know the truth," Davy said.

"Maybe we can put an end to the Hun before he turns 19," Gavin added. Mac folded his letter, lit a cigarette and leaned back to enjoy his smoke.

Jamie had a letter from his young wife. It was in a pale pink envelope. He opened it and took out the neatly folded sheets of pale pink paper. He held them to his nose, inhaled slowly, and smiled. He unfolded the pages and read,

Jamie My Love,

I live each day for the mail to come, and I am thrilled when I receive one of your wonderful letters. Seeing your strong hand and hearing your voice in my head is such a comfort.

I know you don't approve of my decision to get this job in London, but, I just couldn't sit around knitting socks and rolling bandages any longer. My da is still mad at me for leaving Hamilton to come here, but he'll get over it. I just pray that you're not mad, I can't bear to think of you being mad at me. But the day's without you are just too long and I need this distraction or I'll go crazy.

I've adjusted well to being a factory worker. The work is hard and like you said, some of the women are rougher than I'm used to, but the days fly by. I've learned to use a metal stamping machine. We're making ammunition for the Lewis machine gun. (I probably shouldn't have written that, we're not supposed to talk about it, but I'm just so proud to be doing my part). Isn't that the type of gun you were trained to use?

I'm sharing a flat with three other girls. Barb, she's married like me and we've become great friends. Eve, she's younger than us, I think she may have lied about her age to get the job. If I had to guess, she's not much older than 16. Her da was killed in the Battle of Mons and I think her family needs the money. Barb and I have decided to watch out for her. My last roommate is Julie. She's, well, I can't think of a nice way to say this, she's a floozy. She smokes and goes out to the pub with some of the rougher sort of girls. She actually drinks liquor! She is always making eyes at the bosses, which only encourages their forward behavior. Oh, I can see the look on your face as you read that, but don't worry, they leave us married girls alone.

Julie has invited Eve to go out with her, but so far, Eve has been a sensible girl and said no. She has joined Barb and me on our trips to the picture show. I hope you don't mind, but I bought Eve's ticket. Poor dear, first she loses her father, than she has to get a job to support the war that took him.

London is an exciting city. I've learned to use the underground so Barb and I have been touring around on our Sunday's off. We're working 10 hours a day Monday through Saturday, so Sunday is the only day we have off. We've been to the National Gallery and St. James Park. Both were lovely outings. The only thing missing was you by my side.

Remember last spring how horrified we were when we heard how Germany was using Zeppelin's to drop bombs on London. Well, you would be proud at how the country has reacted to protect us. At night, the skies over London are awash with spotlights and anti-aircraft defenses are everywhere. They even drained the lake at St. James Park so the nasty Baby Killers, that's what the papers call the Zeppelin's, well, they drained the lake so they can't use it to navigate to Buckingham Palace. Imagine that! We have blackouts to further confuse the Zeppelin pilots. It's wonderful to see how the people of London have come together to defeat this menace, and its working ...

Jamie stopped reading, grimaced and mumbled, "Damn, bloody Germans!"

"Everything okay mate?" Davy asked.

"Yeah, at least she was when she wrote this, but London has been under attack. Bloody Zeppelins! Bloody hell, the German's are dropping bombs on women and children. And my silly wife has put herself right in the thick of it." Jamie growled. He got up, gave a nearby flower-pot a swift kick so that it exploded in a pile of dirt and dust, then he turned and walked away.

"Bloody hell," Gavin said.

"Meet us over by the pitch in say, half an hour?" Mac called after him. Jamie raised his hand in a half wave, shrugged and continued walking. He read the rest of his letter.

> ... they've been able to shoot down more than one of the dreadful things before they could do any harm. I know what you're think-ing, and I have to admit, it is a little scary, but I still believe I'm where I'm supposed to be, doing what I must do. And isn't that exactly what you're doing? So, forgive me, please, and don't be mad and know that I love you with my whole being and can't wait for the day when I'm safe in your arms.
>
> Love, forever and always, Nora

Davy watched as Jamie walked away, *damn bloody war*, he thought. He had two letters, one from Nana and one from Alice. He had already read the letter from Nana and was looking at the latest newspaper. "Listen to this, Five Auto Bandits Loot Burroughs Car of $37,000," he said.

Mac whistled, "$37,000? Did they get away?" he asked, somewhat hopefully.

"Yeah, I think so, let's see," Davy said as he continued reading, "It says one of the robbers and a clerk were injured in a duel in the street. Happened in the middle of the afternoon," Davy added surprised.

"Wow, I read somewhere that America is full of gangsters. Maybe it's true," Gavin said. Davy passed the newspaper to Gavin and opened the letter from Alice. He read,

Dear Davy,

This is so hard. I just don't know how to tell you, so well, here goes. I'm engaged to Kyle Blackwood.

Davy couldn't believe it. But that can't be, she's engaged to me, he thought. He kept reading.

I'm sorry. And I didn't mean for it to happen, but he came back, he was wounded you know, he has a limp now and can't return to the front. We ran into each other a couple of times. And well, he ask me to marry him and I said yes. I'm sure you won't hold me to our prior agreement seeing is you're over there and who knows...

Davy could tell that the word "if" had been erased and the word "when" put in. He continued in disbelief.

... when you will be coming back. I'm sorry, but I know this will be for the best.

Sincerely, Alice

Dave read the short note again. He was shocked. Not that he loved Alice. No, he had seen the way Jamie's eyes looked and voice sounded when he talked about his wife. Anyone could tell Jamie loved her. No, Davy thought, *I don't love Alice.* But he had gotten used the idea of marrying her. It was easy. It was settled. It was done. They'd get married, have kids, and he'd work in the mine. *Then, I'll die.* Davy thought. *Maybe it will be quick, an explosion or collapse, or maybe the long slow death of black lung disease. The end. At least, if I'm lucky Mac and Gavin will be around, we can have family gatherings and Saturday afternoons at the pitch. Of course, that's if I survive this bloody war.*

Beyond that, he didn't think about the future. None of them did. It was like tempting fate to plan ahead. So, they lived in the moment: one day, one meal, one battle, or one game of football at a time. Now, without Alice, the future was a mystery and he'd have to trust the fate he was so afraid to tempt.

Davy signed. He didn't really want to blurt out that Alice had dumped him, but he wanted Mac and Gavin to know all the same.

"Bad news?" Mac asked. Davy handed him the letter. Mac read it and mumbled, "Bloody, hell." Gavin looked from Mac to Davy and back again. "Alice dumped him," Mac said, he continued, "she's engaged to Kyle Blackwood, the sod."

"Well, I guess I can't really blame her. He's there and alive," Davy said, gloomily. He reached over, took the letter, crumpled it into a tight ball and tossed it into the puddle with Mac's growing pile of cigarette butts. "Let's go see if Jamie's ready for a game of football."

CHAPTER 9

The Telegram
~ Bob Stevens

Bob transferred his and Maggie's book bags from his left shoulder to his right, and wondered why Maggie needed to bring home so many books. It was a beautiful Friday in late September. *Maggie may plan on studying all weekend, but I think I'll see if Henry wants to toss a football around later*, Bob thought. The leaves on the trees were still mostly green, with a hint of red and yellow on the very tips, like a whisper of the spectacular fall color show still to come. The yellow, purple and burgundy mums were giving a show of their own. As Bob and Maggie turned the corner onto Maggie's street, they passed a Western Union delivery boy. Maggie gasped softly. She grabbed Bob's arm, picked up her pace and ask, "Come with me?"

"Sure." Bob said. And they walked on in silence. They went into the side door of Maggie's house. The kitchen was empty.

"Mum?" Maggie called.

"In here, dear." Mum said from the front room. She was sitting quietly on the sofa, an unopened telegram in her hands.

"I can't open it." Mum whispered. Seeing Bob she said, "Oh Bob, I'm glad you're here. Please run down to the construction site and tell Mr. Robinson to come home."

Maggie was staring at the yellow telegram in her Mum's hands. As if by staring at it she could make it disappear. She sat down next to her mum. Bob put down their book bags and headed out the door.

As he had done, when Sara was sick, he ran to the construction site and found Mr. Robinson. Also, as before, Mr. Robinson hurried off. Bob wasn't sure if he should go back to the Robinson's house, or not. He was afraid of the grief he might find there, so he went home instead. Mother wasn't in the house. He found her in the garden. She was humming softly to herself as she stood on a step stool, wicker basket over her arm. She was picking apples. She turned as she heard him approach. "Oh, hello dear," she said smiling. "Here take this basket. I think I'll make a pie for dessert, aren't these apples beautiful? Why, whatever is wrong?"

He told her about the telegram.

"What time did it come?" Mother asked, sadness and concerned replacing the sparkle in her eyes.

"About an hour ago."

"Well, now, we shouldn't assume the worse. Maybe one of the boys was just injured, or maybe it has nothing to do with them at all." Mother said, trying to be positive. "If we don't hear from them in a bit, we'll walk over and see what's happened."

Bob went to his room. He thought about how unfair it was. How Maggie had been so very happy a couple weeks ago when the letters came. He looked out the window. The gazebo was bright in the late afternoon sun. He thought about the first time he looked at it, covered with snow and hidden by the dead, over grown shrubs, paint chipped and peeling. He thought about the fun he'd had painting it with Henry, and playing Pit and Inside Baseball there with Maggie, Jeannie and Sara. He realized that Detroit was his home. A gentle tapping on the kitchen door downstairs interrupted his thoughts. He held his breath and listened. Maybe it was Maggie come with his books to study, maybe everything was okay. He heard Mother opening the door and talking to someone. It was Aunty McLeod. He heard their soft voices, the door closing again. He looked out the window to see Aunty McLeod walking slowly across the yard and into the alley toward her own home.

"Bob" Mother called. He took a deep breath as he went toward the stairs. Mother was sitting at the kitchen table. Apples, some piled and sliced sat in a pile on the large wooden cutting board in front of her. *Was she crying?* Bob wondered. "Mother?" Bob asked softly. She wiped a stray tear from her cheek with the back of her hand.

"It's their son Bill, he's been killed." Mother said, a soft sob escaped, "In a place called Flers, in northern France."

Bob sat down at the table across from her, he reached over and took her small hand in his. She continued, "Oh, this dreadful war. Such a terrible, terrible waste. I can't even image the grief Margaret must be going through. Her oldest son, dead and buried, so young, so far away, and for what?" She wiped her nose with a hankie from her apron pocket and looked into Bob's eyes. "Promise me, please, you won't ever go away to war?"

Bob knew that he might not be able to keep such a promise, but he said softly, "I'll try.

Mother sighed. She handed him the paring knife, "Do you mind helping me for a bit? I need to get these pies in the oven. Peel and slice up these apples, and hmmm, Aunty McLeod said she'd make some shortbread and tarts, let's see some tea sandwiches will be nice." She got up and went to the icebox, "I'm so glad I baked an extra chicken yesterday, it was for you and you're your father's lunches, but chicken salad sandwiches will do just fine. And cucumber sandwiches too, I think." She was busy pulling things out of the icebox and cupboards. Bob sat, paring knife in hand, staring at her, *How could she think of food, he wasn't hungry at all, and he was always hungry,* he thought. She looked over at him. "What's the matter, I need those apples," she said.

"What's all this food for?" he asked.

"Why, we'll take it over to the Robinson's this evening," she said.

"But shouldn't we, well, maybe just, I don't know, not bother them?" Bob asked. He didn't want to go. Didn't want to see the sadness on their faces.

"Why, this is when neighbors really need each other. I'm sure there will be quite a few people. The Robinsons are quite respected in this community. People from McCoy's work, from the women's suffrage group, and from their church will all be stopping by to offer their condolences. And, all those people will need something to eat. Now peel, and I'll need you to run up to the market to get some mayonnaise and cucumbers," she paused, sighed, and then added softly, "this type of gathering keeps everyone busy, so we don't have time to dwell on the sadness before us." She wiped away another tear and pointed to the basket of apples.

Bob started peeling. He'd never experienced death before. When his grandmother died, they were in western Canada. They took a train to the funeral, but he didn't really remember much beyond that. This was new to him. He'd heard about wakes, but he thought they were planned, and you got invited, but now, thinking about it, that would be silly. You don't know when someone is going to die. He finished an apple and picked up the next. When he had quite a pile of peeled and sliced apples in front of him, Mother said, "That should be plenty. Now, can you run to the market?"

"Sure, I'll be quick," he said, and he headed out.

The Wake
~ Bob Stevens

Later that evening, Bob and his mother walked over to Robinson's. He carried a pie in one hand and a plate of sandwiches in the other. They went in through the front door. Mother was right, there were already quite a few people there. Most he knew, some he did not. Aunty McLeod met them at the door.

"Oh, my, doesn't that pie look good," she said taking the pie from him. To Mother she said, "Margaret is holding up pretty well considering. She's in the kitchen, come, she'll want to know you're here." And she and mother went off to the kitchen. He stood there holding the plate of sandwiches, wondering what to do with them, but he didn't have to wonder long. A short, round lady with glasses took the plate and said, "My, don't these look nice. I'll put them on the table for you."

"Oh, thank you," he said absently. He looked around the crowded room. Finely, he spotted Maggie. She was standing at the far end of the front room, by the window. Edith was standing next to her, so was Henry. Henry's parents were talking to some people in the dining room.

He felt a small hand take his, and he looked down. Sara was standing there looking up at him. Her face was pale and sad.

"Our Bill's been killed in the war," she said with a sniff. "That's why all these people are here. They buried him far away. In a place called France."

"I'm sorry," Bob said squeezing her hand gently. She squeezed back.

"You won't go away to the war, will you?" She asked. Her big eyes filling with tears.

"No," Bob answered. His voice catching.

"Promise?" Sara said.

"I promise," Bob said. Again, he knew it was a promise he might not be able to keep. They stood there holding hands. Bob looked again at Maggie. Her face was fixed. Her eyes were dry. People were talking around her, but she didn't seem to be paying attention. He saw sadness and agony in her eyes, and something else. Her jaw was set. Was it anger, fury?

"Come on, let's go say hi to Maggie," he said to Sara. She didn't answer, but let him lead her across the room.

"I'm so sorry," he said as they approached.

"Thank you, and thank your mother for bringing the pie and sandwiches. I saw them when you came in. They look lovey," Maggie said. Their eyes met, then she looked away.

"Um, yeah, I peeled the apples," He said then thought, *Gosh, that was dumb.*

"It was nice of you to help," Maggie said. *Why doesn't she look at me?* Bob thought. Edith and Henry said hello and they talked quietly together about the fine fall weather they were having then fell silent. He wondered where Jeannie was. He looked around the room. Most of the younger people, some of his classmates and some friends of Bill and Sam's were on the front porch. He would have joined them, but Sara was still holding his hand and he didn't have the heart to let go.

In the dining room the older men were drinking what he assumed was whiskey and talking quietly about the war and whether President Wilson would be able to keep the United States out of it, or if he should. Professor Ackermann was there. Bob wondered where the Professors true loyalties lay. As he watched, he was surprised to see his dad enter with two other men. They must have left work early. Dad gave him a solemn nod and joined the men in the dining room. Bob continued looking around the room for Jeannie.

Some of the women had gathered in the small, tidy kitchen. He could see his mother standing next to Mrs. Robinson. And there hidden slightly behind her mum, was Jeannie. She too looked pale and sad, and younger than her 10 years. She caught him staring at her and gave him a weak nod and wave. Maggie's voice startled him.

"Sara, have you eaten anything? Mother told you to eat something," Maggie asked, looking down at Sara.

"I'm not hungry," Sara protested. Maggie shrugged and looked out the window at the people on the porch.

"Gee, Sara, Aunty McLeod brought shortbread. And my mother made some little sandwiches that she said you would especially like. She even cut off the curst," Bob said. Maggie looked at him, and for a fleeting moment, gratitude replaced the anguish in her eyes. Encouraged, Bob continued, "I wouldn't mind one of those sandwiches myself. How about you come with me and we'll see if anything looks good?"

Sara nodded and they walked over to the table. Bob was happy to have something useful to do and managed to get Sara to eat a chicken salad sandwich and a shortbread cookie. He also took a sandwich to Maggie and stood by as she reluctantly ate it. He spent most of the evening standing near Maggie, holding tight to Sara's hand and making small talk so Maggie wouldn't have to.

Eventually people started leaving. Mrs. Robinson and the girls retired upstairs. Bob joined Edith and Henry on the porch with the remaining young people. His mother, Aunty McLeod and a few other women washed the dishes and put the food in the icebox or wrapped it neatly on the table.

Bob, his parents, and Aunty McLeod were among the last to leave. On their way out Mr. Robinson said, "We've decided to go back to Toronto for a week or so. We have family there, and most of Bill's friends, at least the ones who aren't fighting, are there. We'll have a memorial service at our old church," he said shaking his head. To Bob he said, "I want to thank you for fetching me, again. And I wanted to ask you another favor."

"Of course, anything I can do to help," Bob said.

"If you could take care of the yard, water the flowers, rake the leaves that would be very helpful indeed. I, well, would like the house to look nice for the girls when we get back." He said.

"Oh, sure, no problem" Bob said. Mr. Robinson shook Bob's hand.

"Thank you, it takes a load off my mind not having to worry about the house too. We'll be heading out on the morning train," Bob retrieved his book bag, they said good-bye and walked home in silence. Professor Ackermann was sitting on his porch as they approached their house.

"Good Night," the professor said softly. Bob thought about Professor Ackermann. How could he go to the Robinson's if he was a spy? Was he really helping the very people that killed Bill? It just didn't make any sense. But neither did the fact that he spoke German on the phone in the middle of the night and quit his regular job and made mysterious long trips to who knew where. It just didn't add up. Bob swore to himself that he would find out the truth.

❖ ❖ ❖

Please be Safe
~ Aunty McLeod

Aunty McLeod tossed and turned the night of Bill's wake. Finally, she got up and sat in a rocker by the window. She watched the harvest moon track across the sky. *Is Davy okay?* She wondered. *If anything happens to him, how will I find out? How long will it take before Katherine thinks to notify me? Will she send me a telegram or a letter? He may be dead or injured at this very moment? Oh, this won't do?* Aunty McLeod thought. She got up and went to her writing desk. First she wrote a quick note to her daughter-in-law in Scotland. She explained her anxiety and ask her to send a telegram if they ever get news that Davy was injured or otherwise. Then she wrote Davy. She had already written him this week and sent him the latest issue of Bob's newspaper, but she wanted to write again, to tell him that in spite of the miles that separated them and the years that had passed since she last held him when he was just a baby, she loved him.

Dear Davy,

As always, I hope this letter finds you well. Thank you for your last letter. I know it must be hard for you to find time to write. I'm very sad tonight. The son of my good neighbors the Robinson's has been killed. I think I've mentioned him. He and his brother were serving with the Canadian forces. The family received a telegram today. It will be a very sad time for them all.

I hope you are still considering my offer for you to come and visit and even stay. You will love Michigan in the fall. It's beautiful. Do take extra care of yourself, and remember always that I love you.

Love Always,
Nana

Aunty McLeod put down her pen. She felt very old. She looked at the picture of Davy on her desk. He sent it after he enlisted. There he was looking back at her. Smiling in his new uniform. He was a handsome young man, *just like his grandfather*, she thought. She yawned. Even though the eastern sky was starting to brighten, and it was almost the time to get up and start the day, she climbed back into bed and fell asleep. About the same time, around the block, the Robinson family was leaving for the train station and the start of their sad journey back to Canada.

CHAPTER 10

The Corporal
~ Davy McLeod

By mid-September 1916, Davy had been at the front six months. The men of the platoon were standing to on the fire step, ready to go over the top. Davy tried to breathe slowly, deliberately. He tried to steady his racing heart. A hint of the approaching dawn was visible on the horizon. The attack was scheduled for 5:30 am. They would be attacking from the darkness, into the rising sun. Corporal Thomson walked slowly up and down the trench.

"Five minutes now lads," Corporal Thomson said. He patted a pale lad standing a few places down from Davy on the back, and said, "Steady son." Corporal Thomson was an older man, maybe 40. He had been a mine supervisor before enlisting. He was an experienced leader and was quickly promoted to corporal.

Davy's heart continued to race. He felt for his gas mask, canteen, checked his rifle, *Yes, everything is in order,* he thought. They had done this before, but it never got easier. The bombardment had started yesterday, the deafening noise and shaking ground of the last 24 hours heightened the intensity of his anxiety.

"Three minutes," Corporal Thomson said after checking his watch again. To Davy, it felt as if time had stopped. He didn't own a pocket watch; miners didn't need them. They lived by the whistle.

There were fourteen men in their section, and Corporal Thomson made sure they knew what was expected, and that they all knew the objective. He had reviewed it with them two days ago. As a bombing team, they were to take a German trench 200 yards and slightly north of their current location. It wouldn't be easy. He showed them the maps, pointed out the obstacles, ensured them that the bombardment would severely weaken the enemy's ability to counterattack. The landscape was rough, pocked with shell holes and mounds of dirt. Barbed wire traversed the area like lethal lace.

"Two minutes lads," Corporal Thomson said.

The land sloped gently up from the parapet, then down toward the enemy trenches. They would be somewhat protected as they left the trench. Davy peered out over no man's land. The approaching sunrise lightened the eastern sky. He looked at Gavin a few yards to his left. Gavin's eyes were fixed on the horizon.

"One minute," came Corporal Thomson's confident voice.

"Steady lads. Ready ..." and Corporal Thomson moved up over the parapet as his last word left his mouth, "ATTACK!" But, before the men could follow, before they had time to climb over the wall, Corporal Thomson fell back. His body crumbling to the trench floor in a heap. Gavin rushed to the Corporals aide. Davy watched as Gavin put his steady hand under the corporal's head and lifted it gently from the pool of blood that was quickly darkening the trench floor. A bullet had entered near the corporal's right eye and exited the back of his head. Corporal Thomson was dead.

The men of the section had gathered around Gavin as he knelt next to the corporal's lifeless body. Gavin stood slowly, wiped his hand on his tunic leaving a patch of red. Davy watched as the men looked at Gavin, shock, dismay, and fear in their eyes. But, he saw a question in their eyes too; they were looking to Gavin to lead them. To tell them what to do. It made perfect sense. Gavin was the perfect choice. Corporal Thomson had been an experienced supervisor, but Gavin was a natural leader. The men not only respected him; they trusted him. Completely. Davy watched as Gavin looked from man to man, accepting their trust. Only moments had elapsed since the corporal had fallen, the battle raged around them, but in those moments, Gavin became their leader.

"All right boys, we know what we have to do," Gavin said in a deep, steady voice, then he yelled. "STAND TO." The men returned to their positions on the fire step.

"ATTACK," Gavin yelled. And he went over the top.

❖ ❖ ❖

The Bombing Team
~ Davy McLeod

The men followed Gavin without hesitation. A bombing team consisted of nine to fourteen men. Two or three were grenadiers. Their job was to throw grenades into the enemy trenches. Mac and Gavin were grenadiers for this attack. Once a trench was breached, the grenadiers ran down the trench tossing grenades into the dugouts, killing any enemy soldiers that remained. Each grenadier was assigned a carrier who carried extra grenades. Jamie was Mac's carrier. Two or three bayonet or riflemen were assigned to defend the bombing team as they moved toward and into an enemy trench. Davy was a rifleman. Each bombing team had a few 'spare' men in case of casualties.

The team moved in relative safety up the gradual rise. With Gavin in front, they crawled and rolled through the mud and dirt, under and around the barbed wire. They were increasingly aware that the sun was rising and they were quickly losing the cover of darkness. As they came over the low ridge and began the descent toward the enemy trench the illusion of safety vanished. A machine gun at the end of the trench raked the area. Davy and Jamie rolled into the nearest crater. The team was pinned down.

"Bloody hell," Jamie said. Davy signaling for Jamie to be quiet, he could hear Gavin, he must be in a crater nearby.

"Mac, you there? Did you see the machine gun?" Gavin asked Mac. He's voice was low, almost a whisper.

"Yeah, about 30 yards, directly in front of me," Mac replied. Davy could tell they were on opposite sides of the crater he and Jamie were in, Gavin to the right, and Mac to the left.

"Do you think you can hit 'em?" Gavin asked.

"I can bloody well try," Mac replied. His voice was horse and muffled.

"Davy? You there?" came Gavin's gravelly voice.

"Yeah, on your left, Mac is on my right, Jamie's with me" Davy said.

"Can you give those bastards something to think about with a couple shoots, give Mac some cover for the throw?" Gavin asked.

"Sure." Davy said, "Mac, tell me when you're ready, I'll take three shots at 'em, then you take them out."

"Got it." Mac said. There was a pause, then "Ready."

Davy had used his bayonet to dig a small "V" shaped notch in the edge of the crater, now he slowly placed the rifle in the notch, rose quickly, took three shoots, and fell back into the mud of the crater. He waited. A second later, he heard the explosion. Then he heard Mac yell, "Bullseye!"

"Forward," Gavin screamed as he leapt from the crater and moved toward the trench. The rest of the team followed. They entered the trench where the machine gun had been, two dead German lay there in the dirt and destruction caused by Mac's grenade. Davy could see other German soldiers as they disappeared beyond the first zig zag in the trench. The team moved cautiously but quickly after the retreating Germans. Davy, his gun ready, was prepared to fire as he moved through each turn in the trench.

On the third turn, a German soldier emerged around a corner and fired in quick succession.

"Bloody hell," Mac mumbled, hoarsely. The men took cover against the uneven walls of the trench. Davy knelt behind a pile of sandbags, rifle aimed at the spot the German had fired from, waiting and watching. A muzzle of a rifle appeared, then the barrel. Davy waited. When the German's head slowly emerged, Davy fired. The Germans head flew back and he crumpled to the muddy ground.

"Great shot," Gavin hollered to Davy as he continued past, "Keep moving men, we have to take this trench."

Gavin and the grenadiers moved cautiously round the next turn in the trench. But, as Mac passed him, Davy was surprised to see a large patch of blood on Mac's left shoulder.

"Mac, your hit," Davy yelled.

"Don't I bloody well know it! Hurts like hell," Mac said with a grimace. Mac had never been good around blood. As a kid, he had passed out cold when Davy had a particularly bad bloody nose. He looked down at his shoulder, looked away. Davy could see the color draining from Mac's already pale face.

"Steady there mate, let me see." Davy said. He looked around for something to stuff in Mac's shirt and hopefully stop the bleeding. The German he had just killed was lying face down a few feet away. Davy bent over the dead man and pulled at his loose fitting jacket. It was well worn and ripped easily. Davy decided that the inside would be the cleanest, so he rolled it up, and carefully pulled open Mac's shirt exposing his shoulder."

"Oh, shit," Mac said, quickly looking away. "Bloody hell, that shirt's filthy."

Davy snorted, they were in the middle of a hellhole; mud, dirt, blood and bodies, and Mac was worried about a little filth. *We'll probably all die out here anyway*, Davy thought. He looked quickly at Mac's wound, it didn't look too bad, kind of flayed open, but the bullet was not lodged in his arm. Davy worked quickly now, he pushed the bit of flesh back where it belonged, stuffed the dirty shirt up against it and tied it in place with another strip of cloth.

"There, that will have to do, let's go," Davy said and they move down the trench and caught up with the rest of the section.

With Gavin in the lead, the bombing team proceeded the length of the trench, throwing grenades in the dugouts as they passed. As instructed before the battle, they took no prisoners. At the far end of the trench, they meet the lads from another bombing team. They had taken the trench. Gavin ordered them to take up defensive positions on the parados, or eastern wall of the trench, facing the enemy. They would defend the position they fought hard to take.

Davy watched as Gavin moved up and down the trench talking to each man, offering encouragement and con-gratulations. As he approached Mac, who was sitting on a crate, eyes closed, Gavin said, "Hey Mac, that was quite a toss, we were pinned down for sure." Then Gavin noticed the blood on Mac's shirt and added, "Bloody hell, are you hit?"

"Yeah," Mac moaned.

"At the first corner, when that German turned and fired on us." Davy explained.

"Sorry, mate," Gavin said to Mac, to Davy he asked, "Did you look at it?"

When they were kids, Davy was the one to 'look at' their cuts and bruises. He seemed to instinctively know if they needed a mum's special care, or if a little spit, and wrap with a hankie was sufficient.

"Yeah, I think it's just a flesh wound," Davy said.

Mac moaned again and said, "Bloody hell, just a flesh wound. Anyone got a cigarette?"

As they were considering what to do, Lieutenant Payne, the platoons commanding officer, came down the trench. The men stood at attention. "Great job lads, at ease, at ease. We have to hold this position. Where is Corporal Thomson? I want to congratulate him, the way you chaps took out that machine gun was capital."

Gavin stepped up, saluted, and said, "Private Gavin Campbell, sir, Corporal Thomson is dead sir. He was hit as we left the trench."

"Dead, back in our own trench?" Lieutenant Payne asked.

"Yes sir, sorry sir," Gavin said.

"And who led your section into battle?" Lieutenant Payne asked.

"I did, sir," Gavin said without hesitation. Lieutenant Payne shook his head slowly, considering the situation, then he said, "Good job Private Campbell. Can you continue to lead this section until we're relived?"

"Yes, Sir," Gavin said.

"Men, Private Campbell will be your acting Corporal until further notice," Lieutenant Payne said. There was a buzz of approval from the men. Lieutenant Payne continued, "We must hold this position. Take shifts at the fire step keeping watch. We should be relieved within 24 hours. Private Campbell, I need a report of casualties, and injuries. Medics are forming in a dugout a little further down the trench, wounded should report there. And again, good job."

They had lost three men, two when the machine gun opened fire on them in no man's land, and one as they cleared the trench.

The French Girl
~ Davy McLeod

On the evening after the battle, the sector was quiet. Heavy fighting had moved to the south. Mac and the other wounded were being evacuated to the rear, although Mac did not go willingly.

"I'm fine, honestly, it's just a scratch," Mac said as he tried to get up from a stretcher in the makeshift hospital dugout. But, he grimaced, he wasn't fine, the bullet had ripped a large hole in his upper arm. The medic had done his best to clean and stitch the wound, but to heal properly, it needed to be immobilized, and there was always the threat of infection.

"Private Sutherland, I must insist that you go to the rear with the rest of the wounded," the medic said. Davy, Gavin and Jamie watched as Mac tried to stand, then slumped back down.

"Well, I guess I could use a little rest now that you mention it," Mac said sheepishly.

"I wish we were all going," Davy said. His stomach rumbled loudly.

"According to Lieutenant Payne, the entire platoon is being shipped to the rear for R&R as soon as the reinforcements arrive," Gavin said.

"So leave some food for the rest of us," Jamie told Mac.

"First come, first served," Mac chuckled as he laid back on the stretcher. Mac left with the rest of the wounded that evening.

The reinforcements arrived three days later. They came with a welcome supply of bully beef, hard biscuits and water. After devouring their share of the rations, the platoon worked its way back over no man's land, into the trench where they had started. While this section of no man's land was now behind the advanced trench, it was note a safe place to linger, Davy tried not to look at the bodies, both German and British that covered the eerie landscape. As they walked, a chap from one of the other sections told Davy and Jamie that he'd been to this valley before the war.

"You'd never believe what a beautiful place this was. I came here with my mum to visit a cousin of hers. This whole area was fields, some planted with crops, some covered with wildflowers," he waved his hand over the desolate landscape. "There was a stream, I know because my mum's cousin's lad and I went fishing. But the stream seems to have disappeared, or maybe it's just spread out causing this blasted muck," with that he pulled at his boot that was caught in the sticky, thick mud. "And I'm sure there were trees, lots of trees, just over there," he pointed to the low rise they had found safety behind during the attack. "Now look at it," he continued sadly, "not a bloody blade of grass to be seen, every tree turned into splinters and the trout stream is just a sick liquid oozing up from the ground." He shook his head and added, "Just war, waste, death and destruction."

The platoon was sent to a small French town about two miles from the front. Mac was still in the field hospital. He was recovering nicely, the threat of infection had past. He was well enough to enjoy the smiles and gentle, caring touch of the nurses. He flirted with them shamelessly.

Word of Gavin's heroism and fierceness in battle had spread among the platoon and beyond. They called him "The Viking." Even the company captain was aware of "The Viking's" leadership, resourcefulness, and bravery. Gavin was promoted to corporal and sent to officer training.

For the first time in a while, Davy and Jamie were clean, full and well rested. They had just picked up their mail and were back in the makeshift barracks relaxing and reading. Davy only had one letter. It was from Nana. He had just received a long letter and newspaper from her before the battle, so he was surprised to get another letter so soon. It did not contain a newspaper, only a short note. As he read Nana's words, he felt both sadness and anger. Her neighbor's son, Bill, had been killed. *This bloody, stupid war,* Davy thought. *A colossal waste, started by kings, generals, and politicians. For what? So lads from Canada, Britain, France, Germany, Italy, hell, from the whole bloody world could die together in fields of muck.* Davy tossed the letter onto his cot and got up. He was restless.

"I think I saw a pitch over by the mess, want to go see if we can get in a game?" Davy asked Jamie.

"Ah, maybe later, I want to write Nora." Jamie said absently, engrossed in his mail.

"Okay," Davy said. He grabbed his jacket and headed out. It was a warm afternoon for late September, but he thought he might need the wad of cash that was rolled up in the jacket pocket. He walked fast, not quite sure where he was headed, he just walked, his mind racing, *war – waste – death – destruction – war – waste – death – destruction.* Over and over the words circled in his head.

He walked down the narrow streets of the tidy town. If it wasn't for the presence of soldiers milling around and army vehicles rolling up and down the cobble streets, you would hardly know there was a war at all. The town had not been bombed during the initial German attack, and now it lay safely behind the French and British trenches.

The shops were open, and happy to have an influx of soldiers. There were shortages of some things, but basic, simple things were still available if you could afford them. Shop owners called to him in French, but he ignored them. Davy thought about Bill's death, *why does it bother me so much? I've killed men and witnessed men dying. I didn't even know this Bill chap. But now, because of this bloody war, his sisters— what were their names again—* and for some reason, it seemed important that he remember them, *Nana's written about them often enough, Maggie, Jeannie and little Sara, she always put "little" in front of Sara.* The thought of them losing their big brother, losing the future with him, losing the family Bill might have had, all gone. Lost forever. *War – waste – death – destruction – war – waste – death – destruction!*

He discovered he had circled half way around the small town and was by the makeshift enlisted men's club. He went inside, he needed a drink. It took a moment for his eyes to adjust to the darkness. He ordered a shot and beer. Paid, drank the shot and started on the beer, waiting for the numbing effect of the alcohol. *I'll need to drink more, much more,* Davy thought.

At a nearby table a group of men were drinking together and talking loudly. Davy couldn't help but eavesdrop as he drank his beer.

"I can't wait to get to the front," one young soldier was saying, "kill myself a couple Germans."

"A couple?" another man boasted, "I think I can take out more than a couple." The men continued, each upping the ante on the number of Germans they would kill.

Davy looked closer. They were new recruits, fresh off the boat from home. New uniforms, new weapons, all fresh and clean. *Had he been that young? That foolish? How long had it been?* His mind raced. *A year? No, less than that.* He felt so old. *Too old, men don't get old here; they die here.*

Davy couldn't listen any longer. He poured the remainder of his beer down his throat and left. The sunshine hurt his eyes and his head was starting to ache. He started walking again. And before long, he realized, he had come to the street some of the chaps had been talking about. The street with the brothels. He hadn't visited one before, hadn't paid for a prostitute, ever. At first, he didn't think it would be fair to Alice. He grimaced at the thought of Alice, at being fair to Alice. Even after he got the letter calling off their engagement, well, the thought of paying for sex still disgusted him.

But maybe today, he thought. *What did it matter anyway? What was he waiting for? The right girl? Someone special? Bloody hell, I'll probably be dead within a fortnight. Why the bloody hell not?* He needed something, something different, to take his mind off this damn war.

Women, some old, some young were sitting and standing at the entrances of the brothels. *It's still early afternoon, must not be their busy time,* Davy thought. The women smiled at him, and whispered together. Some pointed, some called to him. He wondered how he looked, he'd forgotten the effect he sometimes had. Back in Scotland, in school, girls had giggled when he walked by. In church, the older ladies whispered usually something about him being a catch for their daughters. He rubbed the bristle on his chin. He'd shaved when they first arrived from the front, but not since. He got to the end of the street. *Now what,* he thought, *bloody hell, where's Mac when I need him?* But, he hadn't been standing there long when he felt a soft tap on his shoulder. He turned around, a pretty, young women was standing there. She was short, about five feet to his six. She had long, brown hair, pulled back into a thick braid. Her very red lips formed a pretty bow and her high cheekbones were awash in red. She looked back over her shoulder, embarrassed, toward a group of women standing on the opposite corner. They seemed, to Davy, to be encouraging her.

"Mister, I am, ah," she considered the next word, "purifier," she stammered.

"Purifier?" Davy said, thinking she didn't know much English.

She bit her lower lip, looked up at him through her thick black eyelashes and whispered, "Clean?"

"Oh, fine," Davy said, now he was embarrassed. *Is it so obvious that I haven't been to a brothel before? Does my disgust with them, with myself show on my face,* he thought. He took her arm, and led her down the street away from the watchful eyes of the women on the corner. He had passed a dingy hotel about 50 yards back. Neither of them spoke as he led the way.

The lobby was dark and, once again, it took a minute for his eyes to adjust. Two old men were sitting at a small table inside the door drinking coffee. They chuckled, and said something in French Davy didn't understand, but the young women understood because he could feel a shudder go through her small arm. *What am I doing,* Davy thought, *I don't even know her.* But he couldn't back down now. He paid the receptionist and they were directed to a room on the third floor.

The room was small, not exactly clean, but not filthy either. It contained a small bed, a chair and a small chest of drawers. All the furniture had been painted white at one time, but now, the paint was worn and peeling. A faded quilt covered the bed. The women paused next to it, her hand on the quilt, her fingers pulling nervously at a loose thread. Davy stood with his back to her, looking out the small window. He noticed a faded garden behind the hotel. Still with his back to her, he took off his jacket, tossed it on the chair, then untucked and unbuttoned his shirt. He turned to face her. He reached out, took her arm and gently pulled her toward him. He lifted her chin and kissed her. She parted her red lips and returned his kiss, but not eagerly, as Alice had done.

Davy put one hand on the small of her back and kissed her again, he could feel her trembling. He released his hold on her and looked into her velvety, brown eyes. A tear slipped down her cheek taking some of the red powder with it. The neat bow on her lips was smeared and unnatural. *She's just a child, no older than fifteen*, he thought. He took a step back.

"Please mister, um, you're au debut, first, but I can do it, really." she said and she tried to smile at him. With trembling fingers, she started to undo the buttons on her blouse. Then her stomach rumbled loudly, Davy stared at her. "I am sorry mister, I can do it," she said again.

"No, no, that's fine, you don't have to," Davy almost shouted. And he began to laugh, the situation was so ridiculous, so sad, and so pitiful, that all he could do was laugh. She looked at him, her eyes swimming with tears. He stopped laughing suddenly, *poor thing, she's hungry,* he thought. *She's here, doing this, because she's hungry.* Davy reached out and lifted her chin once again. Fear filled her eyes, and Davy knew what to do. He took his handkerchief from his pocket and wiped the rouge and lipstick from the girls face.

"My name is Davy," he said, and he stepped back and held out his hand for her to shake. "Davy," he repeated, pointing to himself with this other hand. She took his outstretched hand slowly, hesitantly.

"Adele," she said, pointing to herself.

"English?" Davy asked.

"Un petit peu" Adele said. Davy knew that petite meant little, *good, she knows a little English*, he thought.

Then she surprised him, she asked, "Français?"

"Very petite," he said with a chuckle. He asked, "Do you want to eat?" and he made, what seemed to him to be the universal motion for eating, scooping imaginary food into his mouth with an imaginary spoon.

Adele smiled and nodded. The fear and dread melted from her eyes. He re-buttoned his shirt, picked up his jacket and led her from the room. Back in the lobby, the old men sniggered as Davy and Adele past. Davy glared at them, and they fell quiet.

Davy had seen a café just outside the brothel district. He pointed it out to Adele, she nodded happily. They found an out-of-the-way table, and sat down. They hadn't spoken since leaving the hotel, now Davy interrupted the awkward silence.

"So, um, come here often," he joked and chuckled. Adele looked at him confused. Davy smiled and asked, "Is this town your home?" Adele thought for a moment, Davy could see her translating his question, then she smiled with understanding.

"Home, domicile, no," she said shaking her head, and her expression changed to sudden sadness, she continued, "My home is gone, parti."

"Oh, sorry," Davy said, then he asked, "Your family, mum, da?"

"Mon père est parti," Adele whispered. But Davy didn't understand.

"My père, my da, is gone," Adele said. A waiter came. Davy indicated that Adele should do the ordering. She and the waiter talked easily together, then the waiter left. Davy wished he'd taken French in school, but it didn't seem like a terribly important skill for a miner.

Adele asked, "Your mum, da? In England?" And Davy tried to explain that he was from Scotland.

"Yes, Scotland," Adele said, she seemed to understand more English then he originally thought. Encouraged, Davy continued, he told her about his mum and sisters. Adele nodded and said, "Yes, a sister, J'ai sœurs. I have a sister."

"Your sister, is she . . ." and he stopped not sure how to ask or if he wanted to know. He looking down the street toward the brothels.

"No," Adele answered his unasked question, shaking her head vehemently, "I am l'aînée, oldest. Mère does laundry for the soldiers, but it is not enough."

Davy continued talking, sometimes waiting for her to reply, asking her questions, but mostly, he just talked. He realized her petite, little English, was quite a bit more than his little French. English or French, she was a good listener. He told her about Scotland, about how the heather looked in the morning mist. And how the wind and rain swept over the highlands. He explained how his father had died in the mine, and how he hated mining. And Adele listened. The food came. It was simple food, cheese and bread, some dried fish and strong, hot coffee.

Adele ate much of the food, but wrapped some in a napkin when she was sure the waiter wasn't looking. Davy took the bundle of food and hid it safely under his jacket. They sat together for a long time. Davy told her about life in the trenches and Adele told him about the home she had lost. She told him about the small village, with a stone church, school and a few small shops. She had lived on a farm with her mum, da and little sister. It was gone, buried along with her da, under the muck, barbed wire and dead soldiers in no man's land. Davy imaged the highlands of his home being churned into a no man's land and was sad for this pretty little French girl. She had lost so much, and still, she carried on. The sun was low in the sky when Davy picked up his jacket and Adele's bundle of food. He paid the bill and they left the café.

Davy and Adele walked together until they came a dingy street of long, low buildings. Adele turned, took the bundle from him and said, "Thank you. You have been very," she thought for a moment trying to find the right word, then said, "kind." The she turned and started to walk down the street.

"No, wait," Davy called after her. He reached into his jacket pocket. He still had most of lasts months' pay; he had decided back at the café that he would give it to her.

All of it. He didn't need it, the army provided what he needed, food and someplace to sleep.

He took her hand and pushed the wad of bills into it. "Here," he said, "maybe you can figure out something, maybe you won't have to go back, you know."

"No," Adele said, "I can't take this, I didn't . . ." but her voice trailed off and she closed her hand tightly around the money. Then she reached up, put her hand on the back of his neck and pulled him toward her so she could whisper in his ear, "Thank you." And she kissed him, softly, sweetly, then pulled away.

He smiled at her, and he had a thought. Something else he could give her. "Wait," he said. He dug through the many pockets of his jacket and found the newspaper. He'd brought it along, planning on giving it to Mac for something to read in the hospital. It was the one with the last installment of the Fred Norman story, but it also had a page of women's hat fashions. Davy opened it up and showed her the pictures. Her eyes lit up with delight. "I don't know if you can read it, but here, take it," Davy said as he handed her the newspaper. She took it, looked at the cover, smiled at him, then turned and walked quickly down the street. He wanted to call after her, tell her not to go back to the brothels, to be careful, but he didn't. He just watched as she walked away. *I have no right, I can't take care of her, protect her, I belong to the British army,*

Page 1

— The Sunday Gazette —
— Better-than-ever —

APR 30 1916

IN this Issue —

1. The Three City Boys At the lake *complete story*
2. See page 2 — girls, girls girls.
3. Page 3 — AROUND The World —
4. A Pictor — By H. Norman —
5. Rhmmes page 8
6. Instalment FRED Norman of Forestvill
— Six Big Features —
7-8 RHYmes — Pictor —

— SPECIAL —
— Notice —

See Page 10-11-12

FRED Norman
of By
Forestvill

April 30, 1916
www.catherinepaonessa.com/thegazette

Selected
~ Davy McLeod

When Davy got back to the barracks, Jamie was waiting for him.

"Where have you been? Lieutenant Payne was here looking for you," Jamie said. "He said you should report to HQ as soon as you return."

Davy found Lieutenant Payne in a makeshift office in an old hotel that had been converted to the army headquarters. He saluted and said crisply, "Private McLeod, reporting for duty."

"At ease Private," Lieutenant Payne said. Then, to Davy's surprise, he added, "Actually, that will be Corporal McLeod from now on. Congratulations." And he stood and shook Davy's hand.

"Corporal? Sir?" Davy asked.

"You've been promoted. Actually, you've been selected to attend the sniper school in Steenbecque near Linghem, but to attend you have to be a Corporal. We had to get you the promotion first. Sergeant Macgregor recommended you." Davy was speechless. He'd completely forgotten about Sergeant McGregor's promise to recommend him for the sniper school.

Lieutenant Payne continued, "They train snipers in pairs, one man shoots, the other observes. Both the sniper and observer will learn to use high-powered rifles with telescopic sights, telescopes and periscopes that are far more advanced than the standard issue ones. You'll also be trained in map reading and observation skills. You'll be expected to record detailed notes on what you observe in the field. Sergeant McGregor has assured us that you won't disappoint us."

"No sir, of course not sir," Davy said, recovering his voice.

"Your observer should be someone you trust, someone intelligent and organized enough to keep accurate observation notes, we thought you might have a suggestion? Otherwise, an observer will be assigned to you."

Davy's mind raced, Gavin was already at officer training, and Mac was in the hospital. That left Jamie, but Jamie was perfect. *Actually, Jamie was even better than either Gavin or Mac*, Davy thought, feeling somewhat disloyal, but with Jamie's memory and education as a clerk, he'll be a perfect observer.

"Yes sir, I'd like to recommend Private Patterson. But he's a private?" Davy asked.

"No problem, observers can attend as long as a promotion has been requested." Lieutenant Payne explained. He quickly wrote out new orders for both Davy and Jamie. You'll have to leave on the morning train. The next session of training starts the day after tomorrow. The clerk in the next office will give you all the specifics. And good luck."

CHAPTER 11

Headlong into War
~ Bob Stevens

It was late September, and Detroiters were enjoying an Indian summer. The days were warm and sunny and the nights were cool. "Good sleeping weather" they called it. But the cool nights meant that Professor Ackermann had his windows closed. Bob started watching the Professor's house in the mornings. He kept a log of what he saw.

Monday, September 25, 7:00 a.m. – P. A. leaves house with a small leather case, wearing suit.

Tuesday, September 26, – No activity

Wednesday, September 27 7:15 a.m. – P. A. leaves house, suit, no case

Thursday, September 28 7:00 a.m. – P. A. leaves house, leather case, wearing suit

Friday, September 29 7:00 a.m. – P.A. leaves house, leather case, wearing suit

On Friday, Bob discussed what he had observed with Henry.

"He goes someplace almost every day, but where?" Bob explained. He opened his canvas lunch sack and took out an egg salad sandwich.

"Well, we know he's not going to the college to teach, that's for sure," Henry said, looking at Bob's sandwich, he added, "What do you have?"

"Egg salad, how about you?" Bob said

"Jam and butter," Henry said, licking jam from his finger.

"Want to trade half?" Bob asked.

"Ah, Sure," Henry agreed, somewhat reluctantly. They traded half of each sandwich. Henry continued, "And he takes a leather case? What do you think's in it?" Henry asked as he lifted the bread from the egg salad sandwich and looked inside.

"I don't know? Books, papers maybe, but it seems kind of heavy," Bob answered.

"Maybe it's bribe money? Or even a gun?" Henry speculated, eyes wide. "This is pretty good," he added with his mouth full.

"Money maybe, but I don't think he would have a gun. What would he need with a gun if the plan is to blow something up or, well, you know sabotage?" Bob said, then he added thoughtfully, "Unless, the plan was is to assassinate someone? But who would be worth assassinating here in Detroit? All the important diplomats are in Washington," Bob popped the last bite of jam sandwich in his mouth and took an apple from his lunch sack.

"I guess we'll have to follow Professor Ackermann one day," Henry said.

"I was thinking that too, but when? We have school,"
Bob replied.

"We could skip," Henry said softly.

"If he really is a spy, nobody would care if we skipped
school to investigate, would they?" Bob ventured. "When?"

"How about Monday?" Henry said. "We'll tell our
teachers on Tuesday that we were sick."

"I don't know," Bob said. He was beginning to think
that skipping school was not such a good idea, but the headline TWO DETROIT HIGH SCHOOL CHAPS UNCOVER
GERMAN SPY RING with a picture of him and Henry smiling on the cover of the Detroit Free Press flashed through
his mind. "Well, okay," Bob agreed, "Come by my house,
early, Professor Ackermann usually leaves the house by 7:00."

The bell rang and they grabbed their lunch sacks and
headed off to class. Bob walked home from school alone.
Maggie was still in Toronto. He missed Maggie's bright
chatter on their walks to and from school and wondered
when she would get back, they had been gone a week.

It was a busy weekend. He had lots of homework.
Chemistry was a struggle without Maggie's help. They usually talked through the chemistry assignment as they walked
home from school. One afternoon they even stopped at
the pharmacy and sat at the soda counter to compare notes.
They each had a Coke-a-Cola in a funny shaped green bottle. Bob had hoped to stop again; he enjoyed both the bottle of the sweet, fuzzy liquid and sitting next to Maggie at
the soda counter. The telegram had come a few days later.

Along with doing his own homework, Bob copied
out notes from the classes he and Maggie shared. On his

suggestion, Edith and Henry were doing the same for the classes they had with Maggie. *Bother,* Bob thought, *he and Henry would miss the notes for Monday. Well, that couldn't be helped.* When he wasn't doing homework that weekend, he cut the grass at Professor Ackermann's and the Robinsons, watered the gardens, walked Nietzsche, and worked on his newspaper.

On Monday, he prepared for school as usual. Mother packed his lunch while he ate his breakfast.

"You're quiet this morning. Do you feel okay?" Her voice started him.

"I'm fine," Bob said.

"Do you have an editor meeting after school today? Do you want me to put a snack in your lunch?" Mother asked.

"Um, no, I'll be fine," Bob said, distracted.

"And you're sure you feel okay?" Mother said, putting her cool hand on his forehead.

"Really, I'm fine," Bob said, pulling away. "I have to get going, ah, actually, I have an editor meeting this morning. See you later," he added as he grabbed his lunch sack and book bag and hurried out the door.

He took a deep breath as he slipped into the alley. *I'm glad that's over,* he thought, lying to mother was harder than he expected.

Henry met him in the alley. The day was cool and gloomy. They kept their lunch bags and a notepad and pencil, but stashed their book bags under the wheelbarrow at the back of the yard. Then, they hid in the shrubs next to the Professor Ackermann's house. Within five minutes, Professor Ackermann's back door opened and Nietzsche appeared. She bounded over to the fence and barked a friendly hello. Bob and Henry both shushed her. Professor Ackermann called from the house, "Nietzsche, what's the matter with you? Quiet, you'll wake the neighborhood." But he didn't come outside. Nietzsche gave the boys a sad, sideways look, caught sight of a squirrel and gave chase.

"That was close," Henry whispered.

"Yeah, I hope she didn't wake my dad," Bob replied. They waited about 10 minutes, and the door opened again. Professor Ackermann emerged, case in hand. He left through the gate and headed north on Crane Avenue toward Mack Avenue. Bob and Henry waited until he was a block or so up the street, then clamored out of the shrubbery and followed him.

Professor Ackermann walked to Mack and turned west toward downtown. The boys followed on the far side of the street. After walking a couple blocks, Professor Ackermann entered a small café. Bob and Henry stopped and waited across the street behind a delivery truck parked in front of the grocery store.

"What should we do?" Henry asked.

"I guess we have to wait until he comes out," Bob said. "But let's move around the corner. We can still see the café from there, but no one will notice us." They moved quickly to the concealing corner. "We don't want to get caught by an attendance officer. Our names will be on today's truancy report you know."

"Yeah, I was thinking if I write a note saying you were sick, and you write one for me, they won't notice anything suspicious about the hand writing," Henry said.

"Good idea," Bob agreed. He looked over at the café and added, "What do you think he's doing in there?"

"Eating breakfast I suppose," Henry speculated. "They have great pancakes, haven't you ever been there?"

Bob rubbed his hands together, and said, "No, but I wish I was inside eating some now. I'm cold." He looked up at the cloudy sky, a soft drizzle was falling, he continued, "I hope we discover something worthwhile, or at least something that proves Professor Ackermann is okay even though he's German.

"Yeah, especially after what the dirty Hun did to Bill," Henry agreed.

"I hate the Kiser. This whole war is his fault you know. I read that Kiser Wilhelm is considered a war criminal by the English and that they will hang him after the war," Bob added.

"Serves him right. If it's still going on, and if Wilson gets us in, will you join up?" Henry asked.

Bob thought for a moment before answering, "Yeah, I suppose so," he said still thinking. He took off his glasses, wiped the mist that had gathered on them on his sleeve, put them on again. He ran his fingers through his now damp red hair and continued, "For sure I'd go, for Bill and all. It would feel good to make those rotten Germans pay."

"Me too," Henry said.

Bob and Henry talked about the war and kept an eye on the café door. It was about forty-five minutes before Professor Ackermann left the café and continued west on Mack Avenue. Bob and Henry followed. Professor Ackermann boarded a westbound trolley, got off at Woodward Avenue and boarded a northbound Woodward trolley. Bob and Henry jumped onto each trolley, being careful to stay at the back of the car and out of site. They were surprised when Professor Ackermann got off the trolley at the Highland Park Ford Plant, and even more surprised when he approached the main gate, spoke with the gate attendant, and was ushered into the plant.

"What do you think he's doing here?" Henry asked.

"Gee, I don't know. I thought he was writing a book. Doing research and all that," Bob said. "What kind of research would he do here?"

"You know, I told you about the contract my pop has with the Fords to make canvas parts for military trucks," Henry said. "You don't suppose Professor Ackermann is going to blow up the Ford plant?"

"Well, not today at least, I don't think his case is big enough for a bomb," Bob said. He considered, and continued, "But maybe he's getting information about the plant, so he can, I don't know, do something—like sabotage, or something."

"Well, let's wait here and see where he goes next," Henry said. "I'm kind of hungry, let's eat our lunches while we wait."

"Great idea," Bob agreed. They found a spot at the side of a storage building where they could watch the gate, but not be noticed. After finishing their lunches, Bob got the notebook out of his pocket and they wrote the school notes. Each note was the same, but in the others handwriting. They read:

Please excuse my son Bob Stevens for missing school yesterday. He was home sick with a sore throat. Thank you, Mr. Stevens

Please excuse my son Henry Harding for missing school yesterday. He was home sick with a sore throat. Thank you, Mr. Harding

They looked at the two notes, and decided they shouldn't each have a sore throat. Bob rewrote Henry's note substituting toothache for sore throat. Satisfied, they stuffed the notes in their pockets.

Professor Ackermann was in the Ford plant for two hours. Bob and Henry watched the gate and wished it were warmer. At about 12:30 Professor Ackermann emerged from the plant with some other men. The men were all wearing suits, so Bob figured they must be office workers, not assembly line workers. Bob and Henry followed the group as they walked along the front of the Ford plant.

Without warning, Professor Ackermann stopped, put down his case and bent down to tie his shoe. While doing so, he looked over his shoulder, and directly at Bob and Henry. A look of recognition, surprise and puzzlement crossed the professor's face, he began to raise his hand in a wave. Bob shoved Henry and they stumbled into the open door of the shop they were passing. Bob watched through the shop window as Professor Ackermann used his raised hand to scratch his head. The professor turned, picked up his case and followed the rest of the men into a busy deli.

"That was close," Bob said. He looked around the shop. It was a shoe repair shop. A short, bald little man was standing behind the counter.

"May I help you?" he said, as he peered at the boys over his glasses.

"Um, no, sorry," Bob stammered as they left the shop. They waited across the street from the deli behind a car.

"Now what?" Henry said.

"I guess we wait again," Bob replied.

Bob and Henry followed Professor Ackermann for the remainder of the afternoon. They didn't think the professor saw them again, and hoped he didn't recognize them when he stopped to tie his shoe. Professor Ackermann visited two factories along Atwater Street in the afternoon. One was the Armored Motor Car Company where they made the King Armored car, and the other was a casing manufacturer. At each factory the professor was allowed in without question. At the casing manufacturer, Bob and Henry decided to head home. They wanted to be home at their usual, after school, time.

"What do you think he's up to?" Bob asked.

"Could be anything, but he's not teaching, that's for sure?" replied Henry with suspicion.

"We still don't have enough information to prove he's a spy, but it just doesn't seem right," Bob said with a sigh. "I wonder if we can trust any Germans with the war and all."

"Yeah," Henry agreed, then added slowly, "But, I think, my grandmother on my mom's side was part German, so, um, they can't all be bad."

"I guess not, especially not your grandmother, or people who have been here for a while."

"I just hope Professor Ackermann didn't see us over by the Ford plant," Henry said concerned.

"Me too," Bob said. They slipped into Bob's backyard through the alley, retrieved their book bags and Henry set out for home.

Bob checked his pocket for his note, and called after him, "Good luck with the note tomorrow, see you at school.

"You too," Henry called over his shoulder as he turned the corner. Bob headed inside.

The kitchen was warm and smelled like freshly baked bread and cookies. As the warmth of the kitchen hit him, he realized how tired he was. *Spying is exhausting,* he thought.

"Hello Robin, ah, Bob," Mother said, "How was school?"

"Oh, fine," Bob lied, his heart was racing and his stomach ached a bit. *Maybe I'm hungry,* he thought. He reached for a warm sugar cookie from the plate on the table, but looked pleadingly at Mother before taking one.

"Go ahead" She smiled as she removed another pan from the oven. "How is Maggie?"

"Maggie's home?" Bob asked.

"Oh yes, they got in on the morning train. Mrs. Robinson wanted Maggie to stay home from school, but Maggie was anxious to get back, she went to her afternoon classes. You didn't see her? Don't you have some classes together?" Mother said.

"Oh yeah," Bob said, distracted, "Um, but we didn't get a chance to talk much. I have all the notes from last week upstairs, I'll take them over to her now. Maybe I'll take Nietzsche. Sara will be excited to see her."

"That would be nice," Mother said, "And you can take some of these cookies too."

Bob grabbed two more cookies, and headed to his room. His tiredness had faded. He gathered the notes he had been compiling for Maggie and looked out the window into Professor Ackermann's yard. Nietzsche was out, waiting for her after school walk. The professor didn't seem to be home. The drizzle had stopped, the clouds were braking up, and the sun was even shining. Bob headed back down to the kitchen.

"Bye, Mom," he said, as he hurried through the kitchen toward the door.

"Bob," Mother said.

Darn, Bob thought, He didn't want to answer any more questions about school.

"The cookies," Mother said, holding out a box tied with a string. She added, "Now, don't you eat any more, these are for the Robinson girls. You've had enough."

"Yes, ma'am," Bob said, smiling sheepishly. He took the box and headed out. He retrieved Nietzsche and walked down the street to the Robinson's. Sara was on the porch. She bounded down the steps and held out her arms. Bob wasn't sure if her excited greeting was for him or Nietzsche, but he guessed, correctly, that it was for Nietzsche. The big dog pulled away from him and ran into Sara's outstretched arms, almost knocking her to the ground. Bob was happy to see a smile appear on Sara's face.

"Hello, there," Bob said, "Nietzsche missed you."

"Oh, I missed her too," Sara said. Bob frowned, and Sara added, "I missed you too."

The front door opened and Jeannie came outside. She gave Bob a quick, shy wave and a smile. "Hi Jeannie, here, my mom sent you all some cookies," Bob said as he handed her the box.

"Oh, that's nice, tell her thank you for us," Jeannie said as she opened the box and peaked inside.

"Do you two mind watching Nietzsche for a bit? I have some notes to give Maggie. Then we'll take Nietzsche for a walk?" Bob said.

"Sure," Sara said, excited. She was busy rubbing Nietzsche's ears enthusiastically, and Nietzsche was enjoying the special attention.

"Maggie's in the backyard getting the wash off the line," Jeannie mumbled, mouth full of cookie. Bob smiled at her and walked around the side of the house to the backyard. Maggie was taking each article of clothing off the line, folding it quickly and dropping it in the nearby basket. Another basket of wet clothes was ready to be hung.

"Hello," Bob said. Maggie turned and looked at Bob.

"Oh, hi, I thought you were sick," Maggie said, "I looked for you in Chemistry."

"Um, yeah, um, I had a headache this morning, but I feel fine now," Bob said. He found it just as hard to lie to Maggie as it was to his mother.

"Well, don't come to close, I can't get sick, I'm too far behind in school as it is," Maggie said. She started hanging the wet clothes on the line.

"Actually, I, well, Henry and I, we skipped school to follow Professor Ackermann," Bob blurted out in a low voice, he plowed on, talking fast, trying to get it in before Maggie replied. "We think he might be a spy." As he said it out loud, he realized how absurd it sounded, but he continued, "you remember, he was talking German on his phone, so we went over to the college, he doesn't even teach there, so we decided to follow him, he went to factories that are currently making stuff for the war, the Ford plant, and ...” Maggie turned to face him, a wet dress in her hands.

“Stop!” she spat. “I don't want to hear it. I can't stand it. WAR! WAR! WAR!” Maggie's face was red with fury. “It's like a fever. All this talk about war, doesn't anyone really understand? Every family in Toronto, every last one, has a son, a brother, a father fighting and dying in the French mud and muck.” She paused, and continued almost in a whisper, “And I don't care. I don't want to know. I don't want to talk about it.” Maggie stopped, anger and sadness flashing in her eyes, she turned, hang up the dress, reached in the basket, pulled out a small, pale blue dress with dainty flowers on it, gave it a hard shake, so that it snapped in the cool air, then she clipped it to the clothes line.

“Um, I'm sorry. I didn't mean to...” Bob stammered. He put the notes on the picnic table, took off his glasses and wiped them on his shirtsleeve, and put them on again. He couldn't look at Maggie. “I copied out the notes for the days you missed,” Bob said, deciding to change of subject.

“Well, except for this morning,” Maggie snapped, still facing the clothes line.

Ouch, that stung, but I should have been there for her, she looked for me, Bob thought sadly. At that moment, he hated himself. He changed the subject again.

“Sara, Jeannie and I are going to take Nietzsche for a walk. Want to come?” Bob asked.

“No, I can't,” Maggie said her voice almost normal, she continued, “I have to finish this and I have a lot of homework.”

“Oh, yeah, okay, maybe tomorrow then?” Bob said.

"Yeah, thanks for taking Sara and Jeannie though," Maggie said, "And, ah, thanks for the notes."

"See you in the morning, then?" Bob questioned, hopefully.

"Actually, no, I'm going early to meet Edith in the library. She's offered to help me get caught up," Maggie said, she continued hanging the clothes.

"Oh, yeah, that's nice of her. Well, maybe see you at school tomorrow then," Bob said. "Bye," and he left.

Regrets
~ Bob Stevens

Bob was trapped in the school. He ran from door to door. Each one he tried was locked. His heart was racing. He had to get out. Down at the end of the hall someone was yelling something, what was it? "Go home you dirty Hun!" SMASH, the window in front of him came crashing in. Glass covered the floor at his bare feet. He escaped through the broken window. Now, he was running down the street, away from the school. Nietzsche was with him, barking, barking, barking.

Bob woke up with a start. His heart was pounding, he was breathing hard. *Wait, this is my bed, my room,* he thought, *wow, what a nightmare.* But he still heard barking. He sat up and peered out the side window. His room was in the corner of the house. From the window over his desk he could see the backyard, from the window over the bed, the one he looked out now, he could see Professor Ackermann's front yard and down the street to the north. In the dim light of the quarter moon, Bob could see Professor Ackermann standing in his front yard, his fists clinched. "Get 'em girl," the Professor yelled. Nietzsche was running down the street barking ferociously. *What the hell?* Bob thought. He continued watching out the window. Professor Ackermann went back into his house, a light came on, but the shades were drawn, so Bob couldn't see what he was doing. All was quiet on the street. Bob rested his chin on the window-sill and watched. In a short while Nietzsche returned, she stood at the door and gave a soft whine. The door opened and she disappeared inside. Bob watched a while longer, but his eyes wouldn't stay open. Soon he laid down and fell sound asleep.

Bob headed to school the next morning hoping Maggie had changed her mind and would be waiting for him. She wasn't. The day was long. Between running around town the day before, and the activity in the Professor Ackermann's front yard last night, he was tired. He ran into Henry at the attendance office, but they didn't talk to each other. The attendance officer took his note without question. Bob was relieved. He was behind in every class, and really lost in chemistry. He walked home alone loaded down with homework. It had been a crappy day. Mother was busy in the kitchen.

"Hello," Mother said softly

"Hello, Mother. How was your day?" Bob asked her.

"Oh, it was fine. Your father asked me to tell you he would like to talk to you after work tonight," Mother said, questioningly.

"Tonight? After work? That will be pretty late, won't it?" Bob asked.

"I suppose so, he's usually home between 11:30 and 12 o'clock. He wouldn't tell me what it's about, but he seemed very serious. Have you done something to upset your father?" Mother asked.

"Um, no, I don't think so," Bob lied. He thought, *maybe it wasn't about school at all, maybe it was something completely different.* He continued, "Um, I have to walk Nietzsche and I have a ton of homework, so I'd better get at it." He escaped to his room. He decided to walk Nietzsche before starting on his homework. When he retrieved her from the yard, he noticed that the front window of the Professor's house was boarded up. *Wow, that must have been the crash I heard in my dream,* Bob thought.

Later that night, after Mother had gone to bed, Bob sat at the kitchen table waiting for his dad. His chemistry book lay open in front of him, but he couldn't concentrate, which didn't really matter, chemistry didn't make much sense when he could concentrate. *Could dad have found out about my skipping school,* he wondered? *What else could it be?* He thought about when he was a kid. He'd been in trouble before, Dad had even taken a paddle to him, but not often. Luckily, violence wasn't in dad's nature, and the disappointment Bob saw in his Dad's face when he misbehaved was punishment enough. So, he was usually pretty good, plus, school was okay and he didn't have many chores to do, or siblings to fight with, so, being good wasn't exactly hard.

The door opened and Dad came in. He sighed, as if he wasn't exactly happy to see Bob. He said, "I see you got my message. Let's go outside, I don't want to wake your mother. It's raining so let's go in the shed." Together, they dashed through the yard and into the tool shed. The shed was musty and dark. The rain beat loudly on the tin roof. Dad lit a lantern then looked Bob square in the eyes, and asked, "Did you skip school yesterday?"

Bob couldn't lie, not straight to his dad's face, "Yes sir." He said. "But, …" Dad held up he's hand to silence him.

"And you lied to your mother, pretending to go off to school when you planned to do something else entirely?" Dad asked.

"Yes, sir," Bob answered, hanging his head.

"Look at me," Dad said, "And you think you have a good reason for behaving in such a deceitful way?"

Yes, sir, I do," Bob said. Dad waited, so he continued, "Henry and I skipped school to follow Professor Ackermann. We think he's a German spy." Dad's face changed from anger to complete disbelief, Bob continued, more quickly, "First, I heard him speaking German on his telephone, then, we went to his school and he doesn't even teach there, and yesterday he went to …"

"Enough," Dad said. "Professor Ackermann is not a spy. Actually, he's a good neighbor and a friend." Dad shook his head and sighed, "You're right though, Professor Ackermann is German and, because he's German, he misses hearing and speaking German, so he calls his German friends, to talk to them, in German. Is that a crime?" Bob opened his mouth to speak, but closed it again. Dad continued, louder now. "And do you know why Professor

Ackermann doesn't teach anymore, because he had to quit, because ignorant students stopped wanting to learn German and stopped wanting to take literature classes from a Germen teacher, even though the Professor's a leading expert in the field." Dad was shouting now. "And, the manufacturing sites he's been visiting, yes he told me about them, they are for research, for a book about the United States and German industrial revolutions." Dad stopped and took a deep breath, then asked, "Were you home last night?"

"Yes, sir," Bob answered, surprised at the question.

"All night? You never left the house?" Dad asked.

"No, sir, I was in bed," Bob said.

"Because someone threw a brick through Professor Ackermann's window and shouted some nasty anti-German rhetoric. And you didn't have anything to do with that?" Dad asked, seriously.

"No, of course not. I would never. . ." Bob answered, shocked.

"Well, who else did you tell about your spy suspicions?" Dad asked.

"Just Henry, and oh Maggie, but they wouldn't break Professor Ackermann's window," Bob said.

"No, probably not. But who might have overheard you and Henry talking, did you discuss it at school? Can't you see how such talk is harmful? We can't judge people by the language they speak, or their nationality, or the God they believe in or don't believe in, for that matter. Everyone deserves a chance to prove their worth by their actions, don't you agree?"

"Yes sir." Bob said, ashamed.

"Karl, Professor Ackermann, saw you yesterday by the Ford plant. He asked if you were there about a job. He knows one of the foreman quite well. He offered to put in a good word for you," Dad said shaking his head sadly. "He said you didn't see him when he waved."

"Oh," Bob said miserably.

"Now, I've decided that a job is a very good idea. The foreman over at Burroughs is out this week, but when he returns, I'm going to ask if he has an apprentice machinist position for you, after school of course," Dad said.

"But . . ." Bob tried to interrupt.

"Hear me out," Dad said, "This country is rushing head-long into war, and it's time you pitched in. Machinists are always needed, and if, when you graduate, you decide to do something different, well, you'll have something to fall back on. You seem to have time on your hands anyway."

"But I'm an assistant editor on the school paper, and what about Professor Ackermann's lawn, and my newspaper," Bob shouted. He couldn't believe what he was hearing. A job, as a machinist. Once he started, he would never escape.

"The lawn won't need cutting much longer, and you'll have to give up those other after school activities," Dad said dismissively, he added, "Oh, and tomorrow, after school, offer to help Professor Ackermann repair his window."

"But I can't be a machinist, I don't want . . ." Bob was shouting, but a wave of his dad's hand quieted him.

"I'm cold and tired. Good night," Dad said, and he left.

Bob was cold too. Numb actually. He sat in the shed for quite a while. Eventually the rain stopped pounding on the roof and through the little window he could see heavy clouds racing past the bright moon. *A job as a machinist,* he thought. For skipping one day of school. It just wasn't fair. Other fellas did much worse. Eventually his fingers were so cold he couldn't stand it and he headed inside. For a fearful moment, as he walked toward the house, he thought his dad might have locked him out, but the kitchen door was unlocked. He crept in, climbed quietly up the stairs and went to bed.

The rest of the week was long and miserable. Maggie was avoiding him, but he didn't know why. It was like when he avoided her after the snowball. *Was that just last winter?* He thought. *How could I have been such a stupid kid, worried about being hit with a snowball?*

It was Friday before he had a chance to talk to Henry. And it was no comfort to discover that Professor Ackermann was also friends with Mr. Harding and that Henry got into trouble too. His punishment was swifter but more painful, at least in the short term.

"Yeah, my pop was pretty mad. I have the bruises on my backside to prove it," Henry said.

"I'm sorry I started this whole mess," Bob said.

"I suggested we skip school," Henry reminded him. "Sorry your dad's going to make you get a job and quit the editor thing. My pop can't do that," Henry said with a chuckle, "I already have a job working my butt off for him. At least I can still play football. Actually, Pop has been really excited about me making the team."

"I think it's pretty unreasonable. But maybe the foreman will decide they don't want some kid after school," Bob said hopefully.

"Hey, I have a great idea," Henry said brightening. "We're super busy at the shop. Ford doubled their order, and Pop's looking at expanding into canvas tents, cartridge belts, helmet chin straps, stuff like that. Maybe my pop could give you a job? And he works around my football schedule, I'm sure he'd work around the editor schedule. He's always saying he could use five more of me."

"I don't know if my dad will go for it," Bob said, discouraged. "He was pretty mad. Plus, he said learning to be a machinist would give me something to fall back on."

"I'll talk to my pop, and if he thinks it's a good idea, and I'm sure he will, he can talk to your pop and work things out," Henry said happily, as if everything was settled. Bob wasn't so sure.

The Human Spider
~ Bob Stevens

Bob got up extra early on Saturday morning. He thought if he worked really hard in the yard, raking, cleaning out the shed, he even washed the windows for Mother, maybe Dad would change his mind about the job.

By late afternoon his stomach was growling, and he'd run out of stuff to do. He went into the kitchen, partially to see if Dad had noticed all the hard work he'd done, and partially to see if he could get a snack from Mother. She knew about him skipping school, but hadn't mentioned it.

"Hi," Bob said. He took off his glasses, wiped them on this sleeve and put them on again.

"Well, hello," she said, frowning at his haphazard way of cleaning his glasses. "You've been busy."

"Yeah, I thought I'd help out a bit today. Where's dad?" Bob answered.

Mother looked up from the carrot she was peeling and smiled. *How does she know exactly what I'm up to?* Bob thought.

She said, "Your father ran out to pick up some boots he was having re-soled, but I'll tell him what a great job you did on the windows. Why don't you take Nietzsche for a walk? Maybe the Robinson girls would like to join you?"

"Oh, sure, if you don't have any more chores for me to do?" Bob said, excited at the chance to escape.

"Well, I can't think of anything right now, and it would be so nice if you did something with the girls. Mrs. Robinson is worried about them, maybe a walk will take their minds off their troubles," Mother said. "Do you need a snack before you go?"

"That would be great," Bob said happily. He had two thick slices of fresh bread smeared generously with butter and jelly, then headed next store to get Nietzsche. On the way to the Robinson's, he thought, *maybe Sara and Jeannie will be busy, but Maggie will come.* Unfortunately, Maggie was out with her mum shopping. Mr. Robinson was reading the paper and seemed only too happy to have Sara and Jeannie out of the house for a bit.

Out on the street, Sara took Bob's hand and said, "Now, where shall we go?"

"Gosh, I don't know," Bob said, "Jeannie, where do you want to go?

Jeannie had taken Nietzsche's leach from Bob and was walking slightly ahead. She turned and said, "Oh, Belle Isle is my favorite place to walk, and it's so pretty right now."

"Great idea," Bob agreed, "Let's go out to Belle Isle, then we can go downtown." They crossed the bridge to Belle Isle, unleashed Nietzsche and let her run. The sky was a deep blue, and the sun still had some warmth to share. The trees were in full fall color, and leaves were blowing in the soft breeze. It was one of those wonderful Michigan days that makes Detroiters forget about the hot and humid summers and not remember the cold, damp winters. They skipped rocks in the water and played fetch with Nietzsche. After a while, they crossed back into Detroit and took Atwater Street toward downtown.

As they approached Jefferson and Woodward, they noticed a crowd gathering. They edged their way through, curious to see what was going on. Sara tightened her grip on Bob's hand, and Jeannie stayed close with a secure hold on Nietzsche's collar. The crowd filled in quickly around them. Everyone was pointing up at the Majestic Building on the corner of Woodward and Jefferson. Bob scanned the building. *Is it on fire*, he thought, but then he saw what everyone was looking at. High on the buildings side was a man. Sara and Jeannie saw him too. Sara gasped, "What's he doing up there? He'll fall."

"It's the human spider," they heard someone yell.

"I can't watch," Jeannie said. Covering her eyes.

"Gosh, he's crazy," Bob said. The crowd was still growing. He and the girls were getting bumped and pushed.

Bob heard Nietzsche release a low growl. *We need to get out of here,* Bob thought.

"We should go," Bob said to Jeannie and Sara. He kept a tight hold of Sara's hand, with his other hand he caught hold of Nietzsche's collar so that both he and Jeannie had a good grip on her. "Easy girl," he said to the big dog.

Jeannie said, "I don't think she likes this crowd."

"I don't like it either," Sara said. Together the four of them edged away out of the crowd. When they reached a clearing at the back, they turned to see if the man was still on the building. He was, higher now, almost to the top.

Bob realized that it would be horrible if the man fell, and Sara and Jeannie saw it, so he said, "How about we go to the pharmacy and have a Coke-a-Cola? My treat."

"Okay," they agreed, but they kept watching the man on the Majestic Building. Bob gave them each a little nudge, in the opposite direction toward the pharmacy and home. Both girls kept looking over their shoulders to see what was happening and Bob was happy when they turned a corner and the building was out of view.

"Gosh, that was scary," Jeannie said.

"Maybe he had a rope," Sara said. "Like the men who wash the windows."

"Yeah, maybe," Bob agreed, but he didn't think so. He continued, "The crowd was huge. I think it was the biggest crowed I've ever been in."

"Me too," the girls agreed in unison.

They enjoyed their Coke-a-Cola's and headed home. The girls were excited to tell their da about the human spider.

SATURDAY
OCTOBER
7TH

2ND
New Home
Edition

The Gazette —

PRICE
TWO CENTS

Second New OFFICE Editon Oct 7.

CROWDS-SEE-MAN-SCALE
MAJESTIC-BULDING

Notice The Notices	Scales Majestic Bulding By R R Stevens
Page 2 – The Price of this Paper Page 3. Detroit [illegible] [illegible]. page 4. Around the world. Page 2 colum 2 [illegible] notice and others Page 3 colum 2	Mob of [illegible] watch man [illegible] at the [illegible] city could [illegible] side of building as motion picture camera clicks, [illegible] climb on top of cars, bicycles are in center of croud and had pretty [illegible] time [illegible] and I have [illegible]

October 7, 1916
www.catherinepaonessa.com/thegazette

A Job
~ Bob Stevens

At supper that evening, Bob was surprised when Dad said, "Well, I had a long chat with Mr. Harding to-day. He was as disappointed with Henry as I was with you."

"Um, yeah, Henry told me his pop was mad," Bob said. For a second he was worried his dad was going to adopt Mr. Harding's form of punishment.

"Mr. Harding told me he would like to hire you to work at his shop," Dad continued. "He said you'd be able to continue with your editor meetings after school, as long as you worked Saturday mornings instead. What do you think?"

"That will be fine, I guess," Bob said. He was thrilled at the idea, but didn't want Dad to know. It was supposed to be punishment after all.

"If you'd prefer a job at Burroughs, I could still talk to the foreman?" Dad said with a hint of a smile.

"Oh, no sir," Bob said sheepishly, "a job with Mr. Harding will be grand. And, well, I'm sorry I skipped school." He looked at Mother, "And I'm sorry I lied to you." She smiled back, but he realized he had crossed a line that was hard to step back over. He would have to re-earn her trust.

"Well, now, that's settled," Dad said relieved. "Mr. Harding has assured me that you and Henry will be quite busy. Oh, and Karl has to go out of town again. He'd like you to take care of Nietzsche and the yard, as before. Do you think you can manage all that?"

"Yes, sir. Except, well, walking Nietzsche after school will be hard, but maybe Jeannie and Sara will take over that job. I could pay them out of what Professor Ackermann pays me," Bob said.

"Having seen those girls, especially Sara, with that dog, I dare say you won't have to pay them," Mother said.

"Oh, but I'd want to," Bob said smiling.

He started work the following Monday. As promised, Mr. Harding kept him and Henry busy. In the first weeks he learned how to use the industrial sewing machines, did a lot of sweeping and unloaded a large quantity canvas roles.

A Letter from Before
~ Maggie Robinson

Maggie was in the kitchen ironing. She had settled back into the routine of school, but she was moody and cross. It took over a week for her to get caught up with her class work. The notes from Bob had been quite helpful, but she hadn't told him. Actually, she'd been avoiding him since they returned home from Toronto, but she didn't know why. Mum was worried about her and kept stealing looks at her as she the cut vegetables for dinner.

"Mum, stop, I'm fine," Maggie said.

"Aunty McLeod said what you need is a tonic" Mum said.

"Mum, I'm fine, really," Maggie said. Jeannie and Sara came running in, Nietzsche at their heels. The big dog had earned a soft spot in Mrs. Robinson's heart.

"Hi, Mum, do you have some scraps for Nietzsche?" Jeannie asked.

"I do," Mum said, "The lamb bone from the other day is on the shelf in the pantry, but take it outside, she makes such a mess of the floor otherwise."

"Oh, did you hear that Nietzsche! Lamb!" Sara told Nietzsche happily. Mum laughed.

"Here's the mail. Maggie, you got a nice thick letter from Sam," Jeannie said as she tossed the mail on the table. She and Sara headed outside with Nietzsche and the bone.

Maggie put down the iron, picked up the letter and looked imploringly at Mum. She wanted to go somewhere and read her letter, alone.

"Go, read your letter," Mum said.

"Thanks Mum," Maggie said. She didn't want to be interrupted, so she decided to go over to Professor Ackermann's gazebo. The Professor was out of town again, and Bob would still be at work. She grabbed her coat and Sam's hat, the sun was shining, but the air was crisp. She hadn't worn Sam's hat in a while, but it was a letter from him, so she put it on, remembering how he had placed it on her head before he left.

Maggie found a sunny spot on the steps of the gazebo and sat down to read the letter. When she opened it she was surprised to find another envelope inside. It was addressed to her in Bill's handwriting. She gasped. She unfolded the letter Sam had included and read it first.

Dear, Dear Maggie,

    I'm sending you a letter I found in Bill's belongings (the rest of his stuff has been boxed up and will be sent home shortly). I wanted you to have this as soon as possible. I was with Bill you know, when he passed. I wrote mum about it, I'm not sure if she shared that letter. It was hard to write, and I'm sure harder to receive.

Maggie stopped reading and thought, *Mum hadn't shared the letter, was it because I've been so mean and unapproachable?* She felt bad. All she'd done lately was to cause her mum extra worry. She continued reading.

I know you think this was all a waste, but I want you know that Bill didn't have any regrets about joining up. He wanted to do his part, to be with his mates. I don't know if you know this, but he's the one who suggested we join up like we did, instead of waiting to be called. To be honest, when we got over here, and things were hard, to say the least, I was kind of mad at him. But now, I think I'm where I'm supposed to be. The men in my platoon look up to me, they follow me, and I think I can make a difference. Some of the sergeants don't have the respect of their men and I think it puts the men in more danger. They hesitate when they should just follow. I think my men trust me. Anyway, don't be mad at us, and try not to be too sad.

        Love you and miss you,
        Sergeant S. Robinson
        (Doesn't that look smart?)

Tears were streaming down Maggie's cheeks. She hadn't cried. Not when the telegram came, not when they met with friends and family in Toronto, not even at the memorial service. She didn't know why, but the tears just didn't come. She had been mad. Mad at them for signing up, and mad at Bill for dying. Sam knew her so well, knew how she would feel, even with an ocean separating them. With shaking fingers, she opened Bill's letter.

Hello Meg-Peg, (Maggie sighed, that was Bill's special name for her.)

I hope everything is going well there. We're fine over here. The food is miserable, and the weather, well, not so different from late summer at home, hot and humid. Thanks for all the chatty letters. I have one chum over here whose sister never writes him, he thinks she's mad at him for signing up. Poor chap, feels miserable. Sam was really mad at me for talking him into this mess. But I wish you could see him now. He used to be so changeable, didn't know what he wanted, what he should do after school, but now, he is different, so confident, so strong. I rely on him, all the fella's do. Like he'll pull us through, just because he wants to. So try not to worry, and keep the letters coming. I love hearing about all your doings, even if you think it's just boring day to day stuff, it helps so much to hear it. In your next letter tell me more about your classes and

The letter just stopped. Maybe Bill got called away, and planned on finishing later, but that's all there was. Maggie was crying softly. She smoothed the page out on her lap, tracing over some of the words with trembling fingers. Why had she been so mad at him? And she had taken her anger out on Sara, Jeanie, Mum and Da, even Bob. Now she was ashamed.

She heard whistling and looked up. It was Bob. He was holding a rake and looking at the leaf covered lawn, as if he was trying to decide where to begin. Nietzsche was with him, but neither Bob nor the dog saw her. Maggie watched as Bob started raking. He reached the rake out and pulled it in, Nietzsche followed the rake back and forth. Leaves flew everywhere and Nietzsche yelped at them. Bob continued to whistle a lively tune, Nietzsche bounced back and forth scattering the leaves as Bob tried to pile them, and to Maggie, and they looked like they were dancing. She couldn't help smiling. It was the first time she had smiled in quite a while. She felt like a heavy weight had been lifted from her. She didn't have to be mad anymore. Mad at Sam for making Bill join up, because it was the other way around. Mad a Bill for dying, because he was doing what he thought he had to. And mad at Bob for being here instead of there. Tears threatened again.

Nietzsche suddenly stopped chasing the leaves, the big dog had noticed Maggie, and ran to greet her. Bob's gaze followed Nietzsche. Maggie looked up, Bob was looking at her. He stopped whistling, and smiled tentatively. She smiled back. *Gosh, I must look like a mess,* Maggie thought. Bob leaned the rake in the crook of a nearby tree and walked back to the gazebo. He said, "Hello, there, this silly dog is no help at all."

"I can see that," Maggie said. "It looked like you two were dancing."

Bob sat down on the step next to Maggie, he must have noticed her tear steaked face, he asked, "Are you okay?"

Maggie looked away, then back at Bob. She didn't want to tell Bob what was in the letters, didn't want to admit how mad she'd been, she just said, "Yeah. I've had a letter from Sam, and well… yeah I'm okay."

Bob smiled. He reached up and wiped a moist strand of hair from Maggie's cheek. He looked directly into her eyes, she had to look away. Her heart skipped a beat. *Wait, no, they were just friends, right?* Maggie thought. Her mind raced, *do I want him to kiss me, maybe, but then everything would be different.* Maggie jumped up and said, "Wow, you have lots of leaves to rake. Want me to help?"

"Sure," Bob said. "I think there's another rake in the shed."

Bob and Maggie raked leaves until the sun was low in the sky and it was time to go home. Bob walked Maggie to her house before going home himself.

"I'm done meeting with Edith before school, I'm all caught up," Maggie said. She had missed walking to school with Bob. He was a good listener, because he let her do most of the talking.

"That's great, do you want to meet in the morning? At our old corner?" Bob asked.

Maggie smiled at the thought of them having a corner, and said, "Sure."

Bob smiled, "Great."

They walked in silence for a moment, then Maggie suggested, "Hey, I was thinking while we were raking, Halloween is next week. It would be nice to do something, you know, Halloween-ish, maybe have a bonfire, we could burn up some of those leaves? Sara and Jeannie would really like it."

"That's a great idea," Bob said. "We could chip in and get some marshmallows to toast and we could bob for apples. We could invite some of the gang from school too. Edith and Henry?"

"Yeah, and there are some people in the science club, how about some of the editors from the newspaper, they could come too?" Maggie added. They had reached her house.

"We can talk more about it on the way to school tomorrow." Maggie said. She decided it wouldn't due to linger on the front walk too long. Front walks were where a quick kiss could be stolen at twilight, so she ran up the front steps, turned back to Bob, smiled, tipped her hat, and said formally, "Thank you sir, for escorting me home."

For the next week, Maggie, Bob and Henry were busy planning the Halloween bonfire. On the day before Halloween, Jeannie sat at the dining room table working on the huge Halloween edition of Bob's newspaper.

"See," Jeannie said, holding out the newspapers for Maggie. "It has stories, poems and information about tomorrows Halloween party. Bob dropped them off a little while ago, I get to add some pictures and make more copies." She picked up an orange crayon and continued coloring in a jack-o-lantern on the front page of one of the newspapers.

Maggie realized that Jeannie really enjoyed working on the newspaper. *It's nice of Bob to let her help*, Maggie thought, *we all need a distraction, otherwise, we'll go crazy worrying about Sam. Wondering, is he okay? Or is another dreadful telegram on its way?*

"Should I bring my homework down here and work at the table with you?" Maggie asked Jeannie.

"Oh, that will be fun," Jeannie said with a smile. "And if you need a break, you can help me."

On her way to her room to get her books, Maggie thought about how they were all finding ways to move on after Bill's death. *I have my school work, Sara has Nietzsche, and Jeannie has the Bob's newspaper,* she thought with a sigh.

The Halloween bon fire was a huge success. Quite a few friends from school came, the weather was cold, perfect for a big bon fire. A harvest moon set the mood.

And Maggie was surprised to discover that she was happy. Well, maybe not happy in the old sense like when she was a little girl before the war, but the ache she felt was smaller. She didn't think it would ever go away completely, but smaller was better. Like she was carrying a stone in her pocket, instead of a brick on her heart. The stone would weigh on her daily, but it wouldn't completely pull her down.

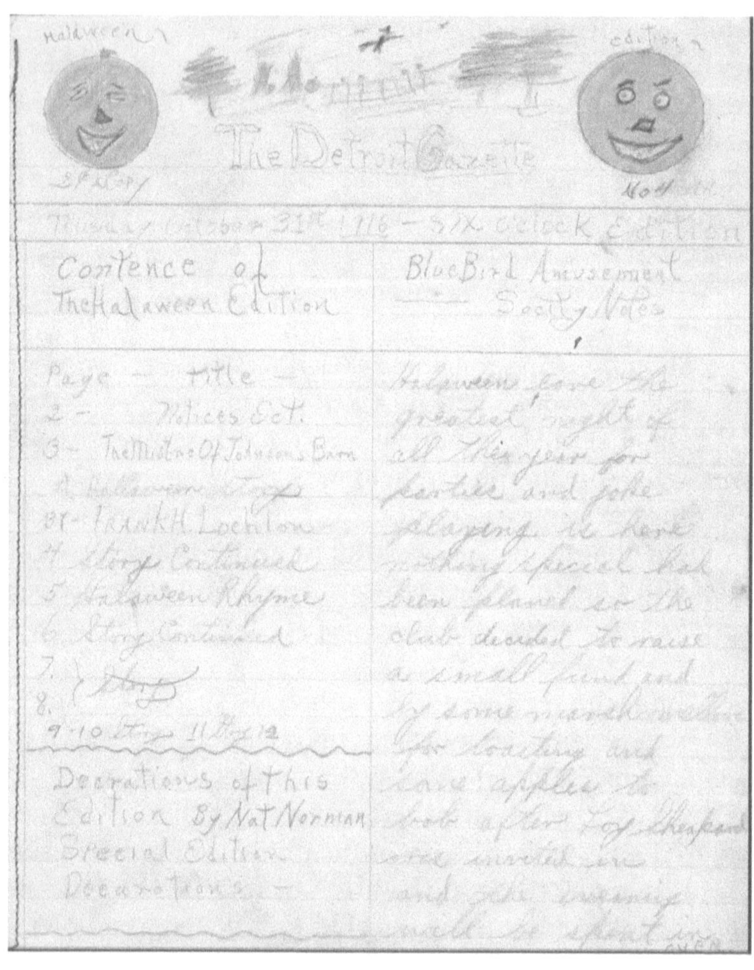

October 31, 1916
www.catherinepaonessa.com/thegazette

The Zimmerman Telegram
~ *Bob Stevens*

The remainder of 1916 came and went quickly. Bob's grandparents visited for Thanksgiving, and the Robinson family went to Toronto for Christmas. At school Bob continued to work as an editor of *The Eastern*, the quarterly school magazine.

Thanks to Maggie, he even managed to maintain a decent grade in chemistry. Bob and Maggie returned to the easy friendship they had before Bill died. They walked to school together most days, and studied together. Bob and Henry often joined the Robinson girls on outings to the picture show, skating in the park and trips to the soda fountain counter in the pharmacy. Bob hadn't tried to kiss Maggie again, although he thought about it, but she seemed to avoid giving him the opportunity. *Maybe being friends okay*, Bob thought.

Every day after school, and on Saturday mornings, Bob worked at the Harding Canvas Works. With help from Jeannie and Sara, he took care of Nietzsche and Professor Ackermann's house, and on Saturday afternoons he delivered Mother's and Aunty McLeod's groceries.

Bob followed the news from Europe where the war raged on. At sea, American ships were lost at the hands of terrifying German U-boats. In France, the two armies were locked in a deadly stalemate. Each trying to get the upper hand in no man's land. And still Wilson waited.

On Thursday, March 1ˢᵗ, Bob was busy shoveling Professor Ackermann's front walk. He had hoped the snow would melt in the afternoon sunshine, but the walk was still snow covered and slippery when he got home from school. Bob was surprised when Maggie came running up the street waving the latest Detroit Free Press.

"Did you see the news?" Maggie called from a few houses away.

"No, what's up?" Bob called back. By the expression on Maggie's face and the excitement in her voice, he figured it was good news.

"Germany tried to make a deal with Mexico!" Maggie said.

"Mexico?" Bob asked.

"Yeah, Britain intercepted a telegram from, um," Maggie looked at the paper, "let's see, here it is, from the German Foreign Minister, um, his names Arthur Zimmermann, to the German Minister in Mexico. Germany offered Texas, New Mexico, and Arizona to Mexico in return for their joining the German cause." Maggie held out the newspaper for Bob.

"Huh? Germany offered Mexico what?" Bob mumbled as he quickly read the first couple of sentences in the article.

"Do you know what this means?" Maggie asked.

"War with Mexico?" Bob replied, still reading.

"Well, it doesn't say that, but, it means Wilson can't wait any longer, he has to declare war on Germany. And with the U. S. in the war. Germany can't win. It means the end of the war," Maggie said excitedly.

Bob and Maggie were both reading the paper now. Heads together, talking excitedly. They were so engrossed in the newspaper, that they didn't hear Professor Ackermann coming up the sidewalk. The Professor had been gone since Halloween, and everyone was beginning to wonder when he would return.

"So you've seen the news?" Professor Ackermann said as he approached.

"Oh, hi," Bob said, surprised.

"Interesting isn't it?" Professor Ackermann said.

"Wilson will have to declare war on Germany now? Won't he?" Maggie asked.

"Well, it may take a little time I would think. He has to make sure the telegram is real," Professor Ackermann answered.

Maggie looked disappointed, then asked, "What do you mean, real?"

"Well, they don't just send this type of information in regular telegrams, I would guess. It's coded before it's sent over the telegraph wires," Professor Ackermann pointed to the text of the telegram that was reprinted in the newspaper, "This telegram must have been intercepted and decoded by Britain. I would hope President Wilson will check to make sure Britain hasn't fabricated the whole scheme to get us into the war," Professor Ackermann explained.

"Oh," Maggie said, dejected.

"Well, we should know is a few weeks either way. Now, I've had a long journey, and I'm tired. Stop by later Bob and I'll pay you what I owe you," Professor Ackermann said. He looked at the house and continued, "As usual, everything looks great."

"Okay," Bob agreed. And Professor Ackermann went around to the backyard and meet Nietzsche with a happy greeting.

When the Professor was out of ear shot, Maggie whispered, "Well, I don't think Britain would make something like this up. And what does he know about telegrams and codes. Maybe you were right, maybe Professor Ackermann is a spy after all."

"Exactly what I was just thinking," Bob whispered back.

"Do you think that's true? About the code? That would mean that the country that could decode the enemy's codes would have a huge advantage, enough of an advantage to even win the war," Maggie speculated.

The Typewriter
~ *Bob Stevens*

But March wore on and still Wilson waited, Bob managed to write and improve his newspaper. Jeannie helped; she copied out the duplicate papers, continued to create a Women's section, and added decorations. By the end of March however, Bob had decided that the newspaper was just too much work. He had enough to do, plus, the days were getting longer, and he didn't want to be stuck in his room working on the newspaper. Bob decided the March 17, 1917 issue would be the last.

Bob delivered Aunty McLeod's last copy of the Gazette when he delivered her groceries. He handed over the paper and said, "Enjoy this issue, it's the last one. I've decided to stop writing it." Aunty McLeod stared at him, shocked. Her reaction surprised him, so he went on, "I've been so busy at school, and with my job, and well, I don't have time to keep it up." Her pained expression made him keep talking, "Professor Ackermann is going away again, and with spring coming, I'll have to start taking care of the yard."

Aunty McLeod said, "You can't stop; you just can't."

"I don't understand. It's just silly stories and family news." Bothered by her suddenly paleness he added, "I'll still visit when I deliver the groceries."

She sat down at the kitchen table and stared at her wrinkled, knotted hands. "It's not for me; it's for the boys at the front." Now it was his turn to be shocked.

"What? What boys at the front?" He asked.

She looked up, her usually twinkling eyes swimming, close to tears. "I have a confession to make. I've been sending your newspapers to my grandson Davy. He's been sharing them with the other boys in his platoon."

Bob couldn't believe it. Grown men, fighting men were reading his silly little newspapers. They were getting a good laugh at the little boy who knew nothing of the war. He could feel his face turning red with anger and embarrassment.

"I know what you are thinking, but it's not like that. They really like the newspapers. Davy says they don't get many British newspapers. He said your papers give him and his mates something to talk about, to think about besides the miserable conditions and upcoming battles." She sighed and looked from her hands to him and went on, "I'm sorry, I should have told you, but I didn't want you to start writing the papers differently, or stop writing them. I've been so worried about Davy, by sending your newspapers I can give him something more interesting than the ramblings of an old lady."

Bob thought she looked old—really old. He said, "I guess I could keep writing them, for a little while." He turned to leave, still feeling dumbstruck.

"Wait," she got up from the table and went to a desk in the living room. From the top drawer she pulled out a small stack of letters. She handed them to Bob. "Read these, than decide. Bring them back tomorrow and let me know.

Bob sat in his room that evening reading through Davy's letters. Aunty McLeod was right; he really did enjoy the newspapers. In one letter he wrote, "The fella's really enjoyed the January issue with the car pictures. We all picked which car we'd buy if we didn't have our feet stuck in the mud over here."

January 27, 1917
www.catherinepaonessa.com/thegazette

And in another letter Davy wrote, "What happened to the last installment of the Broken Bill story? I've been reading it out loud to the fella's, and we want to know how it ends. If it doesn't come soon you'll have to ask Bob to make us another copy."

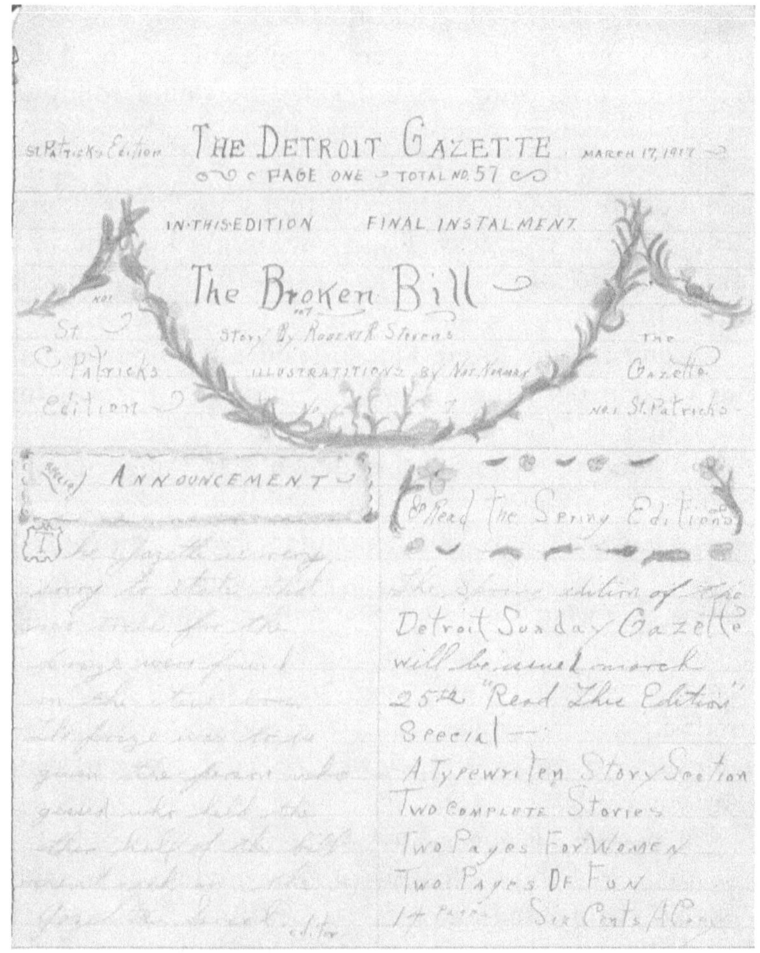

March 17, 1917
www.catherinepaonessa.com/thegazette

Bob was surprised, could they really like the newspapers? Or, more likely, they were so miserable anything different was interesting. Bob decided he would continue writing the papers, but he'd make them even better. His mind raced with ideas for improvements, more pictures and more real news. He carefully folded up Davy's letters. Reading them had given Bob some insight into the war, and he hoped for Aunty McLeod's sake, that Davy made it through safely.

"Come in Bob," Aunty McLeod said as Bob approached her kitchen door the following afternoon. It was warm for March and the door was open to the spring sunshine. Aunty McLeod was busy in the kitchen, and it smelled wonderful. She wiped her flour-covered hands on her apron, smiled and said. "I've been watching for you." She looked brighter today, and the twinkle had returned to her eyes. "Come, see what I found." She led Bob into the dining room. On the table was a small screwdriver, an oilcan, a couple of dirty rags and a large, square shaped lump covered with a flowery towel. Aunty McLeod stood next to the table, lifted a corner of the towel, looked at Bob and said, "Are you ready?"

"Um, yeah," Bob hesitated.

Aunty McLeod smiled, swept away the towel and said, "Ta da!" Under the towel was a typewriter. Bob couldn't believe his eyes. It was a relatively new typewriter, black, of course with the alphabet and numbers on the little round keys and the paper roller. Bob had never used a typewriter. Aunty McLeod continued, "I ordered it a couple of years ago from Sears Roebuck. I thought it would make keeping up with my correspondents, easier, but I couldn't get used to it. I found the keys too difficult. And that awful tap, tap, taping, and having to push the roller back when I finished a line, well with all that commotion, I couldn't keep track of what I was writing. I put it in the attic and forgot about it. Last night I was trying to think of a way to help you so you could keep writing your newspaper, and it came to me. You can use the typewriter."

"Oh," Bob said flabbergasted, he couldn't imagine trying to write his newspaper while sitting at Aunty McLeod's dining room table. He usually worked on it late at night in his night-shirt, and he was often grumpy when he was writing especially if someone interrupted him. "But, I've decided to keep writing them anyway, and well, I couldn't work on it here."

"Well, of course not here, at my dining room table," Aunty McLeod said, as bothered by that thought as Bob was, "You can have the typewriter of course, to take home with you."

Bob's mouth dropped open, "I can have it?" He repeated.

"Why, yes, I would love for you to have it. Especially if it means you can continue with the newspaper, but you can keep the typewriter either way, it's not doing anyone any good in my attic. I cleaned it up, and oiled the keys, it works just fine, see," Aunty McLeod said pointing at a piece of typewritten paper on the table. Bob picked it up. The following line was typed multiple times. "Now is the tim for allgood men to coome to the aidd oftheir contry." There were numerous spelling errors and places where there wasn't a proper space between words.

Bob read the line as a question, "Now is the time for all good men to come to the aid of their country?"

"That was in the instruction book as a good line to type for practice," Aunty McLeod said. She continued, "So, this will be just fine. Just think how nice the paper will look typed. But, don't feel like you have to type it all at once, it takes practice."

"Wow, and you're sure you don't want it," Bob asked.

"No, you take it, please. Now, it's heavy, do you think you can manage it? I had a heck of a time getting it out of the attic. I had to move it down one step at a time, with a break for tea half way down the stairs," Aunty McLeod smiled.

"Oh, I can manage. Thank you, and if you ever decide you want it back, just come on over and I'll carry it back for you," Bob said, he continued, "And, I'll make the best newspaper ever."

Bob lugged the typewriter home. Aunty McLeod was right; it was heavy. He took it to his room, put it on his desk and opened the instruction book. He was trying to figure out how to insert a piece of paper when Mother came into the room. She looked at the typewriter and said, "Oh, my, where did that come from?"

"Aunty McLeod gave it to me," Bob said, distracted, "For my newspaper." He was still struggling to get the paper to advance along the roller and into the machine.

"Here, let me show you." She said, and she sat down, quickly fed a piece of paper in to the typewriter and began typing.

Bob was surprised, "Wow," he said, "I didn't know you could type."

"Oh, well, I had a job in an office back in Nova Scotia before I married your father. I kind of forgot how fun it was." Tap, tap, tap, "Oops, oh dear." She looked at the page. "Now that I think of it, I had a problem with errors, I could get going quite fast, but my accuracy was terrible. Your father saved me," she said with a chuckle. "Here, you put your hands like this, and use this lever when you get to the end of a line. Practice a bit, I'll show some more after supper."

Bob published the first issue to contain typed print on March 25, 1917. He didn't use the typewriter for the entire newspaper, just the story section. Jeannie added a large women's section, and on the last page, Bob included a list of American ships sunk by German U-boats.

As President Wilson waited, Germany's return to unrestricted submarine warfare and the Zimmerman telegram produced a shift in the hearts and minds of the American people. They were ready to fight. Bob wanted Davy and his mates to know that Americas may be joining them soon.

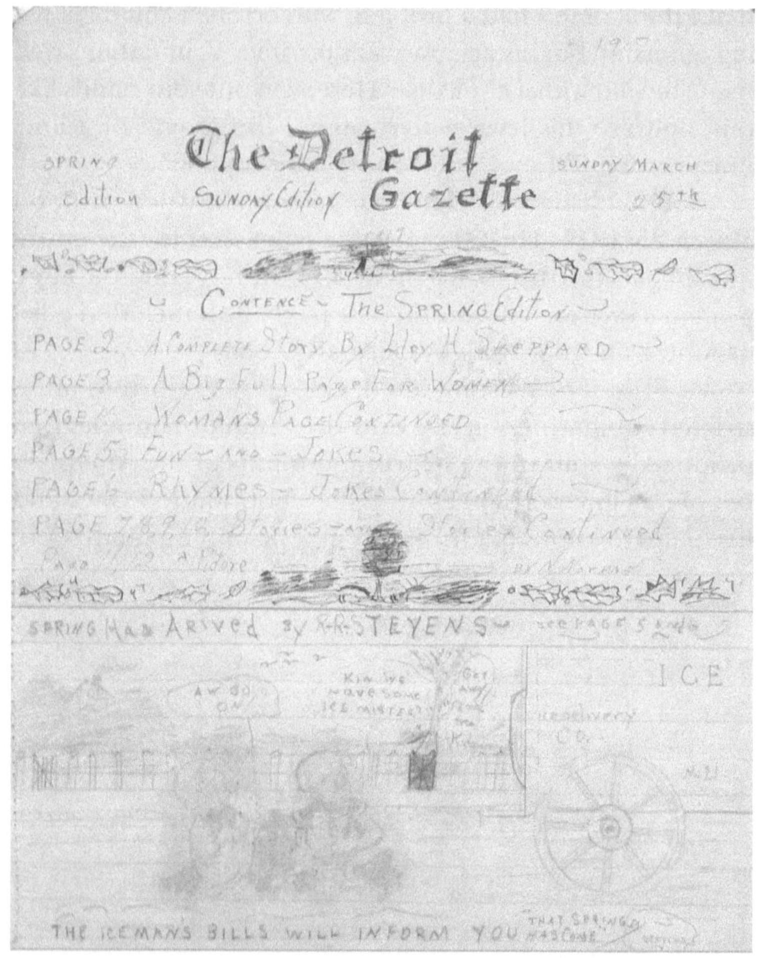

March 25, 1917
www.catherinepaonessa.com/thegazette

A week later, on April 2, 1917, President Woodrow Wilson went before a joint session of Congress to request a declaration of war against Germany. Congress approved the request 4 days later, on April 6, 1917. America was at war.

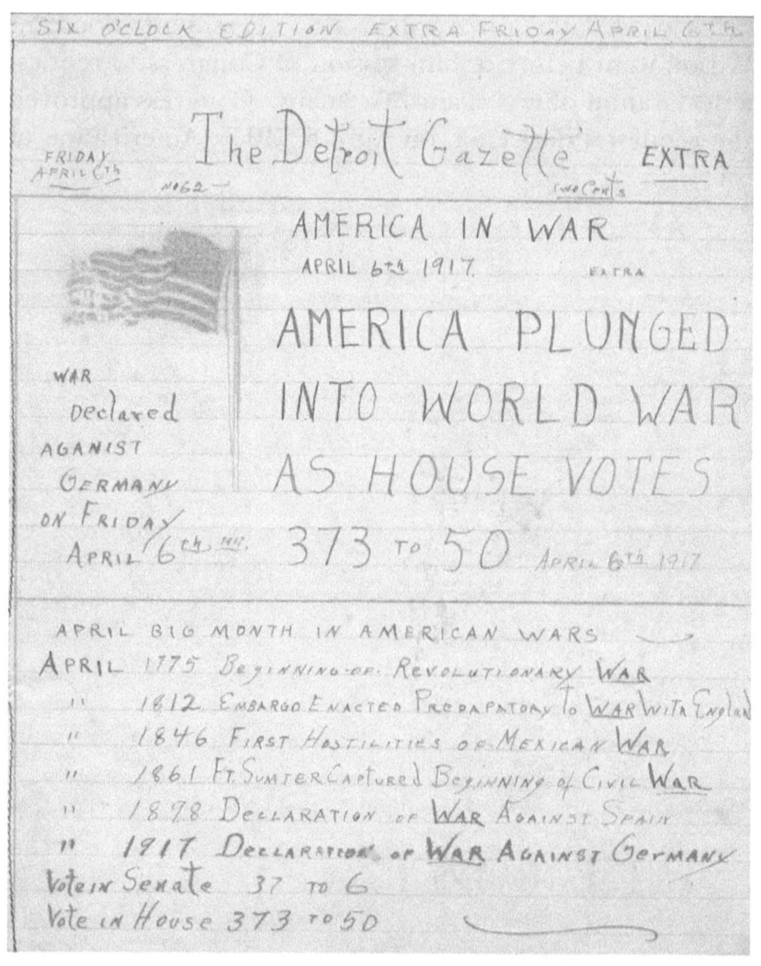

April 6, 1917
www.catherinepaonessa.com/thegazette

CHAPTER 12

Mac and Millie
~ Davy McLeod

Davy and Jamie stopped at the hospital to visit Mac before catching the train to the sniper training school. Davy was worried that Mac would be mad because Jamie was going instead of him. As it turned out, Mac was too busy being in love to care what Davy and Jamie were doing.

"This is Millie," Mac said, smiling. "Isn't she the most beautiful girl in the world?" Millie giggled and turned bright red. She looked from Davy to Jamie and back to Mac, where her eyes lingered and she smiled. Mac was right; she was pretty with blond hair that was swept up neatly under her nurse's hat and bright, friendly blue eyes

"Hi Millie, nice to meet you, I'm Davy McLeod" Davy said with a nod.

"And I'm Jamie Patterson," Jamie added.

"Oh, I know, Mac has told me all about you, and Gavin too. I would've known you fella's anywhere," Millie said. Davy looked from Millie to Mac. Mac was grinning from ear to ear.

"Millie's has been taking great care of me since I came in, and well, we started talking, and just kept on, all night one night, talking that is," Mac said sheepishly.

Davy chuckled, and Millie explained, "I was working the night shift, and the boys were quiet, so I wasn't too busy, and well Mac couldn't sleep. It was after the doctor had cleaned up and added some stitches to his arm. It was hurting him," she looked at him with a little pout, "so we talked and talked to take his mind off the pain."

"Millie's from Bellshill. Imagine that, us living so close to each other, and coming over here and meeting like this," Mac said.

"It was fate," Millie said, "I had to come over and do my part, I have two brother's fighting, and so I came and . . ." but Millie was interrupted by the sharp voice of the head nurse.

"Millie, enough dilly dallying, I'm sure some of the other patients would like a little care, don't you think?" The head nurse said, a twinkle in her eye.

"Yes ma'am," Millie answered, to Davy and Jamie, she said, "Very nice to meet you."

Millie walked away and Mac whispered, "Well, what do you think? Isn't she an angel? I know what you're thinking, that it's just a crush, that it's only because she my nurse, and I'm the patient, but honestly, I think I'm in love with her, and I think she feels the same way."

"Well, then, congratulations," Davy said with a smile. "She is an angel, especially if she's willing to put up with you."

"How's your arm?" Jamie asked.

"Oh, it's getting better, but, I'm stuck in the hospital for at least another week," Mac said. He looked around the room, caught Millie's eye, smiled and continued, "Then I've been assigned to light duty until it's completely healed. They want me to train other chaps on how to handle the Lewis gun. I'll be able to see Millie when I'm not teaching and she's not nursing." Mac hesitated, looked from Davy to Jamie and added, "But, I'm sorry, I won't be with you fella's when you return to the front."

"Well, don't be too sorry, because we've also been reassigned." Jamie said. "You're looking at Corporal McLeod, by the way." Jamie nodded toward Davy with a chuckle.

Mac whistled through his front teeth, then said, "Corporal, you made corporal. Congratulations."

"Thanks," Davy said, "I've been selected for sniper training, and Jamie will be trained as an observer. We leave on the train in a few hours. The school is in Steenbecque, wherever that is."

"A sniper, really, that's great, you're the best shot in this whole bloody outfit, it's about time the blokes up top noticed," Mac said.

"Well, we'll see about that," Davy said, "but thanks. You know it was Sergeant Macgregor who recommended me."

"Really, turns out he wasn't such a nasty bastard after all," Mac said.

Jamie looked at the clock over the door and said, "We better get going or we'll miss our train. Take it easy Mac, I'm sure we'll catch up with you after the training."

Davy held up his fist as if to give Mac a farewell sock in the arm. Mac cringed and Davy laughed, "Just kidding mate, take care," he said. He looked over at Millie, she was busy redressing another soldier's wounded leg, "and be good," he added with a wink. Davy thought about telling Mac about Adele. He almost blurted out about how he had met her and maybe Mac could find her, make sure she was okay, but he didn't even know her last name, didn't even know where she lived, only a street. *No, I'll keep the memory of her, but I'll never see her again,* Davy thought.

Back to School
~ Davy McLeod

The sniping course started on October 4, 1916, Davy and Jamie had a day to get there and get settled. They traveled by train to Aire, France then hitched a ride on an army supply truck to the sniping school in the small village of Linghem. The school was located on a high plateau overlooking the village and surrounding farmland. It was pretty country, and reminded Davy of Scotland. At the school headquarters, they were given their course material and the address of the village home where they would be billeted. They walked back down to the village and found the small, stone, ivy covered cottage. Davy knocked on the door and a short, round woman opened it. Her hands were covered with flour. She smiled at the boys and said, "Bonjour, hello, you must be the officers from the school?" Her English was perfect.

"Um, yes, ma'am, we were told we'd be billeted here," Davy said, recovering from the surprise of being greeted by this cheerful, little English woman. He added, "I'm Corporal Davy McLeod and this is Corporal Jamie Patterson."

"Please, come in. I'm Mrs. Blythe," she said. "You'll be in a room upstairs, but, I must insist that you put your weapons, guns, bayonets and any grenades you might have in your pockets in the shed just outside the kitchen door. I can't sleep a wink if they're in the house." Davy and Jamie must have looked concerned, so she added, "The shed will be locked up tight."

"Yes, ma'am," Jamie said. He and Jamie deposited their weapons in the shed as instructed, noticing that they were not the first soldiers to arrive. Back in the cottage, they followed Mrs. Blythe up a very narrow staircase to a small landing. Two doors opened onto the landing.

"You boys will be here," Mrs. Blythe said, opening the door to the left. In the kitchen below, a kettle whistled loudly. "Oh, dear, make yourselves at home, tea will be ready, well, in five minutes," she said and hurried off. As she passed the other door, she knocked on it and said, "Captain Clarke, Captain Fuller, tea will be served in five minutes."

Davy and Jamie went into the room. It was small, but clean. The ceiling was pitched, and neither of them could stand up straight except for in the first few feet by the door. A small gabled window provided the only light. There were a few hooks on the wall and a wooden cross. Two cots took up most of the space.

"Well, this will be cozy," Jamie chuckled. "It's a good thing Gavin isn't here, he'd have to sleep in the yard." They dropped their gear on the cots and went back into the hall. The other door opened and two young officers emerged. They were both dressed in spotless captain's uniforms, clean-shaven, not a hair out of place. One carried a long, silver topped walking stick. *Mac would be impressed,* Davy thought, *but I know the type.* They were commissioned officers, the younger sons of wealthy gentlemen, here to make a name for themselves.

While the sale of commissions had stopped over 40 years ago, it still took an education from schools like Eton or Harrow, social standing and money to be a commissioned officer. In normal times, Davy would not have meet, let alone socialized with men of their social class. Jamie would have only had contact as a clerk providing a service. But war was different, and now Davy and Jamie trained and served with commissioned officers. There were two types, some were top-notch officers who cared about their men, and others were first rate asses. And a feeling of entitlement can make a first-rate ass a bloody nuisance.

The landing was too small for the four men, so they clambered down the stairs. Once in the small sitting room, they introduced themselves, Mrs. Blythe brought in the tea and they all sat down.

"You chaps been over long?" Captain Clarke asked. He took a cup of tea from Mrs. Blythe, sipped, and, when she wasn't looking, rolled his eyes and looked disappointed.

"It'll be a year come next March, you?" Jamie asked.

"Just came over," Captain Clarke said, he looked disapprovingly at their tattered uniforms and asked, "Did you come directly from the trenches?"

"We were on R&R when we were told to report here for training," Davy answered. Mrs. Blythe handed him his tea, "Thank you," he said. He sipped tentatively, expecting it to be weak or lukewarm, but it was perfect, of course, teatime in the trenches, or the mine for that matter, was probably different than what Captain Clarke was used to.

"I see," Captain Clarke said, "Have you seen any action?"

"Some," Davy said.

"Where did you fella's shoot before coming over?" Captain Fuller asked.

"Pardon?" Jamie asked.

"What club did you shoot with?" Captain Fuller asked.

"I hadn't fired a rifle before enlisting, but Davy here's a crack shot with a slingshot," Jamie said with a smile.

Captain Clarke looked at Davy, "You didn't shoot either? Not at all?"

"No," Davy said, he almost added sir, but didn't. *Bloody hell*, he thought, *I'm off duty*. Instead, with a smirk, he added, "Except for the slingshot." He was beginning to think these arrogant officers fell into the asses category.

"You boys came up from the ranks then?" Captain Clarke asked.

"Yes, that's correct," Jamie said. And the group fell into an awkward silence as Mrs. Blythe passed around a plate of plain biscuits. Captain Clarke and Captain Fuller declined, but Davy and Jamie happily helped themselves.

"Mrs. Blythe," Davy said, "am I correct in assuming you're English?"

"Oh, yes, I was born and raised in Brighton." Mrs. Blythe answered. "My late husband and I came over when he inherited this house and farmland from his uncle. I've been here 25 years now, so it's home. Our children live nearby. The only good thing to come out of this war is the fact that I get a chance to speak English again."

Captain Clarke and Captain Fuller put down their cups. Captain Clarke said, "Well, thank you for the tea, Mrs. Blythe." They both rose. Captain Clarke continued, "We are off to check that our batman found adequate lodging and for a tour of your little village. Is there someplace you can recommend for our supper?"

"Oh my, didn't they tell you, the students take two meals up at the school, and are served their supper at home, where they are billeted. The village doesn't have a proper inn," Mrs. Blythe said.

Captain Clarke looked from Davy to Jamie to Mrs. Blythe, and said, "Ah, I see, what time is supper served, and is formal dress expected?"

"Eight o'clock, dear, and what you have on will be fine," Mrs. Blythe said with a chuckle.

"Very good," Captain Clarke said and he and Captain Fuller left.

When she was sure the door was safely shut behind them, Mrs. Blythe broke out laughing. "Well, those lads are in for a shock," she finally said between chuckles. "Too good for my tea and biscuits I guess. A week in the trenches and they'll be happy for a cup of tea, any tea. Isn't that right lads?"

"Yes, ma'am," Davy said, "This tea is right fine." Mrs. Blythe held out the plate of biscuits and smiled as Davy and Jamie helped themselves to what was left.

"I'm just glad we don't have to dress for dinner," Jamie said mockingly.

"Last time I checked, this didn't look like Windsor Castle," Mrs. Blythe added.

"Shooting clubs, I imagine it's a mite easier to shoot straight when the target's not shooting back." Davy said, then he added reflectively. "But, I suppose a chap could become a good shot if he'd been at it since he was a lad."

"I'm mighty glad to have a pair of nice ordinary lads like you staying here." Mrs. Blythe said, she looked from Davy to Jamie, relaxed back in her chair and said, "Now, tell me all about yourselves. Where are you from, do you have wives, sweethearts at home?"

Davy and Jamie relaxed and told her everything she wanted to know. They were enjoying the feeling of being in a real home, and of being mothered for a bit.

Sniping, Observation and Scouting
~ Davy McLeod

The Sniping, Observation and Scouting, (SOS) course started the next morning. There were about 50 students in the class. The lead instructor, Major Hesketh-Prichard, introduced himself and gave an overview of what would be covered. Instruction would last four weeks.

The major defined sniping as, "the art of very accurate shooting from concealment or in the open." He went on to say, "What was wanted, apart from organization, was neither more nor less than the hunter spirit. The hunter spends his life trying to outwit some quarry, and the step between war and hunting is but a very small one."

Davy remembered his time hunting rabbit, pheasant and squirrel in the glens and highlands around Bothwell, all the time, trying to avoid being caught by Angus Macgregor. *It wasn't big game, and I didn't have a fancy rifle, but, I suppose it's not so different,* he thought. After lunch in the mess, they went to the range for some initial target practice. They would each take five shots at a small, square target placed in front of the stop-butt 100 yards out. The goal was to get their five shots as close together as possible. The range was large enough for ten men to shoot simultaneously, so they were divided into teams. Davy and Jamie found themselves on a team with Captain Clarke and Captain Fuller.

The men took turns shooting with an instructor changing the papers between shooters. Jamie went first, he was a fair shot, but he was primarily there as an observer, the precise shooting would be left to Davy.

Davy shot second. He took the rifle from Jamie. It was still warm. He loaded it, felt its weight and balance. He aimed, slowed his breathing, and fired each shot.

Captain Clarke, Captain Fuller and the other chaps in the group followed. The instructor retrieved the last shooters paper target and distributed them to the men.

"First shooter," he said, holding out Jamie's target, "Four on the square, but those are not badly grouped, not bad from this distance if you haven't had experience as a marksman. Are you training to be a sniper or observer?"

"Observer," Jamie said.

"You will be surprised how much we can improve your shoot in just four weeks," the instructor said. "Second shooter," he continued as he held up Davy's target sheet. "Great job, nice grouping. All shoots were within a 5 inch radius. Well done."

"Thank you sir," Davy said.

"Third shooter," the instructor said as he held up another target sheet and Captain Clarke claimed it. Only four of the shots had hit the target. The instructor continued, "As I told Corporal Patterson, sir, we can make some real improvements in four weeks, sometimes it's only a small correction that's needed."

Captain Clarke took the target sheet, looked it over and said, "This can't be right, you must have gotten the sheets mixed up," he looked directly at Davy and continued, "Corporal McLeod, is that your sheet, do you think?"

"Yes, absolutely," Davy said. He had shot well. It was the best rifle he had ever fired. He liked the feel of it. He was sure he had hit the target with every shot.

Captain Clarke took the remaining sheets from the instructor and reviewed them. They were all better than his, but not as good as Davy's. Captain Clarke handed them back, looked the instructor in the eye and asked, "And you are quite sure you didn't get the second and third sheets mixed up?"

"Quite sure, Captain Clarke, but if you would like to shoot again, that would be fine," the instructor said. Davy could hear the irritation building in the instructor's voice.

"That will be fine, both Corporal McLeod and I will shoot again," Captain Clarke said, his face red with anger.

The instructor was dumbfounded. He looked at Davy apologetically, and said, "Corporal McLeod would you mind shooting again?"

"Not at all," Davy said with a confident smile. He held up the rifle he'd used and said, "To be honest, this is the best rifle I've ever had the opportunity to fire, I would actually enjoy firing it again." While Davy was speaking, Major Hesketh-Prichard had joined them. The instructor explained the problem and left to prepare the target. Captain Clarke nodded to Captain Fuller, indicating that he should go with the instructor, presumably to ensure that the targets were not mixed up.

"Would you like to shoot first or second," Davy asked Captain Clarke.

"Second," he replied.

For a second time Davy aimed, slowed his breathing, and fired each shot. For a second time, he felt the weight and balance of the rifle. And again, he shot well. Captain Clarke shot again. Davy could tell that the Captain was angry. His face was red and a vein at his temple was pulsing rapidly, and this time, it was his anger that disrupted his shot. The instructor and Captain Fuller returned from the target, the latter did not look happy. The instructor held up Davy's target and said, "First shooter," then he held up Captain Clarke's target and said, "Second shooter." Davy's was as good as his first target. Five shots, all neatly grouped. Captain Clarke's was worst.

"Excellent shooting young man, what's your name?" Major Hesketh-Prichard asked Davy.

"Corporal McLeod, sir," Davy said, "This is a fine rifle."

"Wait till we get you one with a scope, you'll be hitting groupings like that from 400 yards or more," Major Hesketh-Prichard said.

"Major, sir, I believe this rifle should be thoroughly checked," Captain Clarke said, "I think there's a problem with the site."

Major Hesketh-Prichard took the rifle, and examined it. "These were all checked yesterday," he said. "It might be the strength of your grip, you have to hold it soft, feel its weight, but don't worry, with practice, you will improve." Captain Clarke was fuming, he opened his mouth to complain, but the Major continued, "Now, as I explained this morning, each afternoon we play football or cricket, we find it both relaxes and invigorates the students and they are able to stay awake for the lecture sessions."

Davy and Jamie were more than happy to escape the shooting range and play some football. They were also relieved to discover that Captain Clarke preferred cricket.

As the training progressed, Davy did well on the range, and Jamie's good memory and organizational skills made him an excellent observer. In one exercise, instructors standing in a trench held up 20 different objects, for example, model heads of French, British and German soldiers, a periscope, a rifle barrel, a pickaxe, a bayonet, etc. and the students had to write a list of what they saw using a telescope from 600 to 700 yards away. Jamie was exceptional at this. He spotted each object and Davy wrote it down. What was especially surprising, was that Jamie could remember the objects, in order, without looking at the list. The other chaps began taking bets on whether he would remember them all.

They learned how to use, calibrate and care for telescopic-sighted rifles and telescopes, and spent hours shooting from different distances and under different conditions. When they returned to the trenches, part of their duties would be to ensure that the telescopic rifles were used and maintained properly.

The construction and use of loopholes was also taught. Loopholes are plates placed in the parapet through which a sniper can shoot. The design of the loophole varied greatly depending on the construction of the trenches. They were often made of iron and camouflaged to blend in with the trench or breastworks.

Lectures on map reading, copying and enlarging, the prismatic compass, enemy insignia, range finder use and aerial photograph reading were given in the afternoons. They learned and practiced patrolling and scouting techniques. As scouts, they would be important assets to the army intelligence efforts.

One afternoon midway through the course, they learned how to use papier mache heads to flush out an enemy sniper. The students had gathered in the simulated trenches. A group of papier mache heads were in a box at the gathering spot. It looked funny, a box full of heads, eyes wide and expressions blank. Before the instructor arrived, a chap named Mick picked out a dapper French head and started entertaining them by using it as dummy. He was pretty good at making it look as if the dummy was talking.

"Hey, one of you blokes do me a favor and pick the chats from the back of my neck, I can't seem to reach, and they are so bloody itchy." Mick said. Mick scratched the back of the dummy's head.

"Thanks mate," the dummy said.

"You're welcome, Captain French" Mick said to the dummy.

Unfortunately, the instructor arrived, rolled his eyes, took the head from Mick and said, "Sorry to interrupt your fun lads, but I think we can start our demonstration now, Corporal McLeod, do you mind playing the part of the enemy sniper?"

"No sir, not at all," Davy said.

The instructor continued, "Go over to the enemy trench, pick a loophole, but don't let us see where you are, then we'll display a head, and you hit it. We'll do that three times, from three different locations. Come back after the third shot so you can hear the explanation of how the heads are used."

"Yes, sir," Davy said. He jumped out of the trench into no man's land and headed to the enemy trench. As he walked away, he heard the instructor say, "As for the rest of you, keep your heads down. We don't want any accidents here."

Davy crossed the fake no man's land. It was eerily like the real thing except for the fact that no one was shooting at him. The terrain was uneven, and pitted with small craters; barbed wire crisscrossed the area. He jumped into the enemy trench, passed one loophole and stopped in the next one. At that moment, a cloud passed overhead.

Slowly, he opened the loophole hoping the sudden change of light would hide the movement. He placed his rifle in the rear opening and aimed through the forward opening. He maneuvered the loophole plates until he could see the area of the trench where dummy would appear and waited. He slowed his breathing. He watched as the head slowly emerged, first the top of the helmet, an English helmet, *this is disconcerting,* Davy thought, *shooting at an Englishmen.* The helmet continued to move upward, Davy waited. He could see the dummies forehead, eyes, and the bridge of the nose. He was surprised at how real it looked. He almost decided not to fire, but then he realized that the dummy was wearing a helmet, and his classmates weren't. He aimed, and fired. The shot flew straight and true, he could see a puff of dust emerge when the shot hit the head.

Davy moved down the trench, picked another loophole. The elevation at this end of the trench was higher. He fired when the head emerged, a Frenchmen this time. It was another direct hit. For the third shot, he moved back to the first loophole, the one he had already passed. This shot was not as clean as the first two. He grazed the top of the dummies head, an Englishmen this time. *Damn, I should've waited just a few more seconds, sorry mate,* Davy thought with a shrug.

Davy walked back to the first trench were the instructor and his classmates were waiting for him. "Now, if we place the first head like this," and he picked up the first papier mache head and placed it on the stand, and continued, "we can see that the bullet entered here, just below the right eye, and exited here, slightly lower, but also on the right side.

Davy looked at the head, its blank eyes staring back at him, and thought, *this is a bloody awful business.*

The instructor continued, "We know that the shooter was almost directly in front of us, and slightly higher. If we look directly through the hole in the head, we may actually spot our sniper, well, if he were still out there." He pointed to the second loophole, and said, "Corporal McLeod, did you fire the first shot from the second loophole?"

"Yes sir," Davy said, somewhat surprised at how easy it was.

The instructor placed the Frenchmen head on the stand, and said, "Now, you will notice that this shot enters the head directly in the left eye, and exits the back of the head below the right eye. Therefore," he peered through the hole in the head, and continued, "this shot came from further down the trench," he pointed, "Corporal McLeod, did you fire your second shot from that loophole, second in from the far end?"

"Yes sir," Davy said. The one-eyed Frenchmen seemed to be winking at him.

The instructor picked up the third head, and said, "Now, Corporal McLeod, I think you rushed this shot a bit, but again, by the track the bullet took across the top of the head we can easily see that the shot came from the first loophole. Is that correct Corporal?"

"Yes sir," Davy said.

"Now that we've identified the sniper's location, we can have one of our snipers deal with him, or order an artillery hit on the spot, or both. Any questions?"

No one asked any questions, it was time for a game of afternoon football. As he walked to the pitch, Davy decided that the use of dummy heads was both captivating and creepy. The sky had clouded over and he hoped they'd get a game in before it rained.

That night he dreamt of the papier mache heads. They floated around his bed, some were talking, but he couldn't understand what they were saying. One head, a French one, kept winking at him. He woke with a start, sat up and bumped his head on the low ceiling. *Bloody hell,* he mumbled. Jamie was snoring softly in the next cot. Davy got up and went to the small window. In the bright moonlight, he could see the rooftops of the village, the bluff where the school was situated, and rolling farmland. He thought about his dream and hoped he didn't dream it again. When he was a lad, after his father died, he'd had a recurring dream where he was in a mineshaft, falling, falling. He never hit the bottom of the shaft, but he would wake in a cold sweat with his heart pounding. He never told anyone about that dream. He sighed and reluctantly went back to bed.

The weeks at the Sniping, Observation and Scouting school passed quickly. Davy would never have admitted it to his mates when they were lads, but he had always liked school, and, except for the time he spent avoiding Captain Clarke, he enjoyed the training.

Mrs. Blythe made the lads billeted at her home feel extremely welcome. While Captain Clarke and Captain Fuller either went out after supper, or retired to their room, Davy and Jamie used the sitting room. They played checkers, studied, and read some of the English books Mrs. Blythe kept in a little bookshelf. Their mail caught up with them, and they shared Bob's newspapers with her.

Too soon, they were headed back to the trenches. Mrs. Blythe was sad to see them go. She gave them each a pair of good socks and made some biscuits for them to eat on the train. She even cried earnest tears all through their final supper together.

They were reunited with Mac and Gavin in time for the holidays and spent Christmas Eve in a dugout together. They had all been promoted, Gavin was their Sergeant, Mac was a Corporal in charge of a Lewis machine gun section, and Davy and Jamie were both Corporals, serving as one of the battalions Sniper/Observer teams.

The winter of 1917 was cold and miserable, but they were alive. The war was raging in places called Khadairi Bend, Nahr-al-Kalek, Baghdad, Samarrah, Falluja and Gaza, but for most of January, February and March, it was relatively quiet in their section. Boredom was the enemy now. Bob's newspapers were a welcome diversion. They read the serial story of the Broken Bill, debated the merits of the different cars in the January issue about the Detroit Auto Show and even joked about the pictures of the women's hats. When the newspaper had been read and reread, they found other uses for the paper.

At the beginning of April, news that the United States had finally entered the war spread quickly up and down the trenches.

CHAPTER 13

Military Training and Junior Reds
~ Bob Stevens

Bob sat at his desk wrapped in the quilt. It was late, but he couldn't sleep. It was too cold. Winter had returned to Detroit.

It was April 14, 1917 and throughout the day the temperature had plummeted. Bob looked out the window. A thick coating of ice covered the trees and glistened in the moonlight. He shivered. The house was cold, and would stay cold until the weather warmed up. The city's coal supply had been used up during the long, cold winter.

But the cold wasn't the only thing keeping Bob awake. He reread the flyer that had been handed out at school that day. MILITARY TRAINING TO BE OFFERED IN

DETROIT PUBLIC HIGH SCHOOLS, it said in bold letters. An informational meeting was scheduled for April 17th. Bob wasn't sure what he thought about the training. A year ago, he would have been excited to join, but now, he wasn't so sure. He decided he'd go to the meeting and see what it was all about, but he knew his parents wouldn't approve, especially Mother. He yawned, and thought, *I'll ask them at dinner tomorrow. I'll tell them it's for the good of the country, it's my duty.* He crawled into his cold bed, shivered and tried again to sleep.

Bob showed the flyer to his parents at supper the next evening and announced, "I'm going to go to this meeting. The country's at war. I should be prepared."

"Military training, in the public schools." Mother said as she read the flyer, "What is this country coming to?"

"We are at war dear," Dad said, he continued, "I can't say I agree with this program, especially for young boys, but Bob is nearly seventeen, if this war drags on, he may be called to serve."

Mother gave a sad sigh, looked at the still mostly full bowl of peas, mumbled something about getting more, and went into the kitchen.

"I haven't decided to join yet," Bob told Dad.

"I understand," Dad said. He laid the flyer aside. The fact that Dad didn't argue or forbid him from going unsettled Bob. Somehow, it made the war, the idea that he might have to fight, more real.

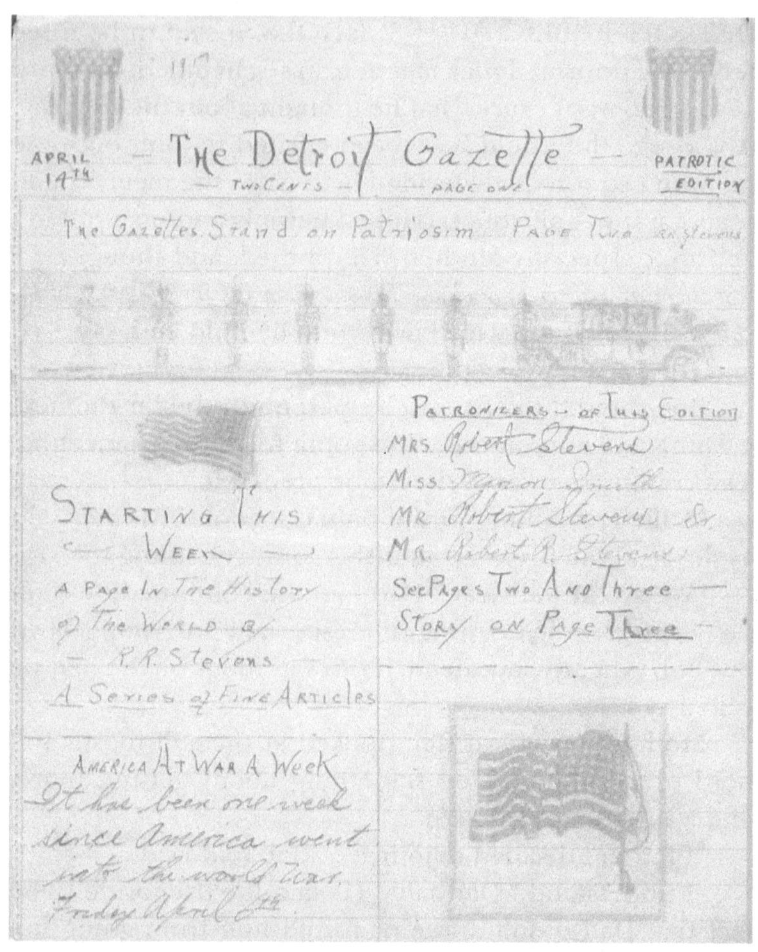

April 14, 1917
www.catherinepaonessa.com/thegazette

Spring returned to Detroit the following Tuesday. The earth was soggy from the weekend rain, but the sun was warm. *It smells like worms,* Bob thought. He was walking to school alone; Maggie had a meeting before first hour. Bob thought about the military training and the war as he walked. He had come to the conclusion that he wouldn't be able to be a war correspondent. Newspapers only hired experienced journalists as correspondents. He was getting some experience working on the school magazine, but mostly he was selling advertising space and working on marketing. *Maybe I'll look for a job with one of the Detroit newspapers when I graduate,* he thought. But with America's entry into the war, life was on hold, especially for Bob and his mates. They may be headed to Europe as soldiers.

Mr. Harding had given Bob the afternoon off so he could attend the military training meeting, but he had told Bob that if decided to join the training, he would have to quit his job. Bob recalled Mr. Harding's usually jovial voice turning serious as they had discussed the possibility of his quitting.

"Darn it, Bob, you're a good worker, and you've learned a lot about the business. I hate to lose you, but if you feel it's your duty to go to this training, well, I guess you have to do what you think is best. But, think about this, you're work here is damn important to the war effort. By filling these contracts, we're helping the lads, soon to be American lads, who are already fighting."

"Important to the war effort," those were Mr. Harding's words. Should Bob give up his job and go to the training?

It would be over a year before he would be old enough to fight. *Maybe, Mr. Harding was right, maybe I shouldn't sign up,* Bob thought, *I'll decide after the meeting.*

In first hour English class Bob was surprised when the teacher, Mr. Taylor said, "Before we begin, Miss Robinson has an announcement." Maggie stood up and walked to the front of the class.

"Good Morning," she started, "I want to announce the formation of a girls Junior Red Cross group. We'll be called the Eastern High Junior Reds. The Red Cross has just begun organizing groups in the Detroit area." As she spoke, a curl escaped Maggie's upswept hairdo and fell gracefully along the curve of her cheekbone. Maggie reached up and tucked it behind her ear. Bob stared at her, she was beautiful. "There will be a lot of important work for us to do. For example, knitting scarves and socks for the soldiers," at this some of the boys snickered, but Maggie wasn't deterred, she glared at them and continued, "rolling bandages, preparing Friendship Boxes for the unfortunate children in the war-torn areas of Europe, and of course raising funds. Please spread the word. The first meeting will be after school this Thursday. Girls, please join us." Bob watched mesmerized as Maggie returned to her seat. She was so confident, so grown up, not the girl with the snowball wearing a boy's hat anymore.

Mr. Taylor's voice interrupted Bob's thoughts, "Thank you Miss Robinson, girls, I hope you will all consider joining this very important effort. Now, your assignment was to read Act II, Scene I of 'A Midsummer-Night's Dream'. Mr. Harding, can you tell me what Puck and the Fairy are doing at the beginning of the scene."

Henry fumbled with his book and tried to locate the correct scene. *Poor Henry,* Bob thought, *he hates Shakespeare.* Class dragged on as Mr. Taylor tried to inspire even Henry to appreciate the prose of Mr. Shakespeare.

Bob, Henry and Maggie met in the hallway after class. "Your Junior Red announcement was really good," Bob told Maggie. "Sounds like you'll be busy. Aren't you going to sign up for the girls first aid training?"

"Oh, no, I'll be far too busy with the Junior Reds. And besides, it isn't very likely that I'll actually be going over to Europe." Maggie replied. "Are you boys going to the military training?" she asked.

"Not me, too much work to do at the shop," Henry answered, looking inquisitively at Bob.

"I'm going to check out the meeting, then decide," Bob said. At that moment, the bell rang and they each headed to class in different directions.

You're in the Army Now?
~ Bob Stevens

Over one hundred boys had gathered in the gymnasium of Joyce Junior High School for the Military Training meeting. Bob looked around the room. Most of the boys were younger than him. He spotted a group of other sophomores on the far side of the gymnasium. Bob would have joined them, but Mr. Downey, the vice principle was standing at the front of the crowd, his arms raised, indicating that he wanted silence.

The room grew quiet and Mr. Downey began, "Germany, although she is our enemy, is not a country which can be whipped overnight." Some of the boys clapped. Mr. Downey raised a hand for silence and went on, "Saying so does not mean, that I am not a good American, I am an American, for many generations back. But, it is to warn you boys. You no doubt are going into this training with a free will. The war may last until you are of age to join the regular army. Our hope is to prepare you if that happens. Now, if there is anyone here who does not wish to join, there is the door." Mr. Downey pointed to the door at the rear of the gymnasium. There was some shuffling and a soft murmur, but nobody left. Mr. Downey continued to talk about the training. He explained that they would be issued uniforms at a cost of $6 and wooden guns that would be made by the manual training department.

Bob listened, and decided that Mr. Harding was right; he could do more for the war effort working at the shop, than by playing soldier. He rubbed the stubble on his chin with the back of his hand, took off his glasses, cleaned them on his shirtsleeve and put them on again. He felt grown-up in this crowd of younger boys. As Mr. Downey rambled on, Bob noticed a commotion among the boys directly in front of him. Bob focused his attention on what was being said among them.

"What's he doing here? Dirty German," a round faced blond boy said.

"Yeah, he shouldn't be allowed to join. He'll just spy on us," added a dark eyed boy. They were talking about a smaller boy with thick brown hair and steely blue eyes standing a short distance away, "Wilhelm, he's even named after the Kaiser."

The smaller boy turned, faced them and said defiantly, "My name's Will," and he quickly turned back around.

The blond boy whispering loudly, "Why'd they let the German kids in?" Mr. Downey noticed the commotion, and said, "Boys, we must have order," and continued with his long-winded speech. The boys were momentary distracted, and Will scooted past Bob and escaped out the side door of the gymnasium.

The other boys rushed after the fleeing Will.

Bob decided he'd heard enough of wooden guns and uniforms. *This is a waste of time,* he thought, *if I leave now, I can still get some work done at the shop.* He left the gymnasium using the same door as the other boys. The sun was bright and it took a moment for his eyes to adjust.

Bob noticed that the three boys had caught up with the boy named Will half way across the school yard and had him encircled. Will had his fists up and was ready to defend himself. The blond boy lunged at Will, but Will was quicker and dodged out of the way.

"Hey, leave him alone," Bob shouted as he approached.

"What's it to you?" said the dark eyed boy. "You his friend or something?" Then he added with a sneer, "Red."

Bob ran his right hand through his thick red hair and brought it down in a tight fist. He raised his left hand and sized up the three boys. They were all younger, but only slightly smaller.

Bob hadn't been in a fistfight since he'd left Beaver Dam. Will had shifted around so that he was standing a few feet away from Bob. His fists were still raised and his jaw was set defiantly. *I hope he's as tough as he looks,* Bob thought, *three against two is never good.*

At that moment, the blond boy lunged again, this time at Bob. Bob brought his fist up in a hard uppercut hitting the advancing boy under the chin and following through to catch him in the nose. The boys lunging momentum added force to Bob's punch. His blond hair flew up as his head went back. He stumbled backward and fell, blood gushing from his nose.

All four boys looked at Bob with surprise. A voice from near the school interrupted the fight, "Hey, you, boy's what's this all about?"

A large male teacher came running toward the group of boys. The teacher was able to grab Bob and Will by the arm, but the other boys escaped, the blond boy holding his hand over his bleeding nose.

"Will Schurz, what is the meaning of this?" the teacher said shaking Will.

"They started it. They ganged up on me. That's the truth. This fella, he saved me. It wasn't his fault at all or anything," Will said excitedly.

The teacher looked Bob in the eye and said, "Is that right?"

"Yes sir," Bob answered.

"You're not in school here, are you?" asked the teacher.

"No sir," Bob said. "I go to Eastern High."

"I see," The teacher said. "Well, save the fighting for the Germans. Did you get signed up for the training?"

"Um, no sir. I can't. I have a job," Bob answered.

"Too bad," the teacher said looking Bob over, he continued, "We may need boys like you over there in a couple of years. Well, if you're not here for the training, you're excused. Go home."

Bob was relieved. He thought he'd get in trouble for fighting, but seems being ready for a fight was popular these days.

"Wow, that was some punch," Will said.

"Thanks," Bob said absently. He looked at his sore knuckles. There was blood trickling down his finger. He must have cut it on the blond boy's teeth. He took out his handkerchief and wiped off the blood. Then he opened and closed his fist. It hurt, but didn't seem to be too bad. That done, he continued, "I think it was, well, mostly just a lucky shot."

"Did you see his head fly back and the blood squirt out his nose?" Will asked with a grin.

"Ah, yeah," Bob said sheepishly. He hadn't meant to give the boy a bloody nose, but well, he deserved it.

"He's the meanest boy in my class. I bet he leaves me alone now, now that I'm friends with you. My name's Will Schurz. What's your name?" Will asked.

"Bob Stevens," Bob answered. He hadn't really planned on befriending the lad. He just didn't think three against one was very fair. He continued, "Well, nice to meet you Will. I have to head to work now," and Bob started walking away.

Will fell into step next to Bob. "Where do you work?" Will asked.

"Um, at a shop down on Atwater," Bob said.

"Oh, great, I'm going that way too," Will said. "Mind if I walk with you?"

"Um, no, I guess not. You live over that way?" Bob asked. Resigned to the idea that he had a new friend, like it or not.

"My mom and I have a flat near Atwater," Will explained. "I'm not German, really, well, my Dad was German," Will hesitated, "he died a couple of years ago. My mom's French, but I was born right here in Detroit."

"Is your name really Wilhelm?" Bob asked as they walked down Mt. Elliott Street.

"Yeah, but my parents didn't know that the old Kaiser was going to start a war when they named me that. Actually, it's my granddad's name. I never met him though," Will lowered his voice, "I think he's still in Germany."

Bob smiled, *Will's more of an American than I am,* he thought. Bob was naturalized when his father took the oath and became a citizen. His mother wasn't a citizen yet, but she was studying for the citizenship test so she could take it next year.

As they approached the Harding Canvas Co. Bob said, "Well, this is where I work," he opened the door to go in-side, "See you around."

Henry spotted Bob standing at the door and hollered over the loud machinery, "Well, are you quitting, or staying?"

"Your pop's right," Bob hollered back, but Henry couldn't hear over the noise, and walked over to join Bob by the open door. They stepped outside and Henry asked, "How was the meeting?" Spotting Will, he added, "Who's he?"

"Oh, it was fine, but your pop was right I'll be more use-ful to the war effort working here than playing soldier with $6 uniforms and wooden guns," Bob said.

"Wooden guns?" Henry asked, raising his eyebrows.

"Yeah," Bob replied with a smirk, and remembering Will, added, "Oh, this is Will Schurz. Some kids were picking on him after the meeting, so I sort of helped him out." Bob didn't want to brag about the fight, but he kind of hoped Will would elaborate.

"Sort of helped me out," Will interrupted, "More like you saved my skin."

"Saved your skin, ah, tell me all about it," Henry prompted.

"Well, three of the boys in my class had me surrounded because I'm German, or they think I'm German because of my name, but I'm not, I'm American, and I could have licked one or maybe even two of them, but not three on one," Will paused for a breath. "But I didn't have to do a thing. Bob came up and Jack, that's the blond boy's name," Will explained to Bob, "Well, Jack lunged at Bob and you should have seen the hook Bob laid on him. Jack's head shot back and blood gushed out his nose. Show him you hand," Will said to Bob, "see, he cut his hand on Jack's weasel face." Will finished with a satisfied grin.

"You decked a kid? Really?" Henry asked Bob, impressed.

Bob held out his rapidly swelling knuckles and nodded in confident confirmation.

"Did you get caught?" Henry asked.

"Yeah, one of the junior high teachers got hold of Will and I, but didn't seem to care much about the fight. I guess, well, its military training after all," Bob answered with a grin.

"Wow, I wish I could have seen it," Henry said.

At that moment, Mr. Harding came out the door yelling, "Henry, what the . . . oh, here you are. They're waiting for the cloth you were supposed to be unloading."

"Oh, yeah, sure Pop," Henry said and hurried back inside.

Mr. Harding turned to Bob and asked, "Well, am I losing you?"

"No sir," Bob said. "I'd like to stay?"

"Great, great," Mr. Harding boomed. "Then what are we standing around for? There's work to be done. Henry could use some help unloading an order of cloth. It was late, and we need it upstairs ASAP."

"Yes sir," Bob said, smiling. He completely forgot that Will was still standing there.

"Excuse me sir, maybe I could help too?" Will said.

"Oh," Bob said, "um, Will, I don't think Mr. Harding . . ."

"Is Will a friend of yours?" Mr. Harding asked Bob.

"Um, well, sort of, we just met at the meeting," Bob said awkwardly.

"Well, I've been thinking about hiring a boy. Someone to do some of the sweeping up, fetching, that sort of thing. Kind of free up you bigger lads to do the heavier work," Mr. Harding said, he added, "Would you be interested, ah, Will, what's your last name?"

"Schurz, Sir," Will said tentatively.

"Nice to meet you Will Schurz," Mr. Harding said, holding out his hand. "The job's yours if you want it. Every day, after school for," Mr. Harding contemplated, "let's say two hours? You're not doing the military training?"

"No sir, I'm not doing the training, and yes sir, I would like the job very much," Will said, then added, "Wow, this is my lucky day. First Bob saves my life, and now I have a job."

Mr. Harding looked at Bob surprised.

Bob shrugged, and said, "I'd better go help Henry," and escaped inside leaving Will to explain.

APRIL 17 1917

THE DETROIT GAZETTE   EXTRA

— page One —   1 O'clock

SCHOOL TRAINING STARTS.

HOUSE-WIVES TO EXPERIENCE

WAR.   MEETING-IN-SCHOOL MANY SIGN UP.

JOYCE JUNIOR HIGH SCHOOL HAS MEETING TODAY
PRINCIPLE SPEAKS,

— BOYS TO TRAIN —

EXTRA   By P.R.Stevens

Joyce Junior High School Detroit:— Today after school over a hundred boys met in the largest room in the building and the principle Mr. Dorey addressed them

continued on Page Two

HOUSE WIVES TO EXPERIENCE WAR ALTHOUGH FAR FROM IT

EXTRA   By P.R.Stevens

Although the house wife of America is far from the horrors and dreads of the great world war, she will never last experience some of war's causes

Con. on Page 3

April 17, 1917
www.catherinepaonessa.com/thegazette

Over There
~ Bob Stevens

During the spring and summer of 1917 America adjusted to being a country at war, and Detroit stepped up to help. The factories heightened the manufacture of munitions, chapters of the Red Cross and Junior Red Cross, like the Eastern High Junior Reds, were formed. By July 3rd, the first wave of the American Expeditionary Force landed in France.

Detroiters began following the news of the war closely. In May, they celebrated when the Australians and British won the Second Battle of Bullecourt, but were disappointed when the Tenth Battle of the Isonzo between the Italians and the Austro-Hungarians ended in a stalemate. On maps, Detroiters located places like the Otranto Straits and Messines. In July, they were horrified by the reports of huge casualties at a place called Ypres. And everywhere, they heard the new, snappy song "Over There" by George M. Cohan.

When the school year ended, Bob and Henry started working full time at the Harding Canvas Co. Mr. Stevens was working overtime at Burroughs, and Mr. Robinson had a job at Selfridge Field, the new military airfield. Prof. Ackermann was back for the month of July, but soon disappeared again on another business trip.

In late June Mr. Harding called Henry and Bob into his office. His desk was covered with a large sheet of paper containing elaborate plans for what looked to be some sort of animal cage.

"What's up Pop?" Henry asked when he saw the plans.

"Pigeons," Mr. Harding replied.

"Pigeons?" Bob and Henry asked in union.

"What pigeons?" Henry continued.

'Well, let me tell you, I received a very interesting letter from my cousin Homer last week. I don't recall if you've ever met Homer," Mr. Harding said to Henry, he continued. "Homer has been recruited to join the Signal Enlisted Reserve Corps."

"Signal Corps, what's that?" Henry asked.

"He'll be working on communications for the army," Mr. Harding replied, "and Homer tells me they need pigeons, lots of pigeons. Seems the French and the British are using pigeons to carry messages."

"Wow, pigeons, really?" Bob said.

"Yes, sirree, the pigeons carry messages from the front lines back to army headquarters," Mr. Harding said, and with a flourish, he added. "So, we're going to raise pigeons and sell them to the army." Bob and Henry stared at Mr. Harding in disbelief.

This must be a joke. Bob thought.

But Mr. Harding continued, "These are the plans for the pigeon lofts. And starting today, you lads are going to build them on the roof."

Henry was looking at the plans more closely, "Yeah, I see," he pointed to a place on the plans, "these are the crates we have in the store room right?"

"Exactly," Mr. Harding replied, "and I ordered some chicken wire."

Henry was getting excited now, "They look like book shelves, or well, pigeon shelves."

Bob joined the discussion, "And the chicken wire goes here," he said pointing at the plans.

"How many pigeons are we getting?" Henry asked.

"Five," Mr. Harding answered.

"Five?" Henry said, disappointed, "This is kind of a lot of room for five birds."

"And 50 eggs," Mr. Harding continued.

"Eggs? We're getting pigeon eggs? What are we supposed to do with eggs?" Henry asked.

"Sit on them?" Bob said with a chuckle. Mr. Harding and Henry looked at him, not amused. "Sorry," Bob muttered.

"We'll start with them in a low crate on a bed of straw," Mr. Harding said. "The salesman assures me they will hatch within a week of delivery. He gave me this booklet. All the information we need is in here," Mr. Harding said, tapping the booklet with his index finger.

"Don't eggs have to be kept warm to hatch?" Henry asked.

"It's 90 degrees out so we should be all set during the day. We'll have to keep them out of the direct sun, maybe you can rig up a canvas awning," Mr. Harding replied.

"But what about at night, it gets cool at night," Henry said, concerned.

"That's one problem I haven't quite resolved yet," Mr. Harding said considering.

There was a moment of silence as they considered how to keep the eggs warm.

"Hot water bottles!" Bob said. "We could get lots of hot water bottles, fill them up and put them in the sun during the day, I bet they get really warm. Then we can move them under the eggs at night."

"Great idea Bob," Mr. Harding said, "that just might be the ticket."

Bob and Henry were busy the next couple of days building the pigeon loft on the roof of the Harding Canvas Co.

The loft was constructed of leftover pieces of shipping crates, scraps of wood and enclosed in chicken wire. They also built what they called a hatching table. Maggie, Jeannie and Sara stopped by with Nietzsche one evening to see the new loft.

"This is the hatching table," Bob said pointing to an odd-looking table with two top boards separated by a space of about 8 inches. The top was fitted with a five-inch frame around the edge.

"Why does it have that shelf underneath? If you put any eggs down there, you can't watch them hatch," Jeannie asked, concerned.

"Oh no, the eggs and some straw will go up here," Henry explained. "And this framing will keep the baby birds from falling off," he added pointing to the edge around the top of the table.

"Why did you put all those little holes in the top?" Maggie asked.

"The eggs and chicks have to be kept warm," Bob said. "The plan is to put hot water bottles in the sun during the day, then move them under here," he swiped his hand in the space between the two boards of the table, "in the evening. The heat from the water bottles will raise up through the holes and hopefully keep the hatching chicks warm."

"Oh, what a good idea," Maggie said.

"Ah, that was Bob's idea," Henry said, winking at Bob behind Maggie's back. Bob rolled his eyes at Henry. *Sometimes Henry could be such an idiot,* Bob thought.

Maggie smiled, and said, "I suppose the canvas awning will keep them from getting too hot during the day."

"Exactly," Henry said. "We've thought of everything."

Sara was standing by a small trap door in the side of the cage. It was rigged with a spring and snapped shut when she lifted it. "What's this little door for?" She asked.

"That's so the birds can get back into the loft when we take them out to train them, but they can't get out unless we let them out," Henry explained.

"Train them to do what?" Sara asked.

"Well, to come back home, to the loft," Bob said.

"Oh, you mean they don't have to live in this cage? They will get to fly around sometimes, oh, that's nice," Sara said.

"Sara, the pigeons aren't going to be pets," Maggie said. "Bob and Henry are going to raise them, and train them, then the pigeons will be sent to Europe to carry messages for the army."

Sara looked at Maggie. Her eyes were wide in disbelief. "You mean like little bird soldiers?" Sara asked, concerned.

"Yeah, I guess," Bob answered.

"How do they carry the messages? In their bills?" She asked.

"Ah, no, in little metal tubes strapped to their legs," Bob said.

Sara considered, then asked, "How long before they are big enough to go to the war?"

"We'll send them to the army in early September," Henry answered.

"Well, then, I guess, maybe, we shouldn't name them. I was trying to think up good bird names, but I guess I shouldn't bother," Sara said, disappointed. She rubbed Nietzsche's head and said, "Let's go. We promised Nietzsche a walk and all we're doing is looking at some dumb bird cages."

The Robinson girls left. Bob and Henry put the finishing touches on the loft. The eggs were scheduled to be delivered in the next day or two.

Bird Soldiers
~ Bob Stevens

Five adult pigeons and 50 eggs arrived a few days later. And, while the adult pigeons were easy to care for, the eggs were a different story. Bob and Henry placed them gently on the hatching table. The sun warmed them during the day, and the hot water bottles kept them warm at night. They started hatching in the morning, two days after they arrived. Bob and Henry had just released the adult pigeons and were moving the red rubber water bottles to be re-warmed by the sun when they noticed some movement in the straw. One of the eggs was wiggling back and forth, a small crack appeared in the smooth shell. The boys watched, amused.

"It's alive," Henry joked.

"This one too," Bob said, pointing at another egg with a crack in it.

"Pop will be happy. He made me come down here three times last evening to see if anything was happening," Henry said with a yawn.

"Look, that one's got a crack too, and this one and over here," Bob said, pointing to the hatching eggs.

"The guy Pop bought them from said they would all hatch at about the same time. I guess he was right," Henry said.

The boys watched as one egg, then another wiggled and cracks appeared. It was a slow process. Bob and Henry went back to work in the shop, checking on the eggs every hour or so. Damp heads and wings appeared. The "Beginners Guide to Pigeon Keeping" provided by the seller said it was especially important to keep the chicks warm, so Bob and Henry arranged canvas tarps around the hatching table to protect the bald chicks from any cool breezes. Fortunately, it was a hot, sunny day.

By late in the afternoon, some of the chicks had emerged completely from their shells.

"They're ugly little things," Henry said. "Especially those big, bulging eyes."

"Yeah, maybe they'll look better when the feathers dry off," Bob agreed.

"Maybe," Henry said, unconvinced.

"I promised Sara I'd let her come and see them hatch, will your pop mind if the Robinson girls come up here this evening." Bob asked.

"Oh, he won't mind, but be honest, you're just using Sara to get at Maggie, you want to share this 'touching moment' with her," Henry joked sarcastically.

"Yeah, right, nothing 'touching' about these ugly chicks," Bob replied, but he hoped Maggie would come anyway.

Henry looked at the pigeon chicks, most still half in their shells, some lying helplessly next to broken shells, he agreed, "Yeah, I guess you're right."

After dinner Bob, Henry, and the Robinson girls gathered in the pigeon loft. Henry had hung more tarps and lit a couple of can fires to keep the pigeons warm. It was a hot evening, so they were all sweltering as they looked at the hatching pigeons. Nietzsche was lying outside the hot loft panting as a soft breeze ruffled her fur.

"They're not very pretty," Sara said, disappointed.

"They're absolutely ugly," Jeannie said.

"How do you feed them?" Maggie asked.

"The book says they don't need to eat for the first day or so, but we have this powder," Henry showed her the can of Kaytee extract, "you mix this stuff with water and make pigeon milk."

"Pigeon milk?" Jeannie asked, eyebrows raised.

"Well, that's what they call it. It's not real milk though. It's powdered seeds I think," Bob explained.

"How do you get them to drink it?" Maggie asked.

"One of us will hold the chick, and the other will put this funnel in its mouth and pour in the milk," Henry explained, holding up a small funnel. "The pigeon book says they have to be fed three times a day for about three to four weeks, then they should be able to eat pigeon food like the adult birds. That's why Pop got the adult birds, so the chicks can learn to eat and fly and, well, act like pigeons by watching them."

Of the 50 eggs, 43 hatched, but of these, eight died in the first week. Bob, Henry and two men from the shop teamed up and took turns feeding the remaining 35 pigeons. The boys were quite happy when about four weeks later most the young pigeons began copying the adult pigeons and eating seeds and drinking water from a dish. Their fuzzy down had been replaced with regular feathers. They now looked like slightly smaller versions of the adult pigeons.

A Pigeon Named Peace
~ Maggie Robinson

To Maggie, the summer was flying by. She and Jeannie were quite busy with the Junior Reds. They organized fundraisers, knit socks for the soldiers and prepared Friendship boxes for children overseas. Maggie especially enjoyed working on the friendship boxes. She felt sorry for children living where the war was so close, so threatening and hoped that in some small way, the boxes helped them.

On a drizzly afternoon in early August, Maggie stopped by the Harding Canvas Co. to see how things were going with the pigeons and, she admitted to herself, to see Bob. He and Henry were so busy caring for the baby birds that

Maggie hadn't seen either of them in a couple of weeks. She missed her walks to school with Bob. She opened the shop door and peeked inside.   It was loud. Women were sitting at big sewing machines, heads bent, fingers moving quickly, guiding the canvas expertly past the quickly moving needles. Mr. Harding saw Maggie and waved her into his office.

"Hello, Miss Robinson," Mr. Harding said with a wide smile. "What can I do for you today? If it's a job you're looking for, I may be able to accommodate you.

"Oh, no sir," Maggie said, "I was hoping to see Henry and Bob and the baby pigeons."

"I see. Too bad, I'm having a devil of a time finding girls. I get one trained, and off she goes, either to a different position, or to get married." He continued, "I think the boys are on the roof. You can go on up."

On the roof, Maggie noticed that the wind had picked up and dark clouds were racing across the sky. They were in for a thunderstorm. She found Bob and Henry in the pigeon loft. Many of the baby birds were happily eating pigeon food that was spread on the floor. They wobbled round, flapping their wings awkwardly, falling over each other to get to the small greenish pellets.

"How's it going?" She asked. Bob was holding one of the birds while Henry inserted a funnel into its open beak and poured in a thick, white liquid.

"Hi," Bob said. Henry nodded.

"Wow, it must take a while to feed all these birds?" Maggie asked.

"You're telling us. I can't wait until these last five start eating the regular food," Bob answered.

Maggie picked up what looked like the smallest of the pigeons and stroked its soft feathers. "They look like the adults now, prettier than the babies I think," Maggie said.

"Yeah, there okay. Pigeons aren't my favorite," Henry said.

"Me either," Bob added, as he picked up the last bird to be fed and held it out for Henry to repeat the feeding procedure. "Especially after having to spend the last four weeks feeding this flock. We didn't think that one would make it," he added nodding toward the bird Maggie was petting.

"It smaller than the rest," Maggie said.

"Yeah, a runt I guess," Henry said.

"We thought you would be back with Sara and Jeannie to see the birds before this. I stopped by last week to see if any of you wanted to walk Nietzsche with me and your Mum said Sara was sick," Bob said. Maggie was disappointed she'd missed him, he added, "I think you were at a Junior Red thing."

"Sara's mostly better now," Maggie said absently, she thought, *He said, any of us, maybe he's just being neighborly.* She continued, "It was a pretty bad cold, and Mum gets so worried about her since last summer. Actually, that's kind of why I stopped by. Sara has been asking and asking about the birds. She wants to know if they got any prettier and if they can fly yet and, well, the questions are endless with her. So, I was wondering if I could well, borrow one for the evening."

"Yeah, sure," Henry said, "just don't feed it anything, if you do, it will get confused about where to fly back to, well, when it can fly."

"Oh, that makes sense," Maggie said. "How should I carry it home?"

Bob looked around, in the corner of the loft was a small cardboard box. "Here," he said, picking it up, "This will be fine." He took off the lid, looked around, found a screwdriver and punched some air holes in the lid. "There, a custom pigeon carrier."

Maggie smiled at him. The wind was rustling his red curls and his blue eyes sparkled behind his round glasses. Their eyes met, he smiled back. He was holding the box out for her to put the bird in. *Oh, God, I'm staring, what will he think?* Maggie thought. "Um," she said, holding up the small bird she'd been petting, "can I take this one?"

"Ah, yeah, sure," Bob said, looking at Henry to see if he agreed.

"Good choice," Henry chuckled, "maybe a little personal attention from some pretty girls is just what it needs."

"Well, great, ah, Sara will be so happy," Maggie said, embarrassed. She looked up at the threatening sky and added, "I better get going. I don't want to get caught in this storm."

She hoped Bob would offer to see her home, but he only said, "Good idea, we have to get these birds in the loft before it hits."

"Bye, and thanks," Maggie said, she held up the custom pigeon box, smiled, and added, "I'll drop it off tomorrow. About the same time?"

"Sure," Bob called. But he and Henry were already busy chasing the pigeons around the roof.

Maggie thought about Bob as she walked home. *Maybe he really was just being nice to us. Maybe he likes playing the part of the big brother, and isn't interested in me at all. Had he really tried to kiss me last fall? Or had I just imagined it? He hasn't tried again.* Maggie resolved that if Bob tried to kiss her again, she would kiss him back. *Other girls let boys kiss them, why shouldn't I.*

Maggie made it home just as big drops began to hit the sidewalk. She took the pigeon box into the kitchen. Sara and Mum were sitting at the kitchen table, Mum was peeling and slicing potatoes, Sara was layering them neatly in a baking dish with flour and small pats of butter. Jeannie was in a chair by the window knitting yet another pair of gray green socks for the soldiers.

"What's in the box?" Sara asked.

"A surprise," Maggie said with a smile.

"For me?" Sara asked.

"And Jeannie, but it's not for keeps, just too look at for tonight. We have to return it tomorrow," Maggie said. She lifted the lid of the box just wide enough for Sara to peek in. Maggie didn't want the pigeon to hop out onto the kitchen table. Mum would have a fit.

Sara gave a little gasp when she realized what was in the box, "Oh, is that one of the baby pigeons? It's so big," Sara said.

"Maggie, a pigeon, in my kitchen! Out, now!" Mum said.

"But, Mum, it's pouring out," Maggie pleaded. "Can't we keep it inside somewhere?"

"Absolutely not, now out, you'll stay dry enough on the porch," Mum said.

Sara, Maggie and Jeannie went to the front porch. Mum was right; a good portion of the porch was dry. Now Maggie took the lid off the box and the baby pigeon hopped out. It flapped its wings as if to indicate that the box had not been a comfortable place for a pigeon.

"Aaah, don't let it fly away," Sara screamed.

"It can't fly yet, at least I don't think it can," Maggie said, watching the pigeon carefully. "It's prettier now," Jeannie said.

"That's what I thought," Maggie said. "Oh, and Henry said we shouldn't feed it. If we do, it won't know where to 'go home' to when it starts to fly."

The girls watched as the pigeon flapped its wings and hopped around the porch. Maggie soon tired of the bird's antics and went into the kitchen to help Mum with dinner. She returned to the porch a half hour later and was surprised to see the pigeon eating seeds off the porch floor.

"Sara, Jeannie, I told you not to feed it," she scolded.

"We didn't," Sara said, "See those black-eyed susans, they've all gone to seed and some of the seeds fell on the porch and Peace just found them."

Maggie looked at the accused flowers, they seemed to be bent and broken and rather pulled through the porch rails, but she decided it wasn't worth arguing about. It was just a few seeds anyway.

"You named it Peace?" Maggie asked. "Don't get too attached to it, remember, it's going to be shipped over to Europe to carry messages for the army."

"Yeah, we know, that's why we named it Peace. So it will carry a message of peace to France," Jeannie said.

"And the war will end, and Sam will come home," Sara added.

Maggie smiled and said, "Good idea."

Ready for War?
~ *Bob Stevens*

It was a muggy afternoon in late August. To Bob and Henry's relief, all the pigeons had graduated to eating regular bird food. The boys took turns going to the roof to let the birds out for some exercise, scatter out bird food and refill the water basin as needed. It was Bob's turn. He enjoyed this break from the loud, busy shop and usually took the Detroit Free Press to read while he watched over the birds. He was greeted by a warm breeze as he emerged on the roof. He opened the loft and chuckled as the young pigeons hopped past his feet, flapping their wings and falling over each other to escape. The adult birds flew away as the chicks watched, Bob thought, with envy.

Bob sat down on a nearby crate and opened the newspaper. With one eye on the active pigeons, he read the front page. He was engrossed in the news of a battle at Isonzo, as one of the young birds hopped and flapped over to the edge of the roof. Bob looked up from the paper to see the bird give one final hop and flap up onto the short wall that surrounded the edge of the roof. Before Bob could jump from the crate and catch it, it hopped off the roof. Bob rushed to look over the edge expecting to see a dead pigeon on the sidewalk below, but instead, he saw the young pigeon flapping hard and landing awkwardly on the two-story building next door. Without warning, another pigeon hopped off the roof a few feet away. In a rush, Bob tried to corral the remaining birds back into the loft, two more flew away, but he was able to secure the rest of the pigeons behind the chicken wire of the loft. To his surprise, one of the birds that had flown off the roof landed next to him, cocked its head and eyed Bob as if to say, "Hey, let me in. Where's dinner?"

Bob picked up the adventuresome bird and put it in the loft with the others. He looked around and spotted two more of the pigeons on the roof next door. He decided to go tell Mr. Harding and Henry that the pigeons had started to fly, he gathered his newspaper that had blown around the roof in the excitement and headed downstairs. Within a few days, all pigeons were flying about with ease.

Over the next few weeks Bob and Henry started training the pigeons. They built three special carrying crates with hinged tops so the pigeons could be easily loaded and unloaded. To train the birds, they loaded them in the company truck and took them a short distance from the shop and let them go. The first time they released the birds, the pigeon Sara had named Peace surprised everyone, and showed up at the Robinson porch looking for dinner. It did this each time the birds were set free. The girls put out a box for Peace to sleep in, and Bob picked the bird up on his way to work each morning.

Besides Peace, only one of the birds did not return to the loft during the early training exercises. It was never seen again. After that, they all found their way home safely. Each week the boys increased the distance. During the last week of August and the first week of September they drove quite far, spending the most of the day in the truck.

Bob and Henry enjoyed these excursions. Henry knew the countryside around Detroit well. He spent many weekends in the fall hunting with his father in the farmland and woods that surrounded the city. They hunted deer, rabbits and grouse. Bob envied Henry. His own father's idea of a good weekend was sitting home with the newspaper, his pipe and a game of chess or checkers. Their family forays into the countryside centered on an occasional picnic or trip to the beach.

Bob was surprised on the last pigeon training trip, to see Henry load a rifle into the truck.

"What's the rifle for? Are we going to go hunting too?" Bob asked, hopefully.

"It's a shotgun, but no, Pop thought it would be a good idea if we made some noise when we released the birds, you know, get them used to it," Henry replied, then added, "but now that you mention it, we could try for a rabbit or two."

"What about a deer?" Bob asked.

"No, deer season isn't until November," Henry said with a sigh, "I'll go ask Pop if we can do a little rabbit hunting though." And he headed back inside. He returned with a smile and another shotgun. "Pop said that was fine. We're going to release birds at three different spots this time. Pop knows lots of the farmers out Woodward Avenue way. Mr. Jenkins was complaining about the rabbits eating up his vegetable garden, so we'll go there last see if we can help him out by shooting a few rabbits."

"But, doesn't he want to shoot and, um, well, eat his own rabbits?" Bob asked.

"Oh, no, you can only eat so much rabbit you know, now, venison, that's another story, some farmers charge hunters to hunt deer in their fields," Henry explained.

They started the truck and headed off. They drove out Woodward Avenue and soon the shops and factories gave way to rolling farms and patches of woods. They turned down a rough dirt road between two cornfields. Once they were a short distance into the open field, they stopped. They unloaded a crate of birds and Henry got one of the shotguns from the back of the truck.

"The trick will be not to shoot the darn pigeons," Henry said with a sarcastic laugh, "Pop will shoot me if I do that."

He retrieved a tin of shells from the truck and Bob watched as Henry showed him how to load the shotgun.

"First, you crack open the chamber," Henry said as he broke open the gun, then he inserted a shell and closed the chamber.

"Is that it?" Bob asked, surprised at how easy it was.

'Yeah, but you have to remember to always point the gun so you don't shoot anyone, especially, like me," Henry said. "Now, when I say go, you open the crate, and I'll shoot. Let's yell too, give them the whole treatment."

Henry aimed the gun away from where the pigeons would emerge from the crate, braced his feet and yelled, "Go!"

Bob flipped open the crate, and Henry pulled the trigger. The shotgun went off with a load bang. The intensity of the shot startled Bob and for a moment, he forgot to yell. Then both he and Henry where yelling at the birds and waving their arms. The pigeons flew off, and were soon high overhead. The noise from the shotgun and boys yelling didn't seem to disturb them.

They repeated this process at a farm a couple of miles away. Only this time, Henry handed the shotgun to Bob.

"Here, your turn," Henry said.

Bob tried to crack open the gun. He discovered it was harder than he expected and tried again with more force. The shotgun hinge gave way and the chamber was revealed. Henry handed him a shell. Bob turned it in his fingers, trying to determine the front from the back.

"The primer goes toward the back." Henry said, pointing at the end of the shell. Bob loaded the shell, closed the chamber, widened his stance and braced his feet as Henry had done. Henry took hold of the lid of the crate. "Say go when you're ready."

"Go!" Bob yelled. He pulled the trigger, the gun fired and hit him hard in the shoulder. Henry opened the crate and the boys yelled as the birds took off. Bob handed the shotgun back to Henry and rubbed his aching shoulder.

"Oh, sorry, I forgot to warn you about the kick," Henry said. "You should hold the butt tight, like this," Henry demonstrated holding the butt of the gun up against his shoulder, "then the kick won't hurt."

"Thanks," Bob groaned, thinking that piece of information was a little late.

"Oh, it'll be fine in a day or so," Henry chuckled. They climbed back into the truck and headed off again.

"Mr. Jenkins farm is about four miles up the road," Henry said.

"That's the guy with too many rabbits?" Bob asked.

"Yeah, we'll see if we have any luck. We should have brought Nietzsche along to flush the rabbits," Henry said.

They sat in silence for a minute or so, then Bob said, "You've shot lots of things, I mean, deer and rabbits?"

"Yeah, well, one deer, when I was 13, but I lost count of the rabbits," Henry answered.

"Do you think you could shoot a German, you know, if the war's still going and we go?" Bob asked.

"Yeah, I suppose, if it was him or me, sure," Henry answered. "What about you?"

"Yeah, me too. Will you enlist when you turn eighteen?" Bob asked.

"Probably, what about you?" Henry asked.

"I think so, I'll be 18 next June, so, well, it's coming up kind of quick," Bob said.

"Wow, yeah, next June, wow," Henry said, then fell silent. They traveled without talking for a few minutes. Bob became mesmerized in the fields of corn rustling in the breeze, his thoughts far away, on a battlefield in Europe. He was startled when Henry said excitedly, "Hey, I have a great idea. You could wait, you know, to join up. I'll be eighteen in October next year. We can enlist together. Go over together."

"That might work," Bob said slowly, thinking, *will people think I'm a slacker if I don't sign up as soon as I'm eligible.* But he added, "Yeah, that's a good plan, we should go together."

When they got to the Jenkins farm, they released the last of the pigeons and spent the rest of the day hunting.

When it became apparent that they weren't going to have any luck without a dog, they set a tin can on a stump and practiced shooting at it. They also practiced shooting at chunks of dirt and clay. The sun was setting when they pulled into the shop. They found Mr. Harding on the roof.

"Well boys, any luck with the rabbits?" Mr. Harding asked.

"No," Henry said, "It's kind of hard without a dog. Did all the pigeons make it back?"

"Yep, all accept one, and we know where it is. By the way, I talked to the army guy. We're shipping them out day after tomorrow. To be honest, I'll be glad to be rid of them. Look at this mess," Mr. Harding said waving has hand over the bird droppings covering the roof.

"Are you going to get more eggs?" Bob asked.

"No, the whole venture wasn't as lucrative as I'd hoped. In fact, once I add in the shipping costs, and the cost of paying you boys to go hunting, I may end up losing money," Mr. Harding said, then he added, "At least we're doing our part to support the war effort. Oh, and the day after these birds are shipped out, you boys can clean up this roof."

It was well after suppertime when Bob got home. There was a note on the kitchen table from Mother. She was at a Red Cross meeting and his dinner was on the stove. He lifted the pot lid and took a deep sniff. The stew smelled good, but he wasn't hungry. The day had grown hot and muggy, too hot to eat stew. He went to his room. It had been a great day, but his shoulder ached, he was hot and tired and he couldn't stop thinking about what he and Henry had talked about. About actually shooting a German. He'd always said, thought, he would be able to, but, he wasn't sure anymore. Not after firing a real gun. Feeling the power of it, hearing the blast, seeing the destruction it caused. He'd even shot at a couple of rabbits, but missed. He questioned himself, *did I miss on purpose? Maybe. Maybe, I'm a coward? Will I be able to kill a man, if I have to, I can't even kill a stupid rabbit?* The more he thought about it, the more disgusted with himself he became.

A warm breeze blew in from the open window and fluttered the papers on his desk. He picked up the latest newspaper he'd been working on. If Aunty McLeod didn't want to send them to Davy, he would have quit long ago. He knew he wasn't going to be a war correspondent. But he couldn't think of anything else to do after graduation, every plan for the future, every idea ended with *but if we're still at war.* So, he held onto his war correspondent dreams.

He tried to conjure up his favorite daydream. Tried to escape in it, he thought, *I am a war correspondent, and Sam has been captured by the Germans. I use my connections to discover his location and help orchestrate his escape. And then Maggie will, will. . .* But it wasn't working, he wouldn't be a war correspondent, and he wouldn't want Sam to be captured, and Maggie would see him as he really was, a slacker and a coward.

He flung the paper back on the desk, and looked out the window. A storm was coming. Lighting danced in the distance and the low rumble of thunder filled the room. *Good,* he thought. He lay down on his bed, took off his glasses wiped them on his shirtsleeve, and tossed them on his desk.

He closed his eyes, and let the cool breeze of the storm wash over him. It blew in the drapes and ruffled his sweaty hair.

He thought about Maggie. He loved her, and not like a brother, and not a silly boyish crush, but he really loved her. He ached when he thought she was hurting and was thrilled when she smiled at him. *This is the real thing,* he thought, *I'm seventeen, that's old enough, but did she, could she. . .* He thought about lifting the strand of moist hair from her check when she'd been crying, about letting it curl around his finger, about its chestnut brown color that was so beautiful in the sunlight. He thought about leaning in and kissing her, about her kissing him back, about her white shirt with the small buttons, about his fingers fumbling with the buttons as they kissed. . . He jumped up from the bed. Rain was pounding on the roof and splashing in the window. He slammed it, and paced the three steps it took him to cross his room. He paced back, then he rushed down the stairs, out the back door and into the dark yard. He lifted his face to the rain, let it run down his neck and arms. He escaped in the sound of the thunder. He wouldn't tell her, he couldn't. Not until after the war was over. The war. Everything was on hold until after the damn war.

Goodbye Peace
~ Bob Stevens

Maggie returned Peace on the day the pigeons were to be shipped east. When she entered the loft, Bob and Henry were loading the last of the birds into the crates.

"Oh, good," Henry said when Maggie opened the door to the roof. "The truck is almost loaded and ready to leave for the train station. Put that one in the last crate." He picked up one of the crates and as Maggie held the door for him he headed down the narrow stairs.

"Hi," Maggie said to Bob, "Henry's in kind of a hurry."

"Yeah, he doesn't want to miss the train. But, I think there's plenty of time, he's really just ready to be rid of these birds," Bob said.

"Oh," Maggie said, "I hope I didn't cause you to be late."

"No, really, like I said, we have plenty of time," Bob said. *God, she's beautiful,* he thought.

Maggie took Peace out of its little box and stroked its breast. She whispered something about Sam in its ear, and her eyes moistened. She handed the bird to Bob and even though the chill of the September morning had past, she shivered. Bob put Peace in the crate and picked up the jacket that he had set aside earlier. He put it over Maggie's shoulders. He was standing directly in front of her. His hands lingered on her shoulders for half a second. It would be so easy to pull her toward him. A single tear escaped Maggie's eye and ran down her flushed cheek. *No,* Bob thought, as he pulled away. *I can't tell her, can't let her know. If she cares for me at all, it will only add to her misery when I enlist.*

Bob picked up the remaining crate and said in a hoarse voice, "Can you get the door for me?"

"Oh, yeah," Maggie said. She took Bob's jacket from her shoulders, laid it on the hatching table, opened the roof door and followed him down the stairs.

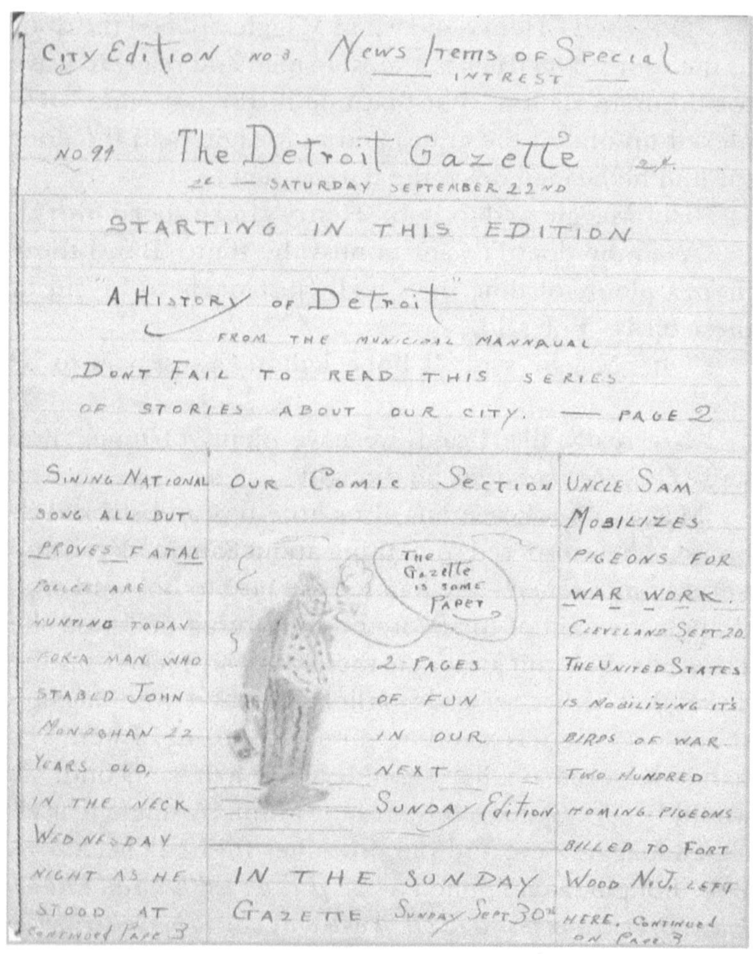

September 22, 1917
www.catherinepaonessa.com/thegazette

A Red Scarf
~ Aunty McLeod

Aunty McLeod sat in her backyard on a warm September afternoon. It had been a busy summer, with Red Cross meetings, and knitting for the soldiers. She was proud of her adopted country and city. She had her writing box on her lap, pen in hand and a blank piece of paper in front of her. She sighed, but was hopeful. Americans were an industrious lot, maybe, just maybe, she could out live this terrible war and, God willing, see Davy again. She wrote:

> My Dear Davy,
>
> I hope everything is going well. Your last letter was quite interesting, and I was happy to hear that you were away from the front, even if it was just a temporary leave. I don't know about this sniper business they're training you for, but I am sure you will be good at it.
>
> Here in Detroit, everyone is doing what they can to put an end to this terrible war. Yesterday Bob stopped by to drop off the enclosed newspaper and told me about the pigeons they are raising to send over to the front. Pigeons, imagine that. They use carrier pigeons to send messages around the battlefield. Bob told me the pigeons are quite clever at it and manage to deliver most of their messages and return to their home bases. I feel sorry for the poor birds, flying around among the dropping bombs and shooting bullets, and, then I remember that you

are among the same bombs and bullets. Not a fit place for boy or bird – seems to me. If you see any of the pigeons, and if you have a few breadcrumbs to spare, maybe you could throw them out to them.

Speaking of birds, I'm sitting in my yard at the moment listening to the chatter of the birds. They are flocking together, getting ready for the long flight south for the coming winter. Except the cardinals, pretty red birds with a very majestic crest. The cardinals stay and keep me company through the long winter months. I sprinkle crumbs out my back window and sit and watch them. Their bright red feathers shine against the white snow. But not yet, today it is sunny and warm still. The seasons in Detroit are changeable, unpredictable and beautiful. I love each passing one.

Take good care of yourself. The ladies of the Red Cross are busy knitting for all of you soldiers, but I've include a pair of socks and scarf that I made especially for you. They're the horrible grey green color recommended by the Red Cross, but the yarn I selected especially for you. They will be both warm and soft. Next year, God willing, the war will be over, and I'll knit you a bright red scarf, just like my cardinal friends.

Stay safe, Love Always,
Nana

P.s. Red socks might be a little much, but if you want some I'll make them as well.

CHAPTER 14

Fritz
~ Davy McLeod

The bombardment had started a couple of hours ago. The ground shook below him. Davy was flat on his stomach in a low depression in no man's land. Through the high-powered scope on his rifle, he could see Fritz. That's what Davy and Jamie named him, the German sniper that was harassing the British trenches in this sector. Fritz had already killed three British soldiers, and Davy and Jamie had been called in to find him, and deal with him, before the pending attack. Davy watched through the scope, but Fritz was good, and it had only been in the last 15 minutes that he and Jamie were able to find his hiding spot.

It was an excellent spot, a crater, with a large tree stump next to it. Fritz was firing through openings in the turned up roots of the stump. But Fritz had given himself away, maybe it was the noise of the bombardment, maybe he was tired, or over confident, but he finally made, what might be, a fatal mistake. As Jamie watched the enemy trench through his periscope, Davy had slowly raised a dummy head. He had placed a lit cigarette in the dummy's mouth hoping Fritz would spot the glowing end and take a shot. It worked, a direct hit. They then used the technique they learned in sniper training to figure out where the bullet had come from, where Fritz was hiding. It was imperative that Fritz be taken out before the attack. He was in a perfect position to hit the British soldiers as they emerged from the trench. He would be able to kill quite a few men before he himself was overrun.

Now, in an effort to get a shot at him, Davy had crawled out into no man's land, inching his way slowly to the left of Fritz. Davy looked through his scope, Fritz was about 250 yards away, not really that far with this rifle. He could see bits and pieces of Fritz through the tangled roots of the stump. Davy watched him carefully. Fritz could shoot from his cage of tree roots without exposing himself. But, Davy also knew that with his own high-powered rifle and scope, he could pigeon hole a shot right between the roots. He watched, relaxed his breathing, finger on the trigger, waiting for Fritz's face or neck to appear in a hole in the roots. *Come on you bastard,* Davy thought, *just a bit to the left, move your head, lower your chin, that's it, just a little more,* and he gently squeezed the trigger. Davy saw Fritz's body fall back.

The attack started before Davy could return to the trench. He stayed flat on his stomach as the soldiers of his battalion came over the top and ran forward. *Bloody hell*, Davy thought, afraid of being hit as they approached. As the attackers passed his location, he got up and joined them. No man's land was filled with fury. The glare of the July sun was softened by smoke and dust that hung in the air, making it difficult to see.

As Davy ran forward, the gap between him and the German trench closed. But the main part of the battle seemed to be shifting toward the south. Davy jumped into a crater, a large tangle of branches loomed over him, and he realized where he was. This was Fritz's hiding spot. The smoke was clearing. Davy's heart was pounding. And, there he was, Fritz. At first Davy thought he was still alive, but no, his face showed the pale, lost expression of death. Davy had seen the face of death before, but never of someone he'd shot. Fritz was on his back. His eyes open, staring up at the sun. He was young, about the same age as Davy. He hadn't died instantly. The shot had hit him in the neck. *A shot in the head would have been better,* Davy thought, *sorry about that chap.* As he lay there dying, Fritz had taken his wallet from his pocket. He had taken out some photographs. The photographs were lying next to him. Davy picked them up as they fluttered in the breeze. There was an older couple, thin and sad looking. *Fritz's parents,* Davy thought. And a family photograph, two girls and a young boy. *Fritz's family.* The brother was holding the collar of a dog, one of the sisters was moving, and her face was a blur. The last photograph was of a pretty, smiling girl. *A sweetheart,* Davy thought. The sweetheart photograph had a bloody thumb print on it. Davy's hands shook as he fingered through the photographs again, for a moment, he thought about putting them in his pocket. *No*, Davy thought, *these photographs need to be with him when someone finds him. So the parents, and the brother and sisters, and the sweetheart know that he still had them, in the end had looked at them.* Davy tried to wipe the bloody prints off as best he could. He put the photographs in the wallet, and tucked the wallet into Fritz's jacket pocket. *I should say something, a prayer or something,* Davy thought. He closed the dead German's eyes and tried to think of a prayer, *Bless this food to our use, no…, bloody hell, years of Sunday school, and that's all I can think of,* Davy thought, *sorry chap, but I guess, it was me or you.*

"Davy," Jamie's voice startled him, "Is he dead? We're moving south, the German's have moved to fortify the trenches down there." Jamie held out his hand to help Davy out of the crater.

Davy took it and said, "Yeah, Fritz is gone."

Killing Dreams
~ Davy McLeod

Davy was sitting on the fire step, head against the wall of the parapet, fast asleep. The battle had been raging for weeks. He and Jamie had been moving up and down the trenches, playing cat and mouse with German snipers. Sometimes Davy felt like the cat, in control, stalking, lethal and sometimes like the mouse, lost and small.

He slept when he could, but even when the guns were relatively quiet and the battle was being fought further up or down the line, his sleep was interrupted by a recurring dream. It wasn't the falling dream of his youth, but it was more terrifying. It was always the same, well almost. In the dream, he was sitting at a table, as if he was waiting for his dinner, but instead of a plate of food, a bloody hand would set photographs before him, one on top of the other. First came the photograph of Fritz's sad parents, then Fritz's family, the blurry girl and the boy with the dog. The sweetheart photograph was next. Always the same, the same photographs, the same faces, the same bloody fingerprint. But, in the weeks since Davy had shot Fritz, more photographs were added. As he killed more Germans, the photographs of their loved ones would appear on the pile. Even though he hadn't come upon their bodies, or seen any of their photographs, in his dream, the pile grew bigger. Two small girls in pretty dresses, someone's daughters? A soldier in a German uniform, maybe a brother? A very old woman with deep wrinkles and sparkling eyes, a grandmother? A happy, girl in a fancy hat, another sweetheart?

He would try to push the photographs away, but the bloody hand wouldn't let him. Finally, in terror and frustration he would overturn the table, the photographs would fly up and float down around him and he would wake with a start.

Davy opened his eyes. Gavin was coming down the trench toward him.

"You look like hell," Gavin said. "When was the last time you had a little R&R?"

"I don't remember," Davy signed. "Everyone seems to need an experienced sniper these days, I can't imagine why."

"Well, you're too good. Words got out and they keep asking for you. By the way, do you keep count? Some of the fella's keep count you know." Gavin said.

"Count?" Davy asked confused, thinking Gavin was referring to the photographs in his dream, but he hadn't told Gavin, or anyone, about the dream. Then it dawned on him, Gavin was talking about kills, "No, I don't keep count," he added despondently, "why?"

"Some of the blokes have a wager going, which sniper will have the most by the first of August," Gavin said. He continued, "I'd put my money on you."

"Well, I don't keep count, I don't want to know, I'm just doing my job," Davy snapped, angrily.

"I guess it's kind of morbid, but this isn't really the place for the high and mighty," Gavin replied, but he continued quietly, "Forget I mentioned it, it's a stupid thing to do anyway." He looked at Davy, and Davy could see the strain in Gavin's eyes. *Maybe betting on sniper kills was Gavin's way of dealing with this living hell, might beat dreaming of dead sniper's photographs*, Davy thought.

"Never mind, I'm just tired out," Davy said, sorry he'd gotten so mad.

"I'll see if I can get you some R&R. You won't be any good to anyone if you don't get a rest." Gavin said. "In the meantime, let's go see if we can get some dinner."

Rain

~ Davy McLeod

Rain, rain and more rain. The rain never seemed to stop during the summer of 1917. It rained on the British, it rained on the French and it rained on the Germans in equal measure. And everyone was equally miserable. The trenches were muddy and an infestation of rats added to the wretchedness. Sniper teams were in high demand that summer. Davy and Jamie stayed on the front lines while the rest of their unit was rotated out to R&R. Since coming to France in March of 1916, their unit had not received a home leave. As the wet summer faded into fall, they were done with war, but the war went on.

In mid-October 1917, Davy, Jamie, Mac and Gavin found themselves in the same little garden they had gathered in over a year ago. The fountain with the statue of the two fat children had fallen over and the chubby limbs of the children were broken and lost. Weeds covered much of the original stone path, so that it was difficult to know where it had been. Actually, it was difficult to tell there had once been a garden there at all.

Davy, Jamie, and Mac had shaved when they first arrived on leave five days ago, but not since. It didn't seem worth the trouble. Gavin still had his thick, red beard. Their eyes were red from the rank air in the trenches, and they all looked thin and tired. Davy sat on a low wall, his boots on the edge of the fountain. He looked up as a cloud swept past the sun, taking the little warmth it had to offer. He shivered. A group of birds flew over and Davy envied them, wondering where they were headed. He heard the motor of an airplane and waited until it appeared above them. Airplanes were much more common now, and the photographs they took were used to track German activity.

Like the last time they sat in this garden, they were reading their mail. Mac's voice interrupted Davy's thoughts.

"Millie's back in England with her parents," he said, as he folded up his letter, put it in his pocket and took out a cigarette. "I'm mighty glad of it too. After her brother was killed, her parents couldn't bear having her over here."

"So, are you going to marry her? After the war I mean," Gavin asked with a grin.

"Actually, I asked her before she left," Mac said with a sly smile.

"And, did she say yes?" Davy asked, surprised but pleased. *Maybe something good can come out of this miserable war after all*, Davy thought.

"She did," Mac said, grinning from ear to ear.

"Well, congratulations," Davy exclaimed, jumping up and shaking Mac's hand. Jamie and Gavin added their congratulations, shaking Mac's hand and pounding him on the back. Davy continued, "Why didn't you tell us?"

"I didn't want to jinx it. Me on the front line, and her on a ship in the English Channel, but, well, we're both still alive, and I'm the luckiest fella in the world. We may even get married before the end of the war. Rumor has it that we're getting two weeks home leave." Mac said, then he asked Gavin, "Do you know if that's true?"

"That's what I've heard," he answered, "new army regulations came out about home leave. Seems they want to improve morale after the rebellion problems the French had this summer, and because we haven't had home leave since coming over, well, we're all due at the same time. There was some sort of mix up, we were supposed to go in stages starting last month, but now it looks like we'll all be going together."

"Great, you can all come to the wedding," Mac said.

They were quiet for a few minutes, lost in the thought of being home. Davy wondered if it was a good idea, would being home, even for a short break, make being here even harder.

Jamie was the first to break the silence, "I haven't written Nora about it, I didn't want to get her hopes up if it doesn't happen." But he held out the letter he was reading and added, "She'll be excited to have me home for a bit. She keeps hinting about starting a family."

"Lucky you," Gavin said.

"Well, a fella's gotta do what a fella's gotta do," Jamie said with a grin, "you know, for King and Country. Someone has to replace the Englishmen that have been lost in this war."

Davy was reading a letter from his mother and his expression caused Jamie to nudge him with the toe of his boot and ask, "Is everything okay at home?"

"Yeah, I guess." Davy answered still engrossed in the letter.

Dear Davy,

I hope you are doing well. We are fine here. We've heard rumors that you boys will be coming home on leave? Is it true? I hope so. I can't wait to see you. You have been away too long. Maybe now that the Americans are there, the war will finally come to an end.

I have some news. Craig and I have decided to leave Scotland and move to Australia. Craig has had it with the mine. His brother went out to Australia before the war, he's been working on a station, that's the Australian word for cattle farm, learning the business and saving up his money. Now, he has a chance to buy a station, and he asked if Craig wants to go in on it. We've sent him the money and everything is in the works. We want you to come. We want you to be part of the whole thing. Help us manage it. Won't that be wonderful? I hear the country is beautiful in a wild way. Craig's brother said it reminds him of Scotland, fancy that. Please think about it. I hope to see you soon.

Love, Mum

"Jeepers, a cattle station, in Australia," Davy said when he finished reading, "My mum and step da are moving to a cattle station and she wants me to come there after the war."

"Wow, do you think you'll go?" Gavin asked.

"I don't rightly know, never even considered it. I hate mining though, so it would be something different. I'm a pretty good sniper, but I don't figure there will much need for snipers after the war." Davy said with a shrugged. He didn't want to discuss the future. It bothered him that he didn't have a plan, but he couldn't think of a time beyond the war. Mac and Jamie had something, someone to plan for. Gavin had always lived in the moment, even when they were kids. He accepted life as it was dealt to him.

Davy folded up the letter and stuffed it in his pocket. He opened the package from Nana. It contained hand-made gray, green socks and a matching scarf. There was also a newspaper and a letter. He held the scarf up to his nose and took a deep breath. He wondered if Detroit had a unique smell. Mac reached over and felt the soft wool. "Now, that's not your regulation army stuff, not even stan-dard store bought, that's quality yarn," he said.

"My Nana knows what a soldier needs," Davy said with a smile. He wrapped the scarf around his neck, passed the newspaper to Mac and read the letter. "She says her neigh-bor, Bob, the chap who writes the newspaper, has been rais-ing pigeons for the war."

"I didn't know the U.S. used pigeons too," Mac said

"I hope they can keep them all straight." Gavin added with a laugh, "Wouldn't want our British pigeons co-min-gling with those American ones."

"There's an article about it in the newspaper," Mac said. Jamie leaned over to get a look at the newspaper.

Davy thought about the birds he'd seen earlier, maybe there weren't free after all. He continued reading, and smiled at the phrase, 'Not a fit place for boy or bird'. She still thought of him as a boy, he didn't fell much like a boy anymore, in fact, he felt old, much older than his 21 years. *Does she really want me to come to Detroit*, Davy thought, *does she realize I'm not the young boy that wrote her letters so long ago? I don't even know where that boy is anymore.*

The clouds thickened and it started to rain, again. They took cover back in the Nissen hut that was home while they were on R&R. The drumming of the rain on the steel roof was loud and steady. Jamie sat down to write a letter to Nora, anxious to tell her about the upcoming leave. Mac and Gavin got up a game of poker with some of the other chaps in the platoon, and Davy dozed using the soft, warm scarf as a pillow. As he drifted off, he thought he could smell the sweet, warm scent of shortbread.

CHAPTER 15

Promises and Secrets
~ Bob Stevens

Bob, Maggie and Henry started their junior year in the fall of 1917. Bob and Henry went back to working part time at the shop. Bob resumed working on the school magazine, *The Eastern.* Henry joined the football team. And Maggie signed up for the advanced science and mathematics courses. After sailing through her classes last year, the teachers didn't question her course choices again. Bob was especially happy when Maggie suggested meeting at 'their corner' to walk to school together. Everything and nothing was the same. The country was at war, and war cast a long shadow.

"Did you hear that Dan Parker enlisted," Maggie asked. It was the third day of classes. Gossip on the first few days revolved around who, from last year's graduating class, had enlisted and who had not.

"Yeah," Bob said. "Did you know his older brother is already overseas?"

"His poor family," Maggie sighed. "I can't decide if I should be happy when I hear about the boys enlisting, or not. Part of me doesn't want anyone to go, but part of me wants everyone to go and just, well, just put an end to it once and for all. To be honest, sometimes I want to go myself."

Bob almost chuckled, but thought better of it. Maggie was determined and smart; she would be a good soldier. He said honestly, "I think you'd be a great soldier." He looked down at her and smiled.

"Oh, you're just saying that so I don't get mad. I would be a terrible soldier. I would talk too much and ask too many questions. The captain would say, 'Fire', and I would say 'Well, should I fire high or low, and why are we always marching around, and couldn't we save a lot of time and trouble if we just invited those fella's on the other side of no-mans-land over for a spot of tea," Maggie said with a laugh. "Maybe we should send Aunty McLeod over to the front with tea and her famous shortbread cookies."

Bob rubbed the stubble on his chin, pretended to be contemplating a serious matter, and said, "Mr. President, I think we have found a perfect weapon – tea and shortbread."

They both laughed. Then Bob said, "Some of the lads were talking about enlisting before graduation, as soon as they turn eighteen."

"Oh, they shouldn't do that," Maggie said, "They should at least finish high school."

"Well, I don't know, will Latin, mathematics and composition help them fight a war?" Bob asked.

"But maybe if they finish high school, they'll fight it a little smarter," Maggie said, then she thought for a moment, grew quiet, stopped walking and turned to face Bob. "You'll be eighteen next summer won't you? Before we start our senior year? But you can't, you won't, tell me, promise me, you won't sign up then." She had grown quite pale.

Bob looked into her eyes and promised, "I can promise that I won't sign up as soon as I turn eighteen, but, I can't make any promises beyond that, I just haven't decided yet." *Is her concern for a brother, or something more,* he wondered?

Maggie turned and started walking again, then she said quietly, "Well, that's something, I guess. Maybe this dreadful war will be over before you have to decide."

Winter came early that year. Fuel shortages and harsh winter weather, forced most people to stay close to home for the holidays. Bob, Jeannie and Sara published a large Christmas edition of the newspaper. Jeannie and Sara added lots of pictures. They even got articles from Mother and Aunty McLeod. Bob's Aunt Marion sent a story all the way from Nova Scotia.

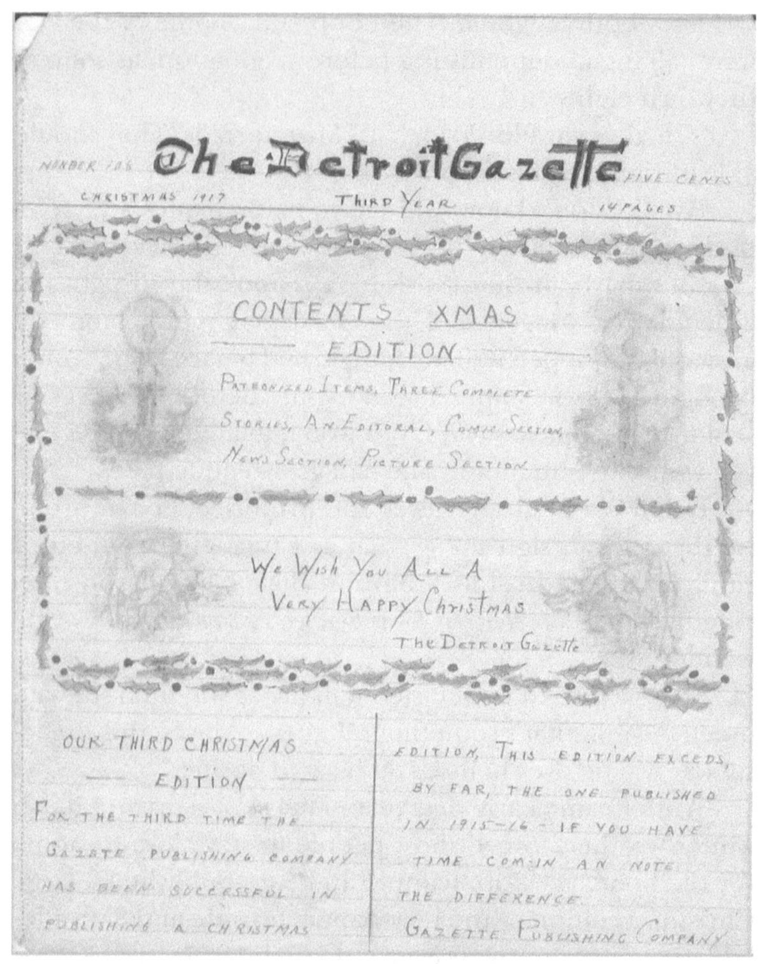

December 25, 1917
www.catherinepaonessa.com/thegazette

The cold weather only worsened during January and February. Coal shortages forced the schools and factories to close for a few weeks in February. Bob took advantage of this unexpected vacation to catch up on schoolwork, work on the newspaper and have some fun. He, Henry and the Robinson girls braved the cold and went sledding and skating. One afternoon, Henry invited them to the ice boat races on Lake St. Clair. He picked them up at Bob's house in the Detroit Electric.

"I've never seen an ice boat?" Jeannie said as she, Maggie and Sara snuggled in the back seat of the car. Nietzsche was on the floor at their feet, keeping their toes toasty warm.

"Me either," Maggie said. "Do they go fast?"

"I guess it depends on the wind, and the ice, the newspapers said 35 mph." Henry said.

"Gosh, that's as fast as a car," Sara said as they sped down Jefferson Avenue. She was looking out the window, trying to get her eyes to focus on the buildings as they flew by.

They pulled over along the lake, and were surprised at the large crowd gathered on the ice. Cars motored up and down, people were walking and skating. A ramp had been constructed for cars to drive easily from the road to the lake.

"Well, what do you think ladies? Do you trust it?" Henry said, looking at the frozen lake.

"It's your car, well, your pop's car," Bob said.

"But it's our lives," Jeannie said nervously.

Henry chuckled, turned the car onto the ramp and said, "Well, if we go through, swim!" In a few seconds, they felt the car leave the wooden ramp and slip onto the frozen lake. Sara giggled. They opened the windows and looked out at the ice and snow speeding under the tires. After a few minutes, they came to a spot that looked like a parking lot. The ice was clearer beyond this point and seemed to be reserved for the iceboats. Henry stopped the car, they flung open the doors and Nietzsche bounded out. She hit the ice on all fours, but her paws didn't catch. Her legs slipped in every direction, she fell, got up, slipped again, but managed to stay up this time. She looked over at Bob as if to say, *Funny, let's see you walk on this.* The rest of them got gingerly out of the car.

Bob walked over to Nietzsche, petted her on the head and said, "Sorry girl, I should have warned you."

They all walked over to where a sort of track had been set up and joined the other spectators. The iceboats were long and narrow, just wide enough for two men. One in front of the other, the men controlled the sails and the rudder. Each boat had two sails, a smaller one in front, and a large one over the main part of the boat. The boats flew quietly back and forth over the ice on pairs of long, narrow blades attached to extensions that stuck out from the sides of the boat.

The girls waved as the boats flew past. When a boat reached the marker at the far end of the course, the sailor maneuvered the sail, it flipped in the wind, and the boat turned sharply. If it was going fast enough, one runner lifted off the ice and the boat tilted into the air. A gasp could be heard from the spectators.

"Wow, they're going really fast," Bob said.

"What happens if they flip over?" Jeannie asked, concerned.

"Getting tossed onto this ice wouldn't be fun, that's for sure," Henry said.

A young couple skated by. Arm in arm. "We should have brought our skates," Maggie said. She looked at Bob, blushed, and then looked quickly away. Sara giggled.

Jeannie, who was busy watching the boats to see if one might tip over added, "Oh, we should have, that would have been great fun."

"Bother, I wish I'd thought of it," Henry said, he added, "Maybe next time."

They watched the boats glide back and forth for a while, then the wind picked up and changed direction so that it was blowing directly off the lake and into their faces. It tugged at the girl's dresses and pulled at their scarves and hats.

"Let's go," Bob yelled over the gusts.

They turned and started toward the car. Bob and Henry held their coats open creating make shift sails and let the wind blow them along the slippery ice. Maggie, Jeannie and Sara linked arms and scooted along, trying hard not to get blown over. Nietzsche barked, tried to run, slipping and sliding with every step. When they reached the car, they piled in relieved to be out of the fierce wind.

"How about we go downtown, get hot chocolate and take a look at the ice fountain on Washington Boulevard?" Henry suggested. "It won't be so windy there," he added.

"Great plan," Bob agreed, he looked at Maggie to see if she agreed.

"Sounds good to me. Schools closed again tomorrow, so we don't have any homework to worry about," Maggie said.

Sara and Jeannie cheered. The car started with a shutter and they were off.

They were surprised at the crowd gathered in the park on Washington Boulevard. Each year the city left the water on at one of the fountains. As the water froze, it formed a gigantic ice sculpture. Because of the exceptionally cold weather, the fountain had grown bigger than it had in many years. People were milling around, many with cameras taking pictures. The park had taken on a carnival atmosphere. Street vendors were selling toasted almonds and roasted chestnuts. Cafes had set up tables with views of the spectacular fountain. They found a table and purchased hot chocolate, except Sara, who had an ice-cold bottle of Coke-a-Cola.

"Wow, it's way bigger than last year," Bob said. He looked over at Maggie, but she wasn't listening. She was standing a few feet away, her hands wrapped around the warm chocolate mug, talking to a tall boy. *Who's that,* Bob thought. At that moment, the boy said something that made Maggie laugh, she turned slightly and Bob could see the boy's face clearly. It was Tom Giddings, one of the smartest boy's in school. He was smiling at Maggie, offering her warm toasted almonds. Maggie took an almond, and looked up at Tom. *What were they saying,* Bob thought. At that moment, he hated Tom Giddings. Henry and Jeannie got up to share in the warm, sweet almonds Tom was offering.

"Bob," Sara said, "let's go see if we can get close enough to touch the ice on the side of the fountain."

"Sure," Bob said. He looked over his shoulder one last time to see Henry, Tom, Jeanie and Maggie laughing together.

A few days later the cold subsided. Schools and factories reopened. And the park on Washington Boulevard became a slushy mess.

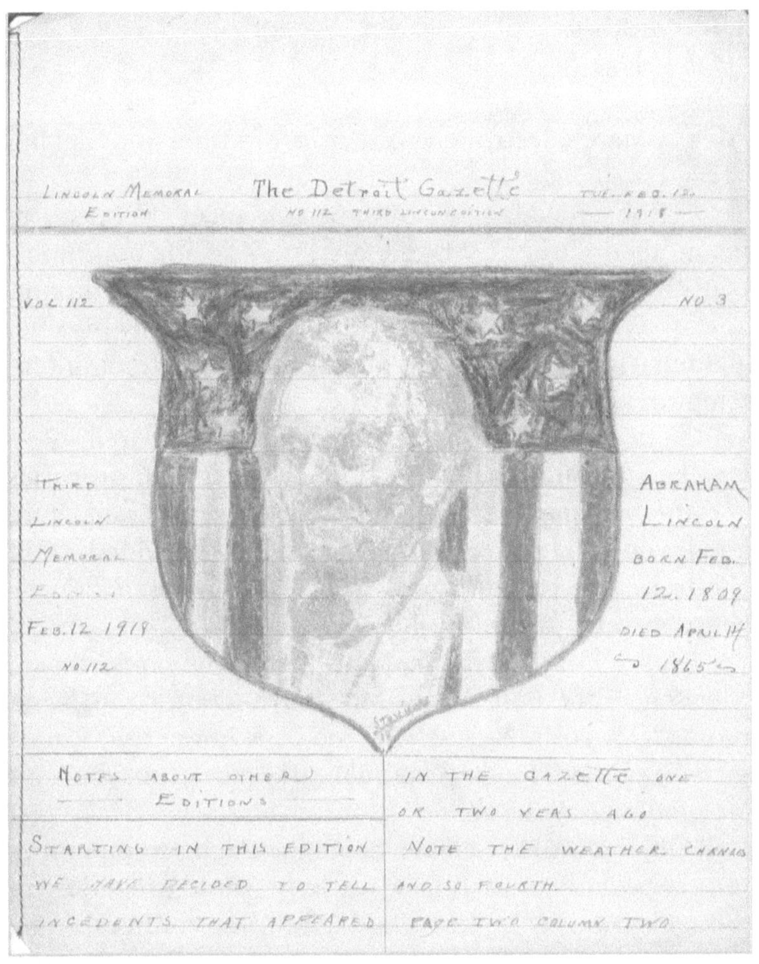

February 12, 1918
www.catherinepaonessa.com/thegazette

The Code
~ Bob Stevens

By March, Detroiters were tired of winter and looking for spring.

Bob and Maggie continued to meet every morning at 'their corner". Maggie didn't ask again about Bob's plans for enlisting, and Bob remained just a little distant, at least as distant as he could with her walking by his side, chatting, smiling and well, being beautiful. He didn't attempt to kiss her again.

On a cold, rainy afternoon in early March, Bob knocked on Aunty McLeod's door to deliver her groceries and the newspaper. She opened the door and said, "Oh, good, you're here." Spotting Nietzsche she added, "Oh, Nietzsche can come in too." Bob was surprised; usually Nietzsche had to wait outside.

"Hello, how are you . . ." but before he could finish, Nietzsche shot past Aunty McLeod and into the living room. "Oh, gosh, Nietzsche come back here. Oh, I'm so sorry." Bob said, looking at the muddy paw prints on Aunt McLeod's kitchen floor.

"Oh, that's okay. Please, come in. We have something very important to discuss. Just leave those groceries on the table," Aunty McLeod said. Bob was confused, *what did she mean, something important.* Bob put down the groceries and followed Aunty McLeod into the living room. He was surprised to see they weren't alone. Sitting on the sofa, looking very out of place, among the doylies and flowered pillows were two army officers. Professor Ackermann was sitting in a chair nearby. All three men were holding teacups and nibbling shortbread. Nietzsche, muddy feet and all, was sitting at Professor Ackerman's feet. Her tail was wagging happily making a steady thumping against the wood floor.

"Hello, Bob," Professor Ackermann said as he put down his tea and rose to shake Bob's hand. "I'd like to introduce Captain Mitchell and Captain Snow. The two captains rose and shook hands with Bob. Aunty McLeod showed Bob to a seat and handed him a cup of tea.

"Now, Bob, let me explain what this is all about," Professor Ackermann said. "I have been working for the War Department . . ."

"The US War Department?" Bob interrupted.

"Well, yes, of course," Professor Ackermann said.

"Oh," was all Bob could think to say, he didn't want to admit that he had thought Professor Ackermann was a German spy and had followed him all around Detroit trying to prove it.

Professor Ackermann continued, "We would like to enlist your and Aunty McLeod's help, you see, we believe there is a spy in the War Department communications office. We think our messages to our British allies are being intercepted and given to the Germans.

A spy, Bob thought, *Professor Ackermann is a spy after all, but for us, not the Germans. Wait until I tell Henry.*

Professor Ackermann was still talking, "Therefore we have started Operation Letters to the Front, or OLF. The plan is to find British immigrants, people like Aunty McLeod, who regularly correspond with British soldiers.

We will embed coded messages in her letters to Davy. Actually, we believe your newspaper would be an excellent place to hide an encoded message."

"Is that the latest newspaper?" Captain Mitchell asked.

Bob had forgotten he was holding Aunty McLeod's copy of the latest edition of the newspaper, "Um, yes," he answered, as he handed the paper over to Captain Mitchell.

"Yes, yes, this will be perfect, just as you said Carl," Captain Mitchell said to Professor Ackermann. He handed the newspaper over to Captain Snow who looked it over silently.

"But . . ." Bob started to ask, but Professor Ackermann interrupted.

"Let me explanation how it will work," Professor Ackermann said. He continued, "We have identified multiple teams of correspondents, people here in the US, mostly British, and the soldiers they write to. We will hide messages in their letters. Some of the letters will hold decoys, and some will contain the real message, in most cases dates and places. The real message will be repeated in multiple letters. British headquarters at the front knows that the information that is reported multiple times is the real message, but you and the others, won't know if you are sending a decoy or a real message. Do you understand?"

"Yes, sir," Bob said, realizing the importance of what was being discussed.

Captain Mitchell added, "The messages will provide information about how our troops will be deployed. It is imperative that the Germans not know where the bulk of the US forces will be joining the front."

"The trick is getting the soldier receiving the message to recognize it for what it is, and report it to their superior at the front," Captain Snow interjected.

"But in this case, we've got an excellent chance," Professor Ackermann said. He continued, "Aunty McLeod has told us that her husband used to send coded messages to Davy when he was a child."

"It was just a game, for fun," Aunty McLeod added. "When Davy was a boy. They kept it up for a number of years. Who would have guessed it would come in handy at this important time."

"I was thrilled with this development," Professor Ackermann admitted.

"So, Bob, will you help us? Will you add the codes Professor Ackermann gives you to your newspapers?" Captain Mitchell asked seriously.

"Why, yes, of course," Bob said with matched seriousness.

"There's one more thing. It is extremely important that you tell no one you are doing this. This includes you Mrs. McLeod," Captain Snow said. He continued, "No one at school," he said to Bob, "or church," he said to Aunty McLeod, "not your parents or your priest or minister. No one. Do you understand?"

"Yes, of course," Aunty McLeod said without hesitation.

"Yes, I understand," Bob added.

"Wonderful," Captain Snow said. "Now, we really must be going or we'll miss our train."

They all rose. Nietzsche circled Professor Ackermann's feet. The Professor bent down, rubbed her head and scratched behind her ears and said, "Sorry girl, I can't stay this time." To Bob and Aunty McLeod he said, "Please, it would be best if you didn't mention I was here. We'll be in touch with the first message shortly. Let's see, we'll use the milk box again, remember, like we did to exchange the newspapers and the ERS magazine." Bob nodded, Professor Ackermann continued, "The message will be in there. Mary, you can explain to Bob how the code will work?"

"Of course, of course, now go, or you really will miss your train," Aunty McLeod said as she shooed the men out the back door.

"Well, now, isn't this thrilling?" Aunty McLeod said after they were gone.

"Um, yes, I guess," Bob answered, "But, I hope I can get the code to work, and how do we get Davy to even look for it?" Bob said. He ran his hand through his thick curly hair, took off his glasses, wiped them with his hankie, put them on again and looked seriously at Aunty McLeod.

"Oh, Davy is quite smart, you'll see, I'll write to him tomorrow. I'll put a hint about the code in the letter. He'll figure it out, I'm sure," Aunty McLeod said with confidence. Bob wasn't so sure.

"How did the code work anyway?" He asked.

"Hmmm, now, let me think, oh yes, it had something to do with the mystery stories of Sherlock Holmes, yes, that's it," Aunty McLeod said. She walked over to a bookshelf in the corner of the living room, lifted the glass door on the top shelf and looked through the books one shelf at a time. Bob watched over her shoulder. "I'm sure it's here," she said. "Let me see, hmm, as I said, it was my husband who sent the coded messages to Davy. Oh, wonderful, here it is," she said as she pulled a blue hardcover book from the second shelf. "I thought Davy was too young for it at the time, but he and Alan enjoyed discussing the stories in their letters."

"Alan?" Bob asked.

"Alan was my husband, Davy's grandfather. He sent a copy of this book to Davy when he was twelve. It was nice that they found something they could share, even over such a great distance. Especially since my son, Davy's father, passed away when Davy was only ten," Aunty McLeod fingered the gold lettering on the book's cover. The title read, 'The Adventures of Sherlock Holmes'.

"But, do you know how the code works?" Bob asked, concerned.

"Well, not exactly," Aunty McLeod confessed as she flipped through the pages of the book, "but, wait, oh yes, they're still here," she said as she pulled a small piece of loose notepaper tucked in the first chapter. "The book has twelve separate stories, I think there's a code for each story." She handed the notepaper to Bob. It had the following letters and symbols written on it,

1.11.1.↑4.Ω.1.12.12.↑4.Ω.1.13.7.↑7.Ω.1.20.7.↑119 .Ω.1.8.1.↑1 ‖

Underneath the code were the words 'Adler is the young man'. Bob looked at the note confused, he turned the paper over to see if there was anything written on the back, it was blank.

"But I don't understand, how can I create a code from this? What do these symbols mean?" Bob said. He was growing more and more uneasy about the whole plan as he realized that Aunt McLeod didn't really know how the code worked.

"I think the code references places in the book. If I remember correctly, the first number references one of the twelve stories, the next number is for the page in the story, or something like that. But I'm sure you can figure it out," she pointed to the note Bob was holding, "Using this as a sample?" She asked hopefully.

"Well, I'm not so sure, I suppose so, just working backward, but that's assuming that 'Adler is the young man' is the solution to this code," Bob said pointing at the code.

"Oh yes, I'm sure it is. I remember, Alan wrote the solution to each code on the note as he figured it out," Aunty McLeod said, confidently. She continued, "Here, you just take this book and the codes, and I'm sure you'll figure it all out." She handed Bob the book, patting his hand confidently and said, "Now, you better hurry on home. Your mother will be wondering where you are. Oh, and remember, don't tell anyone."

Bob walked home in the fading evening light. The rain had stopped and a cold wind was blowing. He shivered. His head was spinning. He took Nietzsche home, feed her and went home for his own supper. When Mother asked about the Sherlock Holmes book, he lied, and said it was for school, but then realized that he'd been home after school so why would Aunty McLeod have given him a book for school. *I'm going to have to be careful,* Bob thought. He hadn't lied to Mother since the day he and Henry skipped school. Of course, he didn't always tell her everything, not about his plan to enlist next fall with Henry, or about his true feelings for Maggie but he hadn't flat out lied to her either.

❖ ❖ ❖

A Special Letter to Davy
~ *Aunty McLeod*

Aunty McLeod wrote Davy the next day. As often happens in Detroit in March, the hint of spring that had blown in with yesterday's rain, blew out with a cold blast from the north. I thick coating of ice covered the city.

Aunty McLeod sat at her desk in the upstairs back bedroom. She looked out into the backyard. The ice-laden trees glistened in the morning sunshine. Aunty McLeod smiled, as anxious as she was for spring to come, the yard was beautiful this morning. It looked like an ice fairyland. She picked up her pen and began her letter.

My dearest Davy,

Detroit is a fairyland this morning. The trees, walkways, roofs and even the crocuses are covered with a sparkling layer of ice. I know it can damage the trees and I feel sorry for all the grownups and school children who have to go slipping off to work and school, but for the moment, I am looking out my window into my yard and enjoying the beauty of it. The trees have grown diamonds instead of buds. The sun is shining and this fairyland will disappear before teatime, and that's okay too, because fairylands never last long anyway. Oh, my, I hope you can excuse the ramblings of a romantic old lady.

To be honest, I'm anxious for spring to come. I've already been going over the seed catalogs and planning out my garden. I miss your Grandfather in the spring. He enjoyed the garden too. And it's hard work without a helpmate. Do you remember the codes he and you used to send back and forth? I ran across his copy of 'The Adventures of Sherlock Holmes' in the bookcase yesterday. The codes you sent are still tucked away in the book, he saved them you know. I hope you remember. It is important, very important, that you remember. And it's funny how the army and government use coded messages too, I wonder if they are like to the ones you shared with your Grandfather.

Well, the sunshine is a blessing and a demon, it's falling on the dresser and I can see a thick layer of dust. I guess it's time I started my spring-cleaning in spite of the weather. I hope you are well, and keeping out of harm's way as much as that is possible. Maybe this war will end soon and God willing, you can come and help me in my garden.

Take Care,
Your loving Nana

Aunty McLeod reread the letter and considered whether it was enough of a hint. Would Davy notice the code in the Bob's newspaper when it came? Would he even remember the codes, he was only twelve. *But,* she thought, *I can't be more specific, if the letter falls into the wrong hands, the whole scheme could be spoiled. This will have to do and I'll just have to hope that Davy catches on.*

Code Breaking
~ Bob Stevens

Bob intended to work on the code the next day, and then the day after that, but there was always some pressing homework, or Eastern magazine work to do. The teachers were trying to make up for the school they missed because of the coal shortage. *It wasn't fair,* Bob thought, *the cold weather and coal shortage weren't his fault.*

He was walking Nietzsche on a warm afternoon in late March. Robins were hopping from tree to tree and the forsythia was in full bloom, but Bob didn't care, he was tired. He was up late last night working on accounting homework, after school he'd worked at the shop unloading canvas rolls, and he still had a composition to write for tomorrow. *Blast,* Bob thought.

Nietzsche pulled at the leash, as if to say, *Hurry up Bob, why are you going so slowly?*

"Sorry girl, I wasn't much fun for our walk today," Bob said as he patted Nietzsche on the head, "I'll be back later to let you in the house," he added as he fed her and filled her water dish.

Bob had been checking Professor Ackermann's milk box every day. He was always a little relieved to discover it empty. As far as Bob knew, Professor Ackermann had not been back to Detroit since their meeting at Aunty McLeod's a couple of weeks ago. Bob looked at the milk box as he was leaving the yard. He thought about not checking it, *it's probably still empty,* he thought. But, he walked over to it anyway, *maybe they changed their minds, or found someone else,* Bob thought as he flipped open the lid. But, there it the bottom of the box was an envelope. Bob pulled it out, opened it and removed a single sheet of paper. Typed in the center of the paper was the line 'Cantigny, April 25 – 1st Div'. He turned it over; the back was blank. 'Cantigny, April 25 – 1st Div' that was all. Captain Mitchell had said the messages would contain information about US troop deployments. So, this meant that the 1st Division would be deployed in a place called Cantigny on April 25th. That's if this was a real message, and not a decoy. Bob thought, *today is March 21st.* He would have to get the newspaper in the mail quickly.

Bob stuffed the note in his pocket and rushed home to his room. Luckily, this Saturday's newspaper was ready. Jeannie had dropped off the finished copies for him that very afternoon. He took the crumpled code paper from his pocket and flattened it on his desk. He looked over his shoulder at the door. Mother was in the kitchen. He could hear her humming softly to herself. His heart was pounding. What if she came upstairs? How would he explain what he was doing? *This won't do,* Bob thought. He looked out the window. The sun was shining on Professor Ackermann's gazebo. *Perfect,* Bob thought. The shrubs had grown up a bit around it last summer offering some privacy, and it was warm enough to work outside. He gathered what he would need, the newspaper, pens and pencil, and 'The Adventures of Sherlock Holmes' book with the sample codes inside, and headed downstairs.

"It's so nice out, I think I'll do my homework over at the gazebo," he said to his mother as he hurried through the kitchen.

"Oh, that's a fine idea," Mother said. "How about a snack to tide you over until supper?" Bob stopped, he couldn't refuse a snack. She spread a thick layer of jam on a piece of warm bread. "Do you have lots of homework?" Mother asked.

"Yeah, I have a paper to write," Bob said as he took the bread and headed for the kitchen door. Before leaving, he turned, smiled, and said, "Thank you."

Bob ate the bread as he walked to the gazebo. Nietzsche was happy to see him again so soon. She attempted to get him to play fetch by picking up a stick, dropping it, as always a few feet away from him, and barking.

"Sorry girl, I have homework to do," Bob said.

He settled down at the gazebo opened the Sherlock Holmes book and the first sample code. He looked at the code.

1.11.1.↑4.Ω.1.12.12.↑4.Ω.1.13.7.↑7.Ω.1.20.7.↑119 .Ω.1.8.1.↑1‖ means 'Adler is the young man'. Bob flipped through the book. The sun was so warm, and the breeze was rustling the tree above him. He remembered how tired he was. Nietzsche had given up the idea of fetch and was napping on the gazebo step in the sunshine. *This will all make more sense if I just close my eyes for a minute,* Bob thought. He took off his glasses, folded his arms on the table and put his head down. *Just a little nap,* Bob thought as he drifted off to sleep.

Adler is the Young Man?
~ Maggie Robinson

Maggie walked into Professor Ackermann's yard. She expected Nietzsche to greet her, but then noticed the big dog sleeping on the gazebo steps. Maggie smiled at the gentle dog that had come to mean so much to her family. She was looking for Bob. His mother had told her he was in the gazebo. She had finished her composition, and was wondering if he was done too. Maggie hoped Bob would suggest a walk to the soda fountain for a Coke-a-Cola on this unseasonably warm March day. A small piece of paper was blowing across the yard. Maggie picked it up and read the following strange message, 1.11.1.↑4.Ω.1.12. 12.↑4.Ω.1.13.7.↑7.Ω.1.20.7.↑119.Ω.1.8.1.↑1 ‖ and below the words, 'Adler is the young man'. *How strange,* she thought.

Maggie quietly stepped over the sleeping Nietzsche and into the gazebo. To her surprise, she discovered Nietzsche wasn't the only one napping. Bob was sound asleep. His red curls, which he usually wore slicked back, were being blown about by the breeze. She held her breath. He was always so busy, so full of energy and movement especially when he was around her. She never had a chance to really look at him, to study him. She liked the look of his high forehead and his bright blue eyes. Eyes that seemed to look right into her and read her every thought. She smiled at the smudge of jelly in the corner of his mouth. As she stood there it dawned on her. She loved him. The realization took her breath away. She loved him. A love that came without fireworks or trumpet blasts, but tiptoed up and met her gently, like a soft caress.

But they were just friends. She almost reached out and touched one of the curls, but stopped herself. *Sometimes, when he looks at me, I think he cares for me,* she thought, *but then he pulls away. If he does care, why doesn't he tell me, court me?* The wonder she felt at being in love quickly turned to wretchedness as she realized he didn't feel the same way. Maggie choked back a sob. *He doesn't care for me, not like that. He just wants to be friends, that's all.*

Bob moved slightly. Maggie panicked. She didn't want him to wake up and find her standing there. She stepped quietly back over Nietzsche and out of the gazebo. She would go home, move on. Just be friends. Some of the other lads at school had asked to call on her, maybe she should let them. *But I love him,* she thought. A tear slipped from her eye down her check and she was about to run from the yard, when she realized she was still carrying the funny note. She turned around trying to decide what to do when Nietzsche lifted her head and gave a happy little 'nice to see you' bark.

"Shhh, quiet, you'll wake Bob," Maggie said.

"Maggie, is that you?" Bob said groggily. Maggie looked up to see Bob standing on the steps of the gazebo. He ran his fingers through his hair and squinted at her.

"Oh, hi, I um, found this in the yard," Maggie said. She was mortified. Did Bob know she had been staring at him while he slept? In an effort to hide her embarrassment, she asked, "What is it anyway?"

A Secret Shared
~ Bob Stevens

Bob couldn't believe it. How could he be so stupid? What was he going to tell Maggie? He didn't know if he could lie to her, didn't have time to think of some explanation for the strange paper she held out to him.

"Um, it's for a project, in um," he tried to think of a class that he was taking that she wouldn't know anything about, but his brain wasn't working fast enough, he was a terrible liar, "in accounting," he finally blurted out. Maggie looked bewildered. Her face was flushed. *She already knows I'm lying,* Bob thought.

"Accounting, this doesn't look much like accounting?" She said staring at the note, not looking at him.

"Oh, what does it matter," Bob muttered. He held out his hand and she handed him the note. Bob took it, examined it, not sure what to do, what to say. He couldn't look her in the eye.

"Well, goodbye," Maggie said, and she turned and started walking away. Nietzsche followed her.

Bob's stared at her back. He didn't want her to go. He needed her. She was better at this kind of stuff. His heart was pounding, and mind racing.

"Wait," Bob called, "I need your help."

Maggie stopped, turned and said, "What's going on? Who's Adler, really?"

"You're not going to believe me," Bob said as he led her back into the gazebo. His glasses were still on the table. He picked them up, wiped them on his shirtsleeve and put them on. He looked at Maggie; his expression was serious.

"What is it," she said. "You're scaring me."

"I'm sorry, but first I have to ask you to promise me that you won't tell anyone about this, not anyone," Bob said.

"Stop teasing, what is it?" Maggie said.

"Do you promise?" Bob persisted.

"Well, of course, but well, if it's something, you know, that I have to tell, well, then I'll have to tell," Maggie said.

"Maggie!" Bob said, exasperated.

"Okay, I promise," Maggie said.

Bob took a deep breath and tried to decide where to begin. "You remember when I thought Professor Ackermann was a spy? Well, I was kind of right."

"What, oh, not that again?" Maggie said surprised.

"Well, yes," Bob said, "Professor Ackermann is a spy, for us! America!"

Maggie just stared at him.

"I knew you wouldn't believe me, but it's true. And he wants me and Aunty McLeod to send coded messages about US troop movement to Davy." Bob explained. He handed Maggie the message from the milk box, and continued, desperately, "This is the first message, and I have to code it into this newspaper, using this code." He showed her the Sherlock Holmes message again. "And to be completely honest, I'm not sure if I can even do it."

Maggie sat down at the table. She read the first message out loud, "Cantigny, April 25 1st Div," and asked, "Where's Cantigny?"

"Well, in France I assume," Bob said. He was getting frantic, he added, "But it doesn't really matter, I have to get this code figured out, Aunty McLeod doesn't even remember how it works. Then I have to create a code for that message," he pointed at the paper she was still holding, "and put it on this newspaper. And I still have to write my composition. So, well, if you want to stay and help, well, that would be great. Otherwise, I guess you should go. And remember, you promised, you can't tell anyone."

"I'll help," Maggie said.

"You believe me?" Bob asked surprised.

"Not even you could make this up," Maggie said. Bob laughed, relieved.

"Now, tell me about this code."

Bob told her about the meeting at Aunty McLeod's and the messages between Davy and his grandfather. She looked at the Adler message and the Sherlock Holmes book.

"And you know that the first number is for the story and the second number is the page?" Maggie asked as she examined the code and the book.

"Well, that's what Aunty McLeod thinks at least," Bob said.

Maggie was looking at the code and flipping through the book. The other messages fell out, "Are these more samples?" She asked.

"Yeah, Aunty McLeod said there was one for each story," Bob said.

"If you want, I could work backwards with these codes and see if I can figure out what these symbols mean? Then you could get started on your composition," Maggie suggested.

"Really?" Bob asked, "You don't mind?"

"Oh, no. This is exciting. Just like the Zimmerman letter." Maggie said. She sat down, picked up a pencil and notebook and was already busy. She copied out the code, quite large, leaving space for notes between the numbers and symbols.

"Great," Bob said. He sat down, pulled the books he needed for his composition from his book bag and got started.

They worked quietly for a quarter of an hour, then Maggie said, "Okay, the first number is definitely the story and the second is the page, and the third is the paragraph. The up arrow means to use the next word."

Bob considered, "That might be tricky to convert to the newspaper, but we'll have to make it work. I just hope Davy can figure it out."

"I think the omega symbol is a space, but I'm still working it out. And this code uses a pi symbol, but I still have to test that out," Maggie said.

They fell silent again. Bob stole a look at Maggie while she worked. She was concentrating hard. He noticed that she chewed on her lower lip when she was concentrating, his heart missed a beat. *Wow, she's beautiful. Concentrate,* he thought.

Nietzsche barked, and they both looked up. "Gosh, it's getting late. I have to go home for supper, Mum will be wondering where I've gone," Maggie said. "Before someone comes looking for me."

"Do you have the code figured out?" Bob asked.

"I think, but I'll explain after supper," Maggie said.

"Is you're Mum going to the Red Cross meeting?" Bob asked.

"Yes, I think so, yours?" Maggie replied.

"Yeah, do you think you could come over after supper to keep working on it?" Bob asked, hopefully.

"Alone?" Maggie asked, surprised. "My Mum wouldn't allow that, but I'll bring Jeannie and Sara."

"We can't tell them!" Bob said.

"Oh, I know, we'll just tell them that we're working on a school project and that you have some newspaper work for them. Could you figure out something for them to do?"

"Sure," Bob agreed.

"Great, see you in a bit," Maggie said as she waved goodbye. Bob gathered up the papers and headed home for his supper.

Later that evening Bob and Maggie were busy at the Steven's dining room table. Bob finished his composition and Maggie worked on the code. Jeannie and Sara sat at the kitchen worktable coping pictures from the Detroit Free Press for the next edition of the newspaper.

Maggie smiled and passed the following note over to Bob. On it she had drawn the following chart.

Character position in the code (Each character is separated by a .)	Location in the book
1	Story
2	Page
3	Paragraph/section
4	If the 4 character is a ↑ followed by a number, count to that word in the paragraph and use it. If the 4 character is a π followed by a number, count to that character in the paragraph and use it.
Space	Space
∞	Use the number that follows the symbol, but subtract 5 (always 5, not sure why)

Bob studied the chart. He looked into the kitchen to ensure that Jeannie and Sara were busy, then whispered,

"So, if we substitute issue number for story, we may be able to make this work."

"That's what I was thinking," Maggie agreed. Then she said under her breath, "Don't whisper, it will only make them suspicious,"

"Oh, right," Bob said, almost too loudly.

Maggie rolled her eyes and continued, "The numbers are kind of strange, it's always the infinity symbol and a number, but then subtract 5, and it's always 5"

In a more normal, but low voice Bob said, "So, now we have to put the first message into the latest newspaper, using this code." He put the latest issue of the paper in front of them on the table. Then he dug the message from the milk box out of his pocket. They studied them together.

"So the first character will be a 5, for the volume," Bob said pointing at the upper left corner of the newspaper. "If we can find the word 'can', we can use it for the first part of Cantigny." He scanned the first page, then opened the newspaper. They both scanned pages two and three. Bob turned the page again.

"Here," Maggie said, pointing to the word 'can' toward the top of page four. "So the second character will be a four, for the page." She found a piece of scratch paper among the notes and books on the table and wrote, 5.4.

Bob looked at the page, the word can was in the second column, and the first column was divided into 3 sections. "I'd call this paragraph four, what do you think?" Bob asked.

"Yes, I think that works," Maggie agreed, she added a 4 to the code. "What word is it?"

Bob counted the words until he got to the word can, "46," he said. Maggie added a $\uparrow$46 to the code. The scratch paper now read, 5.4.4.$\uparrow$46.

"Now we have to add the letters for the rest of the word Cantigny," Maggie said. They finished that and found the word April on the first page. They used the ∞ to add the numbers 25 and 1, but then remembered to add 5, so it was ∞30 and ∞6. They finished with the letters to spell st and Div. The completed code looked like this:

5.4.4.$\uparrow$46.5.1.1.π3.5.1.1.π1.5.4.1.π4.5.4.3.π2.5.5.4.π16 5.1.2.$\uparrow$30 ∞30 ∞6 5.1.2.π6.5.4.1.π10 5.5.1.π12.5.5.1.π4.5.4.3.π5

"Wow, it's kind of long," Maggie said.

"Yeah, but it might just work," Bob said. "Anyone else will think it's just a doodle along the top of the page, I just hope Davy recognizes it. Aunty McLeod wrote him a letter reminding him of the coded messages he used to send to his grandfather, so it will be fresh in his mind."

"I hope so," Maggie said.

"What do you hope?" Jeannie asked as she walked into the dining room.

"I hope we did this assignment correctly," Maggie said. She and Bob quickly covered the code papers with schoolbooks and papers.

"Are you done? Because I'm tired," Jeannie said. "And ..."

"I'm not tired," Sara shouted from the kitchen.

Jeannie rolled her eyes and continued, "And I still have some homework to finish."

"Oh, sorry," Maggie said, "you should have brought it with you."

"It's algebra, and well, I need help." Jeannie said, she looked at Bob embarrassed.

Bob smiled at her, "I would have flunked geometry without Maggie's help."

"Sure, I'll help you, I loved algebra," Maggie said. Bob and Jeannie groaned.

Maggie, Jeannie and Sara packed up their books and newspaper supplies and headed home.

Bob copied the code carefully onto the March 23 issue of the newspaper. Aunty McLeod's lights were on, so he figured she was home. He headed through the yard and alley to Aunty McLeod's back door.

When Bob explained that he had a newspaper with a code for her to send to Davy, she said, "I was beginning to think they had forgot about us, I'll write Davy tonight, I just hope he recognizes the code."

Bob showed her how the code looked written neatly at the top of the first page. "We," he started to say, then corrected himself, "I, I mean I, figured out the code from the samples and used the same basic method to create this code." He didn't want to tell Aunty McLeod that he had told Maggie about the messages.

"Oh, my, that looks fine. Just like the codes Alan and Davy used to exchange."

"It says," Bob began, but Aunty McLeod stopped him with a raise of her hand.

"Don't tell me. The fewer people that know, the better," she said.

"Oh, right, good idea. Well, I should get going. I still have homework to finish," Bob said.

"And I have a letter to write. Good night Bob, and thank you," Aunty McLeod said, patting the newspaper softly, "We're doing our bit to bring an end to this terrible war.

OUR BIG WAR SUPPLIMENT
ON PAGE FIVE AND SIX

The Detroit Gazette

EXTRA ★ ★ ★ EXTRA ★

IN THIS EDITION: —
PAGE ONE ABOUT OTHER EDITIONS, SPRING DAY CALENDAR
PAGE TWO – ANNOUNCEMENTS ADDS ECT.
PAGE THREE WHO IN H — MADE THE KAISER? STORY
PAGE FOUR – NEWS SECTION, COMIC ALTES

NOTES ON OTHER EDITIONS BE WRITEN ENTIRELY
IN TYPE

READ THE APRIL MAY
EDITIONS

THIS IS THE FIRST MARCH
EDITION. THE GAZETTE HAS
NOT BEEN PRINTED FOR
OVER THREE WEEKS, BUT
NEW PLANS HAVE BEEN
MADE FOR COMMING EDITIONS
APRIL + MAY EDITIONS WILL
CONTAIN MANY NEW
SECTIONS. THE SERIAL
STORY WILL BE READY
ABOUT JUNE 5, AND MANY
SHORT STORIES WILL BE
PUBLISHED SOON.
THE EASTER EDITION
NEXT WEEK.

WARM – PLEASANT
WELL SAY IF THIS
WEATHER KEEPS UP WE
WILL SOON BE FORGET
THE COAL SHORTAGE

THE ROBIN SINGS IN YONDER
TREE
THE COWS RUN MERRILY OVER
THE LEA
NOW DAYS GET HOT AND
THE COTTAGE
AND WORK ON YOUR
FARM

March 23, 1918
www.catherinepaonessa.com/thegazette

Bob received two more messages that spring. He and Maggie coded the message 'Belleau Wood, May 25 2nd Div', into the April 24th newspaper, and the message 'Hamel, June 20 33rd Div' into the April 26th issue. Bob carefully wrote the code on the top of the first page of each newspaper. He and Maggie decided that, although it was noticeable, it was better to put it there than hide it and Davy not seeing it. They hoped anyone else looking at the newspaper would simply dismiss it.

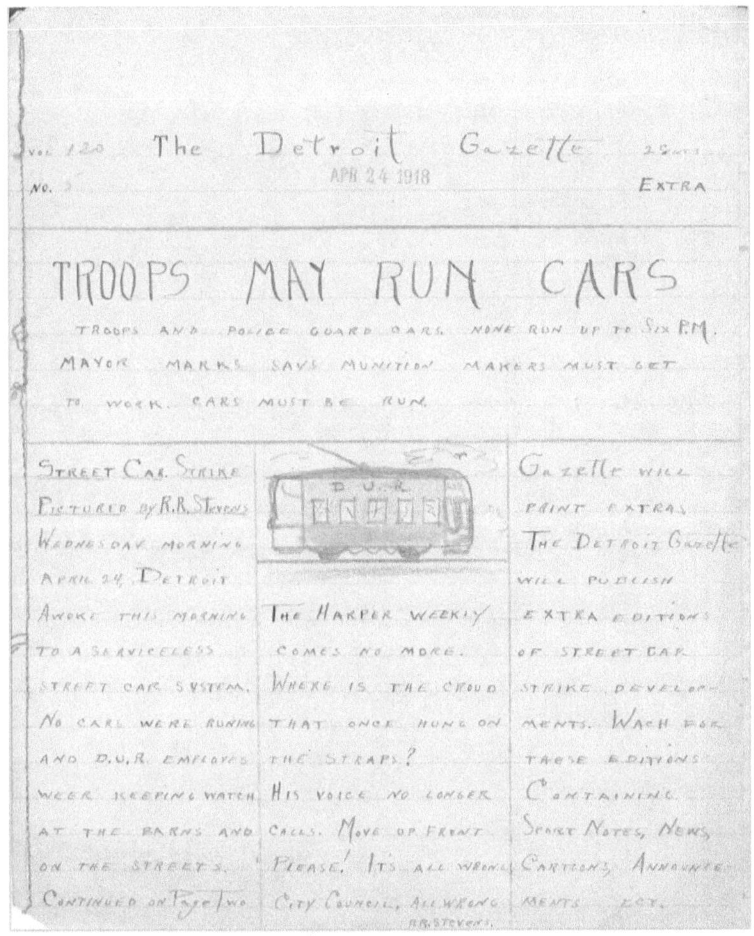

April 24, 1918
www.catherinepaonessa.com/thegazette

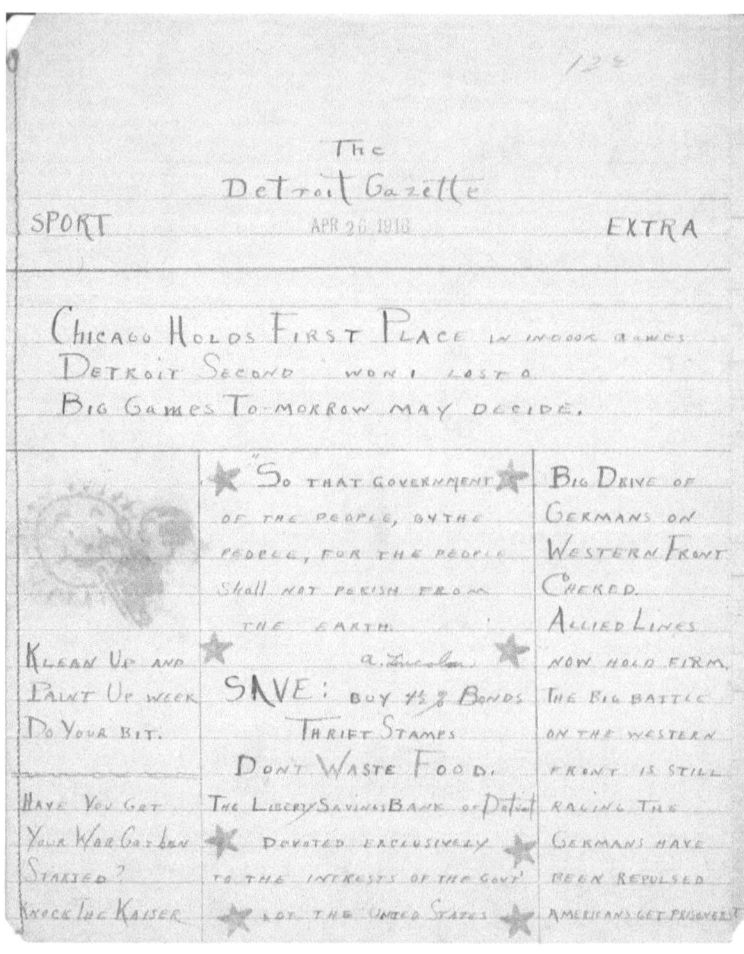

April 26, 1918 – Note, the newspaper with the code was destroyed
www.catherinepaonessa.com/thegazette

CHAPTER 16

A Steamer Trunk
~ Davy McLeod

As hoped, Davy's platoon was sent on home leave for the first two and a half weeks of November. It took three days to get back to Bothwell traveling by train to the French channel town of Calais, then by boat across the English Channel to Dover, and finally by train again to Bothwell. They had 11 days at home before reversing the order to travel back to the front.

Mac and Millie were married four days after they arrived home. Mac, now a sergeant, stood at the front of the small, stone church. Davy, also a sergeant, stood next to him as the best man and Second Lieutenant Gavin stood next to Davy. Gavin agreed to trim his unruly beard for the occasion, but flat out refused to cut his mass of red hair. Jamie and Nora came from London for the event, and for a little while, they all forgot about the war.

Davy spent the rest of the leave talking with his mum about Australia, playing with his stepsisters, reading and walking in the hills and fields around Bothwell.

On his second to last evening before returning to the front, Davy went for a long walk. A soft drizzle was falling. The weather matched his mood but he was determined to think about the future. Make some decisions. His mum really hoped he'd join them in Australia. They were leaving as soon as passenger travel resumed, probably before he returned home again. She suggested he pack his belongings in a steamer trunk, and they would take it with them. That way, she explained, his belongings would be there, ready for him when he arrived after the war. The Bothwell house would be rented to someone else, so he couldn't leave his things there.

Bloody, hell, Davy thought as he climbed a hill and looked down over Bothwell Castle, *I guess the trenches are my home.* He turned up his collar against the wind that was growing increasingly colder.

Davy turned his back on Bothwell Castle and walked north toward the highlands. He thought about Detroit. His grandmother had offered to pay his passage, help him get a start there. But he couldn't decide, couldn't think about what to do after the war. Couldn't get past the war. *I'm too tired,* Davy thought, *I'll decide tomorrow.*

In the end, he packed his belongings: his Sherlock Holmes book and some other books, the letters from his grandparents he'd saved over the years, his slingshot, his father's coat, it still had the big pockets he'd added to hide game in, other assorted clothes and finally, his football. He had fun kicking the football round with his stepsisters before adding it to the trunk. It all fit with room to spare. He locked it, looked at it and thought, *there, my life fits in a steamer trunk.* He lugged the trunk over to Gavin's house. They had offered to store it for him.

❖ ❖ ❖

The Code
~ Davy McLeod

They were back at the front before the end of November and home leave felt like a dream. Christmas came and went without much notice. They fell back into the same routine of rotating in and out of the front-line trenches. Davy and Jamie moved to where they were needed to deal with German snipers. And, the pile of pictures in Davy's dream continued to grow. A young mother holding a baby, a smiling old man with a dog at his feet, a proud German cavalry officer.

Then, in March 1918 all hell broke loose. On the 3rd, news that Russia had surrendered swept through the line and everyone wondered what Germany would do next.

"Damn Russians, if they had just held on a little longer, we might have been able to overtake the bloody Hun once and for all," Mac said.

"The Generals have been saying that for a year now, 'One more battle boys and we'll have them'," Jamie replied sarcastically.

"But you know what this means, it means that Germany can move troops from the Russian front, to this one. They'll be able to hit us hard," Mac said.

The attack Mac had predicted came on March 21st. And it was massive. Even soldiers that had been in the fight since the beginning, said they had never heard anything like it. In the first hours of the battle, the Germans fired one million artillery shells at the British lines. Over 3000 shells per minute. The earth shook and the sound was thunderous.

Davy's platoon was in the supply trenches when they were given the order to fall back. The Germans charged far into France and by March 24th they were shelling Paris with long range Krupps cannons. The British army was in shock, but they were able to stop the advance. The German army had moved too fast, lengthening the area they had to defend and straining their supply lines to the breaking point.

At the beginning of April, Davy and Jamie were assigned to map duty. They had been trained to read and copy maps and aerial photographs at the sniper school, and it was that skill that was urgently needed. It was imperative that information about what ground the Germans now held be mapped and distributed to commanding officers up and down the line. Davy, Jamie and a group of other mappers were assigned to a small room in an abandoned farmhouse. Large tables had been erected and the men were busy copying maps. They were working 16 hours a day, and everyone was tired.

Jamie rubbed his eyes, squinted at the map before him, and said, "I think we're due for a break. If I don't go out and let my eyes focus on something else, anything else, I'll go crazy." He got up, stretched, and said, "You coming?" to Davy.

Davy looked up from the map he was coping, considered, and said, "Yeah, sure." The detailed work didn't bother him. Surprisingly, he enjoyed it. Copying the maps, checking the coordinates, verifying the information against aerial photographs, it took absolute concentration and focus. It was funny but while working on mapping the war, he could forget about the war.

"Let's go over to the mess and see if there's any coffee," Jamie suggested.

"And maybe the mail came in," Davy said.

They walked to the Nissen hut that provided a temporary shelter for the mobile kitchen. Davy opened the door and the smell of strong coffee hit them. They soon discovered that it smelled significantly better than it tasted.

"Ugh, that's terrible," Jamie said. "Like they boiled my boots and a tire in a rusty bucket."

"Ah, but you're missing the subtle hint of powdered mildew," Davy joked, putting on airs with a fake haughty manner. He laughed at his own bad joke.

"Right, how could I have missed the mildew?" Jamie said.

They drank as much of the bad coffee as they could stand and walked over to a large house that was being used as the area headquarters. They were happy to discover that the mail had caught up with them. Jamie had a letter from Nora, and Davy had a nice thick letter from his Nana. *Oh, good, a newspaper,* Davy thought. They walked back to the farmhouse, but before going back to work, they sat down on the front steps and opened their mail. Jamie laughed quietly under his breath as he read. Davy looked up from his letter, Jamie had a wide smile on his face.

"What's up," Davy asked.

"Nora's pregnant," Jamie said happily.

"Wow, congratulations," Davy said. "That's fantastic. Does she say when the baby will come?"

Jamie continued reading, "Let's see, she's known for a month now, but didn't want to mention it until it was for sure, oh here, the doctor put the due date at early August."

"Maybe you can get leave to go back and see the baby," Davy said.

"Maybe the war will be over by then," Jamie said.

"Maybe," Davy said, but he didn't really believe it. They went back to reading their letters. Davy opened the newspaper, and there at the top of the first page, was an odd group of symbols and numbers. He examined it closely and was surprised to discover that it was the code he and his grandfather had created. *Why would Nana send a code now?* Davy thought.

"What's up," Jamie asked, noticing Davy's puzzled expression.

Davy showed Jamie the code and said, "This."

"Looks like hieroglyphs," Jamie said.

"It's a code," Davy said, "Actually, it's the code I used to exchange with my grandfather. He lived in Detroit and we sent coded messages back and forth when I was a lad."

"Well, maybe he thought you'd like the distraction, or maybe he has a message for you he didn't want your grandmother to see," Jamie said with a chuckle.

"But… he died, three years ago," Davy said.

"Oh, sorry, well, maybe your grandmother wanted to see if you remembered it," Jamie said.

"Yeah, maybe, wait," he dug into the pockets of his trousers, after emptying the contents of the third pocket, he said, "here, in this letter, she mentions the code," Davy unfolded the letter and read what his grandmother had written about it being important that he remember the code aloud to Jamie. When he was finished he said, "I think she wants me to solve this code."

"Definitely, but why, why not just write what she wants you to know?" Jamie asked.

"Well, I don't know. She's old, maybe she's not right, you know," Davy said sadly.

"But doesn't her neighbor write the newspapers? He wouldn't put it on if she was, well, crazy, would he?" Jamie said, then he continued, "But, I guess she could have added it before she mailed it. Do you remember how it works? Can you solve it?"

"Sure, if you remember 'The Adventures of Sherlock Holmes'" Davy said, "Let's see," he examined the code, "What's the 46th word in the 4th paragraph on page 4 of the 5th story?" He looked at Jamie expectantly.

Jamie chuckled and said, "Sorry mate, I can't remember that," Jamie continued. "My memory's good, really good, but it doesn't quite work like that."

"Oh, no problem," Davy said, but he was a little discouraged.

"Hey, wait, your grandmother wouldn't expect you to have the Holmes book at the front with you, would she?" Jamie said.

"Why, no, I don't think so." Davy said, he flipped through the newspaper and continued, "Maybe, it refers to places in the newspaper?"

A voice from inside the farmhouse shouted briskly, "Sergeant McLeod, Sergeant Patterson have you finished mapping quadrant 15 yet? We need it ASAP."

They both jumped at the order, hurried inside and started working on the map. When they finished mapping quadrant 15, Davy took a break and discreetly worked out the code. He guessed that the first character meant the page, but that didn't seem to work. Then he noticed that the newspaper was volume 5. The first number was the volume. It went faster after that. The number was hard, for a minute, he couldn't remember what they subtracted, it was always the same. Davy racked his brain trying to remember the number. He put the newspaper aside and worked on a couple maps hoping it would come to him. It did. Five, it was five. His house number. He remembered now, sitting on the porch writing to his grandfather. His grandfather had said to pick a number he wouldn't forget, so he picked his house number, because when you're twelve, you figure you'll live there forever, and never forget. Davy completed the rest of the code. The hidden message was:

Cantigny, April 25 1ˢᵗ Div,

He wrote it on a slip of paper, handed it to Jamie and said, "My grandmother is either completely crazy, or this is, as she said, very important."

"Bloody hell, what's today's date?" Jamie asked.

"April 7, I'm going to talk to the captain about it," Davy said, he stood up and walked over to the captain overseeing the map detail. Davy showed him the message and explained where it came from.

"You mean to say that this code," he pointed to the top of the newspaper Davy had handed him, "is meant for our military? And it came from your grandmother, in Detroit? But that's doesn't make any sense," the captain said, doubtfully.

"I know," Davy said, "but I think it might be worth reporting. Why else would my grandmother send me this? It might be important."

The captain handed the newspaper and the slip of paper back to Davy and said, "See Colonel Irons over at headquarters."

"Yes, sir," Davy said.

Davy found Colonel Irons in a makeshift office of the makeshift headquarters. A door had been laid across a couple of old dressers making a desk. Colonel Irons was a middle-aged man with a receding hairline and glasses. He looked exhausted. He sat quietly as Davy explained how he discovered and deciphered the message.

"Interesting," Colonel Irons said. He rifled through a stack of papers on his desk, "I seem to remember something about an operation, hmm, let's see, here it is," he pulled a paper from the stack, "Operation Letters to the Front, OLF, yes, and your code could be one of these communications. This could be very important."

"OLF?" Davy repeated.

"Yes," Colonel Irons said, "it seems the Americans are having trouble with a mole in . . ." He stopped abruptly, and seemed to consider whether he should tell Davy the details then continued, "Anyway, thank you for bringing this to my attention. I will take care of it from here. If you receive any additional codes, please bring them to me immediately."

"Ah, of course," Davy said, but he didn't leave.

Colonel Irons looked up and said, "Dismissed."

"Um, may I have the newspaper back?" Davy asked.

Colonel Irons looked at the newspaper, tore off the page with the code and handed the remaining pages to Davy.

"Thank you sir," Davy said, and he left.

Colonel Irons called after him, "Sergeant McLeod," Davy turned back, "remember, if you receive any more messages, I will need to see them immediately."

"Yes sir," Davy said. He felt a little let down. He would have liked to know more about the message. *What did it mean? Why was it sent to me, and what did Nana have to do with coded messages? Very strange,* Davy thought.

Davy received two more codes that spring. The message 'Belleau Wood, May 25 2nd Div' was in the April 24th newspaper and a week later he received the message 'Hamel, June 20 33rd Div' in the April 26th newspaper. As instructed, Davy took the messages to Colonel Irons. After receiving the third message from Davy, Colonel Irons said, "Thank you for your help in this Sergeant McLeod. I wish I could give you more information, but, well, the less said, the better. Just know that it is very important, and much appreciated."

By early June the map room was abruptly closed, and the mappers were sent back to their platoons. Back to the front.

CHAPTER 17

Operation Letters to the Front (OLF)
~ Bob Stevens

Bob was playing with Nietzsche in Professor Ackermann's backyard when the big dog ran to the gate and started barking.

"Hey girl, what's the matter?" Bob asked petting her head. Nietzsche continued barking. Bob opened the gate and Nietzsche took off down the street. Her sudden escape surprised Bob. She'd never run off before. He grabbed her leash from a hook in the shed and went after her. Once in the front yard he could see Nietzsche way down at the end of the street. She had stopped running and was making circles around a tall gentleman. She was barking wildly. Bob squinted trying to see who it was, "Nietzsche," he called. As he got closer, Bob realized that the tall man was Professor Ackermann. Nietzsche was overjoyed. She ran circles around the Professor, ran toward the house, and ran back to the Professor.

"Hello," Professor Ackermann called when he saw Bob approaching.

"You must think I never pay any attention to her," Bob said nodding toward Nietzsche, "but, honest, I walk her almost every day and when I can't she gets a real treat; Jeannie and Sara walk her."

"Oh, I understand, actually, I'm kind of glad to see that she misses me," Professor Ackermann said. Nietzsche jumped up and put her big paws on his chest, "Now, down you crazy dog. You're making a mess of my suit," he said.

The Professor shook hands with Bob, "She looks fine, just fine. Thank you for taking such good care of her."

"Welcome home," Bob said. The two men continued down the street. "Are you home to stay?" Bob asked.

"Actually I am, for a month or two at least," Professor Ackermann said. Bob knew better than to ask him what he would be doing. *I'm sure he'll be busy doing spy stuff,* Bob thought. But Professor Ackermann continued, "I've received my manuscript back from the publisher and have much work to do on the edits,"

"Oh," Bob said, disappointed.

Professor Ackermann lowered his voice and said, "You should know, Operation Letters to the Front has been cancelled."

"Oh," Bob said again.

Professor Ackermann continued, "OLF wasn't cancelled because it wasn't valuable or successful, on the contrary, it was quite successful. Many of the messages were received. It just isn't needed anymore. Thank you for your help, and remember, please don't tell anyone about the operation or your participation in it."

"Of course," Bob said, thinking about Maggie.

When they reached Professor Ackermann's front yard. He turned, shook Bob's hand, and said, "Again, thank you for everything." And he disappeared into the yard with Nietzsche at his heels.

Bob was disappointed. The, what did Professor Ackermann call it? OFL Operation Letters to the Front, was cancelled. He had so many questions. Had any of his messages gotten through? Could Davy decipher them? Deliver them? Were they real or just decoys? And it bothered Bob that he would probably never know. On top of that, he would never be able to tell anyone about it.

❖ ❖ ❖

On Deck
~ Bob Stevens

"Aaaa batter, batter, aaaa batter," Bob yelled from the bleachers at Navin Field. The weather was perfect for baseball, sunny and warm, but not too hot. A light breeze was blowing, but not hard enough to affect the game or raise any dust. Perfect. The Yankees were up to bat with one out and a man on first. The Tigers were leading; the score was 1 to 0.

"This is great," Bob leaned over and said to Dad.

"It's been a pitching duel so far," Dad said.

Bob's dad had surprised him with a pair of tickets to a Tigers game. It was an early birthday present. Bob's birthday wasn't until August 9th and the game was July 30th. It was a Tuesday afternoon game, and Bob was even more surprised when Dad suggested that they both take the day off. They headed out early, had lunch in a café on the way to the ballpark and were there in plenty of time for batting practice.

During the 7th inning stretch dad said, "I'm sorry we haven't done this more often."

"Yeah, we used to come, that first summer in Detroit. Remember how I got the Ty Cobb card right after we moved here?" Bob asked.

"Of course, it's still in the china cabinet, although I don't think mother likes it there," Dad chuckled.

"Well, a fella should get to have some things around," Bob said with a smile, he knew mother didn't really mind the baseball card in the china cabinet, but it did look a little out of place among the flowered teacups and saucers.

"You'll be 18 in a couple of weeks, and I want you to know, your mother and I, well, we're very proud of you," Dad said. "You've been working hard, at the canvas shop and taking care of Professor Ackermann's house and dog, and playing the part of big brother to the Robinson girls," Bob tried to interrupt, to say it was nothing, but his dad continued, "No, let me finish, I haven't been around as much as I would have liked, with working second shift, and then the overtime because of the war, and well, we just couldn't be more proud of the way you've stepped up to the plate."

He and Bob laughed, partially because of the baseball reference, and partially to ease the embarrassment of the moment. Talking about his feelings wasn't something Dad did very often, so Bob anticipated what was coming. "That being said, we think you're doing enough, you know, as far as the war goes."

Bob thought about saying, *you don't know the half of it. I've also been sending coded messages to the front. Messages given to me by our neighbor who is definitely not a German spy.* Instead he asked, "You mean, you don't want me to sign up when I turn 18?"

"No, we don't, but, we also know we can't stop you," Dad said. He continued, "But we want you to know that finishing high school is important too, that and the work you're doing at the Harding Canvas Co., the war effort needs that too."

"I know, and actually, I've decided to wait to enlist," Bob said. He could see the relief in his dad's face, the creases in his forehead softened and a sigh escaped with his breath. Bob hated to say the next sentence, but, he had to, "I've decided to wait until this fall. Henry will be 18 on October 30th. We've decided to enlist together."

His dad looked stricken, he was about to say something, but the crowd rose with a cheer making further discussion impossible. The players were taking the field.

Tigers won, three to nothing. On the way home, dad said, "Will you promise that you won't sign up without coming and talking to us first?"

"Sure, but I don't think I'll change my mind. I've been thinking about it a lot." Bob said.

"Of course, I'm sure all you young men have been thinking about it. It's a big decision, and I understand, you want to do your part, hell, I wish they would just end this mess, so much destruction, so much waste," Dad said.

Bob wasn't used to hearing his dad swear. He said, "I promise, I won't make any decision without talking to you and mother first."

"And let's just tell Mother that you've decided to wait. We don't have to tell her your plans for October, not yet?" Dad said. Bob nodded in agreement. They were quiet as they rode the streetcar home, both wrapped up in their own thoughts.

The house was open, but mother was nowhere to be found. Dad asked Bob, "Did Mother say anything to you about a Red Cross meeting? I thought she said she'd be home."

"Yeah, she said we'd have dinner, so not to eat too much at the game," Bob said, his stomach rumbled even though he'd eaten two hot dogs and a bag of peanuts.

"Oh, wait, here's a note," Dad said. He read it out aloud. "I'm at Aunty McLeod's. She's had some bad news. We'll have dinner with her."

As the meaning of the note sunk in, Bob said, "Damn, not Davy."

"Davy?" Dad asked.

"Aunty McLeod's grandson," Bob answered. "Oh, hell, not Davy."

They walked through the alley to Aunty McLeod's kitchen door expecting the worse. Therefore, Bob was surprised to find both mother and Aunty McLeod busy in the kitchen preparing supper, but when Aunty McLeod saw him she wiped her wet hands on her apron, reached up and gave him a gentle hug. He leaned forward, letting her wrap her small arms around his shoulders. Softly she said, "My Davy is missing."

"Missing?" Bob asked Aunty McLeod.

"Yes, but, how, how do you misplace a person?" Aunty McLeod asked.

"So, he could be okay? Maybe he's just well . . ." Bob tried to think of a good way to be missing on a battle field, but he couldn't, so he muttered, "lost."

There was a tap at the door. Bob turned and opened it. It was Professor Ackermann.

He took Aunty McLeod's small hands in his own big ones and said, "Mary, I got your message, I'm so sorry, but don't give up hope. This kind of thing happens all the time. Soldiers go out on patrol, get turned around, and can't find their way back to the right trench. He will turn up."

"Do you think so?" Aunty McLeod asked, brightening.

"Absolutely," Professor Ackermann said, "War is a big operation, men, equipment, supplies, it's a lot to keep track of."

"Oh, thank you, you've given me hope," Aunty McLeod said, as she wiped a tear from her cheek.

"You seem to know a lot about military operations Carl, did you serve at some point?" Dad asked.

Professor Ackermann looked from Bob to Aunty McLeod, as if to ensure they weren't going to blurt out that he worked for the War Department, then he answered, "Actually, no, but I've done quite a bit of research on the subject."

"Well, supper is ready, and it will be getting cold if we don't eat," Mother said as she and Aunty McLeod placed dinner plates on the dining table.

The five of them sat down for supper, the conversation was guarded. They talked about the weather and their gardens. They avoided talking about the war.

As they were leaving, Aunty McLeod said, "Thank you so much for keeping me company tonight. I feel I can face the worry now that I've gotten through the first of it, and Carl, your words were quite encouraging."

Dad was helping Mother pack up a platter she'd brought, so neither of them heard as Professor Ackermann whispered in Aunty McLeod's ear, "It won't be easy, and I can't make any promises, but I'll poke around the department and see what I can discover."

Aunty McLeod gave the Professor a weak smile, patted him on the cheek, and said, "Oh, you're a dear man, thank you."

❖ ❖ ❖

Lost
~ Bob Stevens

Professor Ackermann said that if Davy was just lost, he should show up within a week or two. Therefore, things looked grim when two weeks passed and no additional news came. Through his contacts in the war department, the Professor was able to discover that Davy had gone out on a scouting detail near Ypres and had not returned. One of the other men in his unit reported seeing Davy get hit, but this was unconfirmed and his body was not located after the battle. Davy had simply disappeared.

August wore on and still there was no word. Reports of the war were mixed. The spring began with a mighty German offensive. The Germans advanced deeper into France than since 1914. The Allies retreated, but were eventually able to stop the German advance. As fresh American troops and munitions reached full strength at the front, the tide turned to the Allies advantage. The newspapers were filled with accounts of one Allied victory after another, starting with the Battle of Amiens in mid-August. The Stevens and Robinson families all tried to help Aunty McLeod during this anxious time. Bob, Maggie, Jeannie and Sara visited her often, trying to keep her spirits up, but the worry started to take its toll.

In mid-August the temperature in Detroit soared. After the mercury hit over 100 three days in a row, Mr. Harding decided it was just too hot to work. He closed the shop early. The sewing machines kept overheating and one of the sewers had even passed out. He sent everyone home, and hoped for a change in the weather.

Bob and Henry were thrilled at the prospect of an afternoon off. Unfortunately, it was too hot to do anything. They wandered back to Bob's house hoping to find some cool lemonade in the icebox, but even the icebox had given up in a puddle.

"Wow, what a mess," Bob said. He and Henry entered the Stevens kitchen to find mother on her hands and knees sopping up a large ice block size puddle of water.

"The icebox just couldn't take the heat," Mother said with a sigh, she wiped sweat from her forehead and continued, "And I agree with it."

"Do you want any help?" Henry offered.

"Oh, no, I'm almost done, but thank you dear," Mother said as she got up off her knees. She continued, "Actually, this kitchen is too small for three people, so maybe you boys can find some shade in the yard, or better yet, run this lemonade over to Aunty McLeod." Mother handed Bob a jar of fresh lemonade, and continued, "She mentioned that her throat was sore yesterday, so this might help. Maybe you boys can have a glass with her and visit a bit? She looked rather warn out and I think she could use some cheering up."

"Okay," Bob said, taking the jar, it wasn't as cold as he hoped, but maybe Aunty McLeod still had some ice in her icebox. He and Henry walked through the yard; even the trees were sagging in the heat. They got to Aunty McLeod's and tapped on the screen door. They knew she was home because the main door was open. When she didn't answer, Bob knocked again, harder. Then he heard a crash and a moan from inside. Bob pulled the screen door handle, fortunately it wasn't locked, and rushed inside. Setting the lemonade on the kitchen table, he called, "Aunty McLeod, are you here?"

He heard the moan again, coming from the sitting room. Bob entered to see Aunty McLeod crumpled on the floor, a broken teacup and a puddle of tea next to her. He bent down to help her up, "Are you okay?" Bob asked.

Henry had followed Bob into the room, "I'll go get your mother," he said.

"And the doctor, she's burning up," Bob said. One look at her flushed face and a touch of her warm arm told him that she hadn't just fallen. She was sick.

"Aunty McLeod," Bob said, as he lifted her gently to the sofa. He arranged a pillow under her head, and lifted her feet up on the other end. She seemed to be coming around.

"Oh, Bob dear, I don't know what came over me," Aunty McLeod said weakly.

"I think you're sick," Bob said. "Wait here, I'll get you something to drink."

Bob ran into the kitchen; an empty glass was on the counter. He filled it with lemonade. A dishcloth was sitting next to the sink. He soaked it with cool water and returned to Aunty McLeod.

She had closed her eyes and for a moment Bob thought she was dead, his heart raced, but then he noticed her soft breathing. "Here," he said, "I've got a cool cloth for your head." He had never played the part of nurse before, it was mother who always nursed him, but he knew it felt wonderful when she laid a cool cloth on his forehead. Now he did the same for Aunty McLeod.

She gave a shutter, opened her eyes, reached out, patted Bob's hand and said, "Thank you dear." But then she sighed and closed her eyes again.

"I have some lemonade for you," Bob said, offering her the glass. Mother rushed in at that moment, and Bob was quite happy to hand over the job of nursing to her.

"Oh, my, Mary," she said, bending over Aunty McLeod. To Bob she said, "Henry's gone for the doctor."

"She fell down," Bob said, "I think she's sick."

Now that Mother was here, taking charge, he felt kind of helpless. He picked up the broken teacup and went to the kitchen for a rag to wipe up the puddle of tea. The doctor arrived and Bob and Henry found a shady spot in the yard. They sat down on the grass and waited. Bob brought the teacup with him, it had broken into three pieces. He showed it to Henry.

"Do you think we can glue it back together for her?" Bob asked Henry. It suddenly seemed very important to him that the teacup be mended. As if fixing it would somehow lessen the loss Aunty McLeod had endured since Davy's disappearance.

Henry took the pieces from Bob, fitted them together, and said, "Sure, look it seems to be a clean break. Pop has some great glue at the shop."

"After the doctor comes out maybe we can head over there and glue it back together," Bob suggested.

"Sure, I guess," Henry said, a little confused at the urgency over a broken cup.

"Great," Bob said.

The doctor came out about 20 minutes later. The boys watched him leave then Bob went inside to see how Aunty McLeod was. The kitchen, dining room and sitting room were empty. Bob crept quietly down the hall. Mother must have heard him coming because she emerged from the bedroom closing the door softly behind her.

"How is she?" Bob asked.

"I'm afraid she's quite sick," Mother said.

"Oh, what does she have?" Bob asked.

"Influenza. Dr. Miller said it was a good thing you happened by when you did. It would have been very dangerous, especially in this heat, if she hadn't gotten help right away," Mother said.

"Influenza? It's been in the newspapers, about an especially bad influenza?" Bob asked.

"He doesn't think it's that, doesn't think she would have been in contact with it. It hasn't spread to Detroit, at least not yet. It's probably just plain influenza, but that can be quite risky for someone Aunty McLeod's age," Mother said. "I'm going to stay with her. You'll have to fend for yourself for supper. Can you run over to the Robinson's and tell Mrs. Robinson what's happened?"

"Sure, and then Henry and I are going over to the shop, he thinks his pop has some glue that will mend that broken cup," Bob said.

"Why, that will be nice," Mother said and she headed back in to sit with Aunty McLeod.

Professor Ackermann and Nietzsche arrived at Aunty McLeod's house later that evening. The heat of the day had subsided, but only slightly. There wasn't a breath of air. Bob and Maggie were on the porch. Their mothers were inside nursing Aunty McLeod. Bob fanned himself with a page from the newspaper he was reading, or trying to read. Maggie sat knitting, always knitting, for the soldiers. And they were waiting. Nietzsche laid down on the step, panting in her hot fur coat.

"How is she?" Professor Ackermann asked, somewhat frantic.

"Dr. Miller's been here twice, he just left. She's really sick," Maggie said, looking up from the gray green yarn in her lap, "He said the next 24 to 48 hours will be the worst, that if . . ." but she couldn't continue. She stifled a sob and looked back at the half completed sock she was holding.

Bob finished for her, ". . . that if she can survive the next day or two, she has a good chance, but," his voice cracked and he whispered, "she seems to have lost her will to live."

"Damn, this won't do," Professor Ackermann said, and he went inside. Bob and Maggie could hear him through the open window.

"Carl," Mother said, surprised at his sudden appearance, "She's quite ill."

"Mary, Mary dear," Professor Ackermann said, "Listen to me, can you hear me?"

Bob and Maggie sat stock still on the porch, straining to hear through the open window. They heard Aunty McLeod's weak, throaty reply; yes. She could hear him and something about him taking her husband's books.

But Professor Ackermann's strong voice cut her off, "Now Mary, I'll not listen to any of that. Remember when I lost Hanne and then Gabriele? Remember how I was in a bad way, I wanted to die myself, but you wouldn't let me. You made me keep living. Now, it's your turn to fight."

"Carl, she's quite ill, I'm not sure . . ." Mother said, but Professor Ackermann continued,

"I know you're sick, but I know you, as well as you know me, you're a fighter. So, here's what we're going to do.

I'll sit with you tonight, like you sat with me those many years ago, then, tomorrow I'm off to Washington. I have connections in the War Department. In fact, I've already made some inquiries, I'm going to find Davy. So, promise me, you can't give up until we discover what's become of your grandson."

Bob and Maggie stared at each other. Professor Ackermann was practically demanding that Aunty McLeod keep living. They continued listening.

"Now, my dear ladies," Professor Ackermann said kindly to their mothers, "if you'll let me, I'd like to care for Mary tonight, I nursed my wife and daughter through horrible illnesses, so I know the routine. She'll need you tomorrow when I leave for Washington"

But before they could answer, Bob and Maggie heard Aunty McLeod's weak voice again, "You've made inquiries?"

"Yes, Mary, I've contacted people, who have contacted people, but these things take time, so you have to concentrate on getting well," Professor Ackermann said.

"I guess I could try a spoonful of broth," Aunty McLeod said.

A few minutes later Mrs. Stevens and Mrs. Robinson appeared on the porch. Mrs. Robinson said to Maggie, "Aunty McLeod is in good hands for the evening, let's go home and see what we can find for dinner."

"Bob," Professor Ackermann called through the window, "Can you see to Nietzsche while I'm in Washington?"

"Absolutely" Bob said.

Although Aunty McLeod was still very sick, she improved a little through the night under Professor Ackermann's watchful eye. At the very least, she seemed to have found the will to fight. Her fever broke and she was resting comfortably when Mrs. Stevens returned in the morning. As promised, Professor Ackermann left for Washington on the early train.

CHAPTER 18

The Patrol
~ Davy McLeod

Davy spent the spring and early summer of 1918 back at the front with his original platoon under the command of Second Lieutenant Gavin Campbell. Gavin turned out to be an excellent officer. The men respected him, trusted him and therefore followed him. When the three friends from Bothwell were alone, they joked, tormented and confided with each other as if they were chums on the football pitch, but when they were with the other soldiers under Gavin's command, Mac and Davy happily gave Gavin the respect they would have given any commanding officer. Gavin with his wild hair and beard, easy smile and common manners, had earned the respect of the entire unit.

The scouting and patrolling skills Davy and Jamie learned in the Sniping, Observation and Scouting Course were put to use during that summer. As a result of the devastating German offensive in March, the landscape of the war had changed. Increased patrols were used in an effort to track enemy movement. Davy's duties shifted from finding and eliminating German snipers, to working as a scout on patrols. Patrols were usually sent out at night as listeners, hoping to overhear or witness important information. But, sometimes, they were sent to discover an enemy location. Once located the enemy was destroyed.

In late July, Gavin, Davy, Jamie, Mac and five other men were scheduled for a nighttime intelligence gathering and destruction patrol. During the afternoon, they gathered to discuss the details.

Second Lieutenant Campbell explained the mission, "We'll leave just after sunset. We suspect that a bombed out farmhouse is being used as a German communications installation. Ariel photographs show that someone is in there, we just don't know who. If it's a German post, we're ordered to take it out. The element of surprise is imperative."

"Standard number of grenades, Lieutenant?" one of the men asked.

"Let's take a few extra, if you can get them," Gavin answered, he continued, "The farm is about 6 kilometers northwest of here. Davy and Jamie, you're in charge of directions, the bearing information is here," Gavin handed maps to Davy and Jamie, "I don't want to get lost out there. We'll travel light, water, gas masks, one day's rations; you know the drill. If we confirm that it is a German post, and not some French farmer holed up for the duration, we'll hit it and head back. We'll be back in our beds, well, if we had beds, sleeping like babies before the sun comes up. Any questions?" There were no questions, so Gavin said, "Dismissed, get some sleep this afternoon, we'll meet back here at dusk."

"Sleeping before the sun comes up, ah," Mac said, after the other men had wandered off, "only if I can fall asleep before you start snoring. I swear, you're louder than a bloody Hun attack." Davy laughed, so Mac asked him, "And you've been tossing and turning and mumbling every time you doze off."

"Sorry mate, must be the rich food I've been eating," Davy said satirically.

"Well, I'm going to get some sleep, or at least I'm going to try, 12 kilometers round trip through no man's land isn't exactly an easy evening stroll," Jamie said. They all wandered off to find someplace to rest.

At sunset the same nine men gathered and waited for the sun to disappear in the west. The sky turned from bright reds and pinks to dark purple and finally a deep blue. The first stars of the night began to appear. A nervous energy filled the air. Mac smoked one cigarette, then another. Jamie checked and rechecked the map.

"It looks like we'll be within a kilometer of the German trenches here," Jamie said, pointing at the map, "at about the half way point. Then their trenches veer off to the west and we head north."

"Got that lads, at two kilometers it's absolute silence. And," he looked at Mac who was lighting a third cigarette, "no smoking, they could see the glow."

"That's why I'm smoking them now," Mac said as he took a long drag, "storing up two to remember later."

"Okay, I think it's plenty dark, the platoons to our right and left have been told we're going out, so no worries about getting hit by mistake," Gavin said.

"That's comforting," Davy said.

"Davy and Jamie, you lead, I'll bring up the rear. In, out and asleep before suns up lads." Gavin said.

Davy and Jamie climbed over the parapet and followed the zigzag path that allowed them to pass safely through the field of barbed wire. They emerged into no man's land. It hadn't rained in a couple of days, so the ground was firm under Davy's feet. The sky was bright with stars but fortunately the moon was only a sliver. It had just risen above the horizon.

Davy was in the lead. He walked slowly, cautiously, stopping often to listen. The eight men behind him stopped also. Eighteen ears strained to hear an enemy whisper, or footfall.

Davy felt the breeze as it blew over the barren landscape; it smelled of earth and rot. *Even here, out in the open, I can smell the stink war,* Davy thought. He could hear the buzz of insects, and occasionally, the flutter of a bat overhead. Davy continued walking, checking his compass against the bearings he had memorized. He had been issued the compass after successfully completing the sniper training. It was a night marching compass, with markings made of a material that glowed softly in the dark. He had never owned anything so precise, so intricate. He liked it. His mind wandered as he walked, *an engineer, like my Grandfather, maybe I could be an engineer after the war?* A twig broke loudly under his foot and he stopped, stood stock still, and held his breath. Everything was still quiet. *An engineer, but only if I don't get killed here in no man's land*, Davy thought. He told himself to concentrate.

Davy stopped to check the compass again. They should be nearing a destroyed village. He squinted into the darkness trying to see what remained of a church tower. There, on the left as noted on the map. He turned and pointed it out to Jamie. Jamie nodded. They continued past the church and for about 200 meters followed what was left of an old cobblestone road. As the road disappeared in the muck, they veered right. The ground sloped down; it was wetter here. A bullfrog croaked loudly. Davy's boots squished in the muck, making soft sucking sounds as he lifted his feet with each step. The bullfrog croaked again. He could hear the lads behind him, squishing through the mud. Then the bullfrog, one more time. He continued, a few more steps, the ground was getting firmer, quieter. The bullfrog croaked again. Davy kept walking. He exhaled, softly. He hadn't realized he'd been holding his breath. Everything was quiet, even the bullfrog.

With a flash, a flare rose up into the sky above them and they were illuminated by a bright light. *Shit,* Davy thought, as he dropped to the ground. Shots exploded around him.

Gavin shouted, "Get down!"

There was a grunt, then, "Bloody hell," Jamie said.

"Fall back," Gavin yelled. The flare went out and they were once again hidden in the darkness. "Move, get back,"

Gavin yelled. Davy got up and started to run, but just as his eyes were adjusting once again to the darkness, there was the flash of another flare. Light. As he fell to the ground, he could see Gavin, helping, almost carrying Jamie about 40 meters in front of him.

The world exploded around Davy. A searing pain raced through the left side of his neck and head. The light from the flare faded, and everything went completely black.

To Hell
~ Davy McLeod

The photographs, one after the other, the sad parents and family, the blurry girl and the boy with the dog, the sweetheart, two small girls in pretty dresses, a German soldier, the very old women with deep wrinkles, a happy girl in a fancy hat, a young mother holding a baby, a smiling old man with a dog at his feet, a proud German cavalry officer.

I'm dead, Davy thought, *bloody hell. They will be with me, these photographs, these faces, for all eternity.*

Slowly, the events of the patrol came back to him. It was getting light. He rose up on his elbows, a wave of dizziness enveloped him. He lay back down. *Crap,* he thought. Everything went black.

And Back
~ Davy McLeod

"Sie sin tot," Davy heard, then "Lass uns von hier verschwinden." He stayed completely still, held his breath. He felt a cold shadow pass above him, blocking the hot sun. He lay there, still, the sun beating down. It was quiet for a long time. A breeze ruffled his hair. He heard the call of a crow above, the scurry of an animal not far away. A rat.

His head and neck ached, but he thought he might be okay. Slowly he opened his eyes. His left eye was caked shut with something, *blood,* he thought. He could see the blue sky through his right eye. *A one-eyed sniper,* Davy thought. He moved his head, it hurt like hell, but he could move. He was in a depression or ditch, maybe he could sit up without being seen from the nearby German trench. He took stock of his battered body. *I still have two arms,* he thought, as he opened and closed each fist, lifting them within view of his one good eye, making sure they were really still there. With his arms, he pushed his body up along the edge of the ditch. *Legs, check,* he thought as he surveyed the length of his body. He wiggled his toes, raised each knee and noticed the lack of blood. *Okay, I'm alive, for now,* he thought. He was extremely thirsty; the sun was hot above his head. He felt for his canteen, found it right where it should be strapped around his left side. He shook it; it was empty. A piece of shrapnel had pierced a hole in the side.

The events of last evening returned slowly, the patrol, the stars, and the damn frog. Then the flares and Jamie getting hit. Gavin calling to fall back. He wasn't sure if anyone else was hit. *Were his mates lying dead in the field around him?* Davy thought. Finding them out here would be impossible; he would head back to the British trench. Gavin, Mac and Jamie would be there, all fine, waiting for him to show up so they could play some football. He told himself this, over and over again, trying to believe it. *But can I find my way back?* He wondered.

Davy knew he couldn't get up in broad daylight. He'd have to wait until it was dark. *Bloody hell waiting would be a hell of a lot easier, if it wasn't so hot, and if I wasn't so thirsty,* he thought. He looked at the sun. It was high in the sky. It must be well after noon. He felt around for his compass, afraid to lift his head too high. He had been holding it when the world exploded around him. He found it in the dirt next to him. He brought it up to his good eye, but the glass was broken and the needle bent, *useless,* he thought and tossed it aside. The sun was over this right shoulder, which meant he was laying with his back to the west, with the German trench behind him. So all he had to do was walk due east, in the dark, through no man's land, with one eye and no compass. *No problem,* he thought, *bloody hell.* He closed his eyes against the bright sun and fell into a deep, dreamless sleep.

Davy woke with a shiver, the sun had set and the sky was a deep purple, but it wasn't completely dark. *Good, I have all night to get home,* he thought, *home: a British hole in a field in France.* He sat up slowly, his head and neck ached miserably. He tried to spit in his hand, thinking he could use the spit to wipe the crusted blood from his eye; maybe it still worked. But his mouth was too dry. He thought about pulling the crusted blood away, but decided if his eye could be saved, it would be better to leave it. When he got home, maybe a doctor could fix it.

He waited about half an hour, watching as the sky darkened, and the stars grew brighter. Fortunately, it was a clear night. He looked for the North Star. If he kept it over his right shoulder, he would be walking west. Carefully he pulled himself out of the ditch. The movement sent a searing pain through his neck and head. He gritted his teeth and started walking. Slowly, one step then another. The terrain was treacherous. He tripped several times but didn't want to know what, or who, he tripped on. Turning his head and looking over his shoulder for the North Star was painful. To stay on course, he had to stop, turn his body, check the sky, turn back and keep walking. It was a slow agonizing march. For a while, he forgot to check the position of the North Star and veered too far north instead of west. His head hurt and his neck ached. Swallowing was difficult. He trudged on.

The night wore on, at one point, he thought he heard something in the darkness, a footstep, or was it just the wind. He grew tired. He stopped to check the position of his guiding star and discovered that the sky was completely dark. Clouds, but it didn't matter he couldn't walk any further. He stumbled and fell, jarring his aching body. He didn't get up. *Damn,* he thought, *I can't do it.*

Dr. Mona
~ Davy McLeod

"Oi, this chap is still alive," a gruff voice said. Davy was aware of being lifted. Two hands under his arms, two more at his ankles.

"Watch his neck," the voice said, "most of the damage seems to be there."

"Are you sure he's alive?" asked another voice.

"If he's dead, his heart's still beating," replied the gruff voice, as he checked for a pulse by pressing his finger to the undamaged side of Davy's neck. Davy wanted to yell, tell them he was alive and beg them for help, but his voice wouldn't come. His neck ached worse than ever. They put him on a make shift stretcher and started walking. Each step caused another jarring pain. He opened his eye. He could see the rough, dirty face of the man carrying the foot end of the stretcher.

"Ah, you are alive," the man said to Davy, "well, don't worry mate, Dr. Mona will mend you right quick. You just close your eye there and relax." But Davy couldn't close his eye, couldn't relax. Where were they taking him? They spoke English, but they weren't soldiers, weren't in regular uniforms.

After a while they put him down. He was afraid they would leave him. He tried to sit up, but a firm hand held him down. He heard knocking, then a woman's face came into view. She said, "Well, hello there," she patted his shoulder gently and continued, "don't worry, I'll see what I can do to fix you up. Just relax. Bring him inside." Davy was lifted from the stretcher and carried inside. He watched as the women moved quickly around the room. She put a damp cloth over his mouth and said, "Now, just breathe easy and I'll have you right as rain in no time." Everything went black.

Davy woke to the sound of someone humming softly. *Mum,* he thought. He opened his eyes slowly. They both opened. They both worked. He was lying on a cot in a clean room. The broken windows were covered with white cloth; part of the roof was covered with thick canvas. An oil lamp burned in a corner. There were other cots, other patients. Somehow, he'd made it to a hospital, but it wasn't like any army hospital he'd seen. He tried to remember how he got here, but it was a blur.

The humming was coming from a middle-aged woman. She was busy moving from cot to cot. Checking bandages, gently putting her hand on a forehead here or fluffing a pillow there. The woman had short wavy brown hair, a round face and a friendly smile. She stopped at the end of Davy's cot and said, "Well, hello again, I'm so glad you're awake. I'm Dr. Mona." Davy opened his mouth to talk, but Dr. Mona held up her hand and said, "Oh, don't try to talk, not for a few days." She pulled a stool up next to the cot and sat down. "I'll do the talking for now. You're Sergeant Davy McLeod, at least that's what your tags say." Davy nodded. Dr. Mona continued, "I'm the doctor here. This is an American Women's Hospital, which means its run by American women, not that it's for women patients." Dr. Mona chuckled, and went on, "They found you in no man's land and brought you to me." *Who found me and what's an American Women's Hospital?* Davy thought. Dr. Mona patted his hand and said, "I know you have lots of questions, but they will have to wait. You had a very close call. Shrapnel was lodged in your neck. It's amazing it didn't damage your spine, blood vessels or your windpipe. It completely missed everything important. I was able to remove all the metal and stitch you up. You have a cut high on your cheekbone that extends to your temple. It's superficial, but it bled quite a bit, and caked your eye shut. When I removed the blood, I was happy to see that the eye was just fine. You're very lucky." Davy raised his hand and gingerly felt the bandages on his neck and face. Dr. Mona continued, "I'm afraid you'll have a scar, but it should fade over time. I'm pretty good with a needle." Dr. Mona chuckled and continued, "Your face was a little too perfect anyway the scar will add distinction." She sighed, but gave him a half smile and continued, "Along with the cuts, you've had a severe bump on the head resulting in a concussion. The best thing you can do is lay still and in time, the damage will heal."

"Dr. Mona, there's a French farmer in the yard with a cut on his hand, he's a little wary about coming in," a nurse said as she came into the room, she continued, "Oh good, he's awake."

"Yes, he's going to be just fine. Davy, this is my assistant Marie," Davy nodded, to Marie, Dr. Mona said, "I'll look after the farmer, can you get Davy here some water then, if the water doesn't come squirting out of the holes in his neck," Dr. Mona laughed at her own morbid joke and continued, "sorry, it's been a long war, give him some weak broth." She looked at Davy, raised a finger to her lips and said, "And remember, no talking."

Over the next two weeks Davy grew stronger. As his voice and strength returned he grew both anxious and reluctant to return to his platoon. *Was I the only one hurt, or am I the only one to survive?* He asked himself. He remembered seeing Gavin dragging Jamie from the field, and he was afraid to face the fact that he may be the only one left. He knew he should leave as soon as possible to rejoin his unit, but he couldn't seem to decide to leave. In a strange way, not knowing, meant there was still hope, and for the time being, the hope was easier to live with than the possible truth. His vision, which was blurry at first, became sharp again. The realization that he would once again be able to work as a sniper also caused him to hesitate when he considered returning to the front.

One evening, when the hospital was unusually quiet, Dr. Mona offered Davy a cup of coffee and sat down next to his cot. She explained how she came be in France.

"My grandfather was born in a village near here. He immigrated to America when my father was young. He did quite well in the United States. He settled in Pittsburg, started a steel smelting business and became quite wealthy. The business grew bigger and more profitable under my father's watchful eye." Dr. Mona explained.

"But you decided to become a doctor?" Davy asked.

Dr. Mona laughed softly, "I think I always knew I wanted to be a doctor. When I was a girl I used to bandage up my dolls, the cat, the dog. I even talked my governess into letting me wrap a tight bandage around her poor head. I trained as a nurse, but that wasn't enough, I wanted to be a doctor."

Davy touched the bandage on his neck and said, "I'm glad you did."

"But, I discovered that even though I have all the same training as a man and connections to the upper echelons of society, it's still difficult for a woman doctor to find a position at a good hospital. And many patients are leery of seeing a woman doctor. When the American Women's Hospital advertised for women doctors to come here, I jumped at the chance. I could prove myself as a doctor, improve my knowledge and help the people near where my grandfather was raised."

"But they sent you here, all alone, to a war zone?" Davy asked.

"Not exactly, the main Women's Hospital is about ten miles west of here, but it's a long way for the villagers to travel, so I talked the administrators into letting me move to where I am most needed. As my father is a large donor, they reluctantly agreed. I treat local people and an occasional soldier," Dr. Mona said, then she added, "And I'm not alone, Marie is with me. She's a wonderful nurse." Davy looked around and wondered where Marie was. He hadn't seen her all day. Dr. Mona, anticipating his question said, "Marie has family in a village not far from here, she's gone to see how they're doing."

"Who brought me here? I remember two men." Davy asked.

"One of them was Tommy, but I don't think that's his real name. I don't know the other man's name. They're deserters, I suspect. They scratch out a living on the edge of no man's land, unable to face the trenches any longer." Dr. Mona explained. Davy frowned. "Don't think too badly of them, some men snap under the pressure." Davy realized that the doctor saw distain in his expression, when what he felt was shame in himself for delaying his own return. He would go as soon as possible.

"How do I get back to the British trenches?" Davy asked.

"The front has been moving all summer, which makes travel especially difficult, but the hospital sends a truck out to me once a week. They deliver supplies and take any wounded that need more advanced care. You can ride with them. Once at the hospital, it should be easy for you to locate your platoon. I'm expecting a delivery the day after tomorrow." Dr. Mona explained, then she continued, "You should be well enough to travel, but it will take a bit longer for you to get your full strength back."

"I should return as soon as I can," Davy said.

"You're welcome to stay an additional week, we have room, and if we need your bed for more wounded, you'd be welcome to the shed," Dr. Mona said, she patted his hand and continued, "You do what you think is best, now, I better get back to work."

An English Corporal, an American doctor, a French patient and a German Soldier

~ Davy McLeod

Davy woke up with a start. Someone was pounding on the door of the makeshift hospital. He heard Dr. Mona's footsteps as she hurried to open it.

"Hilf ihr?" pleaded a gruff voice.

"Oh dear, bring her in," Dr. Mona said. The door to the patient room opened, Dr. Mona flew in followed by a German soldier. Draped in his arms was a young girl. Her legs were soaked in blood. She wasn't moving.

Dr. Mona said, "Put her here." The German laid the girl gently on the operating table.

"A landmine?" Dr. Mona asked, but the German soldier had already turned and disappeared out the door. "Bother," Dr. Mona said. She had washed her hands and was busy pulling the blood-soaked clothing away from the girl's body.

Davy realized that she needed help. Marie was away visiting her family for the night. He joined her at the operating table and said, "Tell me what to do."

"Oh, thank you, she's alive, but she's lost a lot of blood. First we need to clean away this blood to see where the damage is," Dr. Mona said. The girl moaned.

"We need chloroform," Dr. Mona ordered, "we'll need to put her under so we can work on her." She pointed to a bottle on the shelf. Davy opened the bottle and poured it into a cloth as Dr. Mona indicated the right amount.

Next he put the cloth gently over the girl's mouth. Before the chloroform took effect, the girl opened her eyes and looked into Davy's face pleading for help. Dr. Mona cut away the blood soaked clothing. There were numerous cuts on the girl's legs.

They worked on the girl through the night. Dr. Mona was able to stop the bleeding and close the wounds. Davy helped by responding quickly as Dr. Mona told him what needed to be done. As light from the rising sun started to peak through the sheet-covered windows, Dr. Mona said, "There, I think she'll be okay." The girl had a long line of tidy stitches from her knee to her hip on her right leg and numerous sections of stitching on her left leg. "She looks like a patchwork quilt, but I think we saved her legs," Dr. Mona said with a frown.

"So she should be able to walk again?" Davy asked.

"Yes, I think so, she was lucky this time," Dr. Mona said.

"I wonder who she is." Davy said.

"Whoever she is, I don't think she would have made it if it hadn't been for your help," Dr. Mona said. "Thank you."

Davy yawned and said, "Doctoring is hard work; I'm beat." He returned to his cot and laid down, soon he was fast asleep.

Davy wasn't on the delivery truck when it left for the hospital two days later. There wasn't room for him. The girl was sent so she could be monitored for infection, and with other patients, the truck was full. Davy didn't want to admit to himself that he was a little relieved. He still wasn't ready to return to the front.

During the week that followed, Davy observed Dr. Mona and Marie as they took care of more patients. The main battle had moved south so they mostly treated illnesses and minor injuries. Davy tried to make himself useful. He chopped a stack of wood for them and re-secured the canvas to the roof. News from the front was encouraging, it seemed the tide was turning in the Allies' favor.

Davy took the next delivery truck back to his platoon. It had been four weeks since the night of the patrol. Before he left, Dr. Mona said, "Be careful," she paused, reached out, lifted his hand so that it was stretched out, palm down in front of her, steady as usual, then she continued, "you know, you have a gift, a steady hand and a keen eye, you would make a very good surgeon. After the war, you should consider going to medical school." She turned his hand over and put a piece of paper on his palm, it had her name and address written on it. She continued, "If there's ever anything I can do to help you, please, let me know."

Beginning of the End
~ Davy McLeod

Davy sat on a cot in a small dark room, elbows on his knees and head in his hands. He didn't know how long he'd been there. He was alone. "It's my fault, all my fault," he kept repeating to himself.

It had taken two days for him to reach his platoon. They were on R&R. He had found Mac, smoking cigarettes in a neglected garden. Davy wasn't sure if it was the same garden they had met in before, it could have been, but the war had changed it beyond recognition. The war had changed all of them, maybe even beyond recognition. He looked at Mac as he approached. He looked older. Older than the boy who had enlisted 3 years ago, and older than the man who had joined him on patrol 4 weeks ago. There was a sadness in his face that hadn't been there before. Mac looked up from the cigarette he was smoking and saw Davy.

"Bloody hell, you're alive," Mac said. They hugged, "Bloody hell," Mac said again, his voice catching in his throat.

"Yep," Davy said with a weary smile.

"But how, we thought you were hit. Where have you been?" Mac asked.

"I was hit and knocked out," Davy said, showing Mac the scar on his neck and cheek, "I wandered around no man's land trying to get back to our trenches, but I passed out, some blokes found me and took me to a hospital. The doctor there, a Dr. Mona, patched me up."

Mac shook his head. He was dumbstruck.

Davy asked the question he dreaded asking, "How's Jamie?"

"Jamie? Oh, Jamie's fine," Mac stammered.

"Oh great, I thought I saw him get hit, saw Gavin dragging him away. That's great," Davy said relieved.

"His leg was pretty banged up, but they were able to save it. He's back in London with Nora and his new baby." Mac said. But, Mac was distracted, not looking at Davy, he stared at his feet, watching a bug at the toe of his worn boot.

"Wow, Jamie's a father, and he's out of it. Safe in London. That's great," Davy said, but something was wrong.

Finally, Mac looked up, stared into Davy's eyes. There was torment and sorrow on Mac's face. He said, "Davy, Gavin's dead."

Davy stepped back, as if Mac had struck him. "Dead," he repeated. "No, no, not Gavin, he's the strong one, the one who would make it." Davy said shaking his head.

"He was hit by a sniper, last week, before we came out," Mac said. "He was walking along the trench and, well it was too low, or he was too tall."

"A sniper," whispered Davy.

"Bloody hell," Mac whispered.

Davy and Mac had sat in the garden. They smoked Mac's cigarettes. Mac told Davy how they had gotten back from the patrol. Jamie and two of the other men were wounded, two were killed and he was missing. They had talked about how the Central Powers were falling apart, that the Allies were winning, that it may all be over soon, but neither of them seemed to care that much. After a while, they had gotten up and walked over to headquarters to report Davy's return. He had wanted to make sure they notified his family that he was safe.

That's when Davy was arrested, accused of desertion, and locked in the small, dark room in the cellar of the farmhouse turned headquarters. When he was awake, he was tormented by the belief that he was responsible for

Gavin's death. If he fell asleep, he was tormented by the photographs of his recurring dream.

Davy was tried by court-martial three days later. By a strange and unfortunate coincidence, Captain Clark, the same Captain Clark that Davy out shot at the sniper school, was one of the three officers that would decide Davy's fate. A makeshift courtroom was set up in the dining room of the farmhouse headquarters. Even as a courtroom, it was a pleasant room. Sunlight streamed in through a big picture window. The scene of a pretty village was repeated over and over on the wallpaper. But the brightness hurt Davy's eyes, and the village seemed to float magically off the wall.

Punishment for desertion was death. Davy didn't have much hope of getting off, and he didn't much care. All he could think about was that if he'd been there, if he'd come back earlier, he might have been able to get the German sniper, before the sniper got Gavin. It was his fault Gavin was dead. Mac was in the courtroom, ready to plead on Davy's behalf, even if Davy would not.

"Sergeant McLeod, you have been charged with desertion. It is a very serious offence," one of the three officers said.

"So, you thought you could wait out the war in some farmer's shed?" Captain Clark asked.

"Captain Clark," we must follow procedure here," the first officer interrupted, "Sergeant McLeod, how do you plead?"

"I was injured," Davy stammered. Davy's mind raced, *I could tell them about trying to find my way back, about passing out, show them my scar and Dr. Mona's neat stiches on my neck, beg them to let me live, or I could let them shoot me, maybe I am a deserter.* Davy stood there, unable to speak.

A commotion in the hall startled everyone. The door flew open and a middle-aged man with a receding hairline and glasses walked in. The insignia on his uniform showed that he was a major. "Pardon the interruption," he said. Davy knew him, but couldn't remember where he'd seen him before. "I'm Colonel Irons, with the Intelligence Corps, Sergeant McLeod, I've been ordered to take you into my custody."

"Now, one moment here, Sergeant McLeod is on trial for desertion," Captain Clark said.

"Not anymore," the major said, "The United States War Department has a need for him."

CHAPTER 19

Hope Again
~ Aunty McLeod

By late August Aunty McLeod began to regain her strength and spirit. The heat of summer had subsided and the evenings smelled of fall. There was no additional news of Davy, but Professor Ackermann's promise to search for him had given her hope. News of the war had been good. The Allies were making progress. There were even whispers of victory.

On the first of September, a telegram came. Aunty McLeod was in the kitchen about to have a cup of tea when the delivery boy tapped on her door. She took the telegram with trembling hands and set it on the kitchen table. She didn't open it. She had promised Susie Stevens that if she received any telegrams she would get her before opening them. At the time, she thought it was a silly request, but now, she agreed. It would be better not to be alone. *I'll just enjoy my afternoon tea as usual,* she thought. *Then I'll take the telegram and run over to see Susie.* She sipped her tea and stared at the telegram. To her surprise there was another tap at the door. It was another delivery boy with yet another telegram. *What can this mean,* Aunty McLeod thought. She couldn't wait any longer. She left her warm tea on the table, tucked both telegrams in her apron pocket, picked up her walking stick and headed out.

The sun was shining warmly in the yard. Birds were gathering in the smoke bush by the alley and the very tips of the trees were starting to show the colors of fall. But, Aunty McLeod didn't notice any of it. All she could think of was the telegrams in her pocket. She could feel the weight of them.

Susie was in the garden, a basket over her arm. She was gathering apples for a pie. "Hello, Mary," she called as Aunty McLeod lifted the latch on the gate and entered the yard.

"I have news," Aunty McLeod said hoarsely. Tears welling up in her eyes. She took the telegrams out of her pocket.

"Two?" Susie asked.

"Yes, but I haven't opened them," Aunty McLeod said anxiously.

"Oh good," Susie said. "Let's go sit down."

The younger woman took the older woman by the arm, and lead her slowly to a stone bench in the flower garden at the back of the yard. Both women were close to tears.

"Do you want me to open them, read them?" Susie asked.

"Yes, actually I suppose you'll have to, I didn't bring my glasses," Aunty McLeod said softly.

Susie's hands trembled as the slid her finger under the seal of one of the telegrams. She pulled the yellow paper from the envelope and unfolded it. She read, "Davy is fine." They each exhaled the breath they hadn't realized they were holding. Tears flowing down their cheeks.

"Oh, thank God," Aunty McLeod whispered. She squeezed Susie's hand. "What else does it say?"

Susie continued reading, "Recovered from injuries in France."

"Oh dear," Aunty McLeod said. Susie read the last line.

"He will be heading home to Scotland soon. – Carl."

"He's going home! Oh, he's made it. I just hope he's not badly hurt, it says recovered, so it can't be too bad." Aunty McLeod said. "It's from Carl, what a dear, dear friend he's been."

"Maybe this one will tell us about his injuries," Susie said. She opened the second telegram and read the short message. "Davy's fine. Returning to Bothwell. He has recovered complete from wounds. Katherine."

"That's my daughter-in-law," Aunty McLeod explained. She took the telegrams from Susie and squinted at them. Reading them each again. "Oh, I can hardly believe it. He's safe."

That evening Aunty McLeod sat down to write Davy a letter. She hadn't written him since he'd been reported missing. How do you address such a letter anyway, 'Davy McLeod, Somewhere in France?' So now, she renewed her request to help him. She knew her daughter-in-law had already left Bothwell for Australia, but had been told to address letters to his friend's home, Gavin Campbell.

My Dearest Davy,

I can't tell you how overjoyed I was to get two telegrams today. One from your mother, and one from my dear friend Professor Ackermann. Both informed me that you were well and heading home to Scotland. I'm so happy. I feel younger than I have in years. Professor Ackermann is my dear friend and good neighbor, he's been looking for you, I don't know how he found you, but he did.

The sun is setting here and I believe it's putting on a show to reflect my joy. Streaks of orange and yellow fading and reappearing as pink and purple. I would love for you to see a Detroit sunset. I think they are the prettiest in the world. I hope you aren't badly injured and that you were treated well wherever you were while you were missing. But, we won't talk of that now.

I want to repeat my offer to send you the money you'll need to make a crossing. You don't have to stay, just visit. If you find Detroit too crowded and busy with excitement after the stress of war, you can go home to Scotland, or to Australia to be with your mother. But, please come. I long to see you. Don't worry about the money, I can afford it. It's been an exciting day, so I'll close now. Take care of yourself, and rest. Then make your decision.

Your Loving Nana

CHAPTER 20

Colonel Ackermann
~ Davy McLeod

Colonel Irons escorted Davy from the dining room. There was a small sitting room across the hall. The sitting room furniture had been replaced by four desks and numerous chairs. Army clerks were working at three of the desks.

"Let's go in here," Colonel Irons said, to the clerks he said, "Take a break lads." Noticing Colonel Irons' rank, they quickly left the room. Colonel Irons took a seat at one of the desks; Davy followed him into the sitting room office. Mac, who had left the courtroom with them stood awkwardly by the door, not sure if he should follow them. Colonel Irons asked him, "Are you Sergeant McLeod's counsel?"

"Um, no, I'm just his chum," Mac said, confused.

"Even better, please, join us," Colonel Irons said motioning for Davy and Mac to take a seat. "Well, it looks like I arrived just in time. Before we get started, however, I would like to personally thank you again for recognizing the coded messages in the newspapers you received from the States, and reporting them. The information was very valuable." *The code,* Davy thought, *I gave the coded newspapers to Colonel Irons. That's where I've seen him. This has something to do with the code.* Colonel Irons continued, "Now, Davy, as I said, the United States War Department has been looking for you, but before I turn you over to them, please explain where you have been since the night of the patrol, because, if you are a deserter, well, the War Department may not be able to have you after all."

Davy, being given a glimmer of hope, seized it. He explained how he was injured, how he ended up at the American Women's Hospital. He told Colonel Irons everything, and half expected the Colonel to decide that he really was a deserter after all. That he should have returned to his unit sooner. Colonel Irons listened quietly.

"Well, considering what you've just told me and the scars you have proving it, I don't believe you intended to desert your post. Also, considering your record as a sniper, that you probably saved the lives of countless British soldiers by eliminating German snipers. I am quite willing to give you an honorable and immediate discharge.

"Discharge?" Davy asked, confused.

"Unless you would like to stay to the end?" Colonel Irons said with a hint of sarcasm, "You have proven to be an excellent soldier."

"Um, no sir, a discharge will be fine," Davy said.

"Ah, very good, the US War Department has requested that you be discharged immediately, but as it's easier to travel as a soldier, your discharge will be effective as soon as you return to England. You will report to army headquarters in London. Colonel Ackermann asked me to give you this envelope." Colonel Irons said. He reached into the inside pocket of his jacket, took out an envelope and handed it to Davy. The colonel continued, "I already notified him that you had been located and I'll let him know that I've seen you and that you are returning to England."

Davy looked over at Mac. He was fidgeting with a pen he'd picked up from the desk and looking out the window, a forlorn expression on his face. Davy said to Colonel Irons, "Sir, actually, I would like to stay on until it's over. Until Mac, Sergeant Sutherland that is, is discharged too. We came over together in 1916, I will not go home without him."

Mac jumped up at this suggestion, "Bloody hell you will," Mac said, staring at Davy.

Colonel Irons sighed, shook his head, and said, "Oh, what the hell, you lads have been here too long, too bloody long, we've all been over here too long, okay, Sergeant Sutherland can have his honorable discharge too. I suspect I'd get hell from Colonel Ackermann and the Americans if I don't insist on your discharge."

"Thank you sir," Davy said. And he smiled.

"I'll have the clerks set up your travel arrangements, discharge papers for both of you will be waiting at army headquarters in London." Colonel Irons said. He stood, shook Davy's hand then Mac's and said, "Thank you for your service." And he left.

Davy and Mac stared at each other, shocked.

"Home, we're going home!" Mac finely said as he pounded Davy on the back. He added, "I'll be in Millie's arms within the week. Millie, I have to contact Millie." Davy grinned; happy Mac was coming with him. *Home,* Davy thought, *where was home anyway?*

"What code was he talking about, and who's Colonel Ackermann?" Mac asked. The clerks were returning to the office, so Davy said, "Let's go, and I'll explain." They left the farmhouse and returned to their barrack. There was an old bench in front of the Nissen hut so they sat down. Mac lit a cigarette and offered one to Davy. He declined.

"This past spring, while Jamie and I were working on the maps, some of the newspapers I received from my grandmother had codes on them." Davy explained.

"Codes, wow. So you're a spy?" Mac asked somewhat envious.

"Well, not exactly, somehow, my grandmother and her neighbor Bob were asked to hide codes in the newspapers and send them to me. I just noticed the code, deciphered it and gave the message to Colonel Irons," Davy said.

"So, Bob and your grandmother are spies?" Mac asked, raising his eyebrows.

"I guess so," Davy said, considering. He continued, "Actually, I think this Colonel Ackermann is the real spy. I remember now, my grandmother mentioned a neighbor whose name was Professor Ackermann. Let's see what this is?" Davy said opening the envelope. A letter and $50 American dollars were inside. Mac whistled, Davy read the letter aloud:

Dear Davy,

If you're reading this, it means you're safe and have met with Colonel Irons. Let me introduce myself. I am Colonel Ackermann. Your grandmother may have called me Professor Ackermann or Carl in her letters. Your grandparents have been good neighbors and dear friends for many years. I still miss your grandfather. He was a wonderful man.

Your grandmother is very special to me and one day, I'll explain how she saved my life. Helping to find you, and hopefully bring you to Detroit to visit her is my way of repaying her for the love and friendship she has shown me over the years. To that end, I would like to offer to pay your passage to the United States. I know she has offered to pay your way, but we won't trouble her with that at this time. I will begin looking into cabin availability immediately upon hearing that you have been found and are safe. When you get to London, visit the US army headquarters. They will have information about your booking. I have enclosed some money. Please purchase what you might need for the trip.

Colonel Irons will notify me after he has seen you in person and I'll notify both your grandmother and your mother in Australia via telegram to tell them you have been found and are well. I believe it would be best if you don't tell your grandmother that you're coming, she is frail from an illness this summer and, with trans-Atlantic travel still somewhat dangerous it will be better if she's not expecting you on a given date. I don't know if she could handle the disappointment if something where to cause your delay.

I know this is all very sudden, and heavy-handed, but if you knew how much your grandmother longs to see you, you would understand. After you visit with her, I'll gladly pay for your passage back to Scotland, or anywhere else you may choose to go. Just please come to see her first. I look forward to meeting you soon.

Sincerely,
Colonel Carl Ackermann

"Wow," Mac said. "Looks like you're going to America."

"Yeah, I guess so," Davy said. He felt a little dazed. In a single day he had gone from thinking he would be killed as a deserter, to receiving an honorable discharge, and now news that he was practically ordered to go to America. "Bloody hell," he mumbled.

"Do you even remember your grandmother, I sure don't," Mac said.

"Oh, we were only babies when she and my grandfather immigrated to Detroit, but I wrote to them when I was a lad, and after my da died, we stayed in touch," Davy said.

"The newspapers she sent were entertaining," Mac said with a chuckle.

"Actually, I was thinking about going to Detroit anyway. I just hadn't decided for sure, now I don't have to bother with the decision or the details, honestly, I'm kind of used to taking orders"

Going Home
~ Davy McLeod

It took Davy and Mac a week to get back to England. Jamie, Nora and Millie met them at the station. After the initial excitement of hellos and hugs, Jamie took a very small bundle from a pram, held it gently out for everyone to see, and proudly said, "Mates, I'd like you to meet, Gavin Patterson."

Mac put a finger under the baby's small chin and said, "You have some mighty big shoes to grow into little Gavin." Davy smiled and nodded, but he was too chocked up to speak.

As directed by Colonel Irons, they went from the train station to army headquarters to pick up their discharge papers. The building was big and busy. After being directed to two different offices, and signing multiple copies of the required papers, they were done. It felt strange to be civilians again.

For two and a half years Davy had been told what to do. What to wear, what and when to eat, where and when to sleep. *For my entire adult life, other people have been making decisions for me, the whistle at the mine told me when to work and when to stop, my Mum told me when and what to eat, then the army told me, well everything,* Davy thought, *but now, now I could sit on a bench in the park for the rest of the day then I could eat a box of shortbread for dinner.* He was almost giddy with the thought of it, the freedom, but the giddiness faded with the realization that he'd have to manage his own life from here on out.

Mac and Millie were heading directly to Bothwell to see Mac's family, then to Bellshill to see Millie's family. Davy planned on staying in London with Jamie and Nora until he got his travel plans from the US army headquarters. So, after seeing Mac and Millie off on the train north, Davy, Jamie and Nora, with baby Gavin sleeping soundly in the pram, headed to Jamie and Nora's small London flat. Nora hurried off to feed the baby and left Jamie and Davy in the tiny sitting room. "Well, how are you, really?" Davy asked. Looking at the cane next to Jamie's chair.

"Actually, not bad, the doctors say I'll regain strength and should be able to walk without the blasted cane," Jamie said.

"That's great," Davy said.

"And, how about you, we thought you were dead, it was pretty awful. Gavin went looking for you. He went out two nights, he would have gone again and again, but the Captain wouldn't let him. He was madder than hell. We all figured you were dead by then, for sure."

Davy told Jamie what happened to him after the patrol. About following the star and the American Women's Hospital. He explained how, when he returned to the platoon, they accused him of desertion and how Colonel Irons had saved him.

"Colonel Irons, why is that name familiar? We didn't server under him?" Jamie asked.

"He's the colonel I gave the coded messages to," Davy explained. "And, he had a letter for me from a Colonel Ackermann. Colonel Ackermann is my grandmother's neighbor. She got the codes from him. Without Colonel Ackermann's help, without him asking for me, searching for me, I would be dead now, shot as a deserter, I'm sure of it."

A Bothwell Goodbye
~ Davy McLeod

The next day they went shopping and Davy replaced a wardrobe he never really had. He used the $50 dollars Colonel Ackermann had given him, plus some of his own money. They went to Selfridges. Nora and Jamie helped him select two suits, shirts, shoes, socks . . . "Everything a dashing young man needs," Nora said.

Davy didn't feel either young or dashing, but the sales girls behind the counter seemed to think otherwise. They smiled and giggled, and stole sideways looks at him through their pretty lashes.

A day later, Davy put on one of his new suits and went to the US army headquarters. It felt strange to be wearing a suit and tie. The jacket restricted his arms, and the tie cut into this neck. He caught his reflection in a large shop window, he didn't feel exactly dashing, but at least he was presentable. He smiled and tipped his hat to people he passed, making the most of it. As it had been before the war, little girls giggled, young ladies flashed shy smiles, middle-aged women stared and old women chuckled.

At the US Army headquarters, Davy half expected to meet the mysterious Colonel Ackermann but instead he was directed to the office of Army Intelligence. They checked his ID and asked to see his British army discharge papers and the letter from Colonel Ackermann. When they were certain that he was who he said he was, they gave him a large manila envelope, and that was it.

Back outside, Davy noticed a bakery. He was hungry, so he bought a large square of shortbread. It was a beautiful fall afternoon. He found a bench in a nearby park, sat down, ate his shortbread and opened the envelope. Inside was a ticket and a note from Colonel Ackermann. Davy was booked on the Corsican. It would sail from London on October 16th and arrive in Montreal, Canada on about November 5th. *Good,* Davy thought, *I'll have time to go to Bothwell and get my trunk and maybe see Mac again before I leave.* It listed his accommodations as second class. He was surprised. He expected to be in the crowded steerage deck. The note said only that Colonel Ackermann would meet him when he docked in Montreal. A smiled spread over Davy's face as he realized that he was excited. This would be an adventure.

Davy sat on the bench for a while enjoying the late afternoon sunshine. He watched the children playing, mothers and nannies keeping a watchful eye on them, the nearby street was busy with busses, delivery trucks and people walking briskly to and from the shops that lined the avenue. It was as if the big city was waking from a terrible and long nightmare. The war was almost over, now it was time to move on. Davy yawned, his own nightmare with the photographs still woke him on many nights. It was time for him to move on too. He was sure it would fade over time, as the one of his father's mining accident had faded, but he wondered how long it would take.

It was mid-September, Davy had four weeks before he sailed, so a few days later he took a train to Bothwell. His trunk was stored at Gavin's house. He was apprehensive about seeing Gavin's family. *Will they want to see me? Do they blame me? I blame myself. I should have been there. I'm alive, and Gavin is gone.*

It was late in the evening when Davy arrived in Bothwell. He checked into the inn. The next morning was beautiful, too beautiful for the task of visiting Gavin's family. Davy went for a walk instead. He walked the fields and hills around Bothwell Castle wondering if this would be the last time he trudged on these trails. Mac and Millie were planning to live in Bellshill to be near Millie's family, so he wouldn't need to come to Bothwell to visit them. After seeing London, and traveling in France, even with the destruction of the war. Bothwell seemed small.

At about 1:00, Davy figured Mr. Campbell and the children would be at work and school, only Mrs. Campbell would be home. He walked anxiously up and down the street trying to get up the nerve to knock on the door. When he could delay no longer he went to the front door and knocked. There was no answer. He knocked again, harder.

A voice from around the side of the small house startled him, "Hello, if you're selling something, I'm sure I'm not interested." Mrs. Campbell said. Then she looked at him more closely, her voice caught as she said, "Oh, Davy, Davy McLeod, I almost didn't recognize you." She leaned the rake she was carrying on the house and held her arms out to him, "Oh, you dear boy, I'm so glad to see you."

Davy went to her and she hugged him, and whispered, "Oh, you're safe and whole." She held him away from her, looked him over, and then hugged him again tears welling up in her eyes.

"I'm sorry," Davy said. "So very sorry."

"Let's go sit in the garden," Mrs. Campbell said as she led Davy to a bench.

"I'm sorry too, we miss him. So many were lost," Mrs. Campbell said with a sigh.

"But, you don't understand, I'm sorry, I should have been there, maybe I could have shot the sniper before he shot Gavin, I should have prevented it," Davy chocked.

Mrs. Campbell took Davy's hand and looked into his eyes, "Is that what you think, that it is somehow your fault?"

Davy nodded, and looked away, unable to look into her sad eyes.

"Well, it's not true. It was a war," she reached up and touched the scar near his temple, he looked back, "you were injured. I'm just glad you're okay," Mrs. Campbell said.

They sat in silence for a moment. Then Davy said, "The garden looks really nice."

"Gavin loved this garden," Mrs. Campbell said.

"I know," Davy said. "He didn't like to admit it, but I could tell."

"He used to sit out here, on this bench, his big frame all scrunched up to fit," Mrs. Campbell said with a sad smile. Again they were silent, then Mrs. Campbell said "I was pulling potatoes, do you want to help?" she asked.

"Sure," Davy said. He took off his jacket, rolled up his sleeves and went to work. They worked and talked about old times. Davy stayed for dinner and afterwards, Bruce, Gavin's brother helped him carry his trunk to the inn.

The next morning, Davy was up and at the station early. He was taking the train to Bellshill to visit Mac and Millie. He had an hour to kill before the train came so he found a seat on the platform to wait. From the platform, he could see the football pitch. It was empty at this time of the day. He smiled as he remembered the time he, Gavin and Mac had skipped school to play football. They got caught, of course, what were they thinking, you could see the pitch clearly from the platform. The station manager had called the school and reported their truancy. But they were just lads, and school days were so long. He opened his trunk, took out the football and walked over to the pitch. He hung his jacket over a nearby fencepost, and went out onto the field. He kicked the ball, ran after it, practiced ball handling tricks. Bouncing the ball from his knee to his toe and back. He must have looked funny to anyone passing by: a grown man in a suit playing football all by himself. After a while he stopped, looked around and imagined Mac and Gavin beckoning for him to send the ball their way. A movement at the far end of the pitch brought him back to the present. Three small boys were watching him. He gave the ball a good hard kick in their direction. They kicked it back. They passed the ball back and forth for a few minutes then Davy realized he should return to the station or he'd miss his train. He walked over to the boys.

"Shouldn't you chaps be in school?" Davy asked.

The boys looked down at their feet, then one asked, "Are you back from the war?"

"Yes," Davy said.

"Mum says it'll be over soon, and everyone will come home," another boy said.

"I hope so," Davy said, he continued, "Hey, will you boys do me a favor?"

"Sure mister, ah what?"

"Well, I'm going to America, and I hear they don't play football there, so will you boy's take care of my ball?" Davy asked. He added, "Make sure you play with it."

"Yes sir," the boys said in unison, excited. Most of the boys in the area didn't have their own footballs, they had to use the community ones, which were often in high demand and usually commandeered by the older boys.

"Great," Davy said. "Now, go out for a pass." He kicked the ball out into the pitch and watched as the boys ran after it.

Davy walked back to the station, picking up his jacket on the way.

Sailing on the Corsican
~ Davy McLeod

On October 16, 1918 Davy was on the deck of the Corsican waving to Jamie and Nora far below. They had come to see him off. The ship was big. It took Davy a while to find his cabin. He was in second class and had a cabin to himself. The room was small, with a bed, small desk, and a porthole. The porthole didn't open, and was splashed with water, but it let in light in and Davy liked it. There was also an electric light on the ceiling. Davy found the switch on the wall, turned it on and off and watched the light with a smile. They were just starting to add electric lighting to miners' houses before the war.

Davy spent the afternoon exploring the ship. It would be home for the next two weeks, maybe longer depending on the weather. Some ships made the crossing faster, but the Corsican wasn't one of them. That was okay with Davy, he wasn't in a hurry. He found the second-class dining hall, a library, game room, music room and a smoking room. He wished Mac were there, he'd enjoy the smoking room although Millie didn't think it was good for him.

His first night at sea Davy fell asleep to the hum of the engines, the vibration and gentle rocking of the ship.

The bloody hands set photographs before him, one on top of the other. First came the photograph of Fritz's sad parents, then Fritz's family, the blurry girl and the boy with the dog. The sweetheart was next, then the two small girls in pretty dresses, a soldier in a German uniform, a very old woman with deep wrinkles and sparkling eyes, the happy girl in a fancy hat, a young mother holding a baby, a smiling old man with a dog at his feet and finally a proud German cavalry officer. Again, Davy tried to push the photographs way, again the table overturned and the photographs fluttered down around him.

Davy woke with a start, his heart pounding. For a few moments, he didn't know where he was. Then it came to him, the ship, and the trip to America. He relaxed a little. He closed his eyes, but he couldn't get back to sleep.

He was afraid. He didn't want to see those faces again. He had hoped he could leave them behind. He got up and looked out the porthole. It was black. He turned on the light, but it was like a scream. *Too bright,* he thought, turning it quickly off. Then he remembered his torch. He bought it for himself as a sort of present. A torch and a compass. He reached into his truck, pulled out the torch and turned it on. It gave off a soft glow. He pointed the torch into the trunk and found the compass, opened it and shined the torch on the face. They were going east, but that was okay because he knew they had to sail east, out of the River Thames then south to the English Channel before heading west to America. He put the torch down on the desk and sat down. The desk had an ink pen, a stack of Corsican writing paper and a stack of envelopes. He had an idea. He started to draw. He drew the sad parents, and the blurry girl and the boy with the dog. He wasn't a great artist, but as long as he knew what the pictures meant, it didn't matter. He drew the sweetheart next, then the two small girls in pretty dresses. He drew each photograph on a separate piece of paper. The soldier in a German uniform, the very old women, a girl in a fancy hat, a mother with a baby, the old man with a dog and a proud German cavalry officer. He drew until his eyes began to close and finally, the pen fell from his hand and he put his head down on the desk and slept.

When Davy woke up the desk and floor were covered with his drawings of the photographs. He turned off the torch and looked out the porthole. It was beginning to get light. He checked the compass. They were going west. He got dressed and went on deck. It was quiet. Not many people were about this early on their first day at sea. He walked to the stern of the ship. The sun was rising in the east. It was a sliver on the horizon, its orange glow reaching out to him. Pulling him back. He watched as it rose higher and the orange trail grew wider, like a road being laid out before him. He took the pictures from his pocket, and one by one he let them go. He watched each one as it fluttered to the sparkling orange sea below and was consumed by the waves and turbulence of the engines. When he ran out of pictures he stood for a long time watching the sunrise. Then, he turned his back on the east, on Europe, and walked west to the bow of the boat. The sun followed him.

Meeting Sam
~ Davy McLeod

The crossing was uneventful. Davy discovered he liked the sea, even when it was rough and choppy. The weather was cold, but Davy sat on the deck most days, moving from deck chair to deck chair to stay in the weakening fall sunshine.

Davy found The Adventures of Sherlock Holmes in his trunk and re-read it. He tried to remember the codes he'd exchanged with his grandfather. When he finished The Adventures of Sherlock Holmes, he got Kidnapped by Robert Louis Stevenson from the ship's library and read that.

They docked in Quebec, Canada and were delayed for a few days before continuing up the Saint Lawrence Seaway to Montreal, Canada. Davy didn't read once they entered the seaway, but watched the Canadian shoreline. He checked the maps in the library and discovered that at this point on the seaway, both shores were Canadian. Had the ship traveled beyond Montreal, the southern shore would become the United States of America.

He found Detroit, Michigan on a map. He recalled finding it on the globe at the Bothwell library when he was a lad, and thinking it was very far away. Now, he studied the map closely. He liked the way Detroit was situated. It was at the cuff of the mitten that was Michigan, under the thumb. Michigan itself was surrounded by the Great Lakes, but after comparing them to the lakes on the map of Scotland, he decided they were like fresh water seas. He was excited to see them.

On the night before they docked, Davy was busy packing his belongings back into his trunk. During the voyage he had made himself at home now his sparse belongs, that didn't seem like much when loaded into the trunk, were strewn all over the room. He didn't want to leave anything behind, and didn't want his grandmother to see his belongs thrown unceremoniously into the trunk, so he was trying hard to fold and pack everything neatly. He wasn't having much success.

There was a knock at the door, Davy looked around the room slightly embarrassed by the mess, and opened it. A steward handed him a telegram, held out his hand for a tip and disappeared once the tip was delivered. The telegram was from Colonel Ackermann. It said, "Welcome to Canada and the US. I will not be able to meet you in Montreal. Proceed to Detroit at your convenience. Send your arrival information to 1534 Crane Ave. and I will meet you."

Davy tucked the telegram in the pocket of his overcoat so he could find it when he arrived in Detroit. He also had his grandmother's address written neatly on a card so he could find her house if needed. Colonel Ackermann had been a mystery so far, and Davy didn't want to find himself alone in Detroit with no way of contacting his grandmother.

After disembarking, clearing customs and with the help of a porter, Davy found his way to the train station. At the station, he studied a large map and train schedule on the wall, trying to decipher the best route. It looked like he would travel from Montreal to Toronto. In Toronto, he would transfer to a connection for Windsor and Detroit. *But, how does the train get from Windsor to Detroit*, Davy wondered, his finger poised over the Detroit River on the map.

"There's a tunnel under the river," a deep voiced answered his unspoken question.

"Ah, thanks, mate," Davy said. He turned and looked in the direction of the voice, and found it belonged to a

Canadian army officer. Out of habit, Davy raised his hand to salute, then dropped it remembering he was no longer in the army, no longer in uniform.

"Are you going to Detroit?" the officer asked.

"Yes, you?" Davy replied. The man was big, built like Gavin, but without the wild red hair and beard.

"I sure am, and can't wait to get there," the officer said, he smiled broadly and held out his hand, "Sam Robinson, pleased to meet you."

Davy was surprised. He'd heard, or at least read that name before, "Sam Robinson," Davy repeated as he shook Sam's hand, "I think my grandmother is a neighbor of your family, at least she mentioned the Robinson family and their son Sam in her letters. I'm Davy McLeod."

Sam said, "Davy McLeod, why my sister mentioned you in her letters. In fact, in her last letter she said you were missing and Aunty McLeod was sick over it," Sam said surprised.

"I was injured on a patrol," Davy said.

"Well, I'm mighty glad you made it through, for you and for Aunty McLeod. She's a gem of a lady, and she makes the best shortbread, my mouth's watering just thinking about it. Imagine that, us meeting in the station like this."

Davy chuckled, and said, "My grandmother often wrote I should keep a look out for you in France, I thought it was rather unlikely that we'd run into each other considering the number of men, and the size of the front, now, here we are."

"Does your grandmother know you're coming?" Sam asked.

"Colonel Ackermann made my travel arrangements, I'm supposed to send him a telegram when I get to Detroit," Davy explained.

"Professor Ackermann you mean," Sam said, he continued before Davy could explain, "With the war winding down, I've been reassigned back here. I've been selected to attend the Royal Military College of Canada. It all happened kind of fast, so I didn't send a telegram to tell them I was coming. Telegrams cause unneeded anxiety anyway." Sam paused, sighed, then brightening, saying, "Hey, I have an idea, let's surprise the lot of them. What do you say?"

"Sure that would be great," Davy said. He looked back at the map and continued with a laugh, "Actually, I'm not sure I could get there on my own anyway."

Sam pounded Davy on the back and said, "Wonderful, let's get our tickets, and I think we have time for something to eat before the train leaves. I'm famished."

The two veterans of what for over twenty years would be called simply "The Great War" traveled to Detroit together. They talked about their time in the trenches, the mates they served with and the ones they lost. By the time they arrived in Detroit, they had discovered that they shared a bond that they would carry for a lifetime.

CHAPTER 21

Endings and Beginnings
~ Bob Stevens

Good news from Europe, which had been trickling in all summer, exploded on the front pages of American newspapers in the fall.

Henry turned 18 last week, but he and Bob decided to wait to enlist. They figured that if they signed up now, the war could be over before they crossed the Atlantic. "I only wish I'd known we wouldn't be signing up when I decided not to study for the first accounting exam," Henry said. "I flunked it and now I have to play catch up."

"Yeah, I'm really behind in Latin," Bob agreed.

"I told you not to take Latin," Henry said.

"Well, I thought we'd be over at Camp Custer by now," Bob said. The weather had turned cold, but they were walking Nietzsche on Belle Isle. They joked around, played fetch with her and acted like carefree boys. Business at the canvas shop had dropped off suddenly. Mr. Harding was considering selling, or converting the shop to something more fitting to a post war economy. He asked the boys if they would mind giving up their jobs to returning soldiers. They happily agreed.

"Be honest, you only take all those hard classes to keep an eye on Maggie?" Henry asked. Bob smiled sheepishly. Henry turned serious. "I'm not kidding. You like her, you know, really like her, right?"

"Well, yeah, actually I, well, I thought it was obvious," Bob stammered. "I really, really like her." He wasn't going to tell Henry he loved her, at least not before he told Maggie.

Henry rolled his eyes and said, "Well, if you really, really like her, you might want to tell her. Did you know Tom Giddings has been calling on her?"

"Tom Giddings," Bob muttered. *Maggie didn't like Tom Giddings, did she?* He thought.

"He was bragging about courting the smartest girl in school, you didn't know?" Henry said.

"Um, no," Bob said discouraged.

"Well, don't look so depressed, do something about it, but you better do it soon," Henry said. "Hey, I'm cold, I'm going to head home, and for what it's worth, I think she really, really likes you too."

Bob wandered around Belle Isle a little longer, *Maggie and Tom Giddings,* he thought. And he started to get mad. Why would Maggie let Tom Giddings call on her, sit in her front room, smile and chat with her parents? Did her mum and da like Tom Giddings? Did Jeannie and Sara like Tom

Giddings? Had Maggie been alone with Tom Giddings? *Damn,* Bob thought. He called Nietzsche and headed home.

Bob didn't sleep much that night, he was mad. He just didn't know who he was mad at, Tom, Maggie or himself. Actually, he couldn't help being mad at Tom Giddings, he didn't really know Tom Giddings, but he hated him all the same.

What started as a cold drizzle ended as an early November snowfall. Fortunately, the next day was Saturday so he didn't have to go to school. Unfortunately, he'd either have to wait until Monday morning to talk to Maggie, or make up an excuse to see her over the weekend.

He got up early and headed out to shovel the three inches of wet snow that had fallen overnight. The trees, some still covered with leaves, were layered with heavy wet snow. Bob was starting on Professor Ackermann's walk when he saw Maggie coming toward him. His heart skipped a beat.

She was wearing Sam's hat and carrying the morning newspaper, "Did you see the news?" Maggie shouted as she approached.

"Ah, no," Bob stammered.

"The Kaiser has abdicated! It's over! The war is over!" Maggie yelled.

"What, wait, let me see," Bob said, taking the paper from her.

He read the headlines, threw it over his head, and shouted, "Whoo, whoo," then he caught Maggie in a big hug, lifting her clean off her feet. He set her gently down;

she tilted her head and smiled up at him. Sam's hat slid to the ground and her brown curls fluttered in the breeze. *But,* Bob thought with a jolt, *she's courting Tom Giddings.*

"What's the matter?" she asked.

Bob didn't know what to say, the war was over, *but have I lost her? Did I ever really have her?* He thought.

Bob blurted out, "Why are you courting Tom Giddings?"

"What?" Maggie asked, confused.

"I heard Tom Giddings has been calling on you, why?" Bob demanded.

"Well, I suppose because he asked," Maggie said sharply, she was getting mad, "But the war's over what does Tom Giddings have to do with anything?"

"I don't really care if the war's over if I've lost you," Bob said softly.

Maggie's eyes widened, and she said, "Lost me, but, I didn't think you wanted me."

Bob took her hands in his and said, "But, all I've ever really wanted was you. I'm mad about you. I couldn't tell you, not if I was going to enlist, I didn't want to hurt you if you cared for me." *Oh, God, I'm not making any sense,* Bob thought.

But Maggie, for once, was speechless. Bob lifted her chin and stared into her beautiful eyes. He bent over and their lips met. They kissed, softly, slowly then eagerly. Bob wrapped his arms around her, kissed her again, and the world disappeared.

Eventually, Maggie pulled away, smiled, and said, "You may call on me, Mr. Stevens."

Bob bowed formally and said with a laugh, "I would like that very much Miss Robinson. Tonight?"

"Well, let me think, yes, I think I can fit you in," Maggie teased.

"Will that be before or after Tom?" Bob said, more seriously.

"Oh, dear, I quite forgot about him," Maggie said.

"Good," Bob said, smiling. He bent down, picked up Sam's hat, brushed the snow off it and placed it on her head, giving it a jaunty tilt, just as Sam had done when he went away over three years ago.

"Oh, dear, poor Tom," she said, biting her lower lip.

"He's coming tonight? Seriously?" Bob asked.

"Well, he asked at school yesterday if he could, and well, you never asked," Maggie said, a little defensively, she continued, "I'll tell him tonight not to come anymore."

Bob wondered, *has she ever kissed Tom Giddings, the way she just kissed me?*

"I have to go, Mum will be wondering what's happened to me," Maggie said. She turned and hurried down the street. Bob bent down to gather up the papers he'd scattered over the yard. Suddenly, a big, wet snowball exploded at his feet. He looked up.

"Come at 7:00, sharp," Maggie shouted. She waved, smiled, then turned and ran down the street.

Bob arrived at the Robinson's home right on time. Mr. Robinson met him at the door and escorted him into the living room. Bob sat down nervously thinking how silly this all was, he'd been here a million times. Maggie came down the stairs. Her hair was done up, her cheeks were flushed and she look beautiful. Her father left them alone in the living room. They chatted quietly, Bob in a straight-backed chair, and Maggie on the sofa. They could hear Maggie's Mum and Da talking in the kitchen and Jeannie and Sara giggling on the stairs. Finally, Maggie said, "This won't do at all. Hey, everyone, Bob's here, remember him."

Sara was the first down the stairs, "Hello," she said, "We're so glad you asked to call on Maggie, you're so much better than that Tom, nobody liked him."

"Sara," Maggie said, appalled.

"Well, it's true," Sara said.

Mr. Robinson came in from the kitchen and said, "Actually, this is a night for a celebration. Bob are your Mom and Dad home?"

"Yes sir," Bob said, "Aunty McLeod is at our house too."

"Well, Maggie, if you don't mind if we impose on your courting, maybe we should invite them to join us and we'll make it a party. Professor Ackermann too."

"I'll see what I can put together in the way of food," Mum called from the kitchen.

"Hooray, a party!" Sara said as she danced around the room, then she stopped and added, "But, we'll have another party when Sam comes home, right?"

"Of course," Mr. Robinson said, "but with him staying in the army, we don't know when he'll get to come home. Maybe for Christmas."

"I'll run to my house and get everyone," Bob said, putting on his coat.

"I'll go with him," Maggie said, she grabbed her coat and Sam's hat and the two of them hurried out the door.

As soon as they were out of view of the house, Bob turned to Maggie and kissed her. They lingered a moment on the dark sidewalk, but Bob saw something move out of the corner of his eye. He stopped kissing, and turned, one arm still wrapped around Maggie's waist. Two men were walking toward them. One average sized, straight and neat, the other taller with vast shoulders. As the men entered the circle of yellow light under a street lamp, Bob could see that the larger man was wearing a uniform.

Maggie said, "Wait, it can't be . . ." then, suddenly she flew out of Bob's arms and sailed down the street. In a moment she was in the large man's arms and he was swinging her around.

Sam, Bob thought smiling broadly. He hurried to join them under the street lamp.

"Can this beautiful young woman really be my Maggie?" Sam was saying, "But it must be, she's wearing my hat," he said, giving the hat a tweak, he added, "What happened to the scrawny kid I gave it to?"

"I can't believe you're here. Why didn't you call or send a telegram? Maggie asked.

"Well, we figured telegrams are rather alarming these days, so, here we are," Sam explained.

"This is Bob Stevens," Maggie said, pulling Bob to her side excited for them to meet.

"Bob, nice to meet you, Maggie's told me all about you in her letters," Sam said shaking Bob's hand, "I appreciate you being a big brother to my sisters," he paused, smiled at Maggie and teased, "But, it looks like she may have left out some important details."

"Sam," Maggie said, embarrassed.

Sam introduced the man standing next to him, "This is Davy McLeod,"

"Davy? Aunty McLeod's Davy!" Maggie exclaimed. She reached out her hand, then said, "Oh, can I give you a hug? I feel like I've known you for years." Davy responded with open arms and she gave him a big hug.

"I feel the same way, my grandmother told me all about her wonderful neighbors. Her letters kept me going," he reached out his hand to Bob and added, "And Bob, my mates and I enjoyed the newspapers."

Bob shook Davy's hand, he wanted to ask about the code, but decided that could wait, instead he said, "Nice to meet you, Aunty McLeod will be thrilled you're here."

"Which house is hers?" Davy asked, looking around the neighborhood, somewhat confused.

"Oh, she's at my house, we were just going to get her and my parents," Bob explained.

"We were going to celebrate the Kaiser's abdication, but now we have something even better to celebrate," Maggie said. She took Sam's arm, "Come on, everyone will be so surprised."

Sam hesitated, "Maggie, I'm sorry, so very sorry that Bill isn't here too."

"We know," Maggie whispered as she pulled him toward the house.

"I'll take Davy over to my house," Bob said. "Then we'll head over. Oh, and we'll get Professor Ackermann."

"And Nietzsche, Sam has to meet Nietzsche," Maggie exclaimed.

She and Sam headed back down the street toward their house, and Bob and Davy continued toward Bob's. They could hear Maggie's excited chatter and Sam's low laughter.

"Aunty McLeod will be so pleased you're here," Bob said.

"Why do you all call her Aunty McLeod?" Davy asked.

"Oh, jeez, I don't really know? But, everyone calls her that, I guess she's like family to the entire neighborhood," Bob said.

"I don't know if she'll recognize me," Davy said. Bob could sense that he was nervous.

"You look just like your grandfather's picture. I'm positive she'll know you," Bob said.

"Maybe you should go in first, give her a little warning, I don't want to startle her," Davy suggested, touching the scar next to his eye.

They went into the house through the kitchen. They could hear quiet conversation coming from the living room. Bob went in. He was glad to see that Professor Ackermann was there too.

"Oh, are you done calling already?" Mother asked.

Bob smiled, "Um, no, actually I came to invite everyone to a small celebration at the Robinson's."

"Oh, how lovely," Aunty McLeod said.

"Actually, I ran into someone on the street who's anxious to see you Aunty McLeod," Bob said.

Aunty McLeod look confused, "Why, who would be anxious to . . ." She stopped as Davy walked into the room and stood next to Bob.

"Oh, oh my," Aunty McLeod stammered. She held her arms out to him and Davy went to her. "My dear, dear boy, you're here," she said as tears streamed down her cheeks. "Look at you, you look just like your grandfather."

"Hello Nana, thank you, for everything. For the years and years of letters. Those letters made me feel like I could belong here, like I have a home here," Davy said.

Aunty McLeod held him away from her, examined him through her tears and exclaimed, "You are home, my dear. Oh, and I'm so glad I made some shortbread today." Everyone laughed, except Aunty McLeod, she added, "Boy's need shortbread, isn't that right Bob?"

"Absolutely," Bob replied.

Bob introduced Davy to his parents and Professor Ackermann.

"Colonel Ackermann, I can't . . ." Davy started to say, but Professor Ackermann laughed heartily, and interrupted him.

"Oh, no it's Professor Ackermann. And I was happy to make inquiries about your whereabouts for your grandmother. And I'm so glad you've been able to make the crossing to see her," the Professor said. Davy nodded, looking somewhat confused, but he didn't say anything.

Colonel Ackermann? Bob thought. *Did I hear that right? Professor Ackermann is a Colonel? And from his reaction, he doesn't want anyone to know.*

Everyone headed to the Robinson's. Professor Ackermann stopped by his house to pick up Nietzsche. Bob and Davy escorted Aunty McLeod, first to her house to pick up the shortbread, and a gift she was saving for Davy. It was a red scarf.

On the way to the Robinson's Aunty McLeod walked with more spring in her step than she had since her illness. Davy, the scarf around his neck, was at one arm, and Bob at the other. A new moon had risen, giving the street a silvery, blue glow. A warmish breeze was blowing. Late fall had returned to Detroit pushing winter back, as least for a while.

"This is such a wonderful evening," Aunty McLeod said with a happy sigh. "I only wish your grandfather was here. He would be so proud."

"I was pretty surprised when grandfather's code showed up on one of the newspapers last spring," Davy said.

"So, you noticed the code?" Bob asked.

"Yeah, it practically jumped off the page at me," Davy said.

"Maybe we should have hidden it a little better," Bob said.

"No, it was perfect, if you hadn't put it right there on the front, I'm not sure I would have noticed it. I figured it out, and reported the messages to a Colonel Irons. He knew what to do with them. But, who gave you the code?" Davy asked.

"Professor Ackermann," Bob said. "He works for . . ."

But Aunty McLeod interrupted him, "Shh, Bob, remember, we're not supposed to talk about it."

"I think I already know who and what Professor Ackermann is and does, and someday, when I have his permission, I'll explain how he and a Colonel Irons saved my life and brought me here," Davy said. Then, he changed the subject and asked, "So this is Detroit?"

"It is, and I do hope you like it," Aunty McLeod said.

"Actually, I feel like I already know it from Bob's newspapers," Davy said. He continued, "They were great, even before the code. Knowing that somewhere, the world was still normal, with normal people, doing regular things, well you can't imagine what that meant. When I was done reading one, I passed it around, so everyone in my section had a chance to read it. The fella's were always asking me for the latest edition. But, I kind of hate to tell you that when everyone had read an issue, we used the paper. It came in really handy."

"Maybe I don't want to know what you used the paper for," Bob chuckled.

"Probably not," Davy confirmed.

They got to the Robinson's and once inside the introductions started again. Bob could tell that Mrs. Robinson had been crying. Tears of joy for the son who had returned, but also tears of loss for the son that was left behind. In spite of prohibition, Mr. Robinson passed out glasses of wine to the grownups, including Bob and Maggie, and holding up his glass, he said, "I'd like to make a toast. To Sam and Davy for fighting and coming home to us, to Bill," he paused, lifted his glass toward Bill's photograph hanging on the wall, a war metal draped carefully around the frame, "for giving the final sacrifice, and to our beautiful neighbors who helped us through these troubled times." Everyone replied, "To Bill, Sam and Davy"

As Bob drank the bittersweet wine, he looked around the room. Maggie and Sara were introducing Sam to Nietzsche. Mrs. Robinson, mother and Jeannie were arranging food on the dining room table. Mr. Robinson was refilling his dad's wine glass as they discussed the pending end of the war. Davy and Professor Ackermann were talking together as Aunty McLeod looked on. Maggie caught his eye, smiled at him, and his heart skipped a beat. Bob thought, *this is my family, wherever I go, and whatever happens, these special people will always be with me, and Detroit will always be my home.* He smiled back at Maggie, crossed the room to join her, and together they told Sam what a good shot she was with a snowball.

No 134   THE DETROIT GAZETTE   WAR EXTRA
NOV 11 1918   No 1.

GERMANY SIGNS TRUCE; WAR ENDS:

REBELS SIEZE FACTORIES, RAILROADS AND
SHIPS; KAISER FLEES TO HOLLAND.

HOSTILITIES END AT SIX THIS MORNING.

THE GERMAN COMMETTE AT GENERAL FOCHES HEADQUARTERS HAS SIGNED THE
PEACE TRUCE, HOSTILITIES CEASED AT SIX O'CLOCK THIS MORNING:

GERMANY IS IN A STATE OF REVOLT, THE REBELS HAVE SIZED THE RAILROADS
AND THE KRUP PLANT IS IN THE HANDS OF REVLITIONESTS, MANY MORE
NAVAL SHIPS JOIN REVOLUTION.

THE KAISER AND A MILITARY PARTY GO TOWARDS HOLLAND ARMORED MOTER
CARS ; DISPATCHES FROM HOLLAND STATE THAT THE KAISER AND THE ROYAL
PARTY WILL NOT BE ALLOWED IN THE COUNTRY.

THE GERMAN REVOLUTION	KAISER RUNS TO HOLLAND
The Revolution in Germany is here at last, The Red flag flies over many german cities and general rioting is going on over the whole country, More naval vasels have declared themselves with the revolutionests, The Social Democratic leaders have controle of afairs , Military Joins inRevolt. A wireless to London this morning stated that the Government was in the hands of people In Berlin.	The kaiser and a military party are on there way to Holland according to a german report, The Dutch Government issued a report on the procedings : Stating that they will intern the Kaiser and his party. It is also reported that the Kaisers special train has reached Madachten, but is under heavy guard by Dutch troops. The Crown Prince and others of the royal famly are with the party.

November 11, 1918
www.catherinepaonessa.com/thegazette

EPILOGUE

B ob stepped out of the foreign correspondents' office on Rue de Rivoli. He paused on the wide steps and looked at the threatening clouds. The Café de Flore was on Saint-Germain, about a 20-minute walk. He checked his watch; he could make it, but he'd have to hurry. He ran his fingers through his thick red hair, pushed his hat down on his head, lifted the collar of his suit coat and started out, hoping the rain would hold off.

It was spring 1945; Paris had been liberated for over seven months. The Allies were on the verge of victory. Bob had been covering the war since the beginning of 1942. A week ago, to his surprise, he received a message from Professor Ackermann. Bob had been quietly using his skills as an investigative reporter to try and discover the whereabouts of Professor Ackermann now out of the blue, the professor contacted him and asked him to arrange a meeting with himself, Captain Davy McLeod, and General Sam Robinson.

Professor Ackermann had left Detroit in 1937. He said he was going to Germany to, what else, do research for a book. But Bob suspected he was spying for the US Office of Strategic Services. Over the course of the war, Bob had heard that the professor was: a US spy, a double agent for Germany, a Nazi, he was working with the French resistance, or that he was in a German prison, and, of course that he was doing research for yet another book. Bob didn't know what, if any of these rumors were true. Bob had also heard that the professor was, well, just plain dead. The professor had asked Bob not to tell the others he had requested this meeting.

Bob entered the Café de Flore as large raindrops began to fall. The café was dim and cigarette smoke filled the air. Sitting in a red booth by the window were two men. Both men were in their early to mid-forties, a little older than Bob. Both in uniform. One a Canadian General, the other an American Captain. Bob walked over, his hands outstretched.

"Davy, Sam, I hope I'm not late," Bob said.

"No, not at all, we thought you might not be able to make it considering the news," Davy said.

"I'm sure you've heard?" Sam added.

"About Hitler, yes, it's been confirmed, he's dead," Bob said.

The old friends greeted each other with handshakes and hugs then sat down.

"I assume the end will come fast now." Davy said.

"Everything points to that," Sam concurred.

"It can't come soon enough, the hospitals are overflowing, staffs have been working double and triple shifts for so long we've all forgotten what sleep is," Davy said. He was head surgeon at one of the American military hospitals in Paris. As an army surgeon, he had saved many more lives than he had taken as a sniper in the Great War.

"The reports out of Germany are very troubling." Bob said, glancing toward the door. He was beginning to wonder if Professor Ackermann would show up.

"I've heard," Davy said, shaking his head.

"It's been too long, this whole damn war," Sam said. He'd been close to retirement from the Canadian forces when the war broke out. But, his services were still needed. Now, he was ready to go home. He changed the subject, "I had a letter from Maggie, sounds like she's busy."

The question interrupted Bob's thoughts, "Oh, sorry, I thought I saw someone I knew. Maggie, yes, sounds like she's very busy. It's all hush, hush, you know, she can't tell anyone what she's working on." Bob looked again toward the entrance, he added distractedly, "She's stationed in Dayton. Wait, is that - excuse me." And he got up and walked toward the door.

An older gentleman had entered the café. Bob almost didn't recognize him, he had a gray beard and round, thick glasses, but when he smiled, Bob knew it was Professor Ackermann. They shook hands and Bob escorting him to the table.

"Professor . . ." Davy started to say, but the professor cut him off, as he had over 20 years ago, when Davy had called him Colonel in front of his Detroit neighbors.

"It's so nice to see you all again," Professor Ackermann said, shaking their hands. He continued, "I was so sorry to hear about your friend Professor Ackermann's death." Bob, Davy and Sam looked at him as if he was mad. Maybe he was, maybe the war had been too much for him. He had to be near 70 years old. The professor continued, almost in a whisper, "It may be for the best however, his work made him very unpopular."

Bob was catching on. Professor Ackermann was changing his identity, becoming someone else. Bob said, "But surely, when we win the war, he would have been safe?"

The professor chuckled and said, "So you think all the Nazi's will be captured and locked up? Not likely, many are already leaving the country. Going to places like Argentina. Eventually, they will find people, people like your friend Professor Ackermann, and deal with him for the trouble he caused them."

"He must have been very good at his job," Sam said.

Professor Ackermann laughed and said, "Ah, he was. Be sure to tell his friends back in Detroit that he talked of them often and that he wished the very best for them." With that, Professor Ackermann got up and quickly left the café.

Davy, Sam and Bob sat there in shock. Bob said, "I guess he wanted to see us again, Let us know that he had survived the war."

"I suppose so," Sam said. The men ordered lunch. They talked about Detroit and Professor Ackermann.

"Do you remember when we arrived in Detroit after the first war?" Davy asked.

"Of course, we met in Montreal, that was a strange co-incidence, wasn't it," Sam said.

"I wouldn't have been there if it hadn't been for the help of Professor Ackermann," Davy said. "If someone told you then that we'd be here now, at the end of another great war, would you have believed it?"

"No," Sam said shaking his head. "But men are strange creatures. Let's just hope that finally, we've learned our lesson." The men fell quiet. The rain had stopped and the sun was shining. A fresh blue mist was rising off the wet pavement.